THE KAZOLA CHRONICLES

 ONE

CAPTURED BY CHAOS

KATHRYN MARIE

For information contact:
Kathryn Namenyi
55 Spencer St
PO Box 342
Lynn, MA 01905
authorkathrynmarie.com

Cover design by Saint Jupiter
Map Design by Vanessa Garland
Developmental Edits by Cassidy Clarke
Copy Edits by Renee Dugan
Proofread by Roxana Coumans 5Dogs Book Editing
ISBN: 978-1-7348323-5-8

First Edition: April 2023

10 9 8 7 6 5 4 3 2 1

Author Note:

Thank you so much for picking up my book! Before you dive in, I wanted to make you aware of a few things. This book contains scenes and talk of sexual assault, rape, suicide, PTSD, depression, anxiety, strained family relationships, grief, and spousal loss. Please be advised.

Dedication

To the readers who need fantasy worlds to
escape from reality.

I hope Kasha, the Faction, and Kazola
brings you on the newest adventure.

Happy Reading!

THE ISLE OF KAZULA

KILERTHE

ADRO

RAVSHIRI

ACCRITON

BROSTE

ARKALEY

VAPALLES

ORILON

CRELANTI

SEATHRIA

RYSTIN

ILFRA

OCHRAT

GAELFALL

LUSPAN

TERLANTHIR

POLANOGH

BILDWIN

PRACHUS

KOBLAR

KORHERELLI

Glossary

Amalgam Blade-*(uh-mal-gm blayd)* The primary weapon of the Onyx Guard

Blackthorn-*(blak-thorn)* An illegal drug primarily used by Shrivikas

Blood Consort-*(bluhd kan-sort)* A person meant to assist a Shrivika or an Ibridowyn to properly feed and stay strong

Faction-*(fak-shn)* A military unit in the Onyx Guard

Fuiliwood- *(fwee-lee-wood)* The strongest tree in Kazola

Futeacha-*(foo-teh-chaa)* Old Kazalonian swear; means tainted blood

Hierarchy-*(hai-ur-aar-kee)* The Leadership team of an Onyx Guard Faction

High Faction-*(hai Fak-shn)* The ruling government of the Isle of Kazola

Ibridowyn-*(ih-brih-doh-when)* Genetically modified soldier created from either a Varg Anwyn or a Shrivika

Iona Silver- *(ai-ow-nuh sil-vr)* The purest silver in Kazola

Kazola- *(ka-zoh-la)* Means Peace-Bearer in the language of the God and Goddess

Keturi-*(kah-tur-ee)* The top four leaders of an Onyx Guard Faction

Lectracycle-*(lec-tra sai-kl)* primary form of transportation for the Onyx Guard

Ogdala Dagger-*(ahg-dah-la da-gr)* The ceremonial dagger of the Onyx Guard

Onyx Guard-*(aa-nuhks gaard)* Special ops section of the military, made up exclusively of Ibridowyns

Shrivika- *(shriv-ick-ah)* Vampire, child of the God Firenielle

Tsio a Chisain-*(si-o ah chee-sahn)* Old Kazalonian for Protect the Peace

Varg Anwyn-*(varg awn-win)* Wolf shifter, child of the Goddess Lunestia

Wolfsbane-*(wulfs-bayn)* An illegal drug primarily used by Varg Anwyns

Faction outline

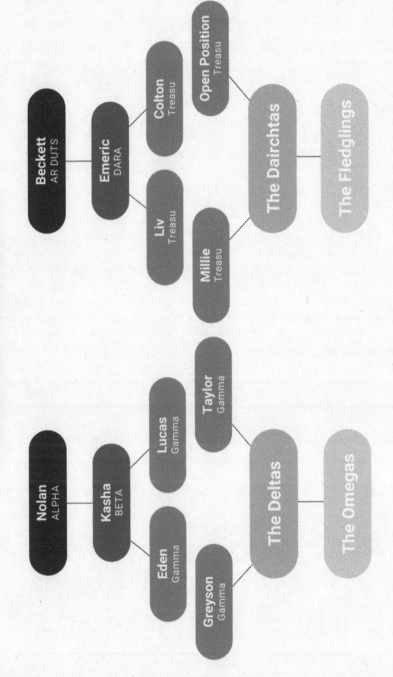

Nolan
ALPHA

Kasha
BETA

Lucas
Gamma

Eden
Gamma

Taylor
Gamma

Greyson
Gamma

The Deltas

The Omegas

Beckett
AR DUTS

Emeric
DARA

Colton
Treasu

Liv
Treasu

Open Position
Treasu

Millie
Treasu

The Dairchtas

The Fledglings

Chapter One

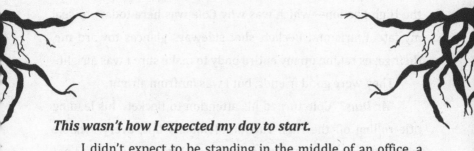

This wasn't how I expected my day to start.

I didn't expect to be standing in the middle of an office, a High Faction Delegate just deciding to "drop by" to deliver the final nail in the coffin that was supposed to be my life plan.

"Do the three of you understand?" Cole, the imposing Varg Anwyn, said, his words commanding an answer from us.

Sandwiched between my fellow leaders Beckett and Emric, Cole's towering build loomed over us as we stood at attention in our full black armor. We were soldiers of the Onyx Guard, the elite military forces dedicated to protecting our Country, The Isle of Kazola—a place where different beings lived together in peace. No one judged, no one let fear get the best of them, no matter what you were: a Human child, a Varg Anwyn wolf child, or a Shrivika blood child.

The Onyx Guard was a separate entity from the traditional military that handled the day-to-day protections. Broken up into nine Factions, one for each territory, we were created and trained to handle the worst of the worst: serial killers, the seedy underbelly of organized crime, and other terrible atrocities that would make most people's skin crawl.

I had dedicated my life to the Guard, to protecting this country with all of my strength.

Tsio a Chisain. Protect The Peace.

I had lived by that motto since I took my oaths into the Guard, but one choice had ruined me in the eyes of our leaders, the High Faction—which was why Cole was here today: to seal my fate. Emric and Beckett shot sideways glances toward me, their gazes raking up my entire body to make sure I was alright.

They were good friends, but I was far from alright.

"*Ar Dtus?*" Cole turned his attention to Beckett, his leading title rolling off the High Faction Member's lips, every syllable laced with impatience. I was fully aware that our silence was not the response he wanted.

"Yes, sir," Beckett replied, his deep tenor rumbling from his chest as he stared Cole in the eye. He looked the part of a dutiful soldier, his white-blond hair shorn at the sides close to his scalp, the longer top part slicked back and away from his eyes. His armor was perfectly polished, covering his tall, well-defined body. No one would ever guess what he had done only months ago. Of course, Cole could never forget, which accounted for the smug gleam in his own gaze at Beckett's words. "I understand my orders."

"Good." Cole paced in front of us, arms crossed tightly against his chest as he moved to stand in front of Emric. "And you, *Dara*, do you understand as well?"

Emric's blushing brown cheek twitched, his bright, aqua eyes glazing over with obedience. "Yes, sir." He was struggling to

14

stay perfectly in a command stance, his fingers twisting behind his back, forced into the submissive position and away from his round face to fiddle with the thin, silver-wired glasses that perched on the edge of his petite nose.

Silence fell as Cole moved to stand in front of me, his hulking form over a foot taller than mine; but by the slight straining of the buttons from his waist coat, he had been indulging a bit too much in the sweets recently. Still, he used our major height difference to his advantage, towering over me like a looming specter. For some, it could intimidate them and make them feel small and weak, but I would never let that happen. I would never let someone think they could break me, even if inside every inch of me wanted to crack into a million pieces.

"Beta?" He rumbled, his pale, sharp-featured face coated in darkness. "Do you understand?"

I stared up at him, our eyes locked in a battle of wills. I used every shred of strength to show him that even though I knew my place, it didn't mean I agreed with their choices. For the first time in many years, I wanted to disobey.

Yet, I still forced myself to say, "Yes, sir. I understand."

"Wonderful." A smirk crawled up his arrogant face before he stepped away, addressing all of us once again. "Your newest partner will be here in three days with all of the information about your next case in hand. This is a time-sensitive and high priority, so we expect you to use every resource your Faction has. Understood?"

"Yes, sir," we answered in unison, our three voices melding together like the united front we were.

"Perfect. We will expect full reports weekly of your progress." Cole reached out to Beckett's glass-top-and-dark-

15

wood desk and picked up his black wool jacket and matching leather briefcase where he had nonchalantly discarded them when he arrived—as if he owned the place. "Have a good day, you three."

He gave us a quick wave before disappearing through the door and shutting it behind him, the frame rattling at the sudden impact. We didn't move a muscle until he walked past the glass wall and disappeared down the hall.

My muscles slacked, collapsing me against the closest sage green wall, the few paintings hanging on it shaking at the thud. I couldn't believe what I'd just heard, what I'd forced myself to agree to. My heart beat against my chest, pounding at me like I was its own personal punching bag. How had I fallen so far...how had I failed so deeply?

"Kasha..." Beckett was the first to reach out to me, his long, pale fingers curling around my shoulder.

I couldn't stop myself from flinching away. "Don't. Just don't."

Both men sighed, resigning to leaving me alone on this subject for now. We had been Keturi together for years, taking up three of the four head roles in the Hierarchy leadership team of our Faction. We were strong together, working as if we were a machine perfectly programmed.

Now the High Faction wanted to blow that perfect machine to bits.

"What do you want us to do, then?" Beckett's onyx-brown eyes were steady as he looked down at me, his arms crossed, shoulders hunched. Emric was to my left, his lean frame propped against the back of one of the gray leather chairs in front of Beckett's desk, both waiting for me to take my command on the matter.

Even though they didn't touch me, their strength started to seep into my imaginary cracks, helping me glue myself back together so I could do what was right for the Faction.

"We go to the rest of the Hierarchy and we tell them the news." I shook my head, invisible steel walls rebuilding themselves around my heart. "They're all probably pacing the conference room while they wait."

"Good thing all the offices are soundproof," Emric murmured, his black eyebrows pinched together.

I grunted in response; at least three of our fellow Hierarchy members would not have been opposed to eavesdropping.

"Let's just get it over with," I grumbled, walking out into the hallway, a long stretch of offices for each of the twelve Hierarchy leadership members lining the way to the conference room.

I led the way, Emric and Beckett on my heels as I pushed through the closed door and emerged into the generic conference room. Its bland, beige walls were unadorned, and nothing more than an imposing cherry wood conference table took up most of the space, twelve black cushioned chairs surrounding it. It was clean and impersonal, perfect for getting work done together as a group.

The half-full room scrambled to attention, chairs scraping and feet pounding, all of our seconds in command trying to move closer to us as if we were about to tell them a deep-seeded secret and we had to whisper as quietly as possible.

"So?" Eden was the first to break the silence, her bright, bottle-green eyes full of questions.

A faint echo reverberated in my mind, telling me someone was trying to telepathically talk to me. I knew instantly who, our special ability allowing us to choose exactly who was and was not allowed in our mind at any time. It was like opening or closing a door to our own personal space; it was our decision who we wanted there, and when.

I opened my thoughts, sending a sideways gaze to him.

"Do you want me to take it? Or would you like to explain?" Beckett whispered in my mind, concern filling every word.

"I'll do it," was all I could say back before shutting him out again.

I wished I could let him take this for me and let him help me through this soul-shattering moment, but I couldn't...because, technically, it was my damned responsibility as the Beta.

With one final breath, I crossed my arms and looked up to my friends. "The High Faction has assigned us a new Alpha. He arrives in three days."

Chaos broke free the moment the words left my lips, shouts of protest and questions slinging at the three of us from every corner—and not just in the room. I stumbled backward at the number of echoes trying to pummel my brain, begging me to open up to them so every single person could privately comfort me.

"Everyone, please!" I commanded, my voice booming off the bland walls. "One at a time, and please stay out of my gods-damned head. I'm not in the mood."

Silence ticked by for a few more seconds before Taylor, my Gamma, got the courage to speak. "This is ridiculous, Kas, you should be our Alpha."

"It doesn't matter now. With Logan gone..." My lips trembled briefly at the mention of our last Alpha before I recomposed myself to push forward. "The High Faction made their choice for his replacement, and I have to live with it."

Half the room stifled retorts, lips pursed or gazes dropping to the floor. I knew what they wanted to say—that it wasn't my fault—but I didn't need false comfort or spoon-fed lies. Technically, it was my decision.

I was the one who committed the act. I was the one who picked up the knife. I was the one who drew the blood.

So much blood...

Nausea whipped through me, dizziness threatening to bring me down once again. I couldn't let that happen, not when I needed to be a leader during what I could already tell would be a tense transition of power.

I steadied my stance, uncrossing my arms and placing my hands firmly on my hips, fingers digging into my sides to solidify myself back in the present. I was safe here. The people around me would keep me safe.

"I know we're used to a certain dynamic in this Hierarchy," Beckett said, the pressure on my spine easing a bit as everyone turned their attention to him. "But that doesn't mean you have to have the same dynamic with this new Alpha. You don't have to be his friend, just his colleague."

Liv, Beckett's Treasu second and wife, moved next to him, his lips cresting into a warm smile as she laced their fingers together, the deep ebony of her skin contrasting with his paleness. "You're right, it will just be an...adjustment, to say the least."

"Great," I clapped my hands together, promptly bringing this dreaded moment to an end. "If anyone needs me, I'll be in the training building."

I spun around, desperate to escape to a place that made me

feel sane, when Taylor's voice drifted toward me. "Can we at least know his name?"

My hand hovered over the doorknob. "Nolan. His name is Nolan."

His name left a poisonous taste in my mouth as I rushed out the door.

Chapter Two

My fists pounded against the supple leather of the training bag, my knuckles protected by nothing more than the fingerless gloves I still wore. I hadn't even changed out of the armor from the meeting, the tight, stretchy shirt and pants clinging to me from the sweat I had worked up, the leather bracers doing nothing to help but chafing my skin even further with each twist and jab I landed. I'd have an angry red rash against my pale skin if I kept going, but I really couldn't have cared less in that moment.

None of it mattered; not after losing the Alpha promotion. The final step I had been ready to take, ripped away.

If you wanted to become a leader in the Guard, it would take years of dedication and tests before you would find yourself in your Faction's Hierarchy of twelve. The top spots were known as the Keturi, the four leaders ultimately in charge of every decision that affected the rest of the Faction. Each Keturi member had two seconds, either Gammas or Treasus depending on if you were Varg Anwyn or Shrivika born, to round out the rest of the leadership team. All twelve members had proven time and time again that they believed in the motto of the Guard.

And after the ten years I had put into making it this far, it still wasn't enough for the High Faction. Not after what I had done.

"Uuughhhh!" I grunted, stabilizing my weight so I could lean back and kick the bag; apparently, my fists just weren't enough today.

My breath was ragged and heavy in my chest, my low ponytail clinging to the back of my neck by beads of sweat, but I didn't care how uncomfortable I was physically—that, I could ignore. It was the gut-wrenching, twisted emotions that I needed to get rid of, that I needed to control. When I wasn't in control of them, I made stupid decisions.

My muscles seized as unwanted memories passed through my thoughts, desperate to bring me back to places of shame and regret. My movements hesitated, fists still poised in front of me, yet I didn't jab. I took a few deep breaths in through my nose, jaw trembling, trying to bring balance back to myself. I wasn't that person anymore; I had changed, I had grown.

My past did not define me. I was stronger than my past.

That mantra had gotten me through the last eight months and had taught me to look forward instead of behind. Yet, it didn't stop my mind from trying to pull me back into the murky depths that I had fallen to, to convince me I was still the weakened girl I had once been.

My fists unclenched, my shaking fingers instinctively going to my neck, gently tracing the long, thin scar that ran along the left side. To those who didn't know me, it looked like a battle wound; they had no idea what this mark truly meant. Every day I walked around with my head held high, pretending that I wasn't ashamed.

Oh, if only they knew...

No, I wasn't that girl anymore.

I shook my head, letting out a few more frustrated grunts, fists pounding into the training bag that swung in front of me. I let the memories linger for a moment before releasing them through my fists, allowing the impact to absorb them.

A whiff of Lucas and Taylor's unique scents drifted to me before they even crossed the threshold into the combat training room I'd commandeered. Located on the second floor of our training building, the concrete walls and padded floors were designed for small group practice in hand-to-hand combat. I had wanted privacy, using the warm-up bag that hung in the back right corner of the space.

I shouldn't have been surprised that they decided to follow me after giving me some time. I was sure everyone wanted to bombard me, but they knew me well enough to realize that would be a terrible idea. So instead, my Gammas came up to me, flanking the training bag, peeking around at me.

I wiped the back of my hand across my forehead. "Can I help you boys?"

"We wanted to check on you, make sure you hadn't torn anything to shreds yet." Taylor smirked, his bright blue eyes gleaming wickedly. He was trying to make me laugh, and it almost worked. Almost.

"You know I can't do that."

"Kas, are you sure you don't want to talk about the news?"

23

Taylor asked. Lucas just stared at me, the quietest one between the three of us but always the most intense. The same question burnished his cerulean eyes, matching his fraternal twin beside him—though you might not guess it, as they had few similarities between them.

Where Taylor was well above six feet and a bit lanky, even with the defined muscles he had built over many years in the guard, Lucas was stalky and only a few inches taller than me, his arms twice the size of his brother's. They had matching russet brown skin and blue-black hair, although Lucas kept his head shaved to the scalp while Taylor preferred to grow it longer, the curly strands secured by a band at the nape of his neck. However, the biggest difference was that Lucas had both arms and his back covered in elaborate, black ink tattoos, and Taylor's skin was mostly free from inkings besides a few I knew were hidden under his shirt, speckling his torso.

So different in both looks and personality, yet they worked as a perfect unit. It made them the flawless seconds—my Gammas.

"I'm positive." I turned around, walking to the open, padded space behind me, feeling the weight of their gazes following my every step. "But if you two want to be useful, then entertain me more than that bag was."

I didn't need words or talking or opening up. I needed action, I needed a reminder of my strength—and the twins knew it. They glanced at each other quickly, most likely telepathically arguing over who was going to step forward first.

With a heavy sigh, Lucas did, rolling his shoulders a few times before bringing his fists up in front of him, the intricate tattoos decorating his knuckles flexing under the pressure.

Taylor stayed on the outskirts of the mat, crouching down and watching us.

"Are you sure about this?" Lucas asked.

I lunged, aiming a few well-timed jabs to his ribs as my answer. He grunted, stumbling back.

Taylor let out a low whistle. "Our girl isn't playing around today."

His words drove me forward, a smirk playing on my lips, baiting Lucas. He shook his head, a low laugh escaping him before he attacked, our movements blurring as we sparred.

Some found it odd that I had chosen a set of twins to be my seconds, but I'd never cared. These two men had been a part of my life for years, ever since we met when we were nothing but baby Omegas starting our training in the Guard. After a few months, they'd started calling me their missing triplet, because somehow we had just clicked when we fought together, not even needing our telepathic connection to synchronize as one battling unit. There was no one else I trusted to stand beside me when I took my promotion as Beta, and they had both earned their positions by my side.

The three of us were Varg Anwyns, children of Lunestia, the Goddess of Moon and Hunt. We were born into her line of beings, blessed not only with speed, strength, and plenty of other sharpened abilities, but with our second form—a wolf. Our wolves gave us freedom and passion and abandon. It was as much of who we were in our soul as our human forms. As a Varg, you never felt fully like yourself until your first transformation around eighteen years of age, when your beast broke through and unleashed all of the potential for your future.

My heart lurched, distracting me for only a moment, but long

25

enough for Lucas to get a swift jab into my side. I let out a deep grunt at the impact before clearing my mind, finding my center, and attacking once again.

"You can keep fighting Kas, but just know we're on your side," Lucas's voice filled my mind.

I looked up at him, eyes widening. *"Excuse me?"*

"If you actually think we're just going to roll over and act as if this new Alpha is welcome, you're wrong."

"He's right," Taylor jumped in. I very rarely kept my mind closed off to them unless I was desperate to be alone, making it easy for the three of us to communicate like this. *"If you hate this guy, then so do we."*

I groaned; that wasn't what I wanted to hear.

"I appreciate the loyalty, I do." I sideswiped, our sparring continuing with less gumption as we talked. *"But I don't speak for you two, and I never have. You need to form your own opinion of this man. He's our new leader..."* I hesitated for a moment, attempting to kick Lucas in the shins, but he blocked me. *"Don't form a negative opinion about him just because you think it will make me feel better about being passed over."*

"Yes, but you aren't the only one who made poor decisions this past year," Taylor countered. *"None of us can understand what you went through, but you know we all fought afterward. We won't look good in the new Alpha's eyes once he reads about our past."*

He was right, a lot had happened in the past year, and although most of the actions were mine, they had caused a rippling of reactions from the rest of the Hierarchy; reactions that had gotten most of them in trouble in some way.

My guts twisted, reminding me that the High Faction could have done a lot worse than just assigning us a new Alpha.

"We are a team, Kasha," Lucas said, sending a punch right to my jaw before I caught it in my hand. He stared down at me, no longer keeping the conversation in our minds. "You don't have to fight alone. You never had to."

I gazed into Lucas's eyes, my grip on his fist tightening. I knew he said these things to make me feel safe, less alone, but he didn't understand. What had happened in the past year was a place I refused to even visit in my mind. I had locked it away in a prison, never allowing it to escape. My psycho-physician told me that not facing it was only hindering my recovery, but she didn't understand, either.

No one did.

Chapter Three

The sun was setting low in the horizon by the time I was ready to leave the Compound, dusty lavender and buttercup yellow melting into a royal blue sky, teasing the appearance of the moon. After working off some of my energy, I was finally able to focus enough to go back to my office and begin preparing for the new Alpha's arrival.

It had been three months since we last officially had one, and I had taken over a lot of the responsibilities to make sure our Faction kept running smoothly. I had hoped the longer an Alpha was unnamed, the more opportunity I had to prove that I was the right choice, to show the High Faction that I was ready for this, even with my past. But it hadn't been enough. I hadn't been enough...

I stopped in my tracks quickly, looking up to the sky and letting the breeze whisper against my cheeks, burning my nostrils when I took a deep breath. None of that. I began walking again, letting the hurt feelings stay where they belonged: in the past.

I pushed forward, making my way as quickly as possible to where my lectracycle was parked. The two-wheel contraption was one of the great perks of joining the Onyx Guard; each member was given one to help them travel quicker through their assigned territory. It ran solely on electricity, a powerful engine shining in between the two wheels, a soft leather cushion running along the top of the body before merging into the handlebars at the front of the cycle.

I threw my leg over, shoving my key in the ignition and flipping the switch to turn it on. The engine purred under my legs, ready for me to unleash its full force. I double-checked my gages, making sure there was plenty of energy stored in the engine to get me home and back to work tomorrow. With one more breath, I kicked the balancing stand up and raced off down the street toward the entrance gate.

"Open," I said into the mind of the Guard currently on duty, a young Delta standing on a parapet that overlooked the tall wall surrounding the Compound. He perked up, flicking the switch so the gate swung open for my lectracycle to race through.

The wind whipped against my face, feeding into me as I gained speed on the abandoned street. I loved my lectracycle; it reminded me of running in wolf form, the thrills of freedom mixed with a touch of adrenaline. In the past few months, I had become a bit overzealous with my speed on the open roads leading to Eroste, the capitol city of the territory Seathra. Most people didn't travel out this way unless they were an Onyx Guard, so I tended to let my desires unleash a bit out here.

I needed it, craved it.

29

All too soon, I crossed the threshold into the city, slowing down to safely wind through the crowded streets. Seathra was best known for its textile creations, becoming a destination for anyone looking for some of the best shopping in Kazola. The center of town had a daily market for the manufacturers and merchants to sell their wares while the surrounding district held the clothing and household shops. I took my time cutting through the market as merchants began closing up their booths with the setting sun, a few waving to me as I passed.

Once I cleared the shopping district, it was only a few more minutes before I arrived at my new residence, located in the artist district where I lived with my childhood best friend, Lea. I parked in the alley next to it and walked up the steps into the house, where a waft of roasted meat and herbed vegetables greeted me.

"Welcome home!" Lea called from the back of the house. I dropped my bag and keys before making my way into the welcoming warmth of the kitchen. Lea's black curly hair was secured at the nape of her neck, a few strands sticking to her forehead as she carved into the meat and placed slices on two plates. "Dinner's almost ready."

"You are too nice to me," I laughed, dropping into a chair at our circular, four-person dining table.

"Nonsense." She placed a plate in front of me before taking the seat across, the two of us tucking in instantly. "How was work today?"

My throat constricted around the first bite, the flavors turning to ash on my tongue. "Could have been better."

"Oh?"

"They assigned a new Alpha," I mumbled, refusing to look up

from my plate. I knew the look she would probably give me, those big brown eyes filled with pity, and I wasn't in the mood to see it from someone else.

"Do you want to talk about it?"

"Not particularly," I said, using my knife to sever a carrot in half. "How was the forge?"

Lea's face perked up as she launched into a story about a couple that had come to her to commission some custom wedding rings. Like me, she was a Varg Anwyn, but she didn't have the calling to join the guard. She loved metalwork, having apprenticed with a blacksmith before taking over her Master's forge here in the capitol. No matter what she created, a delicate piece of jewelry or the deadliest of weapons, it was considered a piece of art to her.

"That reminds me." I leaned down, pulling a dagger from my boot. "Can you sharpen this for me?" I dropped it on the table.

Lea didn't even flinch. "Of course. I should also have your Faction's arrowhead order finished soon as well."

"Perfect." I would have to assign a few Omegas and Fledglings to take on the task of assembling the arrows. "We were hoping to have them before the full moon next week so we didn't have to worry."

"I'm jealous." She stabbed at her chicken. "I wish non-guard people could join your Pack."

"What are you talking about? Your pack is great!" I pointed my fork at her, shaking my head.

She shrugged. "I don't have any complaints, I'm just sick of still being referred to as *baby girl* by everyone 'cause my Father's the Beta."

I chuckled. "Fair, I would hate that too."

"Besides, most of your Pack is closer to our age." She smirked. "Are you sure I can't come once to a full moon? Just to see all you super serious soldiers go wild?"

I cleared my throat. "You know we can't. It's a security risk."

Her shoulders drooped. "Ugh, annoying."

She never asked me too much about my job, knowing the only time she was allowed on Compound grounds was when she was making a delivery or was constantly accompanied by a Faction member. For the most part, I had no issue with the secrets, but there was one that was difficult to carry around—one that was the most classified part of being a member of the Onyx Guard, and we had to keep it protected at all costs.

Technically, I was no longer a Varg Anwyn.

When a Varg Anwyn or Shrivika joined the Guard, they went through a procedure to make them stronger, to make them the best soldiers they could be. Our country's Alchemists—those who studied the way the world worked and discovered new ways to advance our way of life—had created a serum that combined the genetic material of a Varg Anwyn and a Shrivika. When injected with it, we changed, keeping our original self but enhancing it with the strengths of the other. When you came out of the procedure, you were no longer called your base species, but an Ibridowyn.

It had always been weird lying to people about it, but it was the decree of the High Faction. They were concerned that if people found out this was possible, they would use it for selfish and destructive reasons. We were made into Ibridowyns because we were meant to protect this country, not destroy it.

We carried on with dinner, keeping the conversation light until we finished and I grabbed our plates, bringing them to the kitchen. I took my time cleaning everything up and making the place spotless before I retreated upstairs, closing the door to my bedroom behind me.

This was my sanctuary, filled with the things that brought me peace. I walked to the bedside table, lighting the oil lamp perched on top. Electricity had only been discovered a hundred years ago by Alchemists, when they found powerful Ley Lines that ran underneath the core of the island. Although they were working hard to make it available for all, right now the High Faction had to regulate it so only businesses and government official buildings had access to it. The Compound was outfitted with electric lights and fixtures, something that was hard to adjust to when I had moved into town a few months ago, but I didn't care. The peace of mind was worth giving it up.

My fingertips skimmed over the rows of books on the two shelves that sat across from my bed. I considered reading one of my many fiction books, but my mind was still too worked up to focus on it. Instead, I moved to the far corner, sitting on the bench in front of my piano.

My mother had taught me to get lost in the music when I needed an escape. Without even thinking, I placed my fingers delicately on the keys, closing my eyes before I began to play. The melody filled the room, every note and movement memorized from years of practice. It floated around me, through me, bringing me back to my center, to where I felt a whisper of calm.

Chapter Four

My calm was ripped away with the chirp of my portable Comms Unit.

I threw my head back with a groan, hands flattening on the piano keys, a cacophony of mismatched notes clamoring within my bedroom. I leaned down and pulled the palm-sized device from the pocket on my outer thigh, my lips pursing at Eden's name flaring on the screen. Technically, I could ignore it, but I knew she was probably checking in on me or needed help with something. I wasn't one to ignore my friends, even when my insides were all twisted up.

I hit the answer button, but the face that appeared was not the one I expected.

"How do I work this thing?" The smooth, velvety voice came through.

My brow wrinkled. "Benji?"

"Ah there you are!" The bartender at the Blood Moon, the

Faction's favorite tavern in the city, said, his tanned face lighting up through the screen connection. "Thank the God, this thing is impossible to figure out."

"Why do you have Eden's Comms? And why are you calling?" My heart fluttered, unease slicking my forehead with a thin layer of sweat.

"Well, she came in tonight for a drink and has been throwing them back, so I eventually cut her off, but she doesn't look like she should be driving that fancy lectracycle home." Benji's eyes softened. "I don't know if something happened at work, but she keeps talking about how she messed something up."

"Why am I such an idiot?" Eden's husky voice groaned in the background, a thump following the question. My jaw tightened.

"I'm sorry to have called, but when I told her she needed to get someone to help her home, she threw this at me saying she couldn't figure it out." I snorted a laugh, knowing full well that Benji didn't know how to use it either since only Faction and Government employees had access to them. "I knew you were probably closest since you live in the city."

I let out a breath I'd been holding in, my shoulders falling. I wasn't surprised Eden was struggling with the Alpha adjustment too, not after everything that had happened. "Make sure she stays there, I'll be by soon to take her home."

"I'll keep her safe until then." He winked before I hung up and ran out the door.

***

The tavern was packed by the time I arrived, people milling around the long, carved wood bar area, sitting at all of the tables that seemed to be sculpted from the same dark wood, and filling the large open space as the nightly band played music for them to dance to. I made a quick path to the end of the bar where Benji stood, polishing a stack of glasses with a cloth.

"Hey." I leaned against the side, looking up at the tall, muscular Shrivika.

"Hello, lovely." His silver-blue eyes lit up at the sight of me. "You made it here quickly."

"Sounded like time was of the essence," I said. "Where is she?"

Benji quirked his head, walking down the back of the bar while I followed him on the other side. I quickly caught sight of Eden sitting alone at the far end, her head resting against the wall, eyes hooded as if she was falling asleep. "I've been giving her water for a while now to help with what will probably be a terrible hangover tomorrow."

"Thanks, Benji, I don't know how to thank you."

"No need to thank, it's always a pleasure seeing your beautiful face in the tavern." He winked at me again.

I sighed. Benji had gotten this job about a year and a half ago, and since then had always had a fun time flirting with me. His dark brown hair was lightly dusted with gray, angular face radiating a classical handsomeness. At first, the flirtation had been fun and a nice confidence boost, but nowadays I just felt too empty to find pleasure in it. It was nothing against him—he was a kind-hearted man who always made sure we were taken care of—I just wasn't in a place to accept it the same as before.

All I could do was give him a warm smile before walking over to Eden, focusing on the friend who needed me tonight.

"Eden?" I saddled up in the chair next to her.

"Kasha!" She swung her arms out wide, leaning forward and crushing me into a hug. She swayed us a bit, her olive-toned cheeks flushed bright pink with a thin sheen of sweat. Yeah, she was wasted. "I missed you!"

"We just saw each other a few hours ago," I laughed, trying to lighten the mood.

Her hands came forward, eyes glassy as she stroked the ends of my hair. "I don't know why you hate your hair so much, it's so pretty."

"I don't hate it," I grumbled, my cheeks reddening. "It's just so short. And light."

I missed the days when my hair used to be grown to my hips, long and luscious. I used to dye it a dark reddish brown as well, to contrast with the porcelain complexion of my skin and blue eyes. However, I was forced to chop my hair off to my shoulders eight months ago, and it had only grown past my collarbone since then...not to mention the color had completely faded to my natural golden brown. Eden was lucky, her hair was still long and beautiful with the unnaturally blood-red color she dyed over her blonde roots. I knew she would help me dye mine again, but I'd been struggling to find the energy to even ask.

I quickly changed the subject. "What brought you to the tavern alone tonight?"

She flopped back, her head thunking against the wall again. "I'm an idiot."

"Yes, I heard you say that when you had Benji call me." I pushed her glass of water closer to her, staring at her until she wrapped her long fingers around it and took a sip. "But I'm still a little foggy about what makes you think you're an idiot?"

Before she could answer, Benji came up to us, sliding a drink in front of me, a foaming glass of cool ale. My stomach lurched. "Oh, no thanks, Benji, not today."

"Alright, lovely." He pulled it back, giving me a warm smile. "Let me know if you change your mind."

I wouldn't—not now, not ever.

I shook off the shiver that ran up my spine before turning back to Eden, my priority.

"I'm going to lose my job!" she cried, the glass still poised at her lips.

"Oh, Eden," I pulled my chair closer to hers, my hand drawing soothing circles along her back.

Like Taylor and Lucas, Eden was a Gamma in the Hierarchy of my Faction. She had served Logan for almost five years before he transferred. However, the last few months of his time here, Eden had made some questionable decisions against his leadership, as many of us had. My actions had caused so much pain and turmoil, not just to me, but to those around me. They thought they had been protecting me, standing behind me, but in the end it had all been worthless.

"So, I decided that I just had to come here and toast my last few days as a Gamma." She downed the rest of her water, slamming the glass on the bar top.

"And, uh, how many times did you toast?" I waved down Benji, gesturing for Eden's water to be refilled, which he happily obliged.

"I lost count after five," she mumbled.

"Alright, then," I sighed; I could tell she was about to hit her low point of the night, and it was probably best to get her out. "Chug that water and then I'm taking you back to Compound and into Greyson's care."

"He can't see me like this!" Her eyes went wide. "He'll be so disappointed in me."

38

"He's been your Gamma partner for five years now, I doubt he will be surprised." I actually had very little doubt. Greyson was the other Gamma assigned under Logan and was extremely perceptive. Somehow, his quiet nature meshed well with Eden's wildness, making them productive Gamma partners and best friends. "Drink up."

"My lectra..."

"Is chained up and will be safe overnight," I said, forcing the glass back to her lips. "You and Grey can drive back to town tomorrow morning and pick it up."

She downed the rest of her water, turning back to me. "I have to pee before we leave."

"Alright," I said, standing to help her to the back.

"No, no." She stopped me, her hands on my shoulders haphazardly pushing me back down into my chair. "I may be a drunk mess, but I can get myself to the washroom alone. We're close, but not that close."

"You sure?"

"I'll be fine!" She waved to me over her shoulder as she pushed her way through the crowd; my stomach twisted as she disappeared from my sight. I sighed, turning back to look forward at the bar.

"You're a good friend," a deep voice whispered to me.

"Excuse me?" I turned in my chair, my throat drying as I stared into the most intoxicating green eyes I'd ever seen. They were like the forest, but with a lush brightness that reminded me of the way leaves sparkled when the sunlight filtered through them.

They were eyes you could get lost in for hours.

"You're a good friend for taking care of her." He tipped his

39

glass in the direction Eden had disappeared, regaining my attention. "You don't always find that kind of loyalty in people."

I took in a deep breath, pulling in the addicting scent of cinnamon and citrus that surrounded him, with that hidden underbite of nature subtly mixed within, marking him as a Varg Anwyn as well. Heat pooled in my stomach, my heart fluttering a million miles a second. What was happening to me?

I shook my head, trying to form a coherent sentence, which felt impossible in the moment. "I, uh,...thank you?"

"So, is this your favorite tavern? It seems like the most popular one," he said, a few strands of his chocolate brown hair falling against his forehead as he took a sip of his ale.

"It's my favorite personally." I squirmed in my seat, my hands fidgeting in my lap. "Come here a lot with my friends. Are you passing through?"

"Just moved here." He smiled, dimples peeking out. "Seems like a great area, though."

"I like it." I gave him a weak half-smile before turning to look ahead again; yet I could still feel his lingering gaze on me, burning into my side, my shoulders tensing under the attention.

Sweat beaded along my forehead. I was thankful that the bar was so packed, so it didn't give away how nervous I was to be talking to this handsome stranger. It had been a long time since I'd found myself nervous around a man, and over a year since I was in my last romantic relationship. Apparently, in that time I'd forgotten how to act around men I found attractive. Wonderful.

Finally, Eden returned, throwing her arm around my shoulders. "I'm ready to go now!"

Thank the Goddess.

"Alright, let's go." I stood up a little too quickly, adjusting her hold so I could loop my arm around her tapered waist for better stability. I turned back to the man next to me. "Um, well, nice to meet you."

"Hope to see you around." He gave me a quick wink. "Good luck with the rest of your night."

"Who was that?" Eden asked as we walked toward the exit.

"Just some guy who started talking to me." I shook my head, trying to clear my fogged brain of the memory of his beautiful eyes and luscious scent that had made me a bumbling idiot.

Somehow, after a lot of coercing, I was able to get the two of us on my cycle, Eden wrapping her arms around my waist and resting her cheek on my shoulder, wetness seeping through the thin fabric of my tunic. I turned my head, finally seeing a stream of silent tears falling from her eyes.

"Eden..."

"I can't lose my status," She whispered into my shirt. "I can't be demoted, not after everything I went through to get here. If I fall, my family will have been right."

My hands tightened on the handles. "Your family was never right about you. Don't let their hatred control your thoughts."

"You first," she grunted.

I wished I had a good comeback, but she had a point—I had my own family issues, ones that constantly let my thoughts seep into despair. I shook it off; it wasn't the time to think about that, it was time to help Eden.

"Let's get you home," was all I was able to say before I took off down the road.

***

It took a lot longer to get Eden back to Compound since I had to drive slower to make sure she didn't fall off. Although as

Ibridowyn our bodies could withstand basically all injuries—even ones fatal to most—that didn't mean I wanted her to be unnecessarily hurt.

We finally made it back, pulling in front of the townhouse she shared with Greyson. All Hierarchy members had a living space in this sequestered area of the Compound. Traditionally, each Keturi member had their own private townhouse and their secondaries shared the unit attached to their own. However, almost half of the houses were now empty. I had moved out of mine a few months back, Emric lived off Compound with his husband, and of course, the Alpha House had been empty since Logan's departure. My eyes peeked over quickly to the darkened windows of the empty house attached to Eden and Greyson's, my muscles tensing.

It wouldn't be empty for much longer.

I ignored the thought and turned back to Eden, helping her off the bike and toward the house. I kicked the door a few times so I didn't lose my hold on her.

Greyson pulled the door open seconds later, his usually stoic, sharply-edged face slacking in shock, his nut-brown eyes widening with surprise. "What happened?"

"She drowned her sorrows at the Blood Moon."

Greyson sighed, coming forward and untangling her from me before sweeping her up in his arms. "Eden, you should have brought me with you."

"I didn't want to disappoint you," she mumbled into his broad chest, her grip circling his long neck, her fingertips tangling in his coal-black hair. "I'm going to lose my job...what will you think of me then?"

The three of us walked into the entryway, ascending the

42

stairs to their bedrooms. "I'll think that you did the right thing, and I will keep thinking that when I most likely lose my job, too."

Eden grunted. "You didn't nearly act as insubordinate as I did."

"I did." He kicked open her bedroom door, gently placing her on her bed. "I was just a bit quieter about it than you."

"Ha, what else is new," she sighed, burying herself in the small mountain of laurel green and crème pillows she kept on the bed. "You're too perfect to lose your job, the new Alpha will love you. But me..."

"We can't worry about that now," I said, yanking her boots off. "You don't know what the new Alpha will think about us until he gets here and makes his opinions known. Worrying about it now will only make you sick."

My words were true, but like Eden, even I struggled to accept them. Nolan would be here in three days, and most likely would have read the extra thick file detailing all of the transgressions we had achieved over the past year. None of us were safe from his judgment.

Chapter Five

Three days passed too quickly for comfort.

I wished I could have had more courage, could have walked onto Compound that morning with my head held high, acting as if his appearance didn't faze me in the least.

Unfortunately, I was not that person.

I trudged down the steps from my bedroom, the clinking of metal on metal welcoming me as I turned the corner into the kitchen. Lea was already dressed in her work clothes, the plain gray cotton shirt and black pants perfect for a long day at the forge, excellently molded to her curvy body to make sure no loose fabric caught fire but still protected her skin from the heat. Although—even though it was terrible practice—she tended to remove the long-sleeved shirt during her shift and work in the sleeveless top hidden underneath. No matter how many times I chastised her when I patched up a new burn on her lovely, tawny skin, she never cared; she always said scars showed how successful she was as a smithy.

"Morning." She smiled at me, sliding a cup of coffee across the table. "Why aren't you dressed for work?"

I took the cup, pulling a long sip before looking up to her. "Taking the day off."

"But isn't today...?"

"Yup," I said before taking another sip of coffee, letting it help dissipate the usual morning fog that plagued my mind.

"And you're avoiding him?"

"Correct." I leaned forward, my arms braced on the counter, mug still clasped between my hands.

"Too bad, I was going to ask if I could come with you to the Compound today." She pulled a plate from one of the cabinets before turning back toward me with a gentle smile.

My brows furrowed. "Why?"

"Few more resharpened blades I needed to drop off." She shrugged.

I smirked at her, shaking my head. "You just want a peek at him."

"I'm curious who on earth could be better than you." She winked before turning back to the stove to pull off her perfectly golden griddle cakes. "Can you blame me?"

"Still as nosy as ever," I chuckled, my heart lightening a bit as she pulled up a seat next to me, tucking into her breakfast.

"How can I mock him with you at home if I don't know anything about him?" She pointed her fork at me. "It's part of my duty as the roommate-slash-childhood-friend, and I take it very seriously."

"Don't worry, I'll bring you as many juicy details as I'm allowed to divulge," I said. "You won't be lacking for mocking material."

"Promise?" she held out her pinky, wiggling it at me.

A small laugh escaped my lips before I wrapped my finger with hers. "Promise."

"Good." Her dark brown eyes softened as we unlinked. "You know you can't avoid him forever, right?"

I bit my lip. "I know."

And I did know that; I wasn't stupid, and I was too dedicated to my job to avoid him forever. But for now, that was doable.

I just wasn't ready to meet this man. The one who was more competent than me, better than me, who would be my boss; a stranger who probably read about everything that had happened to me over the past year. How would he judge me? Would he take all of my responsibility away? Would he treat me like a fragile doll or as someone whose opinion was worthless? There were just too many unknowns to face.

Luckily, I had found the perfect escape.

***

An hour later, after I had washed and dressed, I raced down the abandoned roads, my lectracycle humming underneath me. My ears perked up at the distant sounds of another cycle coming from my left; technically, it could've been a multitude of people, one of my own Faction on patrol or coming back from a mission. However, I knew it was someone who would help make this dark day a little brighter.

Another driver saddled up next to me, our matching Faction-issued lectracycles keeping pace with each other as we took a sharp left turn, the skyline of Accriton city breaking through the horizon in front of us. Laughter came from my side, and I glanced toward the other cyclist.

46

"Hi, little shadow." He gave me a side-smile, making sure to keep his eyes on the road ahead.

"Hey, big bro." My chest warmed at seeing one of my favorite people again.

Ollie was my older brother, and someone I considered one of my closest friends. He was also part of the Onyx Guard, Alpha of the Vapalles Faction, the territory just to the south of mine. We didn't see each other as often as I liked, but we were lucky to be close enough to visit once or twice a month. He had been there for me always, never gave up on me...unlike a few other family members.

Ollie gave me a wink. *"Race you the rest of the way."*

I let out a deep chuckle before increasing my speed, the wind chapping my cheeks red and drying out my eyes slightly—but I didn't care. The rush of it all eased the weight on my chest and made it all worth it.

I let out a loud whoop when I passed the threshold to town first, slowing down to be safe around the residents that mingled through the street on foot or horseback. We wove through, people waving at us as we passed. Accriton was a lot smaller than the capitol, and most of the residents had lived here for decades.

We pulled up in front of a quaint cottage, the bright white brick exterior and red trimmed windows always a soothing view. I parked my cycle, a teasing grin on my face when Ollie pulled up, his copper brown hair windblown across his forehead.

"I let you win." Ollie pretended to pout at me, but his baby blue eyes held a gleam that let me know he was joking.

"Keep telling yourself that." I wrapped my arms around him, and his encompassed me in a protective hug, my cheek rubbing against the soft burnt orange fabric of his simple, V-neck shirt. I took in a deep breath, filling my lungs with the bright scent that was Ollie: tangerine and vanilla. He wasn't even half a foot taller than me, but still, the comfort of his hug protected me from the rush of anxiety I was holding at bay for the day.

I hesitated one more moment before pulling away. He peeked down at me. "Are you alright?"

"Let's go inside." I ignored his question, knowing I would probably get plenty of similar ones in the house. Might as well save time and only answer them once.

The sweet smell of fresh baked chocolate chip pumpkin muffins was the first thing I noticed, my mouth watering instantly. The second was the smiling, tall and slim, silver-haired woman coming to meet us. "Hello, you two!"

She wrapped us in a group hug, both of us awkwardly hugging her back. "Hi, Nana," we both said.

"I'm so happy you could visit today. Breakfast is almost ready!" She bustled off to the kitchen, her long, plated braid swinging behind her as the two of us silently followed. "Ollie, grab the quiche from the oven so it can cool a little before I serve. Kasha, finish setting the table."

Ollie and I didn't even question the commands, rushing off to do the tasks assigned. The house was bright and open, natural light filtering through the large windows. Nana Aggie loved painting, every room with its own designated color and design to match the mood she wanted each room to portray. The dining room was my favorite, the table built into the half circle window, the rest of the room decorated with a misty blue and silver filigree pattern that she painted freehand. Floral plants hung in different spots, adding pops of bright purples, greens, and pinks. I wasn't usually one for bright colors, but something about the filtered sunlight, fresh floral scents, and cozy seating created a peaceful ambiance; which was exactly what I needed.

As I placed the last pieces of silverware at each place setting, Ollie and Nana joined me, their hands full of different food options. We each loaded our plates, my stomach gurgling with the mingling of sweet and savory.

"Now that we're inside, are you going to answer my question?" Ollie said between bites of spinach and goat cheese quiche.

"I don't know why people keep asking me if I'm alright." I stabbed my fork through a piece of crispy bacon, ripping it in two with my teeth. "It's just getting annoying at this point when the answer is probably obvious."

"I don't know. I didn't want to assume," Ollie said.

"I am here, an hour away from my Compound, having breakfast with my Nana and brother instead of being a proper Beta and welcoming my new Alpha to Seathra." I gave him a pointed glare. "Tell me how that equals alright?"

"Moonlight, we only ask because we care about you." Nana patted my hand, her weathered, wrinkled skin soft against mine.

My chest warmed at the nickname my mother had originally given me, hand gently grazing the black tattoo on my left shoulder: poppy flowers crawling toward the word moonlight scrawled along my collarbone. Lucas had done the design for me on what would have been my mother's fiftieth birthday four years ago. It was my favorite tattoo out of all the designs inked on my body, each one with a specific meaning or representing an important moment in my life. They meant so much to me—to the point where, when I'd received my first one, I'd felt completed in a way I didn't realize was missing. After that, I was addicted, resulting in a half sleeve on my left arm along with some lone tattoos on my ribs, back, and right shoulder.

They told my story, my truths, even when I couldn't speak them out loud.

I focused back on the two people in front of me, their weary faces sending a jolt through my body. "I know, I'm just sick of people asking me. If I wanted to talk, I would."

"That doesn't sound like it will help ease your soul of the burden," Nana said, her long face pinched.

I pulled my hand away from hers, the top burning from the contact. I knew they asked me these questions because they cared about me; they wanted me to open up in hopes that it would make me feel better. Everyone thought if you talked about the pain, then it would just magically disappear, but it wasn't that easy. Maybe you would start to feel heard, maybe you would meet someone who has a basic understanding of the utter turmoil you went through, but it wouldn't make the pain disappear. It would still be there, haunting you, poisoning you, tainting you. So, what was the point? Why burden those you love with your pain when you could contain it within yourself?

When you released pain into the world, it only troubled others instead of healing you. Then, most of the time, they treated you like a little child who needed to be handled with care, as if anything they said would crack you even more. I'd already suffered enough by other people's conscious decisions; I didn't also need it from their unconscious reactions.

I sighed, softening my face with a warm smile. "If it eases your worries, I start my appointments with my new psycho-physician this week. So, I won't be hiding my feelings for much longer."

"Oh, that's good!" Nana perked up. "I'm sorry your other one had to leave town."

I shrugged, pretending it didn't bother me as much as it did. "She was given a research opportunity she couldn't refuse. I can't fault her for that."

"Who's your new one?" Ollie asked, his blue eyes sparkling with a hint of grey from the filtered sunlight.

"I think her name is Vanessa," I said. "The High Faction assigned her."

Another repercussion of my mistakes eight months ago: High Faction mandated psycho-counseling every week. I had been given a break for the past month and a half as I waited for my new physician to move here and take patients. It had been a breath of fresh air, not having to open up about my feelings every week, but that reprieve was at an end.

Nana pointed her fork at me, her gaze grasping mine. "I may not agree with the High Faction, and that idiot son and other grandson of mine, treating their own so horrendously the past few months...but your counseling is important, especially if you won't talk to us."

I looked over to Ollie, the same sullen look on his face that I could only assume was reflected on mine. I hated how my actions had divided my family. My father had dedicated his entire life to Kazola and the Onyx Guard, having served as an Ibridowyn Alpha for over a decade before retiring and taking a seat in the High Faction. Just like his father and grandfather before him. We were a legacy family, groomed and born to serve our country in the Guard.

But, according to my father and my eldest brother, Caleb, my decisions over the past year had brought shame to that legacy.

A lump formed in my throat, remembering the cold stares and distant conversations that had happened. A chill ran up my spine, my head beginning to feel woozy.

Nope, this conversation was over.

"Help me, please, for the love of the Goddess, I am begging you. I cannot handle this right now," I said mentally to Ollie.

"So, Nana, did I tell you about this girl I'm seeing?" Ollie said so nonchalantly, you wouldn't have guessed it was a ploy to shift the attention from me to him.

Nana asked as many questions as she could about what I had to guess was either a made-up woman or a one-night stand. Of course, both Ollie and I knew, the potential for great-grandbabies would steal Nana's attention in an instant. I gave him a quick wink, planning to give a proper thank you when Nana and her Varg hearing were out of earshot.

After that, breakfast continued on rather pleasantly, the conversation and laughter helping to lighten the heavy weight resting on my chest.

That was, until a chirping interrupted us.

"Whose is it?" Nana flicked her fork between the two of us, eyes narrowed.

"Not me!" Ollie threw his hands up in innocence.

"Sorry." I pulled my Comms out, seeing Beckett's name appear. I clicked the answer button. "Nana Aggie is mad at you for interrupting breakfast."

Beckett's full lips frowned. "Well, please give her my sincerest apologies. I would never want to upset Aggie."

"Oh, is that Beckett?" Nana smiled, leaning over to get into view. "Hello, handsome!"

"Hi, Aggie." Beckett waved to her. "I didn't mean to interrupt

Kasha's morning off, I just had a last-minute meeting request that I needed to make sure she was aware of."

"Oh, please don't worry, I know you are all very important." She waved her hands as if it was no big deal, like she wasn't just chiding me for it moments ago. I rolled my eyes; Nana was in love with my Hierarchy team. "I hope you keep your appetite. I'll be sending home plenty of leftovers for all of you to enjoy."

Beckett's eyes lit up, a laugh bubbling from his lips. "We always have room for your cooking."

I turned the unit back to me. "What meeting?"

Beckett sighed, his face falling. "Nolan called it the moment he arrived. He wants to get us all up to date about this new case. You need to be back before five."

My fingers tightened. "Alright, I'll be there."

"Thanks, Kas." He gave me a quick wave before I signed off, slamming the unit down on the table, our plates rattling.

"Sorry," was all I could mumble, heart racing as I began to count down the hours before I came face to face with my new Alpha.

Chapter Six

The Compound was quiet when I pulled back into the drive early that evening.

I shoved my keys into my pocket, looking around at the twilit pathways. I focused my senses, picking up faint voices down near the training building. Heading in that direction, I internally chastised myself for not stopping home to change back into my training armor. Instead, I was about to meet my new Alpha in a plain, long sleeved grey tunic and my old, worn training pants with nothing but one single dagger hidden in my military-styled boots.

Oh, well, there was nothing I could do about it. It was my day off and he'd interrupted it, so he got what he got.

I nodded to a few Deltas and Dairchtas lingering outside, following the conversations that were getting louder and louder with each step I took, finding myself in the main training area on the top floor. The entire space was made for large group trainings, tests, observation, and certain certification processes for the Fledglings and Omegas. The left wall was taken up by a few rows of stadium seating where clusters of Faction members were sitting around and chatting in small groups. The opposite wall had cubby-like storage areas for those who were training to stash certain items along with a few rows of backup weaponry: daggers, Amalgam Blades, spears, and several others that people may have preferred to practice with. It all revolved around the center of the room, taken up completely by a black, cushioned mat. It was big enough to lead a class or have multiple occurring at once without bothering others.

It seemed today, though, it wasn't a class people were observing, but the skills of the new Alpha.

I halted in my tracks the moment I crossed the threshold, overtaken by an intoxicating scent: citrus and cinnamon.

My skin prickled at my first glance of him, throat drying. He was tall, obnoxiously so. I was an average height for a woman at around five-and-a-half feet, but he had to be almost a foot taller than me. His dark chocolate brown hair was slicked back away from his slightly-tanned face, sweat coating his sharp features, staring at his opponent in concentration as they fought hand-to-hand.

It was him—the man from the Blood Moon. The one I had acted like a bumbling idiot around.

Who I had been attracted to…

Oh, Goddess above, just shoot me down.

I quickly looked away, scanning the area for someone to sit with, grateful to see Liv and Eden sitting together. I made a path to them, sitting next to Eden, Liv on the bench behind us in a triangle formation.

"He certainly likes to make an entrance, doesn't he?" I scoffed to the two of them, keeping the conversation private.

"He said he wanted to work off energy from traveling for two days," Liv explained, her arms propped back against the row behind her, her long legs sprawled out, making her look even taller than she already was. *"Invited anyone who was curious to join or spar with him."*

"Who else has he fought?" I glanced back at the show in front of me, where Greyson was currently locked in battle with him.

"Eden was first," Liv said, her sharpened incisor gently biting her lower lip.

I turned to Eden, hunched over so her elbows were braced on her knees, scowling at the fight. *"How'd you do?"*

She just growled at me.

"Oh, not well, I guess."

"Shut up," she mumbled, her fingers twirling a thin, easily-hidden dagger between them. *"I barely lasted any time before he had me pinned."*

"You aren't the only one, Eden," Liv consoled, dropping her legs so she could lean forward. *"He took down Taylor and Emric just as quickly."*

"So, do you, um, recognize him by chance?" I asked Eden, Liv's brows furrowing at my question.

"Oh yeah." Eden gave me another sideways glare, her bright green eyes flashing golden for a brief second. *"I was drunk, not unconscious."*

"Remember what?" Liv poked both of our arms, her brown eyes wide with accusation.

"We, uh, had a..." I tried to find the right words. *"Run-in with the new Alpha at the Blood Moon the other night."*

56

"What kind of run-in?"

"He just talked to me a bit while Eden was in the bathroom."

"Flirted," Eden corrected, my cheeks heating at the word. *"He flirted with you and saw me wasted."*

"Oh my God," Liv said, slapping her hand over her lips, suppressing her giggles in both her mind and mouth.

"I'm so getting demoted," Eden mumbled, finally sheathing the dagger back into her boot.

"He's not going to demote you." I kicked her leg, her eyes raking over to me. *"I won't let him."*

"You don't have a say." Her round face stayed hard, but her eyes softened back to their natural green, looking defeated.

She was right, I technically didn't have a say. Keturi members were assigned by the High Faction, but their Gammas and Treasus were personal choice. The relationship between the three was of utmost importance, the level of trust invaluable to keep the Faction running smoothly and cases properly filtered and solved. It was a freedom you didn't take for granted as a Keturi, and I certainly hadn't when I was able to pick Taylor and Lucas to stand by my side all these years. If Nolan didn't want Eden to be one of his seconds, then he had every right to demote her back to Delta and either promote someone else, or transfer them from another Faction. It wasn't unheard of for Keturi transfers to bring their own seconds, but it wasn't that common.

"If he knows what's good for him, he'll take the advice of his Beta." I winked at her, a whisper of a smile pushing at the edge of her lips before disappearing back into her scowl.

Still, my stomach kept twisting with each moment that passed, tension filling the space as I waited for the inevitable…

A loud groan sounded from the sparring area, grabbing our

attention. Greyson was sprawled on his back, arms reached out in defeat as Nolan pinned him under his foot. People hooted and hollered, giving congratulations to Nolan. I heard whispers from some of the younger members, admiring his strength and agility, a few even saying he was the Alpha we had needed for a while. I swallowed back the acrid taste crawling up my throat, fingers mindlessly scratching at my legs.

I took a few deep breaths, reminding myself that they were probably comparing him to Logan and not me, because I had never officially been named Alpha, I had just taken over a few of the responsibilities over the past months while the posting had been open.

The logical thought did nothing to calm the wave of panic crawling through me.

The crowd in the center dispersed, people going back to their conversations and groups scattering around. My stomach clenched when I noticed Greyson walking right toward us, Nolan in tow. I turned back to Eden and Liv, praying to Lunestia that my face didn't look as pale as it felt, my cheeks cooling from the draining of blood.

"Nice fight," Liv complimented the two of them.

"Nice for Nolan," Greyson said, sitting next to Eden, bumping her shoulder. She gave him a quick jab in the ribs in response. He didn't even flinch, grabbing a towel to wipe the sheen of sweat from his angular face, pushing his black locks away from his eyes.

Laughter rang next to me. "I had a lot of built-up energy, probably the only reason I was able to win so many times."

"Oh, is that all?" Beckett joined us from out of nowhere, although the sweat beading along his hairline told me he was either working out alone or had also sparred with Nolan before I arrived. He leaned over, kissing Liv on the cheek.

A building pressure crawled up my spine, skin prickling from what I could assume was Nolan's gaze lingering on me, beckoning me to look at him—but I refused. I refused to budge until absolutely necessary, a part of me pushing to rebel against the decision of the High Faction, against the choice to keep me from the title that I had earned. I had spent my whole life following the rules, doing what I had been told was right, and look where that had gotten me. It had ripped my dreams from my hands.

The other part was the utter embarrassment that was infecting every inch of me at the memory of the tavern three nights ago.

So, I kept staring at Eden, pretending I didn't feel the weight of Nolan's gaze on my back.

"So," he cleared his throat, sending goosebumps scattering along the back of my neck. "Nice to see you again."

I took in a sharp breath before turning, standing up so I wasn't completely dwarfed by him, although he still towered over me.

"Yes, what a coincidence this is," I somehow managed to say, my throat dry as I caught another look into those forest green eyes I had been enthralled by. "Trying to sneak in some meetings before your official start date?"

"Nope." He shook his head, amusement etched into his features. "Just as you said, coincidence when I needed a drink after a long day of travel."

"But you just moved in here today."

"I wanted to stay in town for my first few days." He shrugged. "Figured it would be good to get a basic understanding of the capital city of my new territory before I started working."

"Mhm." I looked him up and down, begrudgingly admitting to myself that it was a smart idea on his part. Before I let that thought get too far, I reached my arm out to him, his warm hand clasping my forearm as we shook gently in introduction. "I'm Kasha."

"I figured," he laughed, his smile just as warm as his eyes. "Glad to finally meet my particularly famous Beta."

I yanked my arm away. "Famous?" Now what did that mean?

"Of course, your Varg bloodline is fairly well-known in the Onyx Guard." He tilted his chin down at me, leaving my chest unsettled. "Anton was the one to bring the assignment to me."

I bit my cheek at the mention of my father's name, so hard that warm blood slowly pooled between my molars. Nolan's eyebrow quirked, probably smelling it, just like everyone else around me could, which was probably why all of my friends stiffened instantly. They knew my father wasn't the best person to bring up if you wanted to get on my good side, which Nolan probably knew from reading my personnel file. Between my father signing off on a forced hospitalization for three months and his involvement in other issues between myself and the High Faction, only an incompetent idiot would think we were on good terms.

"And where exactly did you transfer from?" I crossed my arms, staring up at him, my spine as straight as it could go. "Nolan...?"

"Carragan, Nolan Carragan." He scratched at his sleeve, my eyes lingering on the tattoos snaking up his forearm and disappearing under his shirt. "From Xoblar. I was the Beta there for six years before I was promoted and transferred here."

Shock rippled through me, my training the only reason I was able to school my expression and keep my jaw from going slack. Xoblar was on the western tip of Kazola. My father barely found the energy to visit me in the hospital when I was being treated, and Seathra bordered the capital territory of Crelanti where he lived. But of course, he had no issue traveling for days to hand over my Faction to a stranger.

My chest ached slightly at that realization, but something else pricked at my mind.

"Carragan?" My brows wrinkled. "That sounds familiar. Have we met before?"

"You mean besides the other night?" He winked at me. My cheeks heated at the gesture. "No, I don't think so. I typically leave a lasting impression when people meet me, and I'm sure I wouldn't have forgotten you."

I snorted. "Wow, I'm certainly impressed by your level of arrogance. Hopefully that's not all that impresses me as we work together."

Beckett let out a muffled groan behind me while Eden and Greyson both hid their laughter. And failed.

"We're going to get along well, I can tell," Nolan laughed, shaking his head before his gaze left mine. I bristled, my scowl deepening.

He stepped around me, his stance shifting from relaxed to Alpha in a matter of seconds. "I'll give you all fifteen minutes to clean up and grab any missing Hierarchy members before meeting me over at the conference room for your briefing on our newest caseload."

Everyone mumbled various agreements, but I just stood there glaring at him. I would go to the briefing—I wasn't *that* insubordinate, after all—but I still couldn't find the strength inside of me to answer him.

He didn't seem to care, giving me that annoying half-smirk of his before strutting out of the room, leaving me to stew in my own frustration.

Chapter Seven

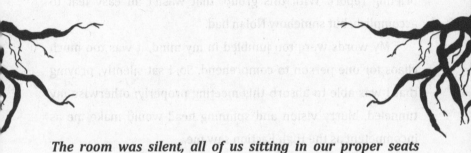

The room was silent, all of us sitting in our proper seats around the conference room.

Everyone's eyes were on Nolan standing in front of his chair at the head of the table, next to Beckett's seat, mine directly next to him. He was shuffling a few papers around from the stack of files strewn out, the rest piled in boxes around the bland room.

However, he must have worked most of the day unpacking in here, because an investigation board was already in progress. Our far-left wall was what we used to lay out important cases, hanging up any pieces of evidence, victim autopsy records, case reports, and any other necessary details so they were easier to find. Somehow, Nolan already had half the wall covered.

He had been busy, the show off.

I tried not to let it bother me. I tried to ignore the crawling, neck-twitching itch that was making its way up my spine. It was perfect, even half-finished and with plenty of boxes still in need of unpacking. Already, I could tell he was meticulous with his work, dedicated and detail-oriented almost to the point of overdoing it. My fingers tapped on the tabletop, trying to avoid the truth that the inky voices in my head were trying to feed me.

He was better than me. I wasn't good enough—he was.

Somehow, this one man had stunned all of us into silence, none of us knowing what to do as we waited for him to start his briefing report. With this group, that wasn't an easy feat to accomplish, but somehow Nolan had.

My words were too jumbled in my mind, it was too much chaos for one person to comprehend. So, I sat silently, praying that I was able to absorb this meeting properly; otherwise my tunneled, blurry vision and spinning head would make me as incompetent as the High Faction saw me.

"Alright, time to begin." Nolan didn't sit down like I expected, instead he walked over to the Investigation Board. We all spun our chairs around, the group of us now staring at him like the most rigid, at-attention audience I'd ever witnessed. "I bring you the Elliot Wells files." Nolan opened his arms, gesturing around the room at the boxes that littered the floor. "Each one of these contains dozens of cases from the past ten years, all of them murder reports linked to this one man, Elliot Wells."

"I'm sorry, did you say ten years?" Beckett asked.

Nolan's jaw ticked. "Yup, this man has killed just under one hundred people over that time across Kazola. He'll start in one Territory, wreak havoc for a time, and when the Onyx Guard finally starts to move in, he disappears for extended periods of time." He pointed to a map of the Isle with small, red pins littering it. "His last known kill was in Ochrat just over a year ago. That was, until last week, when one of his victims appeared here in

Seathra for the first time."

"Is that a typical amount of hiding time for him?" Eden asked, her eyebrows crinkled, arms crossed as she leaned back in her chair. "Seems quite short if he moved three territories over and set up his base here."

"It's always varied." Nolan said. "He's gone underground for as long as two and a half years and as short as five months. He kills his victims by draining them of all their blood, but based on past autopsy reports, it's in a slow, cruel way over a few days. The victims all have bruised wrists and ankles from different restraints. Then, postmortem, he brands them with a crest and then wipes down the body with liquid wolfsbane."

"Thus, killing any potential for a Varg Ibridowyn to track him by scent." I leaned forward in my chair, my mind already trying its best to work out the puzzle hanging before me. Now that I had something to focus on, a case that would give me a purpose, my mind began clearing of the fog that plagued it.

Nolan looked at me, his green eyes glistening, a smirk tugging at the edge of his lips. "Exactly. His patterns are impossible to track. He has no discernible victims either. He has killed humans, Vargs, Shrivs...even a Brido."

My heart dropped into my stomach, a chill sweeping through my veins. I looked around the room, a sea of matching shocked expressions.

"A Brido?" Emric was the first to speak up. "How is that even possible?"

"That's one case that has been a complete mystery to all of us." Nolan's posture tensed, his fingers reaching up to fiddle with a chain that hung around his neck, whatever hung at the end concealed beneath his v-neck black cotton shirt. Well, that was an interesting reaction. "Somehow, he got his hands on the Faction's Ogdala Blade and was able to stab the Brido through the heart."

As Ibridowyn, the genetic modifications we underwent helped to make us almost impossible to kill. However, the Alchemists had found that it was against the God and Goddess's will for creatures to be invincible, that everyone must have a weakness. So, they'd tethered our life to one weapon, The Ogdala Blade. This rare blade was made from a carved piece of Fuiliwood, the strongest tree in Kazola, and then encased in Iona Silver, the purest metal. Where Varg Anwyns could be killed by any form of silver and Shrivikas by any type of wood, we could only be killed by these specific types, and only when they were combined together.

They were so rare, only forty daggers existed: one at each Faction Compound, one for each High Faction Member, and one at each of the Alchemist Labs where the genetic modification procedures occurred. They were well protected, kept under lock and key and only taken out in case of emergencies.

So, how in the Goddess did this killer get his hands on the most unique weapon in Kazola?

I knew that weapon well. I had held it in my hands. I had used it to do a terrible thing...

My fingers clenched underneath the table, my mind plagued with dark memories, my breath going ragged for a moment before I evened it back out. I would not let that happen. This was not the time to remember.

I found something to distract myself with instead: the case.

"How do you know his name?" I asked.

Nolan's shoulders relaxed a bit, fingers continuing to twist the chain near the base of his throat. "Because on some of his victims, he likes to leave the Guards a little note. Not on every one, but some, and they are always signed 'Your New Friend, Elliot Wells'. Plenty of Factions have tried to do digs and checks into anyone using that name and have turned up empty. Now he just needs to leave the branding for us to know who it is."

"Classic narcissistic behavior," Liv said, rubbing her chin, plush lips parted.

"Pretty much," Nolan scoffed. "I suggest all of you take a box of files and start studying the details of each case. We never know when he is going to strike or how long it will be between his kills. We could have a victim show up later today or it could be weeks from now, but no matter when it happens, you all need to be caught up so we can start hunting this bastard down."

I nipped at the inside of my cheek, eyes narrowing. Something about his rigid stance and fiddling fingers mixed with the extra venom laced in all of his words piqued my interest. He was trying his best to hide it, to act professional, but as we continued on with the briefing, it was starting to leak out. I might have just met him, but based on our introduction only a little while ago, I had a good feeling he wasn't one to get easily agitated—and if he did, he could hide it with little effort. So, what about this was causing it to seep from him slowly?

Interesting.

"Where is the most recent victim's body? I would like to have it transferred here," Beckett said, no one batting an eye at his request. He was a trained physician, so with high priority cases he always completed the autopsies. It was a wonderful perk since we received vital information much quicker than if a local clinic or physician completed it.

Nolan wasn't even fazed by the request. "Of course. The

victim was found in Ballaterr, so we'll have to contact the outpost in that area to have her transferred here, but I do believe the autopsy was already conducted."

"I'd still like to have her here, just in case comparisons need to be made or they missed something," Beckett said. "I'll contact them when I get back to my office."

"Wonderful." Nolan clapped his hands together. "That should be all the major details, the rest are better discovered in personal research. Please feel free to come to me with any questions or leads you may have, but besides that, you're all dismissed."

Everyone looked around, unsure if he really meant it or if it was a trick. Finally, Beckett stood up first, grabbed one of the stacked boxes, and walked out the door. Everyone else followed, finding a box to take with them before they silently left the room.

I was the last to leave, giving one final glance at Nolan, his back turned, staring at the board. Between his physical reactions to certain details and his drive to hunt, there was one thing about this case I knew for sure: to Nolan, this was personal.

Chapter Eight

"What's this for?" I asked Beckett, who placed a steaming mug of rich, black coffee in front of me. My eyes wandered up from the load of Elliott case files littering my wood-carved desk; I'd been holed up in my office for hours now studying them, the bright mid-morning sunlight beginning to stream in through the open window that took up most of the wall behind me. The morning had gotten away from me a bit too quickly, my eyes struggling to adjust from staring at nothing but words and paper for so long.

Beckett sat down in the plush black velvet chair across from me, crossing his legs and leaning back to take a sip from his own mug. "I thought you could use a mid-morning pick-me-up."

"And you're coming to check on me?"

"Why would you say that?"

"Because you never share your imported beans with me." I sniffed, catching nutty caramel notes mingling with the bitter roast. "I'd be surprised if Liv was even able to drink this without you biting her head off."

"I let her." He smiled behind his mug, taking a sip. "On our anniversary."

I shook my head. "Making my point—that you are checking up on me."

I took the glass cup next to me, downing the rest of my 'breakfast', also known as a hefty serving of blood. As Ibridowyn, all of us in our Faction needed to feed on blood a few days a week. It was part of the enhancement and exchange of power, but when you gained immeasurable strength, you also needed to accept new weaknesses. As a Varg Anwyn Ibridowyn, I was no longer forced to transform during the full moon, giving me complete control over my wolf no matter the day or time. To balance that shift, I had to drink blood, like the Shrivikas.

On the opposite exchange, Shrivika Ibridowyn no longer had to feed multiple times a day but a few times a week to keep their strength. However, they also felt a calling to the moon, becoming erratic, a bit wild, and impulsive during a full moon phase. It was a give and take that was worth it to gain the strength and abilities needed to protect Kazola.

The ripened strawberry and dark chocolate flavors of Emric's blood mingled on my palette, and I finished it off before moving on to the cup of coffee, the first sip as delectable as the scent.

"I know your first counseling appointment is this afternoon." Beckett's cheeks reddened at the mention. "Between that and Nolan's arrival yesterday, you're right...I wanted to check up on you."

My muscles relaxed, sliding me down slightly in my high-backed chair. For the most part, I hated people hovering around

70

me worried that the wrong move would make me crack again. A part of me knew it came from a loving, caring place. They all just wanted to make sure that I was on the right path to healing. Yet they didn't seem to understand that the more they treated me like a delicate flower, the more I felt like I was about to break. They made me question my own strength, they made me wonder and second guess if I was actually doing better. Were they seeing something I wasn't? Did they know this new me better than I did? It just made my mind jump to the worst conclusions, and it was becoming increasingly hard to ignore with each passing day.

Beckett was one of few exceptions.

He was one of two people that I allowed to approach me like this, and there was a specific reason why: Beckett had been there for me in a way others hadn't. He had stood by me and tried everything he could to protect me.

In the end, he was the one who saved my life.

The memory hit my chest like a well-aimed punch, tugging me back toward that night. Ever since I'd started healing, I knew I would be forever grateful for Beckett. He had seen me at my worst and still helped me take the first steps in recovery; he gave me a second chance. I wasn't sure if I would ever be able to repay him for that, but I'd been working every day trying my best to show my gratitude.

"I wish I could say that yesterday didn't bother me." I swallowed a sip, my throat constricting as it passed through. "But it crushed me the moment I laid eyes on him. He just kept walking around as though nothing bothered him. I felt like I could sense his judgment, looking down on me and seeing nothing but a weak little Beta that he wishes wasn't working with him."

Beckett just stared at me, his deep brown eyes filled with

understanding, his lips pressed together in a hard line.

"Seeing him just act so naturally in his position, as if he had always been the Alpha here, it just..." My fingers scraped across my mug, "it made me wonder if the High Faction was in the right to take the promotion away from me."

"Kas, no." Beckett leaned forward, placing his mug on the edge of my desk. "I don't know Nolan well enough to say if he is deserving or undeserving of this position. But even if he is, that doesn't negate your worthiness of being the Alpha. Which you are, the High Faction's decision was terrible and we all stand behind that."

"Thank you," I whispered, staring at the thin rays of sunlight cast against the dusty lavender walls and the paintings of Nana Aggie's that hung on them. I was trying to accept the words he said with such conviction, but a dark, inky voice whispered in the back of my mind that it was all lies. "Can I admit something terrible to you?"

"Of course."

"A part of me hates him." My stomach twisted at the admission. "I know it's illogical and I barely know him enough to make that judgment, but whenever I see him or hear him or even think about him, my insides feel like they're on fire."

"It may be illogical in some ways, but it's not unreasonable," Beckett said. "Sometimes emotions can get the best of us, and they can surprise us with their intensity, no matter how much we prepare to handle them."

I snorted. "I hate it."

"I know."

"And to make it worse, the rest of you are anxious and stressed over what he plans to do to the Faction." I threw my head

72

back, my neck supported by the top curve of my chair. "If it was only affecting me, I could handle it, but to know that my mistakes and past are haunting all of you, it just makes me want to scream."

"Stop putting all of the blame on yourself." He took another sip of his coffee. "We are all grown adults who made decisions and acted on them. You can't take responsibility for the actions of others."

"Your actions were based on my decisions." My fingers shook, the tips automatically touching the long, jagged scar that ran along my neck. "You were all doing it to defend and protect me."

"Because we love you, Kas! We saw some truly disgusting things happen to you, and the High Faction let you down. We weren't just going to stand by. We weren't going to let him..." Beckett's pale fingers curled around the arm of his chair, shaking, his jaw so tense I thought he was going to break it. His eyes flashed, a bright blood red overtaking the usual deep onyx brown. "You haven't deserved anything that has happened to you, and we all chose to fight against it when you didn't have the strength. That's what family does."

"I know," I whispered, my insides tangling together, indiscernible emotions swirling in the pit of my stomach. "Everything you all did for me is a constant reminder that I can make it through these Goddess-awful moments. I just wish I could erase your pasts for you, make it so Nolan never found out what you all did."

"None of us would go back and change our decisions." Beckett's voice was calmer, his eyes still tinged with red. "Are we nervous and scared how Nolan will treat us in the coming weeks over all of it? Of course. But we don't regret what we did, we don't

73

regret defending you."

The corners of my eyes pricked, tears wanting to escape, but I swallowed them down. Along with Ollie and Nana, the only thing that had gotten me through the past eight months was my Hierarchy peers. They reminded me why I was fighting. Although most days I struggled to accept it, to find my worthiness, it still warmed me. It helped me make it through the bad days.

Chapter Nine

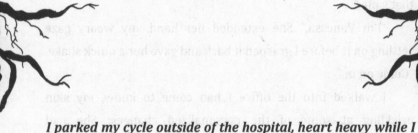

I parked my cycle outside of the hospital, heart heavy while I stared up at the four-story building.

The only way to describe it was clinical, with its bright white brick stacked in a perfect square. Nothing fancy or exciting about it. I walked in, my pulse picking up its pace with each step I took to the psycho-physician ward, a path I'd come to know well over the three months I was forced to stay here. However, this time was different; I would be meeting with a new physician, someone I was expected to profess my overwhelming feelings to.

I'd just started to find trust in my last physician, these sessions actually helping me achieve a sense of calm and normalcy some days. Now I was about to start completely from scratch with this woman, Vanessa. Would she try and take me off active duty if she came to realize how unstable I could be some days? Would she think I was crazy? Or weak?

My hand hesitated over the door handle to the waiting room.

I gnawed at my lower lip, taking a few deep breaths, trying to calm myself down. I could do this, I continued to tell myself, pushing the door open into the tiny sitting room; the four chairs occupying the bland space were empty.

It only took a few moments before another door opened, a middle-aged brunette woman standing in the threshold, smiling. "You must be Kasha."

I gripped the strap of my bag slung across my chest. "Yes, that's me."

"I'm Vanessa." She extended her hand, my weary gaze settling on it before I grasped it back and gave her a quick shake. "Come on in."

I walked into the office I had come to know, my skin prickling at some of the personalized changes; She had rearranged the furniture, so that the two chairs now sat directly across from each other as if we were in an interrogation room minus the table in between. She'd moved her desk to the far right and new, colorful artwork hung along the walls, helping to brighten up the space from the lack of windows. I hesitated, not sure exactly which seat I should be in anymore. It used to be easy with my last doctor—she had a couch she made me lie on.

"Choose whatever seat you want," Vanessa smiled, coming up next to me, apparently reading my mind.

My posture straightened a bit, and I went for the chair facing the door, just in case. One should never have their back to an entrance if they wanted a fair fight. As if she expected it, Vanessa's hazel eyes softened, watching me sit down and drop my bag next to me.

She settled in across from me, a leather-bound notebook in her lap and a stilo in her hand, a fresh pot of dark black ink on the side table next to her. I stared back at her, knowing the expectations that I would need to start talking about the past twelve months. I didn't want to relive it again just because I was forced to see a new physician. I rubbed my palms along my thighs, my pants smooth under my touch.

"Nervous?" she asked.

"Why would you say that?" I retorted, although I knew it was a stupid question just based off the way I was posturing. I leaned back in the chair, crossing my arms and legs, holding them close to me in hopes they didn't give anything away.

"Never mind." She dipped the tip of her stilo into the ink before jotting down something onto the first page of her notebook. "So, how's your day been so far?"

I blinked a few times, convinced I hadn't heard the question right. "My...day?"

"Yes," she said, eyes filling with an unreadable calmness that unsettled me a bit.

My grip tightened around my forearms. "It's been busy. We had a new case come in with our new Alpha."

"Sounds stressful." She jotted something down. "Having to meet your new superior and start a new case at the same time."

I took a good look at Vanessa. By the metallic edge subtly hidden under lemon and lavender, I knew she was a Shrivika. Her olive skin tone matched well with her hazel eyes and rounded cheeks. Her dark onyx hair reached her ribs, but it was half contained by a braid that sat on the crown of her head, keeping it pulled from her eyes. Her slender, athletic build was well suited for the flowing black pants and white silk button-up shirt she wore.

She looked perfect...too perfect. She wanted me to trust her,

77

yet something gnawed at my stomach.

"Have you ever been on the Guard, Vanessa?" I leaned forward, elbows braced on my knees.

She shook her head. "No, but I can only imagine the stress and trauma one can go through during it."

"Stop skirting around the subject." I couldn't help but call her out, her eyes widening a bit before returning to their unreadable calm. "You most likely read my file."

She nodded. "I did."

"Then you know what happened to me." My throat tightened, but I forced my words to come out strong.

"I do. And I stand by my words: you went through something traumatic."

"Then why aren't you trying to force me to talk about it?"

Her perfectly manicured eyebrows quirked up. "Do you want to talk about it?"

"No, not particularly," I said. "I don't even like talking about it to the people closest to me. Which is why I never understood why the High Faction thought I would be so open to talking to a stranger, even if they are a professional."

"Which is why I decided to start simple and ask how your day is," she said, placing her stilo in the spine of her notebook. "Relationships take trust, this is no different. So, let's just get to know each other and see what conversations come from it. Some might be productive, some might be nothing more than small talk or frustrated rants, but that doesn't matter. What matters is that you come here and you talk about what you are ready to talk about. That's how you find yourself on a healing path that you want to be on, not the path others want to force you down."

I stared at her, my whole self still. Something about her

78

words stung me, invisible needles poking into my throat. My last psycho-physician hadn't been like this, she had been insistent that we get to the root of the problem. Of course, she'd started as my physician the moment I had been admitted to the hospital, and at that point what else was there to talk about?

Yet Vanessa just sat there, calm and collected, waiting for me to say whatever I wanted. Maybe she found it useful, or maybe she was just trying to get me to trust her. Either way, I kept my guard up but relaxed my shoulders a bit. I could do this, especially if there was no pressure to talk about what happened.

"So," she picked her stilo back up, tapping it against the back of her hand. "How's your new Alpha?"

I grunted. "Cocky."

She laughed. "He seems to have made a strong impression."

"That's one way to put it." My insides squirmed, my clavicle warming. "His name's Nolan, and he walked in like he didn't have a care in the world, acting like we should just hand over control to him."

I didn't mention that I had met him previously and had found him attractive before I knew exactly who he was. That was a fact that didn't need to be admitted out loud.

"And you don't like handing over control?"

"If you hadn't already guessed, I don't do well with strangers." My fingers tapped along my throat. "On top of that, I've been a part of Seathra's Faction since I was a Delta. I worked my way up through the ranks and earned the trust of everyone there. And this guy thinks he can just strut in and be handed it like a welcome gift? That's not how it works."

"Control seems important to you."

My jaw tightened. I wasn't sure how we got here, but

79

somehow we did. "Control is how I keep my sanity in check. It's how I keep myself safe."

"From?"

"Myself." I bit my bottom lip. "Others around me. Anyone who wants to change me."

"So, what's something that you could do to take a little control back?" she asked. "Doesn't matter how small, just the first thing that comes to mind."

"Start growing my hair out again. Maybe dye it." I had no idea why that was the first thing to come to mind, but memories of Eden drunk at the bar somehow reminded me. "They made me cut it when I was a patient here and the color faded quickly. Maybe if I put it back, I'll feel like myself again."

"Maybe," Vanessa said. "Was that a large part of your identity?"

I shrugged. "I never thought so, I just enjoyed having darker hair."

"Then why would it make you feel like yourself again?" My shoulders deflated at her words, no answer coming to mind, but she continued, "If you want to dye your hair because it makes you happy, then do it. Give yourself a reason to take time and care for yourself even if it's in a little way like changing your hair color."

"But?" I coaxed, sensing there was more.

"You just admitted that before everything happened, your hair wasn't a big part of your identity, it was just something you did for fun." She scribbled something in her book. "Going back to that, it might not bring the normalcy you want it to. It could even have the opposite effect."

My chest tightened. "Maybe that's why I always find an excuse not to do it."

I had always said I was too busy or that it wasn't important, but she made a good point. Why did I want to look like that broken girl again?

She leaned forward. "I'm not telling you to do it or not. But I suggest you take some time to think about what making that change actually means to you. Is it a step forward or back? Only you will be able to answer that."

"Um..." My brows crinkled, words jumbling in my mind unable to form coherent thoughts.

She held her hand up. "You don't have to have the answer this very moment. You don't even have to tell me the answer when you figure it out if you don't want. I just think maybe it's a question you should ponder during a quiet moment, when you feel emotionally and mentally ready to concentrate on it."

We stared at each other for a moment. Vanessa's words rippled through me, bringing me to terms with the fact that these sessions were going to be a lot harder to navigate than I initially hoped.

Chapter Ten

My counseling continued on with typical conversation that kept me on edge for the rest of the appointment. Somehow, I wondered if it was a trick, trying to get me to admit something that I wasn't ready to talk about. It all just seemed too easy, too relaxed, and that made my anxiety spike, sending my mind spinning for the rest of the morning.

Luckily, I got to spend the afternoon leading a training session for the new Omega and Fledgling trainees, which meant an excuse to beat my aggression out on Taylor and Lucas again. For educational purposes, of course.

An hour into it, a slick sheen of sweat covered my entire body, my skin no longer pin-prick sensitive. Thank the Goddess.

I hung back during the next round, sitting on one of the benches to observe the dozen trainees while they tried to recreate the weapon techniques we had just taught them. Taylor and Lucas wove in between each pair, correcting any mistakes or missteps. I took progress notes on each recruit, the stilo slippery between my sweat-coated fingers. Most of the recruits were doing a decent job for it being their first time working with the Amalgam Blade, the main weapon used in the Onyx Guard.

It wasn't the only weapon that we were trained in. Everyone also had to do dagger handling and a few of us even went on to learn and master archery, along with a handful of non-fatal weapons when needed. However, it was the Amalgam that we were known for, just one more thing that made us stand out as an Onyx Guard soldier.

The double-sided weapon was a hybrid of a short sword and a switchblade. Two blades easily nestled into the forearm-length steel handle, each one triggered by an onyx stone button on either end. One blade was forged of pure silver, the weakness of the Varg Anwyns, and the other blade was carved from wood reinforced with a steel core, since Shrivikas were allergic to wood. These weapons were created specifically for the Onyx Guard, although some military units outside of the guard were known to train with them in case of emergencies, since it was one of the few weapons that could be used as protection against the three original species of Kazola.

I put my notebook down, picking up my sheathed Amalgam, twirling the handle between my hands. Like the rest of the team, this blade was my primary weapon, although I was the Archery Master on Compound and led all the bow and crossbow training. But I had been shooting and perfecting my abilities in that weapon since I was a teenager, and I was never allowed to handle an Amalgam until I had officially joined the Guard. The day I got to hold one for the first time was a memory I always cherished, as it was the moment I had finally made that dream of joining this unit a reality.

I loved the design, black carvings embossed on either side of the flattened hilt. The crest of the Onyx Guard was carved into one side, an entwined circle of tree roots and branches surrounding the Ogdala Blade, which was pierced through a crescent moon. On the opposite side was the Onyx Guard Motto in Ancient Kazalonian, the original language of the Isle before it mostly died out centuries ago.

Tsio a Chisain. Protect the Peace.

My thumb gently rubbed over the words, heart lurching. Some days I wondered if I was still worthy of that motto. Did I deserve to protect others when I felt incapable of protecting myself?

"Seems like a good team of recruits." A voice pierced through my blackened thoughts, my body flinching away; I looked up, my shoulders deflating at the sight of Nolan looming over me. His eyes narrowed at me. "I'm sorry, did I scare you?"

"No!" I said a bit too quickly, my skin still prickling from his untimely arrival. "And yes, they're doing fairly well."

He sat down next to me, picking up my journal to make room. "Wow you take...detailed notes."

"Give me that." I yanked it from his grasp, closing it and clutching it close to my chest. "You know, in most parts of Kazola, it's considered rude to read other people's journals."

He chuckled. "Isn't it just notes you'll put in their training reports later for me to review?"

My cheeks flared with warmth, fingers tightening around the leatherbound book. "Some of them, but not all. Only the ones that are necessary for the report."

"Wouldn't all training notes on recruits be necessary?" He

84

gave me a questioning look, one eyebrow raised.

"Not necessarily," I grumbled. "It's..."

I didn't know how to finish that sentence, how to explain exactly what was in this journal. Not every note I took was clear and cut on training. I also wrote about different things I noticed about each recruit, whether it be a sensitivity to a certain word or a particular touch aversion. After what I had gone through, I always tried my best to pick up on other people's...tics. I wanted to make sure that when I was training them, when I had to be close, I didn't accidentally breach any boundaries. I knew the terrible struggle when it came to speaking up about boundaries—that deep, aching fear that someone wouldn't respect it, or worse, would laugh and belittle you for having them at all.

If this past year had taught me anything, it was that too many people had a lack of respect for others' boundaries. That was why I did my best to show my complete respect.

Although I kept them out of official reports, since they were details not asked for, I did try my best to tell my observations to the other Hierarchy members for training purposes. However, I didn't know Nolan well enough to give him such sensitive details. For all I knew, he would think they were utterly laughable, that the idea of boundaries was nothing more than an excuse for our recruits to slack off.

"Just stay out of my journal, please." I slapped him in the arm with it, the smack echoing off the high glass ceiling.

"Alright, alright, I'll stay out of the precious journal." He rubbed his arm where I hit him, humor gleaming in his eyes. "Goddess, I barely read any of it. I don't know why you think so little of me."

85

My stomach tightened, but I didn't have the strength to answer him with the truth. To explain that a part of me wanted nothing more than to fight against anything he said because I didn't want an Alpha anymore. Not after last year.

I couldn't let anyone control me again. I was in control of myself.

Before I could answer with a snarky comeback, conversations from the center of the room grew, the recruits starting to drift over to the storage areas, grabbing bottles of water and cloths to wipe their faces.

Lucas and Taylor walked over to us, their stances going rigid with proper salutes: a fist pound against the heart.

"Alpha," they said in unison, bowing slightly to Nolan. I rolled my eyes at the formality.

"Um, at ease?" Nolan laughed at their posture. "Nice job with training, the three of you seem to have put them through their paces."

Taylor and Lucas exchanged a look, as if not sure if Nolan was telling the truth or not.

I sighed. *"Will you two just act normal?"*

"Oh, shut it, Kas," Taylor relaxed his posture, smacking my arm playfully before grabbing his water bottle from next to me and taking a quick swig.

"Thanks," Lucas answered first, sitting down on the other side of me, using a discarded cloth to wipe his chiseled face and shaved head. "We gave them a fifteen-minute break before shuffling the pairs and having them do a mock sparring match."

"Well, while they're on break, why don't we give them a little show?" Nolan nudged me with his shoulder, my body seizing up at the contact...and the suggestion.

"Excuse me?"

"You're the only Hierarchy member I haven't sparred with yet, so how about a little hand-to-hand?" he winked at me. "Since you find me so distasteful, why not put me in my place?"

"Um..." My eyes narrowed at him.

He made it seem so innocent, even a little fun. Yet too many questions about his motives filled my mind. What if he was trying to embarrass me in front of the young recruits? To prove that I was weak? What if he wanted to find a reason to report me to the High Faction?

There were just so many unknowns with this man, and I hated unknowns.

He leaned toward me, a wicked smirk playing on his lips. "Are you trying to tell me that the idea of punching me isn't tempting enough?"

I cocked my head to the side, lips spreading into a matching grin. Well, that idea certainly made the noise in my mind stop. "Fine, but when I beat your ass, just know you brought this on yourself."

I laid my journal down, placing my Amalgam Blade on top before standing to stretch my muscles out. I didn't even give him a second look before sauntering into the center of the ring, ignoring the growing ache in my stomach. This was an important moment, the moment where I fought the Alpha for the first time. If I won, it would prove to him, and myself, that I deserved that job. That no matter my past, I'd earned the title of Alpha, in spite of what the High Faction decided. Yet, if I failed, it would confirm everything the High Faction believed. That I was unworthy and weak and useless...

I let that thought disappear from my mind, refusing to let it distract me from this moment. This was my time, and I would not back down.

He followed behind me, giggles erupting from off to the left, a handful of the recruits whispering to each other and batting their eyes as Nolan sauntered up to where I stood. I didn't even try and listen into the conversation, the sweet scent of their attraction to Nolan enough to confirm what they were thinking. I glanced back to him, his lips twitching, teeth gnawing at the edges. His gaze flicked over to them for a brief moment, giving them a wave before he turned back to me, as if the giggling that surged on was completely normal.

Ugh. That just added fuel to the fire; I was ready to punch him a few times.

I readied myself with a wide stance, fists poised in front of me, Nolan doing the same. He winked a beat before someone called start from the sidelines, and I watched his face transform in front of me. No longer the joking Nolan, but a predator ready to fight.

Little did he know, I was a predator, too.

I didn't hesitate to take the upper hand, aiming for his left side with a series of jabs and strikes. Unlike him, I had watched my opponent fight multiple people already, and I'd studied his fighting style. He favored his right side, and he relied more on his strength than speed, using his height to his advantage whenever possible. That would be my biggest handicap in this fight, since it would be difficult to counter an attack from above, which he could easily do if I let myself get too close. So, I made sure to keep us moving, our footwork in sync while we threw punches and blocks.

I sent my next flurry of jabs, yet instead of trying to block them, he reached forward, his fingers curling around my wrist and yanking me right toward him. My mind had only a moment to react before his free hand came down toward me, his fist aimed right at my face. I spun away, his knuckles barely missing my face and colliding with my shoulder. I used the force of the impact to my advantage, stumbling backward and free of his grip.

I caught myself before falling to the ground, shoulder pulsing with dull pain, lips curling up into a snarl.

I would not let him win.

I faked to the left before rounding on him, my elbow cutting across, smashing into his face, a growl escaping both of us at the scent of blood pooling in his mouth. I didn't let that stop me, seeing his dazed look and taking advantage with a sharp jab to the ribs, feeling the impact under my knuckles.

"Well, aren't you just a little vicious," Nolan laughed, wiping a slick of blood coating his pouty lips.

"You're so vicious..."

My feet stumbled backward, the memory hitting my mind and body with force, the room beginning to spin. I tried to hold it in, to lock the chaos inside before it captured me in its clutches, but it was no use by this point. I'd been forced back to that night when I'd lost everything.

Whenever I found myself back there, I slipped away from reality and into a place I wouldn't wish on my worst enemies. If I didn't get out of here soon, anything could happen; I could start crying or screaming or even black out. Although I kept blocking his attacks, I could already sense the control over my movements slipping, each one a bit weaker and slower than the last.

This couldn't happen here, not in front of Nolan and the recruits. There was only one thing that would end the fight quickly.

I had to lose.

I aimed another punch, knowing I'd left my weak side open. No surprise, Nolan took advantage, ramming his fist into my solar plexus, knocking the wind out of me. I choked, doubling over. Before I could recover, he leaned back and rounded a kick into my ribs, forcing me off balance and onto my back.

My body shook against the mat, tears pricking the corner of my eyes. This was my moment, and I let it slip away. Because I was weak and undeserving.

I did not belong here.

No, no, no, no, no....

"You win," the words came out strained as I pulled myself up from the ground. I sent a million blessings up to the Goddess that this had happened while I was training, so I could disguise this mind-bending panic as nothing more than exhaustion.

"Well, aren't I just the best?" he laughed, the sound dying on his lips as he stared at me, brows creasing. "Kasha? Are you alright?"

He reached out to touch my arm, but I flinched away, taking a step back. "Yes, I just remembered that I'm behind on reviewing case files. Lucas can finish the class if you don't mind helping."

I tried to keep my pace as slow as possible, my steps agonizing as I walked over to the bench and picked up my bag, shoving my journal and water inside. The pressure on my chest increased, each breath sharp as I tried my best to pull air in and push it out.

"I...um...of course..." Nolan hovered around me, his movements hesitant. He leaned down, lips close to my ear. "Are you sure you're alright?"

"Yes! How many times do I have to say it?" I snapped, my mind recoiling at the unwarranted bite in my words, but I couldn't worry about that at the moment. I needed to get away. "Taylor, come with me, I need your help."

Taylor, bag already in hand, fell quickly into step with me toward the door. I tried my best to walk out of the room with ease, as if there was no other reason than work making me flee. But the moment we were outside of view, I took off, my memory guiding my feet while the world blurred around me. I stumbled into one of the private training rooms, the door slamming against the wall as I entered.

I finally allowed myself to collapse on the floor, my mind and body in anarchy. Everything was muted by the agony screaming inside, raging through me like a storm. I barely registered the door clicking behind me, footsteps approaching, the smoky campfire scent familiar from his skin.

"I've got you Kas," Taylor whispered in my ear, his chest pressing against my back, arms wrapping around me in a protective cocoon. "I've got you. No one can hear us in here."

That was all it took for the tears to flow, a scream ripping from my throat as I let the pandemonium out.

Chapter Eleven

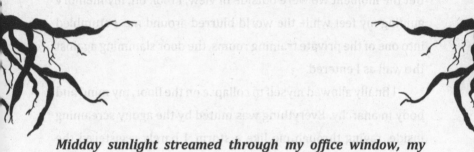

Midday sunlight streamed through my office window, my vision starting to blur while I stared down at the reports in front of me.

I was taking every chance I had to go through as many Elliot files as I could. I wanted to be an expert and catch up as quickly as possible. The more I continued to learn and read, the more my stomach churned at the thought of this man running free in the streets, in my country. This was why I had joined the Guard, why I felt called to take the oath even as a legacy child. I wanted to protect, I wanted to give others safety in life and retribution to those who had been wronged. This man, with the evil that must course through his veins, represented all of that. I would hunt him down with every bit of mental and physical strength I had left if I had to.

A smaller part of me was using this opportunity to prove my place.

I wasn't sure if I was trying to prove something to the High Faction or to myself, but I was determined. I didn't care if Nolan had helped lead it in the past, or if he was some kind of expert on Elliot Wells. Seathra was my territory, it was my home. I would keep it safe.

Pettiness was seeping through every inch of me. I needed to rein it in a bit, and I would, but if it was the thing that drove me to learn more, to protect better, and to hunt this villain down quicker, then what was the harm?

Oh right, Nolan.

He inadvertently had become the representation of my past and the mistakes I had made. He was this living embodiment of failure that I was now forced to follow—something I had never wanted to do again.

Seeing him almost every day made my stomach curl inward, my chest ache in a way I wished I could banish. My mind and body felt out of sync, unable to discern what feelings toward Nolan were truth and which were nothing more than defensive reactions.

The loyal soldier in me wanted to obey, but the swirling turmoil inside wanted me to act out. Nothing seemed to make sense when it came to that man.

Before all of this happened, I had never found myself in such a toxic place. I had been ready to take an Alpha promotion. I was collected and calm under pressure, able to banish feelings and emotions from cutthroat decisions that sometimes needed to be made. I could sacrifice my personal comfort for the betterment of the Faction and Kazola. I had been ready. Now, every time I felt betrayed or hurt or was triggered by my past, my first instinct was to act out, to defy.

I loathed this new part of myself. I wanted it to disappear, and sometimes I wondered if it would just be better if I disappeared along with it.

I shook my head, ridding myself of the terrible thought. I couldn't give in, I couldn't surrender. Not again.

Damn Nolan for his presence bringing this horrid part of me so much closer to the surface.

As if summoned, a knock came from my closed office door, the faint scent of cinnamon and citrus seeping through.

"Yes, Nolan?" I called out.

"Do you have a moment?" Nolan's head peeked in.

I dropped my stilo on the desk, leaning back in my chair. "I suppose."

"I just wanted to see if you had Beckett's blood card." He strode to the front of my desk, fingertips skimming the top. "I searched for it in my office, but I can't seem to find it."

To make sure everyone had access to blood consistently, each member of the Faction was assigned a Blood Consort. In the Hierarchy specifically, matching members between the Pack and the Clan were paired off, each one responsible for keeping the other strong. Every person had a blood card for them and their Consort, which allowed them to access and deposit blood bag donations into the bank set up at the infirmary. You could only access each electrified cooler—yet another wonderful invention from the Ley Lines—with one of the cards.

Doing it this way meant none of us found ourselves in Blood Starvation, a very real and dangerous place for the Shrivikas and Ibridowyns to find themselves in. If we went too long without blood, it depleted our strength and ability to work, just as if we were deprived of food and water. The symptoms of Blood

94

Starvation could be intense, from jittering nerves and twitches to weakened muscles and lethargy, and even hallucinations at the worst of it.

Luckily, with this tight system, none of us ever found ourselves in that place.

While the Alpha position had been empty, I'd temporarily taken over as Beckett's Consort, happy to give anything to the physician who had helped me all those months ago. But now, a new Alpha was here, ready to take over that duty. To make sure his partner in rank was strong and ready to lead.

"Here." I pulled open one of the drawers of my desk, the card sitting right on top. "I just filled his cooler yesterday, so you should have about a week before you have to restock it."

"Thanks." He slipped it into the back pocket of his dark pants. "It must have been hard having to Consort for both Beckett and Emric."

I shrugged. "I only consorted to Beckett. Emric is my Consort, but his human husband is his."

"Oh." His shoulders dropped. "Well, at least it's one less thing you need to worry about."

I couldn't even respond to that, heart lurching at yet another responsibility taken away from me. All my actions, everything from my past was catching up and ripping away my dreams one by one. So I just stared at him, curbing my emotions so they weren't desperately written all over my face. He blatantly stared back, those green eyes appraising every inch, attempting to see through the facade I'm sure he knew I put up every day.

"Is there something else?" I cleared my throat, hoping he would leave me and my jittering nerves alone for the rest of the day.

"Nope," he said, taking a step back. "I'll see you at the camp tonight."

My breath caught in my throat. Pressure built within me, twisting and writhing, pulling my attention inward, toward the ache.

No, not now. Not in front of him.

My past does not define me, I am stronger than my past.

I repeated the words in my head as I unclenched my white-knuckled fingers from around the arms of my chair, leaning forward.

"No, you won't." I picked up my stilo again, twirling it between my fingers to keep them busy. I kept my voice level and cool, not wanting to give away any of the actual panic swirling just below my surface. "I don't attend the campouts anymore. Medical exemption."

Nolan halted in his tracks, turning back around. "It's my first campout, and you're telling me that my Beta won't be there to celebrate?"

"Pretty much," I mumbled, refusing to look up at him. I felt the weight of his stare on me, but I refused to budge. I knew what part of me was coming to the surface—the one that thought it was protecting me. I would usually try to fight it, but this time I let it free. If he wanted to battle against my stubbornness, then he was in for a treat.

"I saw the exemption note in your file," he said, my insides jittering at the mention of that dreadful stack of papers. "But it had mentioned that you didn't always have to attend. Made me believe that you could pick and choose when you wanted to go, not that you didn't attend altogether."

"That is true." I nodded without looking up at him. "And I

made the decision that this is one of those times I am choosing not to go."

He sighed. "I want the entire Hierarchy there so I can get to know all of you better. So we can become a team."

I wasn't surprised he wanted me there; the Full Moon Camp was a Faction tradition that went back to the conception of the Ibridowyn. Although the Varg Anwyn Bridos were no longer forced to turn during the full moon, it didn't make the call to the lustrous orb that looked over us any less alluring. We craved it, maybe even more so with the freedom of being able to turn at will. Since the Shrivika Bridos now felt that same calling, we celebrated under the full moon every month. Factions would camp out in the wooded area of the Compound to drink and laugh and revel together. We would forget the responsibilities from the past and for the future and just be. Except for a few Deltas and Dairchtas who we kept behind to monitor for any issues, everyone was required to go. That was, until my last psycho-physician had given me a medical exemption from the monthly event.

"We *are* a team." I crinkled my brow, my nose scrunching up. "With or without me there tonight, that fact doesn't change."

"No, we're colleagues," Nolan challenged, coming back to stand in front of my desk, his towering form looming over me. "A team is a group of people who work together because they enjoy it, not because they're forced to."

"You've only been here a week, Nolan." I tried to evade the subject, to put it to rest before we went to a place we couldn't return from. "Just give it time."

"Kasha, this is important to me, so I'll ask nicely one more time." The power in his words raised my gaze to finally meet his.

"Come to the Full Moon Camp tonight."

I stood up slowly. "Or what? You'd force me?"

Just as in a typical Varg Anwyn Pack, orders from an Ibridowyn above your station could not be disobeyed, especially a formal command from an Alpha. You either submitted right away or suffered, your strength seeping away from you until you did. As my Alpha, if Nolan gave me an official order, I would have to go.

No, no, no, no...

My mind was spinning. I wouldn't go back. He couldn't make me.

"Of course not." His cheekbones hollowed as he clenched his jaw. "I only use that when absolutely necessary, and with great caution. This is far from one of those moments."

I let out a deep breath, my quivering insides stabilizing a bit. At least he wouldn't do that. At least he wouldn't take away my control over myself. Unlike...

"Good," I said, pulling my shoulders back to try and take a stronger stance.

"What I'm asking of you is tradition, not torture." He shook his head, his dark hair swishing across his forehead. "So why are you acting like what I'm asking would ruin you?"

"Because it would!" I said, my voice piercing. I wished I hadn't answered—it was only three words, but they elicited so much more than I wanted him to know.

"What does that even mean?"

"Nothing." I didn't know how much more I could take before I crumbled, but I would push myself to the edge before I backed down on this.

"Then give me one good reason why you can't make it

98

tonight. If you give me just one, I'll back off." His hands braced on the desk, towering over me, eyes flaring a bright amber before returning to their usual dark green hue.

I was angering him, his wolf seeping out because of it, but I didn't care. I couldn't.

There were important reasons why I didn't go to the camp anymore, why I avoided it as if I would catch on fire the moment I crossed the threshold. The moment everything changed for me was at my last campout, just under a year ago. The incident where every piece of me had been broken and shattered. Where I'd felt everything slip away, forced from my grip. I wasn't ready to go back and face that moment again.

Yet, even if I was, there was something far more shameful that I was hiding from Nolan. Something that I had barely been able to admit to the rest of the Hierarchy.

I hadn't been able to shift into my wolf form since that incident.

That part of myself, the other half of who I was, had disappeared. It was locked away somewhere deep inside me, and no matter how hard I tried, I couldn't seem to make it emerge. My strength and abilities in human form hadn't disappeared, but I couldn't even make my eyes flair their beautiful gold. It was like that part of me had been nothing but a dream, something that my imagination had created to amuse me.

So much had been ripped away from me on that night last year, but losing my wolf form was the worst of all. It was the other half of my soul, my essence, my life. It was my freedom, my fearlessness, and my strength. Every inch of myself was tied to that part of me; my identity couldn't exist without it. So why, *why* did it evade me?

Why did it walk away from me when I needed it most?

Maybe if I could still shift, my life would have turned out differently.

I shook away the thought, reminding myself that it was just my darkness trying to get the best of me. I had tried to argue that with my first psycho-physician, but she had put a stop to that pretty quickly. She'd told me that dwelling on what could have happened wasn't going to bring my wolf back; the only way to gain it was to move forward and heal.

And I was trying. Damnit, I was trying so hard.

But of course, I couldn't say any of that to Nolan. Even if I didn't recoil at his presence, even if I was just fine with him being my Alpha, I couldn't admit that I was unable to turn. What if he reported me to the High Faction? They could demote me even further, or worse, force me to retire and go through the Removal. What then? I would be nothing but a shell of who I once was, of everything I had created for myself. I had fallen far, but I refused to fall that far.

"My reasons are my own," was all I could say. It was pathetic and I loathed myself for it, but I had no other words. It was either give into the protection of acting immature, admit details about myself to Nolan that terrified me, or face the campout.

I'd rather he see me as an immature and defiant Beta than let him know the truth of my brokenness. Of the terrible options in front of me, I had to choose the one that was trying to protect me. So I stood my ground.

"You know what, fine." He threw his hands in the air, backing up a few steps. "If you want to act like a brat, go for it. I guess now I'm starting to see the true reason why you were passed over for Alpha."

100

I snarled, my teeth bared, but I had no words to retaliate with. I wanted nothing more than for him to take back those words, even though every bit of my heart and soul knew there was truth in them. This new me, this person that had been forced into existence a year ago, wasn't an Alpha. I barely had any control of myself, and my wolf had abandoned me. That wasn't a leader, that was a failure.

I was no Alpha.

And that was a truth that was impossible to accept, but Nolan finally calling me out for it meant I was no longer able to ignore what was fact.

He growled right back at me, "I'll see you tomorrow, then...hopefully in a better mood."

His words sliced through me like a dagger, my body collapsing back into my chair the moment he slammed the door behind him.

Chapter Twelve

On the night of the full moon, I went to the one place that seemed to bring me peace.

I walked down the cobbled streets, my boots clicking against the rough stone, moonbeams bathing me in Lunestia's warm light. I could take my lectracycle to arrive quicker, but a small part of me always hoped that the longer I spent under the moon, the more likely my wolf would come back.

Yet it never seemed to happen.

I crossed through the closed marketplace, wrapping my wool coat tighter against my body to protect myself from the whistling fall wind. My path was an easy one, my destination rising above me as I made my way to the most beautiful building in our city.

The Temple of Tranquility.

Every major city had a Temple dedicated to Lunestia and Firenielle for people to come and worship and celebrate them whenever they wanted. They were all set up in a similar style; two towers made of dark black stone, one for Lunestia and one for Firenielle, rose above the town. They were connected by an arch, bridging together the God and Goddess who watched over us every day.

I veered to the left, heading to Lunestia Tower. The doors were pitch black with the moon phases painted along them in a circle, to remind us that we were forever evolving and changing. I took a deep breath, my fingers shaking as I pushed the door in, the dark sanctuary welcoming me. Seathra's temple had been decorated to match the night sky, midnight blue walls embossed with diamonds and silver filigree patterns swirling together, as if the stars still sparkled and comets danced in celebration.

I walked about halfway up the aisle before settling onto one of the black painted wooden benches. I stared up at the ceiling, my neck barely supported by the wooden back as I let my eyes scan over the ornate ceiling, detailed pictures telling the story of Kazola and the God and Goddess who had saved us centuries ago.

It had all started so simply: when a God fell in love with a Goddess and made her his Mate. They wanted to spread their love to celebrate, so they found a beautiful Isle off the coast of an overpopulated continent and helped create safe passage for humans to travel there, giving them the opportunity at a new life. When the humans arrived, Firenielle and Lunestia gave their new home a name: Kazola. Meaning Peace-bearer in the language of the Gods.

But the Isle was overrun with wild animals and creatures that hunted the humans. Unable to protect themselves, they were slaughtered before they could even settle. Knowing they must intercede, Firenielle and Lunestia had decided to bless the Isle once more so the humans could protect themselves, by each giving a drop of their blood to a handful of humans, creating new beings to protect and watch over the Isle.

Lunestia, Goddess of Moon and Hunt, was able to fortify her beings with the same strength as the animals who plagued them, allowing them to take the animal form of the wolf while they still held the control of a human. She'd also blessed them with the ability to hunt down wrongdoers by giving them the sight to see her Mark, her crest that only those with a guilty conscience would bear in the moonlight of blessed moons.

She'd named these new beings Varg Anwyns.

Firenielle, God of Blood and Truth, had wanted to create beings who could blend into the world as humans but held the strength of a God. He gave them speed, inhuman strength, vision, and hearing. He also gave them the ability to seek the truth, honing their ability to taste it in the one thing that brought life to a person: their blood.

He'd named these new beings Shrivikas.

My Isle was one built on peace and love and unity. We had been blessed from the beginning, and every day we continued to prosper with our Alchemists' advances and our thriving economy, we gave thanks to the Mated Gods who watched over us.

Yet, as I sat in that beautiful temple, I felt out of place. I felt wrong and shunned, disgraced.

Was I even welcome in this place, now that my wolf had abandoned me?

I'd started coming to the Temple every full moon since my last camp, when I realized my wolf had disappeared. At first, I would spend the entire time on my knees, praying to Lunestia for answers. Begging for a sign that my wolf would return or answers as to why she had taken it from me. I needed hope, I needed something to live for.

But as the months went on, as my hope dwindled, I'd stopped praying as hard...but I still came. I had nowhere else to go, nowhere else to turn. At least here, I felt less alone in my disgrace; I could still remind myself that once I had been a child of Lunestia and maybe one day I would be again.

Maybe, one day, a miracle would be bestowed upon me.

I sat there for Goddess-knew how long, wishing and praying and hoping to no avail. Another full moon had passed and my wolf was still nowhere to be seen.

My heart ached, my mind bleak when the creaking of the front door jolted me upward, the warm orange rays of the rising sun peeking in as someone entered.

"I knew I would find you here." Lea's voice drifted down the aisle, her curly hair caked with a bit of dirt, her clothes wrinkled and sweaty from her own Pack's full moon campout. She sat down on the bench in front of me, turning to look in my direction.

"You didn't have to come," I muttered, my hands twisting in my lap.

"I wasn't going to leave you here," she whispered, leaning her arm along the back of her seat. "Anything?"

I shook my head. "I don't know why I keep trying."

"Never lose hope, Kasha." She reached out to me, our hands linking. "You'll make it through."

Lea's confidence in me was just as strong as my Faction's. They all believed that one day I would find my way back to my wolf. Yet none of them seemed to understand the pit that I lived in every day, trying desperately to get out of it. Every time my emotions started to rise, I would hope that was the moment my eyes would glow again or my claws would start to push against my fingers. I searched every moment of every day for a sign that I hadn't been abandoned.

And yet, nothing.

There was only so much hope one person could hold before going insane, and I was starting to reach my limit.

"Want a distraction?" She nudged me. "You're off today, right?"

"Yes." I narrowed my eyes at her. "What did you have in mind?"

***

Lea knew exactly what I needed when she made me drive us out to Nana Aggie's house for the day. Apparently, they had been communicating via Falcon mail, planning to get me away for the day.

My hands clutched the cup of coffee that Nana had welcomed me with, sitting at the counter while I watched her and Lea attempt to cook lunch. I would've offered to help, but they had permanently banned me from the kitchen long ago when I had burned an entire pot of turkey meatball sauce they had worked two hours on.

I never complained; watching the two of them try and cook together was more entertaining anyway.

"Aggie, how many times will it take me coming here for you to finally go and get your knives sharpened?" Lea asked as she struggled to cut a cucumber for the citrus garden salad.

"Pah." Aggie waved her hand, dropping a few herbs into the simmer soup on the stove. "Too much of a hassle."

"I am a blacksmith! This is physically killing my soul," Lea grumbled, her hazel green eyes widening, teeth gnawing at her bottom lip. "I gave you a list of local smithies with wonderful rates."

"She even offered to sharpen them for you and have them done in a day," I pointed out.

"You are not helping, young lady." Aggie pointed her knife at me, a laugh playing on my lips at her frustrated scowl marring her usually gentle, sweet face.

I lifted my hands in innocence. "I'm just pointing out the facts."

"My kitchen, my rules." Aggie shook her head. "If I don't want to part with my knives, then I don't have to, and that's all I have left to say."

"I'm over this!" Lea dropped the knife, the metal clattering against the stone countertop before she headed for the back door.

"Adelaide! Where are you going?" Aggie scolded.

She stopped by the back door with a huff. "To find a decent rock so I can somewhat sharpen these pieces of dull metal you claim are proper knives." And with that, she disappeared into the backyard.

"That girl hasn't changed since she was a child." Aggie shook her head, a smile playing on her lips as she continued to flit around the kitchen.

"Do you want her to?"

Aggie's blue eyes sparkled with amusement. "Of course not."

I let her continue on in silence, wandering away from the savory aromas and into the sitting room that took up the front room. Like every space, she had painted and decorated it herself, the light coral walls contrasting with the indigo couch and chairs. I stopped in front of the grey stone mantle, my heart heavy as I stared up at the painting that hung there: Caleb, Ollie and myself, smiling brightly.

To the Goddess, it was realistic. People were always shocked when they learned Aggie wasn't an artist by trade, but had actually spent most of her professional life as a State Alchemist until she had retired about fifteen years ago, when my Papa had passed from a hunting accident. She was a genius both scientifically and artistically.

She had made us sit for the painting a week after I took my oath into the Guard, wanting to commemorate her final grandchild following our legacy. That was ten years ago, and this painting hadn't moved from this spot since she finished it. I stood in the center, Ollie to my left with his arm slung over my shoulder and his mischievous grin playing on his angular face. Caleb stood at my right, holding my hand tightly, his head gently tilted close to mine. His posture was a bit more rigid than Ollie's, but his smile burned brighter than the sun, his dirty blond hair falling slightly against his forehead.

I could never forget this moment; I had felt fortified and strong, like I could take on the world knowing my two big brothers would always be there to hold me up when I needed them. We had made a promise that day: Born by Blood. Bound by Loyalty. It had meant that even though we would find new family in our Faction, we would always remember where we started and would end—with each other. To solidify it, we each had it tattooed on ourselves, mine running along the length of my left bicep, blending in with my Moonlight tattoo.

Ollie had stayed true to that promise. Caleb had not.

It broke my heart every day, knowing that his love for me was conditional. When he was forced to make a decision between what I told him and what others said, he had chosen to turn his back on me, to believe the lies that were spread about what happened. He broke his loyalty to me to stay the perfect oldest child my father saw him as. He'd made his choice, and every day since I've had to live my life with that broken promise inked on my skin.

Yet, no matter how much I hurt from the betrayal, I still wished every day that Caleb would come back into my life. That I would have both of my brothers back, the way it was supposed to be.

A clattering from the kitchen pulled my attention back, Aggie bickering with Lea that she didn't have to take the time to sharpen the knives when lunch was almost ready. I gave one last look at the painting, wiping away the stray tears that had escaped, before heading back into the kitchen to try and enjoy the day they were creating for me.

Chapter Thirteen

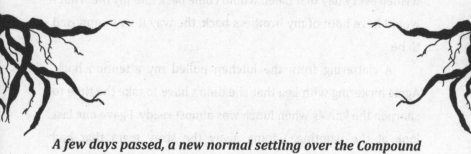

A few days passed, a new normal settling over the Compound with Nolan's presence after the full moon. Although, something still hung in the air, a muddled tension that no one understood.

The more he acted like nothing was wrong, the more confusion rippled through the Hierarchy. Did he think that pretending everything was fine would make it that way? Was he trying to lure us in with a sense of false security before showing his true, ruthless colors, using our past to blackmail us into submission?

I rolled my neck a few times, the muscles stiff from staring at my desk while filling out our armory inventory. I hadn't talked to Nolan since our little fight before the Full Moon Camp. I'd expected him to show up in Lunestia Tower and try and drag me there, but my guess was someone had convinced him not to. Each day that passed, more unease formed in my chest every time I thought about him. He had just been a man in a tavern when I first met him; now every time I saw him, I second-guessed myself and my place in the Faction. The power he had over me made me slick with sweat and left me buzzing with an energy I could barely comprehend. I wasn't exactly sure why, but my guard wasn't going to drop any time soon.

Voices drifted down the hall, my ears perking up at the sound, pulling me from my weary thoughts. I had closed the curtains on the windows of my front office wall, wanting privacy, but as the voices got closer, I realized exactly who it was, his laughter drifting to me, bringing me back to childhood.

"Well, if it isn't my favorite little sister!" Ollie's effervescent presence instantly lit up my office as he let himself in.

I leaned back in my chair, my skin prickling. "I'm your only little sister."

"So?"

"So? I just win by default. Where's the fun in that?"

He laughed, bending over to kiss the top of my head before rounding my desk and plopping into the chair across from me, his long legs sprawled out in front of him. "Fine, then. How is my favorite person ever to exist doing?"

"Better, now that her true status has been recognized." I stuck my tongue out at him. "Seriously, what are you doing here?"

"It was my day off, and I wanted to come visit you."

"And check up on me?" My eyebrow peaked, staring him down.

His shoulders sagged. "Maybe. Forgive me for caring about you."

"It's fine." My heart warmed; Ollie knew I hated being coddled, even more so this past year, but I still appreciated where the concern came from. "You're always welcome here, you know

111

that."

"I figured I could try and twist your arm to go into the city and grab lunch at some pub." He leaned forward, bracing his elbows on his knees. "And I also hoped to get a good look at the imbecile who stole your job. Maybe teach him a lesson or two. That is, if you haven't already kicked his ass so hard he ran away screaming."

My stomach sank, trying to remind me of the dark realization I came to a few days ago. Still, I forced a laugh. "I tried, believe me. But he seems to be stubbornly sticking around."

"Eh, you'll probably wear him down eventually. What's his name, anyway?"

"Nolan." A deep voice came from the doorway. "But you knew that already, didn't you, Mallanis?"

Ollie and I both shot out of our chairs, my hands bracing on my desk as he swiveled around to see who was talking. Damnit, Ollie always forgot to close the door behind him.

"Carragan?" Ollie's eyes widened in disbelief.

My insides rumbled, heat sizzling along my arms. "Do you two know each other?"

"We were Omegas together," Ollie laughed, completely forgetting that mere moments ago he was threatening to beat Nolan up.

Nolan came forward, the two men clasping forearms before embracing. "We were also quite the degenerates back then."

Ollie threw his head back, bellowing a deep laugh. "Oh, did we get under the skin of our Hierarchy! Remember when we snuck into the training rooms one night and painted their names onto the dummies?"

"Oh, Goddess, I almost forgot about that."

112

The two couldn't seem to stop talking, going back and forth trying to outdo each other on who could remember the most deviant act.

"Well, just perfect," I gritted through my teeth. A part of me had hoped Nolan would never learn about pieces of my life outside of the Faction, but it seemed that wish would never come true.

"So, wait," Ollie took a step back at last, his gaze shifting between the two of us. "You're the new Alpha here?"

"Sure am." Nolan's chest puffed out a bit, an eyeroll escaping me at the motion.

"Oh, Goddess." Ollie scraped his hand down his face, realization finally hitting him, shocking the smirk right off his face. "Well, this is certainly awkward."

Nolan leaned against my desk, arms crossed. "You mean because your sister despises my presence?"

"Don't be so dramatic, I don't despise you." A half-truth. That wasn't the word I usually used to describe how I felt about him.

"Oh?" His eyes shifted to look at me. "What would you call it, then?"

I wasn't in a mood that this conversation would end well, my defiant impulses clawing to the surface. I stared down at my fingers, hoping for a brief moment to see my talons lengthen from my fingertips or feel the sharpened shift of my eyes glowing gold, but nothing; I stayed completely human.

I squashed down the impulse to jump at his challenge, biting back my fighting words. "Did you know that Ollie was my brother when you met me?" I asked, changing the subject.

"I guessed," he sighed. "I knew he had a younger sister around your age, you both had a father who's on the High Faction,

113

and you have the same eye color and last name. Though technically it was never confirmed, I sort of just assumed."

"And you never thought to mention it to me?" I flicked my hands out in a sarcastic gesture.

"I wanted to see if you could piece it together." A wicked gleam shone in his dark green eyes. "I was also curious just how much Ollie had told you about me."

"Not enough for me to know that his idiotic friend Carragan was my new boss!" I let the words fly, even though they weren't completely true; when Ollie had talked about him in the past, the last word I had ever used to describe him was idiotic.

When Ollie would come and visit me on breaks from training, he always used to regale tales to me about all the mischievous things him and his friend Carragan had gotten into during their Omega training. I remembered laughing at it as a teen, thinking that my older brother was the coolest and that his friend sounded like the funniest person around...so much so that I had begged Ollie to bring him for a visit.

"Idiotic?" Nolan's jaw dropped. "Half the ideas were your brother's, and he's been an Alpha for longer than I have!"

"Well, I see you two have really bonded over the past week and a half." Ollie cleared his throat, taking a step forward as if to break us apart even though a desk separated us. "Come on, Kas, Nolan's a good guy. I bet if you two stopped butting heads for a minute, you'd actually work well together."

I gave him an unamused stare. "Oh, yeah?"

"You both have the weirdest ability to weave together clues." Ollie let out a whistle. "Him and I worked a few smaller cases together before we were transferred. His instincts are sharp, just like yours."

I let out a huffing breath through my nose, mostly because I had no other response. Ollie didn't have to tell me that, because, unfortunately, I had already noticed. The more I read Elliot's files and researched through Nolan's notes and the theories he had written on the case board, the more I had to pretend I wasn't impressed with how well he blended creativity with sharp instincts.

He was good. He was great, actually, and that fact made my throat tighten. He was a man who, under normal circumstances, I could admire. Yet admitting that felt like a betrayal against my own self, and after everything, I just couldn't do it.

"Keep saying things like that," Nolan smirked at my silence. "Maybe she'll finally put away her claws now that she knows I'm old friends with you."

"That certainly helped me last time," I said sardonically to Ollie, his sapphire eyes widening, face paling, body shrinking away at the jab. My gut twisted a bit—I didn't want him to feel guilty at all, it wasn't his fault that my last Alpha had been best friends with Caleb.

And Caleb had chosen him over me.

My fingers tightened over my left bicep, burning against my palm at the reminder of what was branded there.

"I didn't come in here just to bug you or to see Ollie again." Nolan turned back to me, his spine straightening from a joking friend to an Alpha right before my eyes. "We got a call on the Comms."

"And?"

His eyes darkened. "Elliot's latest victim has been found."

Chapter Fourteen

Our lectracycles blared through the streets as we raced into the town center of Kelna.

The hour-and-a-half journey seemed much longer as we made our way to the crime scene. Kelna was a quaint town right on the border of Adro Territory; five miles northeast and this case would have been investigated under a completely different Faction.

Crowds were already forming in the town center, people standing on the carved, circular water fountain that was the centerpiece of the area, encircled by colorful buildings with different business signs hanging above them. Chattering increased as we slowly wove our cycles closer to the building, people whispering behind their hands as if we couldn't hear them even over the rumbling engines.

"The Guard..."

"I can't believe they're here!"

"Was someone attacked?"

"Was there a death?"

So much speculation; rumors would be flying through the tiny streets in a matter of minutes about what possibly could have brought us here, what evil act was committed to summon the Onyx Guard. Our units were meant for specialty cases only. Typically, our younger Faction members—the Deltas and Dairchtas—were sent out alone or in pairs to assist local guard units in investigations where help had been requested, but they never officially took over. When a group of our size arrived, outfitted in the official black armor of the Guard on our obnoxious lectracycles, everyone knew that whatever had happened was serious. They knew we were here to take over, and it scared them and thrilled their gossiping hearts all at once.

This time, though, no one would be able to guess the treachery that had been committed right under their noses.

We parked our cycles in a street that was protected by local guards, the eight of us securing them. We didn't want to overwhelm the small town by bringing the entire Hierarchy, yet Nolan wanted as many people as possible to come and see one of Elliott's victims firsthand. So, all of the Keturi had come, along with one second of our choosing. I had brought Taylor this time, Eden accompanying Nolan, Liv with Beckett, and Emric had brought his second, Colton. We silently walked past the barricade of local soldiers keeping the crime scene safe, all of them saluting us as we passed by.

The moment I walked into the crime scene, my senses heightened, my eyes taking in every detail around me. You never knew what would become an important part of the case; sometimes the smallest details were the biggest pieces to find the monsters we hunted.

Everything about the bakery was perfectly in order, down to the beautifully decorated display case not yet filled with fresh pastries, frilly curtains hanging around the different windows filtering in the midmorning light, and the pastel green walls that matched the white marble tables and chairs strategically placed around the room. Nothing was out of place, not even the front door, no tampering of the lock or signs of forced entry. If someone had peeked into the window this morning, they would have assumed it was any other day at the bakery.

We crowded in the entryway, Nolan and Beckett standing at the front of the group, waiting for someone to bring us to the victim. Soon enough, we were approached by a middle-aged Shrivika soldier, his black curly hair cropped close to his scalp and a matching bushy beard well-groomed to highlight his round face.

"Hello, I'm Lieutenant Felix, I'm the ranking officer here." He came forward, his face already covered in a sheen of sweat, hand quickly reaching out to shake all of ours in rapid succession. "Thank you for coming so quickly."

"This is a priority case for the Guard," Beckett said, face calm and schooled, giving away nothing about how important this victim was to us.

"Can you walk us through what you've done so far while you show us the victim?" Nolan asked, foot tapping, arms crossed tightly against his chest, fingers brushing over the hidden pendant on his necklace.

He seemed anxious. Interesting.

"The victim, Melinda Graves, a human woman of thirty-two, found in the kitchen of the bakery she owns by her assistant baker, who came in two hours ago," Felix explained, walking us to the back of the open space. "She was completely drained of blood, and the initial report from our local physician is that she died from blood loss. We couldn't find any traces of blood in the entire building, leading us to believe this was a drop site, not the location of the draining."

He hesitated by a door for a moment, looking wearily over his shoulder before pushing it open, all of us following him inside.

My eyes burned the moment we entered the kitchen; all of us Varg Anwyn Ibridowyn instantly recoiled and covered our faces. The scent of wolfsbane was powerful, filling the enclosed space, my eyes and nostrils burning with it, head dizzy just from inhaling the scent of acid-soaked floral. Even the Shrivikas winced at the potency.

Wow, Nolan had really undersold how intense the wolfsbane cleanup was with each victim.

"Victim was rubbed down with wolfsbane," Felix stated the obvious as we moved closer to the body. "No other scent has been detected in the room or anywhere around the bakery. We are in the process of contacting her next of kin, hopefully that will get us more information about her and her past."

"Once you find them, we'll need to interview them before we leave," Nolan said.

Felix nodded emphatically. "Of course, of course, Alpha."

"We'll also need a group of your men to transport the body back to the Faction Compound once we're done here," Beckett instructed, the lieutenant writing everything down in a palm-sized notebook. "I'll take care of the autopsy myself."

"Yes, *Ar Dtus*." He nodded once again. "I'll begin assembling a team now and will get a status update on her family right away."

He gave us a quick salute before shuffling out of the room, leaving the eight of us alone with the young woman.

"So," Nolan was the first to speak up, circling the victim, his booted footsteps echoing in the room, "what do you all notice?"

"She was killed within the last twelve hours." Beckett said, being the first to get close to the body. The poor woman was lying on her back, everything about her perfectly positioned, down to her hands gently placed on top of her stomach, eyes closed, hair wildly splayed around her. Beckett leaned forward, adjusting his black leather gloves, making sure they were secure. "The branding is right here," he brushed Melinda's hair aside, showing off the fresh, blackened burn mark right under her left ear. "This is Elliot."

I had seen a few crude drawings of the branding, but this was different, clean and perfectly pushed into the skin: the letters *E* and *W* entwined together with a circle of thorny vines around them.

"As if that was ever in question." Nolan grumbled.

"Her hair was dyed within the last few days as well." Eden pointed out the strands. "And not well, her roots are terribly done, it's still peeking out as blonde. That makes me think it was done while she was held captive, or after she was killed."

She was right; Melinda's hair was mostly a honey brown, but the roots were bright blonde. If the scent of wolfsbane wasn't so overwhelming, we would probably be able to smell the chemicals of the dye.

"Is that common for Elliot?" Liv asked from next to me, directing her question at Nolan.

"Not always, but there are a handful of cases where he's been known to change the appearance of his victim." Nolan

120

crossed his arms again. "We've never been able to pinpoint why."

Beckett moved away, wiping his hands on his pants, giving me space to move forward and finally crouch near Melinda to get a better view of the details.

"I think he knew her," I said, my eyes never leaving the poor, lovely woman, heart aching to know her life had been cut too short.

"How did you come to that conclusion?" Nolan crouched down on the other side of the body, the muscles in my legs tensing at his nearness.

"Look at the way she's situated." I gestured up and down the length of her. "It was with care. He put her in a relaxed position...if she was alive, this would be a natural way to lie in bed or somewhere more comfortable than the floor."

His hands once again brushed over the bulge of his necklace beneath his shirt before dropping to rest on his knees. It was as if he didn't even realize what he was doing. "I suppose."

"Plus, what serial killer takes the time to bring a victim back to a familiar place?" I pointed out. "We know she wasn't killed here based on the lack of blood spatter. Even with the overwhelming wolfsbane scent, we would have seen traces of cleaning solution if he had tried to clean up the blood, but there are none. So, he not only took the time to place her body in a respectable position, he brought her back to a place that mattered to her. If this was just a random attack, he would have dumped her body on the floor, more likely in an alley or somewhere hidden where no one could find her."

Nolan looked up at me, our gazes connecting. "It's always been obvious he wants us to find the bodies. It's his way of bragging."

"True." My jaw tensed. "But I still think his intentions run deeper, which may be the key to finding the motive."

Nolan's jaw dropped, his face twisting as he processed my theory. Finally, after a few moments of silent tension filling the room, he lets out a chuckle, leaning forward slightly. "Your mind is fascinating." He looked at me with blatant awe, lips pulled up in a loose smile.

My insides churned at the attention, my muscles going rigid. He thought I was...fascinating? Really? My heart fluttered a bit at the prospect...

Nope, none of that.

I cleared my throat, standing up so for once, I towered over him. "And you're the lucky Alpha who has the privilege of working with me and my fascinating mind. Try not to swoon every time I say something brilliant."

"Oh, trust me, I'll try my best, but it sounds like you'll make that a difficult promise to keep." He stood as well, his posture looser than before, shoulders relaxed, hands resting gently on his hips.

By the Goddess, what was happening?

"I'll be able to do a comprehensive autopsy," Beckett said, bringing the conversation back to the important topic. "I don't know how much it will expose that we don't already know, since first glance shows this is standard for Elliot, but it's something."

"Maybe we need to focus on how he got close to her," Emric suggested, him and Colton still hovering by the doorway. "He didn't break in. He could have been stalking her for a while, and they had plans to meet somewhere outside of here last night. Then, after he was done with her, he brought her back here. He would have had her keys if that was the case, which would explain the locked front door."

"That's been one of my theories, but past victims have rarely led us anywhere deep." Nolan rubbed his forehead. "But I agree, it only takes one victim's past to help break a case like this."

"I can stay behind." Eden said, straightening. "I can lead an investigation, get a better understanding of her past and what she's been up to. Her next of kin probably won't have much, but if we can interview neighbors, friends, or other people connected to her, we may get a better understanding of how Elliot grabbed her without breaking in or anyone seeing."

Nolan smiled. "Smart idea. Spend the day here and then write up a report for everyone. We can reconvene this evening."

"Yes, Alpha." She nodded, tucking a few strands of her bright red hair behind her ears, eyes downcast.

"Kiss up," I said to her privately, giving her a wink.

"You're damn right. I like my job," she winked back at me before turning toward Emric and his second. "Colton, will you help me?"

"Sure." The skinny redhead nodded, following her out of the room.

I turned back to Melinda, taking in a dose of horror for the day. I had dealt with murder cases before, but never had I seen something so meticulously executed. This man was a perfectionist, he was a deviant mastermind playing a game he proudly continued to win each day he walked free on the streets. Every little move he made was a taunt, every victim he collected a prize.

I knew that darkness existed in this world, and I was rarely afraid of it, but it was men like Elliot and the crimes they committed that made me shudder with dread.

Chapter Fifteen

That evening, we all came together once again, the conference room filled to the brim waiting for Eden and Beckett to go over their investigations from the day. I stood near the investigation board, ready to mark down any important notes that might need to be front and center to help. I tried not to pay attention to the fact that Nolan was on the other end, a stilo in his hand as well.

"Alright, I'll start." Eden flipped through the report in her hand, quickly thrown together judging by the mismatched handwriting scribbled all over it that must be both hers and Colton's. They had only returned from Kelna two hours ago after spending most of the afternoon there. "We were able to track down four people from Melinda's life: her parents, her fiancé, and one of her close friends. All of them said Melinda was a strongminded young woman. She had dreamed of opening that bakery but refused monetary help from anyone...she was determined to earn all the money needed to gain the lease and start the business. According to her fiancé, Larson, it was one of the reasons they delayed their wedding. She was so busy with starting everything up, they decided to postpone."

My heart ached at that; this man had put his future wife's happiness first, letting her achieve her goals. He sounded like a good man who understood the importance of Melinda's dreams. And now, all because of one maniac loose on the streets, he would never get his happy ending.

I might not be able to give him that happy ending, but I could help him achieve some peace by catching the man who took his love from him.

"Did they all have alibis?" Nolan asked, leaning against the wall.

"Parents were out on a double date with some friends at a local tavern. The friend was working. And her fiancé is a Delta in a local pack and was helping clean up from the recent full moon. We were able to confirm all of them."

"Not surprised, but always good to check." Nolan shrugged.

"Also," Eden leaned back in her chair, fingers curling around the armrests, "I was able to confirm that Melinda never changed her hair, and based on her partner's statement, never had plans to. So, it confirms that Elliot was the one who made those changes."

I picked up my stilo, marking a question on the overgrowing list that we kept on the board—questions that we believed could be key answers into identifying and catching this killer. I ignored Nolan standing only a few feet behind me, watching as I wrote: *Who is he trying to make these victims look like/remind him of?*

"Do we have a list of the different cases that involved bodily changes post-death?" I asked, looking over the board to see if anything popped out, even though I didn't remember seeing anything.

"No, they were few and far between in the past, so focus wasn't necessarily put on it." Nolan tapped his own stilo against his thigh.

Emric removed his glasses and dropped them on the table, rubbing the bridge of his nose. "I remember reading a past case that had a body change to a victim: a male, and a tattoo had been added to his body."

"Of what?"

"It was just a circle, but the way the skin was absorbing the ink made the physician rule it a pre-death marking. But his family confirmed that he hadn't had the tattoo before he was taken."

"We should collect all of the cases that have any kind of body disfigurement or change," I said. "We might be able to get a pattern put together."

"Agreed," Beckett said, running his fingers through the tips of his white-blond hair. "Any volunteers to stay up tonight and read through the reports again?"

Everyone let out a deep groan, a laugh escaping all of us Keturi members. This was something we could get out of easily— typical delegated work. Sometimes it was simple to give this type of project to Deltas and Dairchtas, but with it being a high priority case, only Hierarchy members were allowed to work on it. So, all of our seconds knew this would fall on them. If I hadn't had counseling the next day, I would have offered to help; but showing up to Vanessa's about to fall asleep might not be the best idea, even if I didn't want to go.

"You know, the more of you that volunteer, the quicker finding everything will take." My eyes went directly to Lucas and

Taylor, their gazes strategically trying to avoid mine, but I didn't relent until I caught one of them: Taylor. I stared him down with a mix of pleading, guilt and authority. It rarely ever worked on Lucas, but his twin tended to crack.

"Alright, fine, I'll do it!" Taylor relented, dropping his head on the table.

"Taylor!" Lucas smacked him on the back of the head. "Can you please grow a spine?"

Taylor rubbed the spot Lucas had just hit. "You know I can't say no to her when she looks at me like that."

Lucas rolled his eyes. "Fine, looks like I'll be helping, too."

"We might as well all help," Milly, Beckett's other second, said. She had been away for a few weeks, traveling home to take care of her mother after an operation. Liv and I had spent a part of the previous afternoon catching her up on the case so she would be ready to jump right in. She had an attention to detail we would need. "It's just over a hundred case files...if we hit it together, we can be done in a few hours."

"It's not like you need to memorize them, just look at the autopsy reports and find any mention of bodily changes," Nolan pointed out. "Although, since Eden and Colton spent most of the day interviewing locals and then wrote up this report, I would say maybe they could be excluded."

"Thanks, man." Colton smiled, giving Nolan a smack on the shoulder.

"Yes, thank you." Eden said, barely above a whisper as she stared at Nolan, her brows pulled inward, eyes narrowing.

The rest of the seconds agreed to meet at Lucas and Taylor's house, finding it easier to spread out in the comfortable location. Eden finished up with a few more details before leaning back, adding her report to the case file we had already started to put together this afternoon for Melinda.

Beckett came forward next, weary lines etching deeper on his face. "As expected, the autopsy didn't bring up anything we didn't already know. Internally, everything looked normal for a woman her age..."

He continued on as we all listened intently, my body now leaning against the board, waiting to hear any details I should write down on it.

"Excuse me," Nolan whispered, tapping me on the arm with the end of his stilo as he tried to get past me to the other side of the board.

My body seized at the touch.

I kept trying my best to focus on reading the report in front of me, but the constant tapping of a stilo against the wood surface itched at my skin.

"Stop it, Logan!" I threw my hand over his stilo, his mischievous smile telling me he was far from apologetic for the annoyance.

"What's wrong with tapping?"

"It's making me feel violent," I said through gritted teeth, trying to return my focus to the order report we needed to send out in an hour—or else we wouldn't be able to get another shipment of arrows and bolts until next week.

"Shocker," he laughed. Next thing I knew, his stilo was no longer tapping against the desk, but me, knocking against my hand, my wrist, my arm.

"You are such a bother!" I ripped the thing from his grip and threw it clean across my office, yet a laugh escaped my lips. Somehow, he could get a rise out of me but make me laugh at the

128

same time...

No, no, no, no, no, no...not here.

My mind fogged over, the inky clouds brushing in, blurring all of my coherent thoughts into nothingness. Pressure built in my chest, spots forming in my vision as I tried my best to keep my breathing as easy as possible.

"Kasha? Sorry, can you move? I need to check something." Nolan sounded like he was half a mile away, yet he stood right next to me.

"Sorry, yeah, I, um..." I rushed away from him, moving to the other side of the room, my eyes focusing on the door. Just get to the door, get out of here, and then I could break down. That was all I needed to do. "I think I'm going to read the report tomorrow, I completely forgot I, um...need to go and check on the archery training Rylan's hosting right now."

Everyone was staring at me with puzzled or concerned expressions. Most of them could tell what I was trying to conceal, since this wasn't the first time I'd had a panic attack in front of them. In the past, I might have let myself ride it out here, letting their support seep inside and help me feel safe, but I couldn't this time. Not with Nolan around.

I didn't want him to witness this. Ever.

"You're going to leave?" Nolan stared at me, eyes wide, face covered in disbelief. "You seemed so invested in the details all day."

"Yes, but I, um, I do better reading the report, so I can just take a look later." I scrambled for the door.

"It's alright, Nolan. There isn't much in the report that's pressing." Beckett shrugged as if it was no big deal.

"We can catch her up if needed, but she's read a million of

these before." Emric backed Beckett's claim up. More people nodded, acting as though it was completely normal for me to be leaving a meeting early and rapidly.

My stomach rolled, threatening to release everything within, my throat burning. I needed to get out. I needed to escape to safety...

"I promise, I'll catch up." I stared at him, trying my best to keep eye contact, my hand behind me, clutching the doorknob to remind me that I was only steps away from freedom.

His face fell, shoulders slumping. "Alright, I suppose if this is normal for all of you..."

"Thank you," I said as quickly as possible before ripping the door open and escaping through it, running down the hall and out of the building. But I didn't go to the training building. I just ran into the woods, and I kept running until my lungs burned and my chest hurt and the tears streaming down my face coated my cheeks. I ran until the pain of my emotions and the pain of my body were one.

Chapter Sixteen

The next morning was spent locked in my office, papers littering my desk, notebook already filled with scribbled theories, and half-empty coffee mugs on any flat surface I could find. I was determined to keep working, my mind and body buzzing the farther I got into the investigation.

There were too many questions running through my head after spending countless hours reviewing and memorizing the reports from the most recent murder. How did Elliot get into the bakery? When did he grab Melinda, and how long did it take him to drain her and prep her before putting the body back? How long would he stalk his victims before finally taking their lives? Why did the wolfsbane cleaning burn my senses so badly?

That was the only question I seemed to get more concrete theories on, listing out the many ways he could have treated the corpse after death. He could have drenched them or bathed them in some way with wolfsbane liquid, but that led to more questions. How did he obtain so much liquid? How often did he have to purchase it? Was he even purchasing it, or was he brewing it himself? That train of thought had been my main focus for the last hour, wondering how it could possibly lead to a new line of investigation, bringing us closer to catching this monster.

My concentration shattered when my Comms buzzed at the edge of my desk. I threw the file down with a huff, a touch of annoyance slowly creeping in at the forced break. I grabbed the handheld device, turning it over to see who was calling me.

Caleb.

Bile rose in my throat, a cold sweat breaking out across my forehead. I didn't have to answer it; I could just let it ring and go back to what I was doing. Why force myself to talk to a man who was supposed to be there for me, support me through anything, but let me down in the end? I could just ignore him, show him that his opinion of my past didn't matter—that he didn't matter to me.

But I couldn't do that, no matter how he hurt me.

I clicked the answer button, regret filling me the moment the screen switched to the call.

My heart sped up at the sight of him, his dirty-blond hair perfectly groomed and slicked back from his round face, silvery eyes staring at me with an intensity that would rattle even the most seasoned Guard. There was no love or even familial recognition in that look, just cold professionalism. From most, it wouldn't bother me, but not with Caleb.

"Hello, Kasha." He nodded to me, clearing his throat.

"Caleb." I was lucky to be sitting down, allowing me to come across as composed when my legs felt numb and my stomach rolled, threatening to throw up the gallon of coffee I had consumed in the past few hours.

"I'm calling to request a few files." He leaned back in his chair, notebook poised in his free hand. "We have openings for a Delta and a Dairchta, and I wanted to review some of your trainees for possible promotion."

My fingers curled around the edge of my seat. "Alright, what are the names?"

"Let's see here." His eyes turned away from me, focusing on his notebook as he read out the name and Guard numbers, my free hand shaking with each one I wrote down for myself.

I tried my best to focus on my strength, to remember all of the people who had been there for me: Ollie. Nana. Beckett. Eden. Liv. Taylor. Lucas. Emric. Greyson....

They all loved me, supported me during my lowest times and still stood by me each day while I battled for my sanity. I had my people, I had my loved ones. So why did it still hurt? Why did I miss the gravelly sound of Caleb's laughter? Or the way he only smiled with one side of his lips, the other side barely twitching, yet I always knew that meant he was happy?

"That should be it," he said, his notebook disappearing from view, jaw twitching as awkward silence filled the void. He cleared his throat again. "So, how are you?"

"I'm fine, Caleb. Working, as always." So many angry words came to the forefront, things I wished I could say to him, my stomach lurching at the silence in my soul that my wolf had left behind in these moments. I tampered them down; this wasn't the time, it might never be the time. "How's Father?"

"Good. I'm having dinner with him tonight."

"Oh." I nodded, the dagger in my heart twisting deeper. "Tell him hello from me."

"I will."

"Make sure you send something to Nana in a few weeks." My eyes flickered away for a moment before returning to stare at the screen. "It's her birthday."

"I will, thank you for the reminder." He sat forward, lips still fashioned in a straight line, tension etched into every muscle. "Well, have a good day, Kasha."

My insides quivered, the cracks in my strength starting to give away, but I pulled myself up, straightening my shoulders. "You, too, Caleb."

And without another word, my screen went blank.

I let out a scream into the empty silence of my office. I released the pain and betrayal that I was reminded of every time I was forced to speak to Caleb, my throat raw by the time I calmed down, panting in my desk chair.

At least one thing came from this: I would have something to talk to Vanessa about this afternoon.

***

"Are you alright, Kasha?" Vanessa asked after five minutes of silence into our session.

She sat across from me, her perfectly-tailored burgundy slacks matching well with her black-and-gold button-up shirt and black boots; once again her whole style perfectly put together, finished off with two braids stitched along either side of her head before combining into a bun, her lovely face perfectly complimented by the light cosmetics she had applied.

Every little piece of her was perfect, professional. And I had to sit across from her, in my black stretch workpants that I pretty much wore every day, and a steel gray cotton shirt that wrapped around me, cutting into a V at the neckline. My hair was thrown up in an unkempt ponytail and my face was devoid of any cosmetics. I was a mess next to her.

I shrugged, settling further down into the soft velvet cushion. Questions about if this was the right time and if Vanessa was really the right person to talk to kept bombarding me, sabotaging my original motivation to vent about Caleb and everything that'd happened.

"Did something happen?" she prompted, my skin prickling.

"It's not that big of a deal." But I had decided to talk about this, so why was it so difficult to do when the moment had finally come?

"I told you before, we don't have to talk about anything you don't want to." Vanessa wrote something down in her journal, my eyes tracing the pattern to see if I could discern what it was. Of course, I couldn't. "But you seem like you want to, yet something is holding you back. That is, if I'm reading you correctly...we're still rather new to each other."

Goddess, this woman was sharp.

Why was I hesitating? For years I had lived off my instincts, I had trusted myself, but all of that had morphed in the past year—yet another thing that had been taken from me. I needed to fight against the second-guessing.

My insides squirmed, but I leaned forward, "I talked to my brother Caleb this morning."

"I see." She nodded, her face softening. "And why does that cause you distress? Do you not have a good relationship with him?"

I scoffed, rubbing my forehead, an ache settling behind my eyes. "No."

"Has it always been like that?"

"I can't say we've always been close," I admitted, a truth that never used to bother me. "But I always knew I could trust him, go to him when I needed him most. He was my brother...just like with Ollie, we had this unspoken agreement to always support each other."

I was always closest with Ollie growing up; Caleb and I having a seven-year age gap had made it difficult to bond at such different stages in life. Yet, I remembered him sitting with me for hours in the woods when I was seven, after I had run away from Mama because she told me I wouldn't be allowed to see the wolves during a Full Moon until I was ready to turn. Caleb had let me cry it out and have my temper tantrum, stomping on flowers and leaves and anything I could kick. And when I was finished, he'd walked me to the lake behind our house and given me a swimming lesson, splashing me and tossing me around until I was giggling so much, I completely forgot why I was upset with Mama.

"When did all of that stop?" Vanessa asked.

My body vibrated with uneasy energy, feeding into me like a poison I wished I could escape. I stood from my chair, pacing to the back of the room to find anything to look at besides Vanessa's weighted stare. I finally stopped when I got to the area by her desk, a landscape painting of what looks like the Vapalles coast at sunset.

"Kasha?"

"When he didn't believe me," I whispered, my eyes still tracing the pattern of the painting, arms clutched around me, fingernails digging into the soft fabric of my shirt. "He didn't stand behind me when I...brought the, um...with the investigation."

"That must have been hard. To have someone who was a constant in your life not believe what happened," she said, the honesty and support laced in her voice sending a shiver up my spine.

She didn't use the typical language I heard from other people. She didn't say "alleged occurrence" or "your side of the story". She accepted what had happened as if it was complete fact...as if I hadn't shattered my whole family dynamic because I spoke up, because I told the truth.

"It was heartbreaking." I swallowed a lump in my throat. "My father, it wasn't even that he didn't believe me or not, he just hated the—as he called it—*shame* I brought to the family over bringing my 'personal problems' into the public eye."

"That wasn't Caleb's reaction?" Vanessa asked.

My skin crawled. Why was I talking about this?

Oh, right...because some weird part of my instincts was telling me to.

"Partially, yes, it was. Caleb has always been one to follow my father wherever he goes. His perfect little soldier." A bit of bite laced through my words; I rubbed the back of my neck. "But he was also friends with um, with...him, um, Logan."

"Really?" Vanessa said.

"Yes, they worked as Deltas together for years." Tears pricked at my eyes. I had never said these things out loud. I didn't talk, I kept it all in.

"So when he had to choose a side to believe, he chose his friend?" Vanessa asked.

"Yeah, I suppose." I shrugged as if it didn't bother me to the core, tainting me with sadness and anger.

137

A part of me hadn't even been surprised, and it pained me to admit that. Logan and Caleb were best friends, they were brothers not born from blood but forged through struggles and strength. It was why I had once been close to Logan, too; it was part of the reason why I had enjoyed working with him for almost four years, why I had been proud to be his second.

And all of that had been taken away, stripped into nothingness in one night. One night when Logan showed me and the rest of the Faction who he truly was. And when I'd decided to bring that truth to light, Caleb didn't believe me. He chose Logan, not me. Every time I thought about it, I was smothered by shame and rage all over again.

He had been there for me through everything, so why couldn't he have been there for me through this? Why was *this* the condition that made his love for me disappear?

I wasn't sure if I was ready for the answer, to know the truth. So, I shoved the questions back into the depths of my mind, praying to Lunestia that eventually I would forget them. Caleb and Logan were the past, and I wanted to focus on the future.

"It doesn't even matter." I swallowed back the tears, tampering down the tangled web that Caleb always seems to bring out of me. "I have too much to handle right now, we have a big case and that is much more important than Caleb being a bad brother."

"Oh, well, that certainly sounds like extra stress." Vanessa shifted in her seat, tapping her stilo against her notebook.

"Unfortunately. But working on cases actually helps calm me down." I finally settled back into my chair, the tension slowly easing from my shoulders.

"Why is that?"

A smile tugged at my lips. "I like solving things. Bringing together pieces, discovered clues and using all of that detailed information to create theories and ideas that ultimately lead to helping others or catching some evil creep."

"You like the control," Vanessa pointed out. "And helping people. No wonder you adore the Guard so much."

"Even as a Legacy, I've never doubted my desire to follow the path of my family." I said, my heart twisting.

Even with everything that happened this past year, one thing I knew for certain: being in the Onyx Guard was always my destiny, and I would hold on to it for as long as I could.

Chapter Seventeen

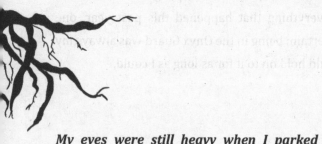

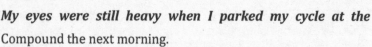

My eyes were still heavy when I parked my cycle at the
Compound the next morning.

After my talk with Vanessa, I could barely sleep, riddled with
vivid dreams bringing me back to days and nights I never wanted
to relive. I didn't remember waking up at all, but when my day
started, I was convinced I'd barely slept a wink. I hated these
mornings, my muscles sluggish, my mind foggy, making it quite
obvious that I would need a few extra cups of coffee to make it
through. Bless Lea's kind soul, the hearty breakfast and strong
coffee she made were the exact thing I needed, and we'd enjoyed
it over our typical conversation of what our days would look like.

I made my way past the Barracks that housed the rest of the
Faction before emerging into the office circle. My Comms buzzed
in my pocket, the vibration zinging up my leg; I pulled it out, a
smile forming on my lips when Ollie's name appeared on the
screen.

"Hi, big bro," I said, pulling open the door to the Hierarchy office building to begin my ascent up the three flights of stairs.

"Hey, little shadow." A smile was plastered on his face, but his eyes were filled with something I couldn't quite make out over the virtual connection, his reddish-brown hair already mussed even though he had probably styled it this morning. "Just thought I would check in."

"On?" I hesitated on the first-floor landing, fingers tightening around the sleek black unit.

"Life, work, anything else that may be bothering you?" Ollie's voice was a pitch too high, the unit shaking a bit like he was pacing or his leg was bouncing. Either way, he was nervous about something. "You know, I'm here to talk if you need it."

"I know." I took a few more steps upward, my eyes narrowing at him. "But what would make you call me this early to check in? Anything in particular?"

"Can't an older brother just check in with his sister?"

"Of course, but you don't," I pointed out. "At least, not in this stressed-out, high-strung way. So why are you really calling?"

"I'm not stressed out." He tried to slacken up, his body moving in a weirdly fluid way. "We're all loose here, see."

"Oliver!"

"Fine!" he groaned, throwing his head back before righting himself to look at me. "Look, I talked to Nolan last night..."

My chest tightened. "Excuse me?"

Ollie winced. "He may have mentioned that he's noticed some odd behavior and brought up some concerns."

"He told on me?" I snarled, my teeth clenching. "Like I'm a misbehaving child?"

"Kas..."

141

"Oh, it is too early in the morning for this."

My vision tunneled, a haze overtaking me as I stomped up the rest of the stairs, taking them two at a time. I could hear Ollie yelling at me, but I barely registered the words, my determination fueled by the hot churn boiling deep in my stomach and growing with each wide step I took to Nolan's office. That little voice in the back of my head—the one I tried to stifle when it convinced me to rebel—was screaming at me, begging to give in.

I was listening this time, letting the defiance take control, feeding it. I didn't even knock when I arrived, swinging the door open with so much force, it slammed into the wall behind it.

"What in the Goddess were you thinking?" I yelled, slamming my free hand on Nolan's desk.

He didn't even look up, scribbling notes on a loose piece of paper. "Good morning to you, too, Kasha. What have I done to upset you today?"

"You called my *brother* and *told* on me?" I shoved the Comms unit in his face, showing Ollie's image. "Seriously? What are you, my babysitter?"

"Hey, Nolan," Ollie said, voice shaking a bit.

Nolan gave a little wave. "Hey, Oliver."

"Stop the pleasantries and answer the question!" My arms were shaking, fingertips numbing with each second that passed.

"I didn't tell on you." Nolan leaned back in his chair, steepling his fingers in front of him. "I was missing some information from one of the Vapalles case files, so I called Ollie to see if he could send a falcon over with the missing pages. And I may have mentioned you seemed extra stressed recently."

I slammed the Comms unit on the table, face-up so I could

142

still see Ollie and his stunned expression. "You don't know me well enough to know when I'm stressed out, let alone extra stressed."

"True, although not for lack of trying to get to know you." He glared at me, prompting an eyeroll. "Still, with your behavior recently—dropping out of meetings, refusing to come to Camp, and purposefully losing our sparring match—it all seemed like you were carrying something heavy, and I wanted to help. And before you try and claim you didn't throw the match, don't even start...it was obvious. You're too good of a fighter to leave your weak side open like that."

My arms shook. "Fine, maybe I did throw the match, but you crossed a line going to my family and tattling on me."

Ollie cleared his throat. "Can I please...?"

"I knew you wouldn't talk to me if I brought the subject up," Nolan cut Ollie off. "I can't get anyone in this Faction to talk to me about anything besides work, so I went to the one person I knew would listen to me that you were close to. How can that be such a bad thing?"

Haughty laughter escaped my lips, my head shaking. "Because I am not a child, and I will talk to people about my problems when I'm ready to, not when you deem me ready, understand?"

"Fine, I won't concern myself with your wellbeing anymore. Happy?"

"Ecstatic!" I yelled. "You should be more concerned about your own stress levels, because it seems I'm not the only one letting the pressure get to me."

"Get to me? What's getting to me is the fact that it seems everyone in this Hierarchy hates me."

143

I pressed my lips together, my insides tightening. "We don't hate you."

"Then tell me." His face darkened, eyes flashing gold for a second. "Why does everyone around here seem to base their opinions on me around your reactions?"

I choked. "Excuse me?"

"Don't think I didn't notice." He braced his hands on the desk, bringing his face closer to mine. "Whenever we're in the group, everyone looks to you, they gauge your reaction to whatever I do or say. Care to explain why that is?"

My eyes widened. I couldn't help but be impressed at his examination, not only of the Hierarchy's reactions to his arrival, but also mine. Clearly, he had been analyzing every little detail since his arrival—maybe even since the day we met in the tavern—and he remember them all.

Goddess above, he was an incredible investigator. Yet another thing I admired about him—my cheeks reddening at the thought.

"You know, this sounds like a private Faction matter, so I'm going to go," Ollie said before the screen went black, leaving Nolan and me alone.

"You seem like a smart man, so can you explain to me how you can be so oblivious to other people's feelings?" I seethed.

"Other people's feelings? For the love of the Goddess, Kasha!" He dropped his chin to his chest, taking a few deep breaths before looking back to me. "All of you keep acting like I'm some kind of enemy who's about to kill all of you at a moment's notice. I try to get to know everyone, I invite people over for dinner or out to a bar or to train, and everyone in this Hierarchy seems to have an excuse as to why they don't want to welcome me as a member of their Faction. And for the life of me, I cannot figure out what I could have done to warrant that behavior."

"After everything you learned about us, and what happened this past year..."

"This past year?" His brows crinkled. "If you're talking about your hospital stay..."

"Yes, that," I cut him off, not in the mood or state of mind to be able to go into detail about that; I barely wanted to talk about any of this. "But also, with our last Alpha and how everyone reacted."

He froze, the muscles in his arms tensing below the tight, long-sleeved tunic he wore. "What are you talking about?"

A chill swept through my body. "What do you mean, what am I talking about? What are *you* talking about?"

"I know nothing about your last Alpha, except that he transferred about a month before you came back to work." He straightened. "Is there something else I should be aware of?"

My mind floundered for a moment. "Plenty. So much so that I am *shocked* the High Faction was even able to find an Alpha who wanted to transfer here."

He narrowed his eyes at me, his mouth gaping for a moment before he shook his head. "I wish I had a better answer for you, Kasha, but nothing in the Faction File made me concerned to come and work here." He fell back into his chair, his fingers curling around his knees.

It didn't make sense—that file should be stuffed full with unpleasant reports about all of our behavior, from an incident report I'd filed almost a year ago that led to a nasty investigation, to everyone's behavior after I was hospitalized. We'd all rebelled against the High Faction and those involved. We should've been

145

marked as one of the worst Factions to transfer to; we should've been considered anarchists in the eyes of the Onyx Guard. So why was Nolan acting like he knew nothing about it?

Something wasn't right, and I needed to figure out what it was. Immediately.

I walked around the desk, kicking his chair leg so he faced me. "Give me the File, Nolan."

"That's not protocol..."

"I don't care!" I could barely control my movements, blind fury taking over as I kicked the chair again before bracing my hands on the armrests, bringing our faces inches apart, his spicy warmth surrounding me. "You are too confused about our behavior, and trust me, we feel the same about you. My gut is telling me the answers are all in that Faction File. Now hand. It. Over."

His jaw ticked, eyes hardening as he took in every inch of my face, gaze lingering on what seemed like every detail. I wasn't sure if he was trying to read my reactions or what, but I didn't dare move, even if my skin vibrated from the closeness, my insides trembling. I couldn't back down, not when I had made this move in the first place. It would show weakness, and I wasn't weak.

Finally, after what felt like hours, he sighed, his fingers gently brushing mine to loosen them from around his chair. I pulled away from his touch, straightening myself and wrapping my arms around my torso. He rummaged in his desk for a few moments before emerging with a file, standing up to face me; our chests barely grazed, his eyes downcast to stare at me. "Here. Whatever you're looking for, I hope you find it."

His low, rumbling voice sent a jolt down my spine, but I

146

ignored it. This wasn't the time to lose control.

I yanked the file from him, taking a few steps away to put the desk between us once again. I stared down at the folder in my grip, my first instinct telling me one thing: it was too light.

I shook away the thought, my eyes scanning each document as quickly as possible. With each page I turned and each note I read, my heart grew heavy, bile burning my throat and nostrils, my mind spinning to dark depths.

No. No, no, no, no, no....

"What...no...this...I can't..." I didn't even know what I was trying to say, sentences unable to form in my mind, the room tilting around me.

"Kasha, what's wrong?" Nolan's voice sounded dull and lifeless, barely making it through the anxious haze racking through my body and mind.

I finally made it to the last page, my grip barely strong enough to hold onto the folder. I looked up at him, his bright green eyes full of distress, pleading for answers—both to if I was alright and what in this file was making me panic.

But that was the problem, it wasn't what was in the file.

It was what was missing from it.

I didn't even think; all I could do was run out of Nolan's office, the Faction File still gripped in my hand, his shouts of concern following me down the hall as I raced out of the building.

Chapter Eighteen

Somehow, I made it out of the office building without tripping down the stairs, the cool fall air biting my cheeks as I rushed across the circle and down the path back toward the townhouses. I opened my mind to the Hierarchy, finally able to let out a breath when I connected to all of their presences on Compound.

"I need to talk to all of you, now!" I yelled within the privacy of our minds. *"Tay and Lucas, can we meet at your place?"*

"Sure," Lucas was the first to answer. *"We're just cleaning up after training this morning."*

"Kas, what's wrong?" Emric asked.

"There's too much to explain. Just meet at Taylor and Lucas's." I cut everyone off, not ready to face an onslaught of questions before we were all face-to-face. I couldn't explain this quickly, and they needed to see the file or else they wouldn't believe me.

The door to Taylor and Lucas's house was already wide open, Lucas sitting at their dining table with a cup of coffee,

Taylor emerging from the kitchen a moment later with Emric on his heels. Taylor immediately pulled a chair out for me, my body falling limply into it without a word. I clutched the file to my chest, my gut twisting so quickly I felt sick.

How was I going to tell everyone the truth?

Beckett, Liv, Greyson, and Eden all arrived within minutes, eyes wild and bodies tense with concern. The other seconds weren't here, but truth be told, this didn't concern them; Colton and Milly had only been in their posts for ten months, their promotions happening just before I was hospitalized. Emric was also down a second, his last one transferring with Logan to Dalchus. Emric had been so concerned with my return that he had procrastinated promoting one of the Dairchtas.

The silence was thick with tension, unsaid questions written all over everyone's faces. All eyes were on me, but no one spoke or moved an inch. They were waiting for me to open up, to give them the reason I had called them in a blind panic.

I released the folder, placing it on the table in front of me. "The High Faction redacted almost everything that happened over the past year."

I could've given a lengthy explanation, but I didn't have the energy. So, I said the words, plain and simple, hoping that was all anyone needed.

Of course, it absolutely wasn't.

"What in the God's name are you talking about?" Emric was the first to bellow, his tawny skin mottling with bright red dots, wire-rimmed glasses slipping down the bridge of his nose.

"How could they have redacted everything?" Liv shook her head, leaning into Beckett, who had his arm around her shoulder. "That's impossible. After everything we did, they couldn't have

149

redacted it."

"But they did." I opened the folder, spreading out the handful of reports and papers inside. "This is all Nolan was given. It's mostly filled with some statistics, training reports, and different budgets. But when it comes to our personal dossiers, almost everything was taken out." I handed out everyone's personnel file, most of them still silently gaping at me with disbelief. "The only part that was mentioned was my...the hospitalization and the sign-off from my physicians and the High Faction that I could return to active duty. They didn't even mention the reason why I was in the hospital for so long."

"That's it?" Liv asked.

I nodded. "Yes."

"But what about..." Beckett bit his lip, his fangs peeking out. "What about what happened last year? The investigation?"

Tears pricked the edge of my eyes, one rolling down my flushed cheek. "All removed."

"But...but..." Taylor's file sat in front of him, his elbows braced on the table, his fingers scratching at his scalp. "No, this...why would they even do this?"

I wiped away the tears, trying to pull myself together, focusing on the facts in front of me. The High Faction had done this on purpose, and although they might try to claim that they'd redacted all of this information for our benefit, I knew that was a lie.

"I have no idea," I shook my head, looking around the room at my friends. "I have guesses. I'm sure the investigation was removed by Cole. The last thing he needs are rumors spreading about Logan."

Beckett scoffed. "Typical Cole, abusing his power for his own benefit."

"As for the rest?" I scratched my fingers along my thighs, my mind clouding with fog, but I pushed myself forward. *Focus on the theories.* "My guess is they were desperate not to put me in the position of Alpha, but they knew if our Faction File had all of the information about this past year, qualified candidates wouldn't want to transfer."

"No surprise," Greyson mumbled, his file clutched so tightly it was almost crinkled into a ball. That would be fun to explain when I returned the File to Nolan. "What new Alpha wants to come in and deal with a defiant and insubordinate team?"

"And with the Elliot case popping up, they didn't want a Faction they couldn't control completely in charge, so they did everything possible to make sure a new leader was put in place." Liv's hazel eyes shifted bloody red. "Unbelievable!"

The weight on my chest grew, pressure building unbearably fast as people shouted and ranted about this news around me. It was pulling me back, bringing me to a place I rarely visited in my past.

My fingertips grazed over the inch of scar peeking out from the collar of my black tunic. All of these truths, these exposures into the High Faction's negligence, were hidden from the rest of the world. I knew everything would be buried from the public, but from the rest of the Guard? Although I didn't need every person knowing the truth about my past, something about this whole thing soured my stomach, making my fingers twitch uncontrollably.

This wasn't right, this was...I didn't know what it was, but my instincts told me that it wasn't good, and that terrified me.

"So this entire time, Nolan has just been trying to be nice to us?" Eden whispered, pulling me from my thoughts; she was still looking down at her file as if everything missing would magically appear, red hair framing her face.

My gut twisted at those words, the weighted truth behind them. For so long, a part of me had hated the idea that Nolan knew what happened, that he was given such intimate details about my past without my permission. Those moments—what had happened to me over this past year—was my history, it was my story to tell, not the High Faction's.

Yet, to know that Nolan had only been given a piece of the story—the piece that made me look weak and fragile—made things swirl inside me, a cacophony of emotions that didn't blend well together: anger, fear, confusion, sadness. Even if the allegations I had brought forward had been dismissed, they'd still happened. It was that one night that changed everything for me, that made my wolf retreat and tore me down from the inside out. It was that night, and the High Faction's inaction afterward, that had led me to some of the darkest parts within myself.

There was so much to my story that Nolan didn't know. Now that the decision to tell him was mine once again, did I want him to know the truth? Did I want him to see the whole story?

Somehow, I had no answer, not even a theory to go off of. Everything was just...blank.

There was no way to know what I was ready for, not when it came to Nolan and my past.

The voices around me brought me back to the needs of the moment. *Focus on the facts. Focus on what you can control around you.*

" We all assumed he was acting oblivious as a way to manipulate us...none of us were willing to trust him," I whispered, all eyes falling to me, burdening me with the weight of their gazes. "But we were wrong. He wants to be here, to be a part of this Faction. He deserves to be given a chance."

"Kas..." Lucas's chair scraped closer to mine, but I flinched away when he reached out to touch a tattooed hand to my shoulder.

"No, don't pity me, you all know it's true." I shook my head. "It's one thing to have known all of that about us, but he knew nothing. The High Faction chose to keep secrets, and it led to a gross miscommunication over these past few weeks. He doesn't deserve to be treated like an outsider, not when he's trying so hard to find a place here and the only reason he can't is because no one will give him a chance to."

He still had the job that I had earned, he'd taken something from me without even realizing it. But he wasn't as terrible as I'd thought; he wasn't pretending to be our teammate or acting as if he was going to hold all of this information over our heads as blackmail. He was just a man who transferred to a post, who wanted to find his place here—and who wanted to lead the Elliot investigation, that much was clear. Yet, it didn't stop him from being genuinely interested in the Faction.

"You all need to get to know him and form your own opinions about him without wondering what I'll think." I had said from the beginning that I didn't want any of them to be influenced by my own personal feelings. Yet once he'd arrived, I'd let that disappear. I could try and make up excuses, say that when I thought he knew all of the truths, he deserved to feel like an outcast; but a voice in the back of my mind told me it was a lie. I had let everyone treat him like an outcast because I had wanted him to feel that way, I had wanted to get back at him in a little

153

way. It was petty and immature, not the qualities of an Alpha.

I wasn't even a little surprised; I was no Alpha.

Nolan didn't deserve that treatment from us. That was pure fact.

"Kasha's right." Beckett circled the room, collecting everyone's files from them. "Nolan is here because he wants to be. He wants to help us hunt down a killer and become a part of this family. He's smart, a hard worker, an impeccable fighter. If it was under normal circumstances, you all know we would be welcoming him with open arms."

Everyone's gazes shot to the floor, proof that they all knew Beckett's words were true even if they refused to admit it.

"You don't have to like him, but you do need to give him a chance." He stopped in front of me, picking up the folder and slipping everyone's files back inside, his gaze lingering on me before turning back to the room. "He's earned that much from us, don't you agree?"

Everyone mumbled in agreement, something in the room shifting from weighted anxiety to fresh clarity. I didn't know how to move forward with Nolan myself, but at least I felt a settling in my chest, knowing everyone else could.

Chapter Nineteen

I had wanted privacy that evening, the nighttime peace my favorite time of day on the Compound. When people were either winding down from a long day or on overnight patrol, I had the run of the training house.

But not tonight, it seemed.

I was drawn to the distant sound of daggers whipping through the air wafting down the hall from one of the target rooms. I didn't know why my legs took me there, beckoned like a siren song. No one else on the Compound usually worked out this late, which meant there could only be one person I would catch. Yet, no matter how much I had been avoiding him all day, I still found myself in front of the glass wall, staring at him while he threw knives against the fake human target.

He never missed, each tip lodging in the main kill areas. The heart, the head, the carotid, the stomach.

Why did he have to be so damned good at his job? It still

irked me to the core.

He peeked over his shoulder, that stupid smirk hanging on his lips as his words filled my head. *"See something you like?"*

I pushed the door open. "More like hear." I forced myself not to slap my face for that comment the moment it left my lips. His brow arched, the glint of his green eyes reflecting in the harsh lighting. How could I be so awkward? "I meant you practicing. I heard your daggers flying from down the hall." I wanted to cross my arms, but my bow case kept them planted against my sides, my grip tightening around the black plastic handle.

"Ah." Nolan nodded, his fingers twirling the hilt of his next blade. "Were you going to shoot?" He gestured to my bow case. "Kind of late, isn't it?"

"I could say the same to you."

"Fair." He smirked, the dark strands of his hair shaking against his forehead, a deep, rough laugh escaping his lips. "You could share this room with me."

I frowned. "There are half a dozen others to choose from."

"True, but I've been here two weeks and have yet to see the legendary Beta Kasha show off her skills." He leaned against the far wall, propping his left foot against it. "I'd like to see what my archery master can do."

"I'm not *your* archery master, I'm the Faction's. And I don't have to prove anything to you."

"Semantics." He waved his hand at me, my nose twitching at the gesture. "Still, I'd like to see for myself. If you're willing."

The urge to rebel poked at my insides, begging me to act out—to tell him to go do something inappropriate to himself and then stomp out of the room to find my own sanctuary to practice. I fought against it, dropping my case on the back table, clicking it open and pulling out my bow, the tight strings and soft black metal feeling like the missing limb it always was when it was out of my grip.

My hand hovered over my case of bolts, the fabric of my long-sleeved tunic itching against my skin—and I had no idea why I wrapped my fingers around the edges and pulled the thin fabric over my head. I convinced myself it was because I always shot like this when I practiced, in nothing but my black, crisscrossed tank top and breastband; it had absolutely nothing to do with the fact that most of my tattoos were now on display for Nolan to see. My array of artwork and meaningful words scrawled across my body, showing off the highs and lows of my life so far.

I felt his hot gaze scanning me, taking in every inch of the skin I had just exposed, the tattoos and the jagged scar running down my neck and collarbone. His breath hitched, but I shook that off, slinging my bolt case across my back and picking my bow up once again, my heavy, booted footsteps echoing against the walls as I took my place in front of the target.

I took three deep breaths in as I nocked my first bolt and raised my bow so my left hand barely grazed my lower lip, staring down my target. I forgot that Nolan was there. I forgot about Elliot and his terror; I even forgot about my past. All I thought about was what was in front of me: my intended target.

I let one of my favorite piano songs dance through my mind, remembering the highs and lows of the melody, the music thrumming through me even just from memory. As it came to its first crescendo, I released, the arrow whizzing through the air and lodging straight into my dummy victim's chest.

A smirk danced on my lips as I rapid-fired three more, all of them lodging in the same spot on the other dummies. Nolan exhaled loudly. "Goddess. People weren't exaggerating when they talked about your skills."

"I told you I didn't have anything to prove." I pulled my shoulders back, forcing myself to stare at the target instead of him as I leisurely pulled another bolt out and nocked it. "Not sure why you think I do."

His boots thumped against the floor, echoing closer and closer as he moved behind me. "Tell me, what exactly do I think of you? Since you apparently know my mind better than I do."

"I don't know for sure."

"Then tell me your theories."

My fingers tightened around my bow, letting another arrow fly. "Who says I have any?"

"Call it instinct." His footsteps faltered, sweat beading at the back of my neck at his nearness. "You seem like the kind of woman who always has a few theories for the unknown."

Well, he had me there.

"Let's see." I pulled up a few ideas I had thought briefly about over the past few weeks, not pausing to second-guess myself. "Maybe you think I'm a spoiled legacy who relies on her bloodline and political connections to get ahead. That I'm Ollie's sweet little sister. That I'm weak." I didn't look back; I couldn't watch as his forest eyes confirmed all of it. A zip of electricity snaked down my spine, his broad build hovering behind me. "Go ahead, take your pick."

"Huh." The sound was odd in his deep voice, making the strength in my arm falter, my bow arm falling down to my side. "You don't know my mind as well as I thought you did."

My grip started to loosen, my obsession with maintaining

my bow to perfection the only thing keeping my fingers wrapped around it. "Oh, really? Then what *was* your first impression?"

Silence fell as he circled around me and forced his way into my line of vision. I stared at the dark, heather gray of his shirt, refusing to look into his tanned face. He was so close, only inches away, his spicy cinnamon scent mingling with the musky vanilla of mine.

"That you must be one of the strongest Ibridowyns in the country to survive what you did and still come back to the Faction," he whispered, his arm twitching at his side, his eyes carving along the length of my scar.

I gulped, trying to force the lump to dissipate in my throat. "You don't even know why I was in the hospital for so long."

"No." He shook his head. "But my previous statement still stands."

I chewed on the inside of my cheek. "Not many people in the Faction know the truth about my past."

"Including me, apparently?" I could feel him staring down at me, the magnetic pull forcing my gaze to finally meet his...and I realized that in my haze of rage from the High Faction's lack of communication, I had neglected to tell Nolan what exactly had sent me running from his office with a confidential file he wasn't supposed to show me.

He was calling me strong, for Goddess only knew what reason, but I wasn't ready to admit the truth to him. He hadn't earned that part of me yet, and I doubted he ever would.

Still, he at least deserved to know that the High Faction had been lying to him, that was more public knowledge than personal. "Yes." I took a step back and turned to face the target again. "The File was missing a few details that I think may have been pertinent to the team you chose to lead."

"At least it explains why everyone stares at me like I'm a charlatan."

I snorted. "Everyone was just...shocked that you were acting like everything was completely normal about you being here."

"And it's not, I take it?"

"Nope." I pulled back the bowstring, sending an arrow whizzing through the air, the thump of it hitting the dummy sending a rush of needed calm through me. "But it's not just my story to tell."

"Then why does it seem like the core of the story revolves around you?"

His words sliced through me, puncturing where it hurt the most. My fingers clenched around my bow, the cool metal biting into my palm, helping to keep me centered in the situation.

I straightened my spine, pulling out another arrow as if his words didn't almost annihilate me. "No idea."

"Kasha..."

His hand gently brushed over mine, the pressure asking me to lower my bow. For some reason, I did, turning back toward him. I thought he was going to say something, but he hesitated, just staring down at me, confusion wrinkling his face. He looked at me like I was a mystery to be solved, but he had no idea how complicated my life was. I wasn't just a scattered puzzle waiting to be placed together; I was full of mismatched pieces and plenty missing from the box.

"Kasha..." he said again, taking a step nearer.

My breath pulled sharply through my teeth, hand shaking so violently, my bow quivered.

Something was happening.

But what?

Before my question was answered, the echoing of boots rushing down the hall gained on us. Nolan cleared his throat, stepping away and running his hands through his hair. I turned from him, my dazed mind resharpening itself from whatever trance he had put me in. Had he commanded me somehow as my Alpha, and I hadn't realized it? It didn't feel like it, but why else would I hesitate? Why else would I let him touch me and willingly lower my weapon?

"Alpha, Beta." Rylan, a Dairchta, came rushing into the room, his face flushed.

The panic in his voice snapped me from my overthinking. "What's wrong?"

"We just got a call through the Comms," Rylan panted, and Nolan came up next to me, his posture rigid. "There's a hostage situation in Sanlow. They need backup right away."

Nolan and I glanced at each other for a mere moment before we both rushed out the door.

Chapter Twenty

The race to Sanlow was a frenzy. All Hierarchy members on Compound were called to action, along with a handful of Deltas and Dairchtas as extra backup. Our group of fifteen was hard to miss as we passed towns and others traveling along the streets on their way home from work, the roar of our cycles echoing into the dark night sky. It might've looked excessive, but we had little information, so we needed to be prepared for anything.

The tavern was luckily not located in the center of this town, making it easier for us to maneuver our lectracycles to the outlying area, the local guard already creating a half-mile wide perimeter to keep the general public safe and allow us to work. We crossed through, heading to the large central group that was set up a quarter mile away from the tavern front. We didn't waste any time, clustering our bikes together before marching right into the fray.

"Who's in charge?" Beckett asked, Nolan and I right beside

him, the rest of the group hanging back to keep the area as organized as possible.

"I'm Commander Reya." A tall, lithe woman approached us, shaking our hands in quick succession. She was dressed for battle already, sporting a similar leather armor to ours, except where ours was black, hers was a combination of brown bracers matched with a steel blue undershirt, pants, and boots. Her dirty blonde hair was cropped to her head and streaked with magenta and purple. "Thank you for arriving so quickly."

"Status report, please," Beckett said. The ride had been just under an hour, but so much could've happened in that time, especially for a sensitive situation like this.

"We've been on the scene for the past hour, canvassing the area and trying to get as many details about the suspects as possible," Commander Reya said. "With the glass front of this particular tavern, we've been able to monitor the occurrence since we were notified about it a little over an hour ago."

I leaned over the barricade of carts lined in front of us, some filled with weapons and others empty, most likely used to transport the troops here. Multiple guards were crouched behind them with spyglasses poised at their eyes, the long cylindrical tube enhanced with glass orbs allowing people to see sharper images at a distance.

The tavern was mostly constructed of white and grey river stones, yet as Reya had pointed out, the front wall was made of glass, opening up the whole main floor to the public's eye. Although it was too far away for even our sharpened gazes to see clearly, I had a general idea of what was going on without any form of magnification. People cowered along the bar that took up the back wall or hid under tables; three men paced throughout

163

the room, their movements erratic. Although I couldn't make out what they were saying, the booming of their shouts drifted toward us on the wind.

"Are those bodies I see?" I pointed to the still forms lying on a few of the tables.

"Unfortunately." Reya nodded. "First death was confirmed about ten minutes ago."

"Why haven't you infiltrated yet?"

"We got one of the guards closer to try and negotiate." She ran her fingers through her hair. "He was able to confirm that all three suspects are Shrivikas, and based on their erratic behavior and the blackened veins running up their necks and faces, all three of them are currently high on blackthorn."

"*Futeacha*," Nolan swore in Old Kazalonian, his fists clutching around the handle of his Amalgam Blade; mine did the same as I pulled my bow from my back.

Blackthorn was one of two illegal drugs we were constantly fighting against the distribution and use of. The crushed gray powder was incredibly addicting to Shrivikas, giving them a sense of invincibility or euphoria. To them, everything felt possible, which led to dangerous and erratic behavior that not only put them in danger, but the people around them. Even worse, when high concentrations of it were taken, Shrivikas became insatiable for blood, their lust for it heightened to a point that they could drain multiple people dry and still feel unsatisfied. Many mass-murder cases had been linked to a blackthorn high, one of the many reasons we wanted to keep it off the streets.

If all three of these men were high off blackthorn, it made this whole situation even more contentious. One wrong move,

164

and they would kill everyone inside if they felt it was for the best in their altered state of mind.

My finger tightened around my bow, eyes scanning the area around the tavern, looking for any spot that might have allowed me to get a sniper's view. It wasn't our best option, since the suspects were keeping themselves covered between the other patrons and victims, most likely making it too dangerous for me to take a clean shot at them. Still, we were taught to exhaust every option before infiltrating, knowing that an act like that could cause more harm than good if the suspects were enraged enough. And by the way these three were feeding and the darkened veins on their skin growing larger, their blackthorn high wasn't dissipating anytime soon.

Something off to the side caught my eye, a chill sweeping so suddenly over my body, I barely believed what was right in front of me.

"Commander?" I turned to her. "Can I borrow your spyglass?"

"Of course, Beta."

She handed over the long cylinder before I brought the small opening to my eye, scanning the area to the right of the tavern, bile rising in my throat as I confirmed my fear. "Goddess, no."

"What is it?" Beckett asked, nudging my shoulder.

"That's Lea's cart." I pointed to the wooden cart, black-dyed canvas covering the top of it to protect all her wares, the slats painted a bright green with the words 'Adelaide's Armory & Blacksmith'.

"Who's Lea?" Nolan asked.

"My roommate." My fingers tightened around the spyglass, my eyes searching for any sign of her through the front of the tavern. I couldn't spot her, my stomach lurching. "She told me this morning she had a delivery today at the local garrison. She must have stopped for dinner on her way home."

"Are you sure?"

"I can't spot her in the crowd, but there are plenty of blind spots she could be in." I handed the spyglass back to Commander Reya. "I know that's her cart."

Why? Just *why* was all I could think, constantly repeating it in my mind. Lea had been there for me throughout my entire life. She was my best friend growing up, she had come over almost every night after my mother passed to keep me company. She had been there when I transformed into my wolf form for the first time and we had briefly been in the same pack until I joined the guard at eighteen. Throughout it all, she had been a constant, and she had showed up when I needed to get away from my Faction after being released from the hospital. When I felt hopeless and lost, she gave me a sanctuary to run to. And now her life was at risk for no other reason than three men decided to go ravage a tavern.

Goddess, why was life so unfair?

"We're gonna get her out." Nolan gripped my shoulder, shaking me from my thoughts, my imagination getting the best of me at the idea of her lifeless body splayed across the bar with the stack of others already piling up.

"I know." I nodded, trying my best to believe it myself, but the pained cry that pierced the air from inside the tavern made it difficult.

"With the dead piling up, I think the best thing to do is infiltrate," Beckett said, his arms crossed tightly against his chest. "Negotiation didn't work, and we can't wait for their high to wear off, not when it's obvious they still have a ways to go before they crash."

"They could kill half the tavern by then," I whispered.

"Exactly." Beckett nodded. "Better to try and save as many as possible then sit back and let them be picked off one by one."

"I agree." Nolan nodded, giving my shoulder one last pat before pulling away.

"There's a back point of entry that my soldiers were able to scout out during the preliminary investigation," Reya said. "They're so distracted by their own bloodlust, they shouldn't see a team sneaking around the side, even with the windows."

"Perfect." Beckett nodded, waving the rest of our team to move closer, all of them crowding around us for next steps. "We're infiltrating, with the local guard staying outside to help usher out any captives and get them to safety."

"The goal is to get everyone out alive, even the suspects," Nolan said, his fingers twitching at his sheathed blades. "But the captives are our first priority."

Everyone murmured in agreement, the final details of the plan hashed out as quickly as possible among the group. We then broke off into teams to collect our weapons and wits, our tense silence speaking volumes about how we really expected this infiltration to end.

As long as we saved even one of them, it would be somewhat of a success. We would get answers and save lives.

My group was almost ready when a tug on my arm pulled my attention away from them.

"You should sit this out." Nolan's eyes scanned over the top of my head before returning to me. "It's personal, and that will make it more difficult for you to focus."

"No way." I ripped my arm from his grip, straightening my spine. "I'm not abandoning my friend. She needs my help."

"It's not protocol." He narrowed his eyes.

"I don't care, you need me in there." I took a step toward him, our chests barely grazing. "I have some of the best aim and I'm one of three archers in this group, which we need for long-range dangers. And even with all of that, you're not stupid enough to actually believe that I'll listen to you."

He stood up a bit straighter, jaw tensing.

"Don't act like you would sit this out if you were in my position," I challenged, my chest tightening even as I held my strong stance.

He huffed, shaking his head in defeat. "If you get hurt, I will never forgive you."

"I don't need your forgiveness." I took a step back, tightening the strap of my quiver across my chest. "I need you to fight."

Chapter Twenty-One

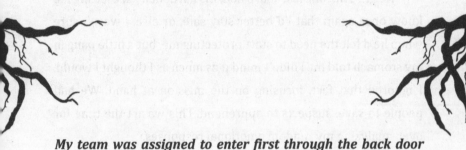

My team was assigned to enter first through the back door that let into the kitchens. I took the lead with Nolan right beside me, followed by Lucas, Greyson, and Eden along with Rylan and another Dairchta, Beth. We made it inside without incident, the oven still aflame, abandoned pots overboiling with liquid, and chopped vegetables and herbs scattered across the counters.

"Two entrances to the front." Nolan pointed to two doors, one to the left of the kitchen and the other at the front.

"One probably leads behind the bar, the other directly into the dining area," Eden theorized.

"We should split up," I said. *"I'll take the left door, hopefully that leads to the dining entrance. If I'm lucky, it will give me a clear shot so I can injure them before attacking."*

"Good point." Nolan nodded, Eden and Greyson already moving behind him, angled to the door in the front.

"Rylan, go with Nolan, just in case," I directed my other

archer, the Dairchta nodding as he pulled an arrow from his quiver.

"Do not act unless you have a clear shot," Nolan instructed. *"If you don't, tell me, and I'll give the command when to ambush."*

I bit the inside of my cheek; it was the smartest choice for this mission, making it easier for me to quell the need to rebel. *"Alright."*

He gave me one last sharp nod, his hardened gaze letting me know once again that I'd better stay safe, or else. I wasn't sure when he'd felt the need to start protecting me, but a little pang in my stomach told me I didn't mind it as much as I thought I would. I ignored that fact, focusing on the mission at hand. We had people to save, suspects to apprehend. This wasn't the time for over-analyzing my random emotional responses.

Lucas, Beth, and I moved to the side door, Lucas pushing it open a crack to get a look. *"It's a hallway."* He peeked out a little farther. *"Right around the corner is the dining room. You should be able to get a shot."*

"Perfect." I soundlessly snuck out, using the corner to hide myself, getting a better view.

My first instinct was to find Lea, pulling in a deep breath to catch a whiff of her bergamot aroma mixed in with all of the spilled blood and other scents swirling through the space. I found her huddled in a corner with two other women, her arms around both of them, holding them tight to her chest. Of course, even in a dangerous situation, she was protecting and soothing others.

After confirming that she was alright, I put my attention back to the three men. A tall skinny one, with long blond hair down the length of his back, sat at a table with his back to me, his fangs deeply embedded into the neck of the squirming man. His whispering pleas for mercy showed that he only had a few moments left before he passed out and eventually died from blood loss. The second was strutting around in front of the bar, his hands grazing over the few people that were cowering there, all of them shuddering each time he touched them.

"None of you understand right now, but oh, you will." His words were rushed, his brown and green tunic completely drenched in a mixture of blood and sweat, his olive-tan skin flushed red, black veins protruding from his thick neck. "You will join us, revel with us! Celebrate your freedom!"

The third was huddled in the corner, rocking back and forth, his curly red hair sticking up and plastered to his sweaty forehead. He didn't blink, arm wrapped around his legs, two people sitting in front of him like a barrier. From here, I could see that he had a knife in one hand, pointed at both of them, so I could only assume he was forcing them to sit in front of him. He kept repeating the same phrase over and over. *"Chu Fui na Déithe. Chu Fui na Déithe."*

"Do any of you know what the redhead is saying?" I asked the group inside, all of them whispering their no's. The words were Ancient Kazalonian, but the old language had all but died out. Besides a few phrases and curses, most words had been lost to common society. Maybe he was a scholar of some kind?

"Status?" Beckett connected to Nolan and me, his team close by and ready to attack from the front.

"I have clean shots of two of them." I made note of the pacing brute and the skinny one feeding. *"I'm going after the blond first so I can maybe save the man with him."*

"We won't be able to get anyone out before attacking," Nolan confirmed my diagnosis of the scene. *"Not without alerting any of*

171

the suspects. Best move now is to try and take them down before too many people get hurt and hope the hostages can escape while we keep them preoccupied."

"Good. Go," Beckett said, the only prompt I needed to nock my arrow, not willing to waste one more second.

I released with my next breath, the thin projectile whipping through the air for only a moment before lodging into the skinny man's shoulder blade.

He let out a howling grunt from the impact, releasing his victim and kicking his chair backward, whirling around, searching for the person who shot him. Searching for me.

My group didn't hesitate, charging into the fray as I shot the blond again in the opposite shoulder, this time through the front. His eyes found me instantly, a growl escaping his lips as he charged at me, the two arrows protruding from his body not slowing him down in his altered state of mind. I swung my bow in an arc in front of me, impacting him square in the jaw. Yet, he continued throwing erratic punches at me. They were easy to avoid, but he was fast, most of my movements forced on the defensive. Out of the corner of my eye, I caught sight of Beth moving around him, grabbing the half-dead man from the table and running out the front door with him to safety. Good, maybe he would survive.

Lucas took advantage of the man's focus on me to sneak behind him, our gazes connecting for a brief moment to confirm what he was about to do. This man would fight until he had nothing left, and with the drugs within him, he felt very little pain.

At my sharp nod of approval, Lucas triggered the wooden side of his Amalgam Blade and shoved it through the man's stomach. It wasn't a killing blow, but there was no coming back from it to fight more.

His eyes bugged out, Lucas pulling the blade from him, the entire length of it coated in crimson blood tainted with black swirls. The man stumbled for a moment before falling onto his knees, lips snarling as he stared up at Lucas, his dagger still pointed at the man's chest. I nocked another arrow, aiming it at the back of his head, just in case.

"Don't move," Lucas warned, but the man didn't listen, shooting himself up to impale himself on Lucas's dagger.

I choked on air as I watch the life die from his eyes, his body going limp around Lucas's blade.

"Goddess! *What?*" Lucas screamed out loud. My thought exactly, but it wasn't what was important, my attention turning to the chaos filling the room.

"Evacuate this half of the room through the kitchen," I directed him. *"I'm going to assist with the other two."*

He nodded, rushing to the scattered people, directing them and pushing them to run to the door, promising that the suspects are too preoccupied to notice. He took Lea's hand, running by her side for the exit. My heart slowed its erratic beat slightly now that she was safely out of the fray, allowing me to turn back to the battle with a clearer mind.

I wasn't the only one to send my seconds to help the hostages, Beckett fighting the paranoid redhead with only Milly to back him up, which was better than Nolan who fought the ranting brute all alone while his team got people out. Nolan fought better, but the man was able to keep his distance by using a broken table leg as means to block Nolan's wooden blade. I could tell he was trying to subdue the man without killing him, but the man's recklessness was making it difficult, forcing Nolan to be careful.

Well, that made my choice easy on who to assist.

I jumped over a table, lifting my bow and shooting my arrow, the tip lodging in the back of the man's right knee. He collapsed onto it, Nolan landing a punch across his face before poising the dagger against his throat.

"Be careful," I warned him. "The other guy just killed himself on Lucas's blade."

"Well, that's lovely." Nolan's face was hard as stone as he pulled the blade away so the suspect couldn't use it, but still poised it at the ready just in case.

"Aren't you just a treat," the suspect spat out at me over his shoulder, my next arrow already nocked and aimed at him.

"Be smart and surrender." I walked a few more steps forward, Nolan and I on either side of him with no means of escape.

We had him cornered. Even with the drugs taking over his system, he should be lucid enough to drop the weapon and turn himself over. One of his partners had killed himself and, from the corner of my eye, I saw his second one also lying on the ground, Beckett kneeling next to him with his fingers pressed against the suspect's neck.

Yet, a devious grin spread on the man's face, his dilated eyes gleaming.

"Chu Fui na Déithe!" He screamed at the top of his lungs, his reddened face making the blackened veins covering his cheeks even more prominent.

He raised his fist in the air, letting out a guttural cry before taking the sharpened wooden table leg and driving it straight through his heart.

Chapter Twenty-Two

I rushed to Lea's side the moment the infiltration was cleared.
She was with the rest of the victims, protected behind the line of wagons and soldiers that had been set up during the situation.

"Are you alright?" I asked, flinging my arms around her and pulling her into a hug. She sat on the edge of a wagon, her feet dangling off the side.

She grasped onto me tightly, her fingernails digging into my back. "I'm fine."

"You need to get checked out by a physician and we need to..." My words rambled out, my eyes scanning over every inch of her, looking for the tiniest scratch.

"I know, I know," she said, her curly black hair matted against her sweaty forehead. "But there are others who need your help first. Go and do your job."

"No, you're my priority right now. Besides, you're a witness, too...no one will question me staying by your side."

"Please." Her voice wavered, her hazel eyes avoiding my gaze. "Just...go do your job."

I wouldn't have listened to her, but the desperation in her voice was potent; a need for alone time, a need to process the shock that was settling deep in her bones. I knew that feeling; it was painful and slow, infecting every inch of you from body and mind to soul, until you could finally accept what had happened.

"Alright." I patted her hand, taking a step back. "I'll be back as soon as possible."

I spent the next hour helping the local forces document the crime scene and move the suspects' bodies into a wagon. As directed, we were having all three of them brought to the Compound so Beckett could do the autopsy, all of us curious just how much blackthorn had been in their systems, hoping it would lead to an answer as to why all three of them committed suicide.

Once all of that was cleared and the rest of the Faction was working on interviewing the other witnesses, I went back to Lea, a smile spreading on my lips when I saw Beckett personally giving her the wellness check everyone was mandated to have.

"I see you got lucky and nabbed yourself the best physician here." I hopped onto the edge of the wagon next to her.

"Lucky for me, I have the best connections." She tried to laugh, but her typical bright chuckle came out shaky, strained against her full lips. She was shivering, a fuzzy red blanket wrapped loosely around her.

"Here." I leaned over, pulling it tighter against her shoulders. I kept my arms there, locking her in a side embrace in hopes that some extra warmth seeped through.

"Sorry to interrupt," Nolan came up behind Beckett, "but I wanted to come and introduce myself. I'm Nolan, the new Alpha

176

of Kasha's Faction."

"I'm Lea." She gave a little wave through the blanket. "I've heard a lot about you."

"I'd ask if they were all good things," Nolan's gaze flicked to me, amusement filling those green eyes, "but knowing who your roommate is, I think I'd rather stay in the dark."

She laughed again, the shaking in her voice lessening. "That's probably smart."

"I know it's a lot to ask, but do you mind if we ask you a few questions?" Nolan said. "I can leave, of course, if you're more comfortable with just Beckett and Kas."

"No, it's alright, I suppose you'll all find out my answers anyways." She looked over to me. "I've learned enough about Kas's job to know whatever I'm about to say will end up in a report of some kind."

"Can you tell us anything that stood out to you about them?" I rubbed her arms, trying to subdue the shivers that continued to rack her body. "Besides the obvious drug use."

"Barely." She scrubbed her hands up and down her tawny face, smothering the word. I moved the blanket back up her shoulder. "At first, they were just ranting about some of the most outlandish things, but you could tell they thought they were making complete sense."

"Consistent with the amount of drugs they seemed to have in their system," Beckett said, handing her a waterskin, urging her to drink. She took a few tentative sips, the jug shaking in her grip.

"I know it's difficult, but do you happen to remember anything they said?" Nolan's words were gentle and kind, his face soft, giving all his attention to Lea. Nothing about his stance seemed agitated or stressed as if he was desperate for information. I wasn't sure if it was because Lea was connected to me, or if this was how he always treated witnesses, but I couldn't help myself—I was impressed with his tender manner.

Lea fiddled with the cap, her eyes downcast. "Mostly just about how we were all lucky they came in to save us. How we would thank them once they introduced us to the truth that would set us free."

I stiffened. That didn't feel right, not typical for those of blackthorn addicts. When they went on rampages, they didn't care to talk, they just wanted blood and pleasure.

"And then they kept chanting those odd words." Her shoulders tensed. "Something like...*Chi Fan na* something."

"Yes, we heard." I had already written the words down with notes to contact local Universities in hopes of finding an Old Kazolanian Linguist who might know what they meant.

A well-known chirping interrupted us, my hand instinctively going to the pocket at my side, but my unit was still.

"Excuse me," Nolan pulled his Comms out, the screen lit up. His eyebrows wrinkled as he walked away for privacy.

"You need lots of rest," Beckett instructed. "You weren't injured, but your body isn't used to the loads of adrenaline it's working through. Along with the shock, I suggest taking a few days off from work."

"But I have orders to fill," she mumbled, her fingers tightening in the soft red blanket. She was a workaholic, but judging by the weakness in her voice, she wasn't going to fight this battle hard.

"Don't care. Physician's orders." Beckett checked her pulse one more time, his long fingers pressed gently into her wrist. "If any of your customers have issue with you taking a few days off to recover from a traumatic event, then send them my way and I'll set them straight."

"We both will," I snorted. "I'll make sure she follows orders."

"Thank you," Lea sighed, her eyes closing. "Both of you."

Silence fell as Beckett finished a few more steps of the exam, checking for concussion and sluggish reflexes.

As he started asking her more medical questions, I peeked over my shoulder to find Nolan pacing back and forth, his fingers once again twisting in the chain of his necklace as he talked to someone on his Comms. I gave Lea's shoulders one more squeeze. "I'll be right back, are you gonna be alright?"

"Yes." She nodded, wrapping the blanket around her a little tighter, her shivering dissipating slightly.

I walked over to Nolan, my stomach tightening. By the way he held tension in his jaw and shoulders, I knew the call wasn't a positive one. "What's wrong?"

"That was Liv," He shoved the Comms back in his pants' pocket. "Another body showed up with Elliot's marking. Looks like a few of us have to get over there."

My stomach bottomed out, my veins running cool. This day was just getting worse and worse as it went on. How would it end?

The Elliot case was my priority; I wanted to know every detail and experience everything firsthand so I could help track him down. However, my heart lurched, knowing that I couldn't just leave, not with everything Lea had just been through. We were always there for each other, no matter what. She had been there when I needed her, and I wouldn't abandon her.

But what about all those people who Elliot had taken from

life? Didn't they deserve my attention too? They deserved retribution, even in the Gods-blessed Afterlife. I wanted to bring their souls peace, so they could finally enjoy paradise with Lunestia and Firenielle. I couldn't just give up on them.

But I couldn't abandon Lea, either.

"We don't need the full unit this time," Nolan said, taking a step closer, lowering his voice to a murmur. "You should take Lea home, she needs you right now."

My chest lightened at his words, letting me know that my instincts were right—that the decision I wanted to make was the one he agreed with. Instead of letting me struggle, he read me like an open book and confirmed what I needed to hear.

"Don't worry," he smirked, giving me a wink. "Liv is meeting us there, and I'll take Eden and Greyson with me. Since you probably won't trust any report I write, I'll make sure they report everything."

I scoffed. "My, how generous of you, delegating all of that work for my benefit."

"What can I say." He leaned down, his warm breath tickling my ear. "I live to make you smile one day."

"You're a dork." I shoved him away, ignoring the fluttering beat pulsing in my gut. I punched his shoulder for good measure, reminding myself *that* was how I treated Nolan. "Try your best not to mess anything up while my fascinating mind is preoccupied with other things."

He shook his head, an amused chuckle escaping his grinning lips. "I'll try my best. Now go and take care of your friend."

"Thank you," I whispered, the fluttering intensifying as I turned around; and, somehow, I felt the lingering warmth of his gaze on my back as I walked away.

***

I brought Lea right home, arranging to have a soldier transport her cart back to her forge. I planned to head on over there and make sure everything was closed and locked after I got Lea washed up and to sleep.

I tried my best to keep the conversation on other topics, not wanting her to feel forced to talk any more than she wanted. It was one thing asking her questions in a professional capacity; I needed those answers to investigate, to get her retribution and closure on what happened. But I had taken my armor off the moment we walked through the door, removing any trace of my Onyx Guard status. At that moment, I was just her friend, meant to support but not pressure, giving her the space to process and think while also being a place to fall just in case she needed it.

We sat in silence on her bed, the glowing embers of the fire in her bedroom hearth illuminating the space as I gently brushed the tangles of her freshly-washed curls. Her fingers hadn't stopped shaking, even after the warm bath she had just taken and the thick fleece shirt and pants she'd put on. She needed rest and sleep; hopefully that would help.

"How do you do it?" she whispered, her hazel eyes staring into the fire, legs crossed in front of her.

My fingers stilled, the brush in my other hand hovering above her hair. "Do what?"

"Fight those people. Risk your life." She shook her head.

I shrugged, returning to one of the pesky knots, being as gentle as possible. "It's my job, it's what I was called to do."

"I always knew it was what you did, I knew the logistics of the Guard...everyone does. But I never really saw you until today.

181

The focus and courage and heart it must take to be willing to run into danger like that just to help others. To face people who...who want to hurt and kill. You were a sight to see, Kas. It was awe-inspiring."

My chest tightened at her words. Plenty of people had told me that over the years, told me about my skills and my natural abilities, how I was born to be an Ibridowyn. I always believed it, and I would mimic their words; because this was always what I had been called to do, with or without my family's legacy. But in the past year, with my doubts, along with those of my family and the High Faction, it was easy to forget. Even with my fellow Hierarchy members around me, it was easy to convince myself that they were only saying those words to make me feel better. My mind always tried to persuade me of that.

Yet, when Lea spoke them—someone who saw me as a protector not someone to be protected—they lifted me. Her faith sang to my soul, calling it forward again. It reminded me why I wanted to sign up for the Guard in the first place and why I kept fighting today, even when my darkness tried to convince me to give up.

I was born to be an Ibridowyn, to follow through on the oath I had taken to my country and its people.

Tsio a Chisain. Protect the Peace.

I would never stop.

I held my breath for a moment, hoping for a whisper of my wolf.

Nothing.

I tried not to let it ruin the heartwarming words Lea had just said, focusing on the happiness the moment had just brought me.

"Thank you," I said, finally breaking apart the gnarled mess, able to smooth the brush through her beautiful black hair. "It's what I was meant to do. But I feel the same way about your job. We all have our own callings, and we are all meant to follow through on them. It doesn't make yours any less important than mine. Plus, I bet no matter how many years I learn, I could never perfectly sculpt and design the works of art you call weapons that come out of your forge. That's not just a calling, that is a gift from Lunestia."

"Thank you." She fell silent for a moment as I finished with the brush, moving on to braid the length of her hair. "Can I say something you probably don't want to hear?" she asked at last, and even though I couldn't see her face, I knew she was smirking from the teasing tone of her voice.

My eyes narrowed. "Sure."

"Nolan actually seems very nice, or at least his witness manner is." She let out a chuckle. "Although I suppose it helps that he's quite pleasant to look at."

A lump formed in my throat, the burning difficult to ignore as I swallowed. I tied off the end of her braid. "I suppose, if he's your type."

"Kasha Mallanis, I've known you for over twenty years." Lea twisted around, nudging my shoulder with hers, a kiss of pink dotting her dark, bronzed cheeks. "Don't act like I don't know exactly who your type is."

I balked at her, eyes and mouth wide. I wished I could tell her she was way off, but then I would be lying.

In a different life or during a different time, if he had just stayed that stranger in the tavern, Nolan would be the one my eyes would go to.

But my life was never that simple.

Chapter Twenty-Three

I took the next day off, refusing to leave Lea alone.

We spent the day at home, part of it together playing chess or cards, and other times giving her space when she needed it. I worked on cleaning the house and cooking a very simple dinner, hoping it would take some of the stress away. It seemed to help, being there for her without constantly suffocating her. By the time dinner was over, she seemed a little less anxious and had decided to go to bed early.

I finished wiping off the last clean dish and storing it in the cupboard when the faint chirp of my Comms rang from my bedroom upstairs. I raced up, taking the steps two at a time, trying my best not to miss the call. The whole Faction knew why I was here, so if they were calling, it might be about Elliot or some new piece of information about the hostage situation. The screen was still lit up as I entered my bedroom, grabbing the unit from my bedside table to see who exactly was calling.

Nolan's name flashed across the screen.

A part of me wanted to ignore it, but the stronger, more curious part hit the accept button, Nolan's smirking face appearing before me on the screen.

"Hello, what can I help you with?" I dropped down onto my bed, my legs a bit shaky. "Something about the case?"

"Uh, no, nothing too pressing," he said.

I squinted, noticing that he was walking outside, somewhere that wasn't the Compound by the look of the buildings around him. "Then this call is for…?"

"I wanted to see if you were available to meet me tonight at that bar you all seem to enjoy."

My eyes widened, my heart pulsing a beat faster. "The *Blood Moon*?"

"Yes, that's it." He nodded. "I think there are some things we need to get out in the open and talk about, which might be better discussed outside of our professional environment."

"I don't know how I feel about discussing my personal life in a public place." My skin itched, and it took all my self-control not to scratch at the rising pressure on my throat.

"I reserved one of the private rooms they have. I figured you wouldn't want me coming to your house…"

"Sharp instincts."

"So, I found a public venue that offers privacy for people to talk in." Nolan stopped in what looked like the entryway to the bar. "Look, a lot's happened since I arrived. I have questions for you, and I can tell you have plenty for me, even if you haven't asked them. We're going to be stuck with each other for who knows how long, so we might as well take a step toward civility and mutual respect. I think the only way to get there is to try and break some of the stress that seems to be surrounding the idea of getting to know each other. So, if you're willing, I think I have an idea of how we can do it, but it involves you meeting me tonight."

"Well, um..." I looked around my room as if some magical answer to my dilemma was going to appear on the walls.

I didn't want to leave Lea alone. Even if she was planning to spend the rest of the night in her room, I had no idea what she might need. Yet, Nolan made a good point. We were stuck with each other, no matter how much I had been in denial since he arrived. If I wanted to try and move on, find a way to regain my composure in the Guard and get back on the path I had been on, then I would need to learn to play in this new team dynamic. The only way to do that was to make an attempt with Nolan.

I wasn't sure if we could ever be friends, but he was a good solider and investigator. All I needed to do was take a step out of my comfort zone and try...

My heart pounded as my mind ran through the pros and cons of going. It could help me move forward or it could remind me about everything I'd lost. I could learn to work with my new superior, or I could resent him even more for taking the Alpha position. So many what ifs; I needed to shut off my mind and go off instinct, even if that felt impossible most days.

"I'll ask Lea if she's comfortable with me leaving," I said, the words dragging from my lips. "But if I get even an inkling that she needs me to stay, then I'm not coming."

"Completely fair," he said. "Call me if something changes, but if not, just ask the bartender where to find me."

And with that, the screen went blank.

***

Lea basically pushed me out the door when I asked her if she was alright alone in the house for a while. Apparently, I'd misread how much space she had wanted today.

For a weekday, the space was packed, the bar a few people deep waiting for drinks. Lucky for me, I wasn't planning to order anything, so I did my usual trick of standing at the edge of the bar, quickly catching Benji's attention.

"Hey there, lovely," he winked at me, his dark salt-and-pepper hair sticking up a bit. "I already know why you're here."

"Your hospitality is beyond words some days." I smiled at him, his cheeks reddening slightly, although it was probably from the increased body heat in the space.

"Your friend is waiting for you in Room Two." He gestured to the back hallway, lined with private rooms for different uses. "Need a drink before you go?"

"Just sparkling water with lime."

The glass of my new usual was cool to the touch as he slid it over to me. "Have fun," he said, turning back to the increasing crowd.

I walked down the hall, doors lining either side of the short expanse. There were six rooms in total, each one with a different size capacity and purpose. Some had game tables, others were just separate lounge areas for private parties and events. I had been in most of them over the years, the Faction taking them over to celebrate different cases closing or the promotion of trainees and other members. I swallowed a sip of water, attempting to wet my severely dried throat as I approached door two, trying to remember exactly what was in this room. Knowing Nolan, he'd chosen it for a reason.

I took one more breath before pushing open the door into the well-lit space.

The room was almost soundproof, the noises of the bar disappearing the moment I closed the door. The space had a few tables along the perimeter, but the main focus was the large billiards table in the center, the bright green top harshly contrasting with the hand-carved cherry wood base. It was perfectly lit with sconces along the wall, all of them dimmed so the occupants could properly play the game without painful lighting ruining the ambiance of the bar right outside.

So apparently, we'd be playing a new kind of game tonight.

Nolan already had a cue stick in hand, bent over the table, hitting casually. He wasn't playing for real, just hitting any ball depending on their ease of sinking into one of the pockets.

"What's this?"

"It's called a billiards table, although by what a few of our colleagues told me, you already knew that." He straightened, propping his smooth cue stick against the table before walking over to me, a pint of ale in his hand. "I thought we could play a round."

"You asked me to meet you here to play a game of billiards? Something we could do literally any night if we wanted?" Although Lea had wanted me to leave, I was a little peeved that he'd asked me to come just for a round of a game. Granted, it was one of my favorites, but it still didn't seem like a good enough reason.

"Besides the fact we could actually talk while we play," he leaned his hip against a corner of the table, standing a few feet away from me, "I figured we could put a little wager on it. But instead of coin, we play for an answer."

"An answer to what?"

He smirked at me. "Any one question the winner has been

desperately tempted to ask the loser."

Now that certainly got my attention.

A voice in my head screamed at me to run away. I didn't want to tell him anything, even if he did win the right to a question. I had too many sensitive secrets, ones that should be off limits until I was ready to tell them. Who knew if that time would ever come?

However, I had questions of my own—ones that I had been wondering since the first day I met him. I'd never felt comfortable prying into his past even when I thought he knew mine, and now that I was aware he knew very little about the past year, it made me even more reluctant to ask. But he was offering—he knew all the questions I could ask or what I might be interested in. He was analytical enough to have gone through all of these possibilities before extending this offer to me, which meant he was alright with me learning more about him.

But was it worth the risk?

Maybe I could negotiate the arrangement more in my favor.

My spine straightened. "I only have one limit that is non-negotiable."

"That being...?"

"You can't ask anything about me from the past year."

He stared at me for a moment, scratching at his chin as he contemplated my caveat.

"Deal," he said. I stuck my hand out, but he didn't reciprocate. "If I can break."

I huffed, rolling my eyes. "Fine, deal."

We shook quickly before silently moving away, me to the wall to pick out my cue stick, him to the table to rack and set. Once we were both settled, he put the cue ball down, and, without hesitating, took a direct shot, sinking two balls in the process.

I grunted in annoyance; apparently, he knew his way around a billiards game, too.

"Looks like I'll be taking stripe colors, then." He winked at me, my stomach churning at the impressive break.

"Yup," I said between gritted teeth, trying my best not to growl.

"Also," he leaned over, taking his first shot, missing the back right pocket, "I felt it was fair that you get to ask me a few questions beforehand. I already know a decent amount about you, between your family's history and my friendship with Oliver, but you haven't been given the same courtesy."

I kept my eyes on the table, circling around it to decide the best shot to take. At least, that's what I made it look like while my insides quaked. His offer was unexpected and immensely generous. He was offering up answers, not because I had a right to them, but because he wanted me to feel comfortable with the fact he already knew stuff about me. He wanted me to feel as if we were equals in a way.

A tiny voice tempted me to take advantage of his generosity, but the churning in my gut let me know that wasn't what I really wanted.

"Then let's make it fair." I finally picked my first shot, leaning over to line up my cue stick. "Think about what you know about me and tell me the same answer for your life."

I shot, my solid red ball sinking into the left side pocket.

"Well, alright then." He sipped of his ale, taking a few silent moments. "I grew up in Rystin as an only child with my fathers. One was in the guard before retiring to open his own archery training school. The other is a craftsman, primarily working in

190

carving and designing furniture. I joined the guard when I was eighteen, training in the Rystin Faction with Oliver, although that fact you already knew. Once I completed my Omega training, I transferred to the Xoblar Faction, first as a Delta before going through promotions, ultimately becoming the Beta. I don't play any instruments, but my favorite is the lyre and I wish I had been able to learn growing up. Just never seemed to find time."

I wasn't surprised about most of the facts he knew about me, seeing as half of them were common knowledge throughout the Guard and the others were easily pieced together from Ollie's life. However, there was one fact he had added that I wondered where he learned it.

"How did you know I played an instrument?" I watched him line up his next shot.

"Oliver," he said. "He used to talk about how much he loved watching you practice the piano and how he missed the sound of your songs in the house, that you used to play them when he struggled to fall asleep."

It was something I had done for him the year after mother had passed and I heard him wandering around the house late at night. It had been one of the few things that had helped during his grieving process. "That was sweet of him."

"You were one of his favorite subjects to talk about." Nolan straightened, taking a step back so I could lean into my next shot.

My cheeks heated, words jumbling in my mind—not the exact state I wanted to be in. So instead of focusing on the conversation, I turned back to the colorful table in front of us.

As the game continued, and we each shot and sank our balls, the quieter we became. We each fixated on winning, my competitive drive stirring and brewing just below the surface. I wanted that question; I wanted to hear his answer almost as much as I wanted to avoid having to answer his. So, I kept all my focus on the table, mapping it out and setting myself up for the best shots.

We ended up tied by the end, fighting to see who would sink the eight-ball.

I cursed my bad luck as Nolan got to take the first shot. The cue ball was decently lined up, although it wasn't the easiest. I sucked in a breath as he took the shot, the sharp click of the two balls colliding echoing in the room as they raced across the tabletop. My pulse pounded for a brief second before the eight-ball knocked into the side instead of sliding into the pocket.

He groaned, his chin falling to his chest. "Your turn."

I bit my lip, hiding the smug smirk that attempted to escape. I didn't want to get ahead of myself; a lot could happen if I got too brash, leading to stupid mistakes. Instead, I kept my focus on what was in front of me, leaning over to get the right view, the cue ball lined up. If I did this right, I could bank shot the eight-ball, making me the victor. I took my time, finding the right angle and making sure everything was perfect. I took one, two, three breaths before pulsing my cue stick forward, sending the cue ball flying.

My heart stopped for the second the eight-ball shot across the table before falling perfectly in the front right pocket.

"Yes!" I slammed the bottom of my cue down on the floor, letting out an exasperated sigh.

"Nice shot." He was no longer smiling, yet I could see a hint of pleasure twinkling in his green eyes. He might not be happy he lost, but he didn't seem too broken up about it.

"Thanks."

"A deal is a deal." He leaned against the edge of the billiards table, dropping his cue on top. "Go ahead and ask away."

I clutched my cue still in my hands, fists twisting around it as if I was trying to strangle it to death. I knew what question I wanted to ask, but a part of me held back. Was it too intrusive? Was I overstepping? He had told me I could ask anything, but it seemed like a trap.

Well, there was only one way to find out.

"Why is this case so personal to you?"

He nodded, as if expecting this to be my first question. "Do you remember the death counts of each species from the Elliot case?"

Odd question. "Forty-two humans, twenty-three Shrivs, thirty-one Vargs, and one Brido."

He reached for the chain at his neck, yanking it up to reveal the pendant on the end. Except it wasn't a pendant at all—it was a sparkling gold ring with a round cut diamond nested in the center.

"That one Brido was my fiancée. Her name was Cleo."

"Oh, Goddess." My breath rushed out of me, my mind blanking for a few moments as I stared at the ring still dangling from his fingers, processing what he'd just said. "So, you didn't just transfer here because there was an open position, you took the job because you wanted to catch the killer who..." I couldn't even finish the sentence.

"Correct." He nodded, letting the chain fall from his fingertips to rest against his heart, above his steel blue shirt. He walked away from the billiards table and over to a pair of leather chairs in one of the corners. "I had been consulting whenever I could over the past four years, trying to be a part of the investigation."

I followed him over, taking the seat opposite him. With the way his posture sank into the chair, his shoulders sagging, it seems this was something he had wanted to talk about for a while. Of course, it was only now that he felt safe to, once the strain of hidden facts finally came to light over the past few days.

"She was the Alpha of our Faction, and we had met as Deltas both transferring to Xoblar at the same time." He twisted his fingers in the chain, a tick I had picked up on whenever we were talking about Elliot or the case. "We hadn't set a date for our Mating Ceremony, we were both getting so wrapped up in the Elliot investigation. We kept saying that once we caught him, we would know that time was right. But that day never came."

"I'm so sorry, Nolan," I whispered, a part of me wanting to reach out and do something, anything, to show how much I truly felt his sorrow and hurt. My chest was aching, my eyes misting over.

"Thank you." He gave me a weak smile. "I had been offered her position as Alpha, but I turned it down...it just didn't feel right to take it. So, I continued on as Beta of the Faction, grieving and learning to move on in some ways and holding on to the past in others."

"That makes sense." I nodded. "Grief isn't linear, we can't just follow steps no matter how hard we try. We can't force the process, we just have to pass through it no matter how long it takes."

"When I heard about the Alpha opening at first, I didn't consider taking it." He looked me up and down. "I liked my team and I was comfortable there. But when I heard that the first Elliot case had officially been confirmed in Seathra, I realized I couldn't

194

pass up the opportunity, so I applied that day. I thought it was a long shot, since they already had a Beta eligible for the promotion, but they put in my transfer almost immediately."

I snorted at that, but it wasn't for his actions—it was the High Faction's. Now I understood, and although I still wanted his job, I could no longer fault him for his choice, for the simple fact that I would have done exactly the same if I were him.

"You made the right decision coming here." The words felt natural coming from me, even though his wide eyes told me he was not expecting that. "You deserve to get Cleo justice. I can't fault you for that, especially now that I know how much information you were actually given about all of us."

He chuckled, fingers brushing over the smooth top of the diamond. "Yeah, that's a whole mess we can save for another day."

"Agreed."

"It's not just bringing him to justice, although that is a part of it," he added, his gaze starting to linger elsewhere. "Really, I just want to know what happened that night. There are so many questions that we can't figure out. How did he get her alone? How did he get his hands on our Ogdala Blade? Why was she even in a position to be facing him? No one knew how she got there, not even me. And the only person with an answer is..."

"Elliot," I finished for him, my mouth going dry.

"They're questions I may never get answered because I have no idea how this whole chaotic hunt will play out." He leaned forward, staring at the wall for a brief moment before softly looking over to me. "But I won't stop. Not until I catch him or we find his body."

His words struck a chord in me, an ache settling deep into

my body, reminding me of a fact I had been ignoring for the past few days. The bitter taste of eating my own words and accepting my unplaced grievances were hard to swallow, but after tonight I couldn't pretend.

Nolan deserved to be Alpha.

Chapter Twenty-Four

Lea was already back to her old routine two days later, flitting around the kitchen making breakfast, dressed in her work clothes and ready to start her first day back.

"Are you sure you don't want to stay home for another day?" I asked, sitting at the counter, sipping the coffee she had woken me up with. "I can stay with you."

"I'm sick of sitting around here." She shook her head, dropping a plate of breakfast-sausage gravy and biscuits in front of me. "I need to get moving, and the forge is the best place for that."

I sighed, picking up my fork. "Alright, then." I trusted Lea to know exactly what she needed, yet it didn't dull the flair to protect her.

"Besides," she rounded the corner with her own plate, dropping in the seat next to me, "I appreciate you taking these days off with me to keep my company, but I know you're just as desperate to get back to work, too."

I chuckled, spearing a piece of sausage. "And here I thought I was hiding it so well."

I was already dressed in my black shirt, stretchy pants, and military boots underneath my armor, ready to get back to the Compound and resume the Elliot case. I had taken a quick call on my Comms with Eden yesterday, having her catch me up on the victim they had found the night of the hostage situation. It sounded like a typical Elliot killing, with the branding, drained blood, and an uncomfortable amount of wolfsbane used to clean up.

The perfection of it all made my head spin. I'd spent my alone time for the rest of the day sitting in my room and trying to come up with any idea on how to move forward, attempting to find any little thread to tug on and find a new path. All that work made my skin buzz, anxious to get back there as soon as I could to help.

Unfortunately, I had a counseling appointment to attend first.

***

"Last time we talked about your family a bit," Vanessa said after we'd both settled into our usual seats in her office. "But I was wondering how everything with your Faction was going. Now that time has gone by, how are you feeling about your new Alpha? Nolan, right?"

My fingers curled around the cushion below me. Was Vanessa a mind-reader? "Yes, Nolan." I took a deep breath, unclenching my fingers and placing them in my lap instead. This was supposed to help me—it *could* help me, if I wanted it to. "Things have...developed."

"Care to explain?"

I let out another deep breath. "It was hard at first, which is probably no surprise. But we both learned that my anger toward him was more due to a...miscommunication on the High Faction's part."

"That's good, isn't it?"

"I don't know." I scratched at my hairline, staring at Vanessa's perfectly polished black leather heeled boots. "I spent time with him outside of work. He wanted to break that tension and he took the steps to try to do it. We played a game of billiards together the other night with a sort of bet where the winner could ask the loser one question."

Vanessa chuckled. "How did you fare?"

"I won." I smirked. "And it helped me learn a bit more about his motivations to come here. It made me realize that his reasons are valid, even if I couldn't understand at first. I was being stubborn, letting my past cloud my judgement. I didn't like having to admit that, but at least I was able to realize that my qualifications didn't make him any less qualified."

"How did that realization make you feel?"

I tapped my finger against the chair for a moment, thinking about the right way to describe it. "Calmed, at least a little. Having that clarity definitely helped. At least now I don't doubt his skills as much. I know he can lead, even if I wish he wasn't here doing it. It's not the best, but better. I think we'll at least be able to work together."

"You seem unsettled by the whole thing even though you're saying it ended well." Vanessa tapped her stilo tapping her knee. It wasn't a question, but an observation, her powerful, inquisitive gaze bearing into me, my skin pricking at the scrutiny.

She wasn't wrong; I was unsettled. In the moment, it was good for me, my mind settling a bit once I learned more about Nolan. It at least helped me feel better about being his second-in-command even if I wasn't one hundred percent alright with it. But once I had gotten home, lying in bed staring at the ceiling, I couldn't seem to figure out exactly how I felt anymore.

"It just made me feel...odd." I fell back in my chair.

"Odd, how?"

"I'm not sure, I can't really explain it."

"Can you try?" Vanessa leaned forward, shifting in her seat a bit. "Maybe explain what different emotions you were trying to process during and after the time you spent with him?"

"No, I can't. They all feel too tangled." My foot began to tap against the floor. I tried to bring myself back to how I felt the other night, but when I did, it all felt muddled and twisted together, lodged within my chest. "It's frustrating, because I know I would feel better if I gained clarity on it all, but it seems out of reach. Every time I think I'm getting close to understanding, it's ripped away."

A jittering buzz spread up my arms, thumping against my chest in an uncomfortably smothering way.

"Is this the first time you've struggled to name emotions like this?"

I bit my lip. "No."

"Hm." Vanessa wrote a few things in her journal. "Did that start within the last year?"

My fingers began to shake, the pressure on my chest deepening. I hated this, thinking about how I'd been forced to change and adapt. I didn't want it, I didn't like it. My head was spinning, the room around me blurring at the edges.

"Kasha," Vanessa whispered, "take all the time you need. Just breathe. and when you're ready to answer, I'll be right here."

I let that soothe me in a way, reminding myself that there was no pressure. This was at my pace, it was my journey. No one could tell me how to heal, not when it came to my own sanity. I took a few deep breaths, the air burning my nostrils, but I didn't care. I pulled them in long and deep, holding them in for a few seconds before releasing. Things began to sharpen around me slowly, the tapping of my shoe against the floor, the slight scent of the lavender candle burning on the table next to Vanessa, and the tickling of my hair blowing against the back of my neck.

I let the calm wash over me and through my mind, allowing myself to finally think about an answer.

"Yes." My voice was shaking, but at least I could speak again. "I suppose there were instances beforehand, but they were isolated. Now it feels like it happens in any situation that's even slightly overwhelming."

Vanessa tapped her stilo against her lips this time, her brows crinkling. "Have you noticed they affect you physically in any way?"

My muscles seized. "What do you mean?"

"If something has happened, then you would know what I mean."

My eyes narrowed at her, my first thought wondering if she suspected I was struggling to connect with my wolf. I had kept it from my last psycho-physician, terrified that they would report it to the High Faction even though these sessions were supposed to be confidential. I only let that shame out when necessary, or when I trusted someone. I could never let the truth show.

Yet, Vanessa was insinuating that she was already aware of

it, that she had somehow deduced it from our past sessions. Maybe she had, and I couldn't help but wonder...did that mean it had happened to someone else?

I supposed there was only one way to find out. Even though my mind screamed at me to keep the secret bottled up, my desperation for answers was stronger. Vanessa was the first person to give even the hint that she might know more about this burden I had been forced to carry for a year. Maybe I could actually learn something that would help me.

"I..." I closed my eyes for a moment, letting a beat pass; then I looked back up at her, all of her attention on me. It was now or never. "I haven't been able to sense or transform into my wolf since the...the incident."

"I see." Vanessa nodded knowingly.

"I've tried but nothing seems to work," Tears pricked at the edges of my eyes, but I didn't let them fall. My voice was shaking, just like my insides, but I didn't care. "After everything that was taken from me, this was...this was the worst part of it all. I feel like half of me is missing and I don't know what to do. What if I can never be whole again?"

Vanessa pulled her chair forward a bit, leaning over to grasp my hand. I stiffened at the contact. "I know you think that makes you a failure, but I want you to know, you are not the first Varg Anwyn I've met who has had that problem."

My throat tightened. "Really?"

"I won't lie to you and say it's normal...it is fairly rare." Her face was calm and relaxed. I could tell she was being honest; she knew me well enough not to sugarcoat the facts, it wouldn't help me. "However, it has been to known to happen."

"Why?" I needed answers, my fingers tingling, not wanting

to waste another second.

"Wolves are meant to run free, live without inhibition—"

"I know that."

"Well, studies have shown that when Vargs suppress extremely potent emotions, ignoring them, it causes an imbalance with their wolf side." She leaned back in her chair. "When the wolf feels such a shift, it goes into survival mode, pulling away from the suppression, ultimately leading to a dormant wolf."

I stuttered a bit. "You make it sound like my wolf is sleeping, or...in a coma."

"No, not at all." Vanessa bit her lip for a moment, the tips of her fangs peeking out. "When your wolf feels you suppressing such strong emotions, it doesn't know how to react, because that goes against the core of what the wolf is. And just like a human, it learns to lean away from what makes it uncomfortable. That's what your wolf is doing. Until you can create an environment for it that's less uncomfortable, it won't return."

I let the new knowledge and facts process. This was good, it was a step forward, which meant I could find a solution. "So, what do I need to do?"

"You need to face what the wolf is trying to escape." Vanessa gave me a weary smile. "You need to cope with the trauma and learn to process the emotions, fears, and other pain that you've been internalizing. The longer you try to ignore it, the bigger a problem it will become."

It all made sense; being able to access that part of myself again, to set it free, seemed so simple. Face your past, face the emotions and thoughts you refused to think about and process. Live through them, feel them, set yourself free from them. It was easy to speak the steps, but it was difficult to even accept the idea was achievable.

In fact, it felt impossible.

So instead of saying anything, of telling Vanessa I could do that, I pulled away and stayed silent.

I didn't want to face myself. I didn't want to look back.

I knew it was wrong, I knew it wasn't helping, and that's what made it worse. Somehow, after everything, the idea of facing my past and digging into my complicated, entangled emotions was even more terrifying than the idea of never shifting again.

Chapter Twenty-Five

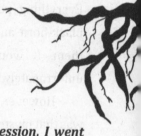

When I returned to the Compound after my session, I went straight for Lucas's office.

Lucas and Taylor had called me the day after the hostage attack, letting me know they had taken point on the post-investigation. I had appreciated their initiative, but was also happy that it was a case the three of us could work together primarily alone.

Both of my boys were already there, Lucas seated behind his desk and Taylor standing next to him, poking him in the arm about who knows what.

"What does he want from you now?" I grinned at Lucas.

His unamused look said enough. "Who knows?"

"You never listen to me." Taylor mock-pouted, a few dark curls escaping the tie at the nape of his neck and framing his angular face.

Lucas looked up at him, little amusement in his cerulean

eyes. "Of course I do, just not about inconsequential things when we're supposed to be working."

"You two are ridiculous some days," I laughed, dropping into the other vacant seat, picking up one of the case files that sat on top of it. "Catch me up."

They told me everything they'd collected, from the scene to witness testimonies to Beckett's autopsies. It was all as I had expected based on my own experience at the crime scene. Everything pointed to three idiotic druggies overdosing on blackthorn and letting the bloodlust rampage get the best of them. It would be an open and shut case, one we had unfortunately seen before.

However, the one thing holding all of us back from closing it was that mysterious phrase all of the suspects had been chanting: *Chu Fui na Déithe.*

"Have we been able to locate a linguist who can translate what they were yelling?" I asked, reading through the witness statements, all confirming it seemed to be their driving reason to commit this act.

"Not at the Seathra University." Taylor flipped through a few pages in front of him. "We thought about sending out falcon messages to other territories universities. Emric is helping us compile a list of academics who may be able to help."

"Perfect." I nodded. It was a shame that we had to use Falcon Mail, but since only military and government personnel had access to Comm units, we had to rely on our trained falcons to get these messages across the Isle. Hopefully, they would respond as quickly as possible. "Once he—"

The office door slammed open, cutting me off, all of us spinning to see who'd interrupted. A giggle attempted to escape my lips at the sight of Emric, doubled over trying to pull full breaths through his lips.

"Morning, Emric." I walked over to him.

After a few more huffing breaths, he straightened, his tawny cheeks mottled with red splotches, glasses slightly fogged. "High Faction..." He wheezed a few more times. "Spotted."

My blood ran cold, the air around me thickening. "Where?"

"Just outside of Eroste, heading straight for the Compound."

"*Futeacha*," I cursed, my fingers curling against my legs. "Why didn't they inform us?"

I walked out of Lucas's office, heading for mine to put on the last of my black armor, wanting to be fully presentable before they arrived. All three men followed behind me.

"Not sure," Emric straightened his own armor, dusting it off as if it wasn't already presentable. "Nolan is cleaning up the conference room in case they want to meet there and look at the Elliot case. Beckett and the rest of the Hierarchy are making sure anyone on Compound is at the ready before they meet us here. They're expected to arrive within a half an hour."

My fingers trembled as I attempted to latch one of my arm bracers. "Was...was he with them?"

I didn't have to say his name, they all knew who I was talking about. I looked up to Emric, my insides clenching at his somber nod.

My father was coming to visit.

***

None of us moved, standing at the ready in the conference room with the three High Faction members. They had walked into the Hierarchy office area as if it was a completely typical day, but we all felt the tension that coated every area they touched. They ordered a meeting with the Keturi, locking the rest of our team outside of the conference room as the four of us stood in a line on the opposite side of the room.

"So, you have nothing new," Violet said, her tightly-pulled bun making her stern face even more intimidating.

The High Faction had sent three representatives, one from each species branch. Violet was representing the humans, her well-pressed burgundy silk top and tailored black pants complimenting her dark skin and russet eyes. Standing next to her was Terrence, the alabaster Shrivika dressed in a simple pair of black dress pants and a silver-gray button up shirt. Unlike Violet, who could be intimidating with just a sharp look, Terrence's round face and stocky build tended to give the opposite effect. He had an approachable air about him, even when he was meant to be serious or upset.

And to represent the Varg Anwyns, Anton. My father.

He exuded power, demanding attention from everyone wherever he went with his tall, slender form complimented by his navy-blue vest, black button up shirt, and matching pants. His dirty blond hair was well-groomed and slicked back from his face, his chiseled features hardened by the frown set on his full lips. He paced slowly in front of our investigation board, his pale silver eyes scanning over every detail. If a stranger walked into this room, they wouldn't have guessed that this man stood in front of his daughter with the chill wafting from every little movement he made.

"This is a case spanning over ten years." Beckett was the first to speak up, his smoky voice pulling the attention of all three High Faction members. "We're still catching up, learning about his habits, his past cases, attempting to build a—"

"And in that time, two people have lost their lives at the hand of this monster," Violet scolded, Beckett's mouth closing over the rest of the explanation he was trying to give.

"What about you, Alpha?" Terrence turned to Nolan. "This isn't your first time working on the Elliot case, how have you not caught them up faster?"

Nolan cleared his throat, and I glanced to my side to see him standing up a bit straighter, if that was even possible. "It was never going to be a quick turnaround, not with so many backlogged cases to get through," Nolan said, backing up Beckett's claims. "With a hunt this large, it takes more than one expert to make it successful. Even with a Faction as skilled as this one, you can't expect us to work miracles. Not with a master manipulator like Elliot."

"You seem to have a lot of faith in this Faction, Alpha," Father said, turning around slowly to face us. "Although past actions have proved perhaps you shouldn't."

"I'm not exactly sure what you are referring to, sir," Nolan said, my heart skipping a beat. "The Faction I've been lucky to work with over the weeks seems to be well-represented in the file you gave me. It did seem somewhat lacking in details, but of course with a group this close how can there be anything too terrible to report?"

Awkwardness filled the air, Terrence's face paling, Violet's lip twitching. I held my breath, waiting for them to react—because although he didn't say it out loud, he was calling out the High Faction for their decision to redact information from our Faction File.

"Hm." Father gave Nolan an appraising look. "And I suppose even with the details you did know, you feel as if everyone has met your expectations?" His gaze flicked to me briefly before returning to Nolan.

"Most have exceeded my expectations," Nolan said. "I didn't think I would be so lucky to be a part of a team like this, especially with such a well-respected and competent Beta such as Kasha. But of course, you shouldn't be surprised by that."

I tensed at his words. Did he actually mean them? So much had changed with Nolan since I'd met him, I could no longer figure out what was real and what was a figment of my anxious imagination. I wanted to believe him, yet the darkened doubt that slithered into my mind tried to convince me he was bluffing...and sometimes it was just easier to listen to it than ignore it.

But that couldn't be my focus. I kept my eyes trained forward, reminding myself that I just had to make it through this meeting. I could do that, I was strong enough for that.

At least, I hoped I was.

"Well then, what do you have to say for your Faction, Beta?" Father's chilled gaze bored into me, his hands braced on the conference table in front of him as he stared me down.

I swallowed a lump forming in my throat, hoping desperately that the words in my head made sense to everyone else. I couldn't tell on my own anymore.

"I think you underestimate us." I kept my shoulders pulled back, trying my best to seem strong. "We are putting as many resources as possible into tracking him down and stopping the terror. Like every Faction before us has. Just because we haven't been able to work wonders in the unrealistic timeframe that you've apparently set for us, doesn't mean we aren't determined to get the job done."

His gaze hardened, the air thinning around us, the room

blurring. All I could see was him, his weighted stare filled with all the accusations and expectations he had put on me since that fateful day a year ago. Every time I saw him, that look got heavier, more accusatory, and stung me just a bit deeper. Yet, no matter how much it hurt, I couldn't look away. He pulled me in, forcing me to feel every inch of his judgment, the silent weight almost smothering me.

Finally, he sighed, looking away as he straightened his vest. "I guess I shouldn't be too surprised by the disappointment anymore."

He acted coolly and spoke under his breath, as if none of us in the room had overly sensitive hearing and could understand everything he said—passive aggressive words referencing the same thing he felt the need to bring up every time we saw each other.

I tried to shake off the painful reminder that every decision I'd made recently had brought nothing but disappointment to him. No matter how hard I tried, no matter how hard I worked to redeem myself, it never seemed to be enough. What would I have to do to be the daughter he praised again?

The gazes of my fellow Faction members slowly grazed over me, checking to make sure I was okay, gauging my reaction to my father's harsh words. But even with the best of intentions, their lingering eyes stung every inch like needles poking into me, crawling up my arms and legs toward the building pressure settling on my chest.

Just make it through the meeting. I could do it.

Emric cleared his throat, thankfully, pulling the stares of the leaders toward him. I could hear the faint sound of his voice, but all his words blended together. I figured out that he was talking through some of the facts about where we stood, trying to get the conversation back on the line of thought the High Faction originally came here to discuss. It worked; all of them were back on the details of the case and no longer on questioning our team...questioning *me*.

A faint whisper of someone's voice attempted to sneak into my mind, wanting to talk to me, but I didn't let them in. Emric and Beckett knew me well enough not to try that, so it could only be one person; and after the way Nolan stood up for me, I couldn't look him in the eye. Not when he'd just witnessed firsthand my father's true feelings about me. I couldn't explain without breaking apart, and this wasn't the time or place. Not when I had spent the past eight months trying to prove I was strong, that I could still fight.

So, I blocked him out, focusing on the three leaders in front of me, pretending that my father's words didn't cut me deeper than any dagger could.

Chapter Twenty-Six

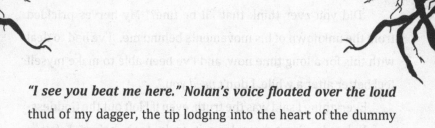

"I see you beat me here." Nolan's *voice floated over the loud* thud of my dagger, the tip lodging into the heart of the dummy thirty feet in front of me.

I rolled my eyes, tensing the minute he walked over the threshold. "Go away."

"I just wanted to make sure you were alright." The door clicked shut behind him, his fist grasping the privacy curtain and pulling it across the window. "I'm sorry the High Faction arrived without your knowledge."

"Pft." I pulled my next blade out from my thigh sheath, the hilt smooth in my hand. "The High Faction and I haven't been on the best terms since they hospitalized me."

"Alright, fair." His boots clicked against the tiled floor, my own feet digging in deeper to the mat that framed the shooting area. I lined my blade up, thrusting it forward with all of my strength, whizzing it through the air and lodging in the carotid artery of my fake victim. I tried to ignore him as I pulled out my next blade; I didn't want him here.

Right?

"Kasha..." His presence loomed behind me, his towering body only inches away. "Please, tell me how I can help you."

"I don't want your help." I gripped the hilt tighter as I raised my hand to throw. Yet my arm just stayed there, fingers gripping the weapon like it was grounding me to reality.

"Why not?" The low rumble of his husky voice sent shivers up my spine.

"Did you ever think that I'll be fine?" My nerves prickled from the unknown of his movements behind me. "I've had to deal with this for a long time now, and I've been able to make myself feel better after a while. I don't *need* you."

Everything I said was the truth, even if I left out the Goddess-awful details about how long it truly took before I felt a semblance of calm again after a panic attack. How the next few days would be spent with irritable, nightmarish sleep, dark thoughts, and such jittery, sensitive nerves that any light touch to my skin could set me off. It was a burden I had been dealing with for a long time; I could take care of myself.

I didn't need him.

I turned around slowly, ready to kick him out of the room. He stared down with those swirling green eyes, like a forest ignited by the summertime heat. I made the disastrous mistake of taking a deep breath, his intoxicating cinnamon citrus scent enveloping me the second I did. His eyes trailed over my face, taking in every inch of me, my spine stiffening at the scrutiny. Whatever he thought he was looking for, I didn't like it; yet I still just stood there silently, letting him take in his fill.

He leaned forward, bringing his face closer to mine, penetrating my personal space, my breath hitching at his nearness. A part of me wondered what he was doing, that intense gaze so powerful it had me frozen. He stared and stared and stared to the point where I wondered if he would do anything else.

Then he shoved me backward. Hard.

My feet stumbled, barely able to catch me so I didn't fall right on my ass.

"What in the Goddess?" I screeched, my muscles tensing as I glared up at him.

"You don't need anything, huh?" He strode toward me like an animal stalking its prey, my instincts pulling me to take a few steps back. "Holding in the anger isn't going to help you! It won't make things better."

My chest tightened, fingers curling into fists at my sides. "You don't know what you're talking about."

"Maybe not with what you went through, but I know what pent-up anger looks like." He rushed forward, throwing a punch aimed at my face. I dodged it effortlessly, putting a few more feet between us, his steps falling back into pace. "I know what it feels like, and you need to let it out or it'll drown you."

"Nolan, stop! I'm not angry!" I yelled, hoping desperately he believed my words more than I did.

"It's alright to hate them, Kasha!" His eyes were wild, transitioning from green to gold with each heated word he spoke. "Even your father. After everything he did to you, everything he's put you through, it's alright to be so angry at him that you hate him."

A chill swept over me, even with the sheen of sweat trickling

215

along my hairline, my fingertips numbing. No one had ever said that to me before. "I don't. I can't."

"Then hate *me!*" he yelled, slapping his hand against his chest twice. "I know you do, and it's okay to. I took the job owed to you. I took your Faction and title."

"Stop it." My voice was low, rumbling from my chest, something hot and dark brewing inside me, rising closer to the surface. I needed to rein it in, push it back down into the depths of my mind.

"Fine. If you won't fight for it, then maybe *I* deserve this job." His words were venomous, slicing into me as roughly as his Amalgam Blade would. "I won't apologize for taking it from you. This is my Faction now, not yours."

The howl that ripped from my throat thundered off the walls as I charged him, my tightened fist swinging in an arch before colliding with his jaw. The impact didn't budge him, his head whipping slightly to the left before he turned back to me.

He could have dodged that easily, but he didn't. He took it...he took my anger.

I choked on air, stunned by the violence I let slip from its cage. I took a step back, my eyes darting toward the door, desperate for escape.

"Don't run away." He grabbed my arm, forcing me toward him, locking my arm behind my back.

"Let me go," I begged, struggling to loosen his grip. I needed to get away from his berating attempt to uncap my ire. It was seeping out, and if I stayed here even a moment longer, it would escape from me, a tornado of pent-up rage I wouldn't be able to control once I let it go.

"Show me how much you hate me." The words rumbled from

his chest, his body pressed against my back, my locked arm the only thing dividing us. "Show me."

That was all it took, those final words. That was all I needed to accept the dark thoughts I had hidden for too long. I unlocked them from the back of my mind and let them free.

I leaned forward, kicking out behind me, my heel crashing against his knee, tilting him off balance enough for me to jab him in the stomach with my free arm, pulling away from his grip. I whipped myself around to face him, my legs hip-width apart, arms already up in a defensive position ready to attack, his stance matching mine. He was ready for me.

Or so he thought.

I snarled, attacking with abandon, letting my movements flow free, my fighting instincts taking over. I didn't think, I didn't analyze, all I could do was fight. I aimed for his face once again, my punch landing against his jaw, a trickle of blood now seeping from his lips. But unlike last time, he didn't just take it, he fought back, forcing my feet to move, my body to react. We threw jabs and blocked punches, my mind focusing on only him and what he was doing for me at that very moment. In his own special way, he was giving me a gift...and instead of thinking too hard about the repercussions of it all, I accepted it.

I did exactly what he asked, I showed him how much hate and anger I had stored up.

But the more I punched and jabbed and thrashed, the more I knew deep in my soul that he was not the one I wanted to be fighting. No matter how much I once believed that I hated him, that was not the truth. He was nothing more than a proxy for those I was truly angry with, for those who had taken away everything from me. My strength, my freedom, my happiness, my

217

light. All of those who had forced me into silence, into the darkness that now tried to consume me every day. They had tainted me, body and mind, each of them in their own uniquely cruel way.

The High Faction. My Father. Caleb.

Logan.

I hated them, all of them. Even Father and Caleb, who I still held a sense of love for—a part of me hated them. The two opposing emotions swirled together, dueling inside of me, colliding and struggling. I didn't know which would win, I didn't know how all of this would end, and for once I didn't care. I just let it out. I let the anger and the hurt and the hatred pool deep inside of me before it fueled my next attack, the power of those dark emotions released with each impact. I didn't have to hold it inside anymore, I didn't need to give it a piece of who I was. I had held the anger in for so long, I hadn't realized that I was just giving all of them even more control over me. But not anymore.

I accepted the anger, I held it for what it was, and then I set it free.

Finally, after Goddess-knew how long, I stumbled away from him, wiping at blood trickling slowly from my nose. My breathing was labored and rough, body buzzing from the release I hadn't known I needed. And it was in that moment, I felt it, something I'd been missing for so long. Something I craved deep in my soul.

My eyes were glowing their beautiful golden hue.

Even though I couldn't see them, I knew they were—my vision sharpening, my mind turning from panicked anger to impulse-driven. Every inch of my body was alight with freedom, a whirlwind of energy swirling around desperate to be released. It was empowering and perfect and completely intoxicating.

Yet, after a year without this intense freedom, it was also overwhelming. Everything was on fire, twitching and pulsating to the point of almost pain, that fine line between pleasurable and unbearable. I didn't know what to do, my mind spinning with so many thoughts, I feared it would make my wolf flee again.

I needed to go off my instinct, I needed to follow my passions. It was the only way to keep my wolf, to follow the freedom to a place where overthinking wasn't allowed and all I could do was feel. Feel anything I wanted, be anyone I wanted to be. No more fear getting in the way, no more second-guessing.

Feel. I just needed to feel.

I didn't think, I acted. Which was the only way I could explain why I rushed at Nolan, his eyes wide with surprise as I pushed him roughly against the wall, his body impacting with a loud thump. I held him there, my hands pinning his shoulders, his body still as he stared down at me, his own wolf-golden eyes watching for my next move. A moment of brief silence passed, stillness settling as we just stood there, staring.

Until I pounced, pulling his neck downward and crashing my lips against his.

I had no idea why that was the first thing I wanted, but I didn't question it. He stiffened for a brief moment before melting into the kiss, his arms snaking around my waist to pull me closer. I started slow, explored him for the first time, moving gradually so I could remember every little movement. Something wet and sticky mingled between us before seeping through the crack of my lips, the luscious taste of his blood tantalizing my tastebuds. I let my tongue dart out, craving the sweet, dark flavor, licking the small stain from the corner of his lips, a moan raking through his body at the contact.

This was my first time tasting him in more ways than one, and already I found myself wanting more. Yet, for all I knew, he didn't feel the same; my stomach clenched at the thought.

I pulled away a mere inch, our breaths still mingling. My body trembled as I looked up, desperate for more of his lips. For once, I didn't want to be fighting for power or control, I just wanted to give in.

Nolan looked down at me, his eyes glowing like embers, just as intoxicated as mine.

In our next breath he whipped me around so I was the one pinned against the wall, his body flush with mine. He didn't even hesitate before crashing our mouths back together. His lips were hard and sure, moving against mine as if they belonged there. He explored every inch of me, his tongue sneaking out to trace me, a groan escaping as I parted my lips and allowed his tongue to dance with mine. He tasted like he smelled: spicy and exotic and addictive.

Seconds passed between us while I savored having someone near me again. For so long, I had been terrified that my body would be scared of everyone, forcing me to cower away from even the idea of being intimate. But with Nolan, with his body so close and his lips so tantalizing, I couldn't stop myself from craving more, from desiring more.

I pressed myself further against the wall if that was even possible, my hands slowly moving to explore the hard form of his chest and stomach through the soft fabric of his short-sleeved shirt. I didn't care about what was happening outside this room. I didn't care that technically someone could walk in and find us. All of that, the responsibility and need to control, left my body as if it never existed.

220

All that mattered were the jolts of electricity coursing through me.

A slam from outside sent us jumping apart, my arms pushing him away just as he took a step back. It was nothing more than the door to the practice area closing shut. No one had found us, no one was even close to the private room we occupied.

But with that collision back to reality, I felt the golden beauty of my eyes slip away, back to their steely blue color.

"No!" I screamed, my body crumbling against the wall, legs half crouched, arms braced against the cold concrete to keep me upright.

I was so close to having my wolf back, and it all just disappeared in an instant. My mind and body were warring once again, everything that had happened just now all crashing down, pulling me with it. My head was spinning, my stomach churning so violently, I dry heaved a few times, but I kept the bile from escaping. I gasped for air, for anything that would calm me down but it was too late. I'd overwhelmed my senses for the first time in a year and now my body was reacting.

Violently.

"Kasha..." Nolan took a step forward, but I didn't give him the opening to touch me again. I didn't even have the words to explain to him what had happened. Everything pounded inside of me at once, trying to escape. It was all too much. So, I did the only thing I thought to do.

I ran.

Chapter Twenty-Seven

My lungs burned with each step I took, but I ignored them, determined to get anywhere that wasn't the training building. I darted to the woods, my steps quickening the moment I crossed the threshold, the underbrush crunching under my boots.

I ran for about a mile, avoiding the camping area and losing myself instead in the thicket of trees that surrounded the Compound. Leaves and twigs brushed against me, nicking my exposed arms, one even scratching my face, but I didn't care. I was determined to see if I could transform.

Even though I had a feeling I knew the disappointing answer already.

I slowed, then stopped in a minor gap in the trees, and waited under the glowing, waning moon, my breathing labored, heart pounding erratically. In the past, calling my wolf was an instinct, a natural part of who I was. I never needed to think, just act. I kept holding onto the small sliver of hope that I needed to focus more since it had been so long; I reminded myself of my limbs cracking into place, the effortless glide of my body switching from one form to the other. I remembered the cool whipping of wind blowing through my soft silver fur, the crunch of twigs under my bare paws. I remembered every moment, every favorite.

Yet, nothing.

I tilted my head back, shouting so loud, the entire Faction could probably hear it. The howl was filled with my sadness, the warbling cry released to Lunestia's crescent hanging above me. I cried out for my wolf, begging the Goddess to bless me with it once again. Was I being punished? Did she no longer find me worthy of her blessing?

As my howl dissipated, the tears finally fell, my body collapsing against the nearest tree. All I could do was curl up, my legs pulled to my chest and forehead falling to my knees, my pants catching the waterfall that escaped from my eyes. I didn't know what else to do. I'd let the anger out, I'd set it free, just as Vanessa said I would need to. So why was my wolf still hiding?

I was so tired of trying to figure it out, tired of being forced to go back through everything that happened to discover what was keeping a vital part of me hidden. Tired of having to prove myself. Tired of having to show everyone that I was still strong, that I could still do my job.

Would it ever end?

I didn't know how long I sat out there alone before the crunching of leaves echoed in the distance. I counted down the seconds until the sound was right in front of me.

"Why are you two here?" I whispered, not looking up, but knowing exactly who stood in front of me.

"Because we care about you." Liv dropped herself next to me, Eden settling in on the other side. "What happened?"

A part of me didn't want to talk about it, many voices in the back of my mind yelling at me to keep my mouth shut. I rocked myself a few more times, trying to even out my breathing. Liv and Eden had been there for me through it all; they had defended me, but most importantly, they had believed me and never questioned my truth. They knew every sordid detail and still loved me, they saw me as strong and capable. I could trust them.

I kept telling myself that, over and over, in hopes I would believe it.

"My eyes glowed." I peeked up to settle my chin on my knees.

"What?" Eden sat up straight, shifting herself to face me directly. "Kas, that's amazing!"

My jaw quaked. "I know, but it's already disappeared again. I tried, I tried so hard to transform, but nothing happened. Not even a small buzz to give me some hope."

"But your eyes glowed, which is the first step," Liv said. "That alone is reason to hope."

I leaned back, my head resting on the trunk behind us. "I suppose."

"Well, what happened?"

I rubbed my temples, a dull ache settling behind my eyes. "After the High Faction left, I was trying to let off some energy in the training room, throwing daggers. Nolan came to check on me."

"He mentioned he was going to," Eden mumbled.

"We talked for a bit, and the next thing I knew he was pushing me around, trying to get me to fight." The memories already felt distant, as if they hadn't happened less than an hour

224

ago. "He said I was holding my anger in and that it wasn't healthy. He wanted to try and help me let it out, hoping it would make me feel better."

And of course, he was right—it did.

"At first I didn't want to, but it seemed like a sign from the Goddess, because Vanessa only this morning educated me on the fact that wolves had been known to retreat when a Varg had gone through trauma and was struggling to process and cope with it." Another tear escaped me, my heart aching to return to that moment, to feel that heated burn I had been so desperate for. "So, I gave in and started fighting him back. After a round of sparring, everything felt alive again, and I could sense it: my eyes were glowing."

"That's incredible," Liv said, leaves rustling under her as she adjusted to stretch her long legs out in front of her. "Repressing intense emotions like that can really mess with a person. I guess it only makes sense that the ramifications are linked to both of your forms."

"You sound like Vanessa," I chuckled, my shoulders loosening a bit. "No, *worse*...you sound like Beckett."

"She's right," Eden laughed, winking at our friend.

"Twelve years of marriage, I suppose it was bound to happen." Liv shook her head, twisting a lock of obsidian hair around her fingers. "Well, whoever I sound like, the words still hold plenty of truth."

Both Liv and Vanessa were right—and it was the only thing that made sense. The problem was, I could barely decipher my own emotions, all of them blending together in a sticky mess, refusing to untangle so I could try and accept them. They each tried to assault me at once, and it was always just too damned much. It made me ache and cower away from them. Even though logically, I knew the steps I needed to take to help bring my wolf back, it was easier to force my emotions aside than to face the pain I would have to go through to understand why they were there.

Even though I knew that mindset was unhealthy, I kept running from them. But if today had taught me anything, it was that running from those messy emotions was never going to be the answer.

"I don't want to face them," I groaned, banging my head lightly against the tree, my hair catching in the rough bark. "What if I don't like what I find?"

It was the question I had been avoiding for so long, the one I had refused to speak until now. Until I had finally been called out for it.

"Would you rather take that risk, or force yourself to continue living this way?" Liv looked at me with such care, her eyes full of love and support; I could sense it from both of them. "Which life do you choose?"

For once, the answer wasn't difficult. "I choose the one that sets me free."

"Then fight for it," Eden said, her olive cheeks mottled red from the cold. "We all believe you can do it. Take our strength if you need to, but don't give up. Take back what they took from you."

I reached out to both of them, looping our hands so we formed a three-person chain. "Thank you."

They both whispered acceptances, a few moments of silence passing, nothing but the whistle of the wind and the brushing of passing animals filling the void. I let my nerves relax and my tears began to dry, giving me a moment to accept what I has discovered today. It felt heavy, but not unbearable. I could do this; I would make it through. Sometimes alone, and other times with help, but either way, I would survive the battle warring within me.

I would not give in.

"Why do I feel like you're not telling us something?" Eden's eyes narrowed.

Goddess above, she knew me too well.

My skin prickled at the thought of telling them. But I needed to talk this out, and if I was going to tell anyone about it, two of my best friends were the perfect ones to listen.

Goddess save my poor pride.

"I wanted to try my to keep my eyes glowing as long as possible, hoping I would feel the call to transform." I let go of their hands and picked at the hem of my shirt, twisting it between my fingers. "So, I figured the best way to do that was to not think and just do the first thing that came to mind."

"Which was—?" Liv asked.

I bit my lip. "Kiss Nolan."

"*What?*" They both screeched, the high pitch grating against my sensitive ears.

I told them the technical details of the whole thing, but kept the truth of how it felt to myself. That was something I needed to figure out on my own—why it felt so good to be in Nolan's arms. Why I had craved his touch. Why even now, a little part of me jolted at the idea of kissing him again, of wanting him.

That was a discovery for another time, when my heart and mind weren't so exhausted from the tumultuous day. But there was one more thing I still needed to do, my heart settled, knowing it was the right move.

227

"I need to go apologize." I rubbed my eyes, wiping away a few remaining tears while stifling a yawn.

"You need to rest first." Liv wrapped her arm around my shoulder. "Your body has been through too much, it needs sleep."

"I'm fine."

"No, you're crashing," Eden pointed out. "You're shivering, your cheeks have no color, it looks like you can barely stand up, and you have dark circles under your eyes like you've been punched."

"To be fair, it could actually be bruises...Nolan did get a few hits in."

"Doesn't matter." Eden shook her head, red hair rustling against her shoulders. "It's not even safe for you to drive."

My breathing hitched. "I can't sleep here."

"Liv can drive you home on your bike, and I'll follow behind. That way, you have no issue driving to work tomorrow."

I wanted to argue, but they were right. My muscles ached with fatigue, my mind clouded and murky, each movement feeling like the most strenuous activity. I needed sleep and rest, time to reflect on what had happened today. It was the only way I would be able to give Nolan the overdue apology he deserved, something that I would most certainly give him tomorrow.

Chapter Twenty-Eight

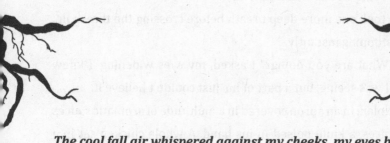

The cool fall air whispered against my cheeks, my eyes bleary as I stared at Nolan's front door. He probably could sense that I was standing out here, pacing back and forth, yet he gave me space. When I focused hard enough, I could hear clanging through the walls, but I had no idea what I was about to interrupt.

When I had finally made it back to the Compound midmorning, Beckett had yanked me into the infirmary to give me a quick check-up and make sure I wasn't harboring any repercussions from the partial transformation. I'd then had to dive right into work and lead an archery lesson with the trainees in the morning before spending the afternoon with Taylor and Lucas, talking to the wife of the most recent Elliot victim. She had been away on business when the body had been discovered and only just made it in to give a statement, her cheeks mottled red from most likely many days of crying. It had been a heartbreaking yet powerful moment, pushing me to fight my hardest in this case.

The sun was already setting by the time I was able to find this moment to talk to Nolan. Alone. My feet stopped, my hand reaching toward the door. I just had to do it, to get it over with.

Before I could convince myself otherwise, I knocked rapidly, my knuckles numb to the biting pain of rapping against the rough wooden door.

"Come on in!" Nolan called out.

I took one more deep breath before crossing the threshold, then stopping instantly.

"What are you doing?" I asked, my eyes widening. I knew what I was seeing, but a part of me just couldn't believe it.

Nolan. In an apron covered in a multitude of aromatic sauces and juices, a knife poised in his hand. A whole chicken sat in a roasting pan on his stove, a colorful array of chopped vegetables sprinkled around it.

"Uh, cooking?" Nolan looked at me, a goofy half-grin teasing at the edges of his lips. "Is there another reason I would be holding a chef knife?"

I took a few steps closer to the kitchen counter he was working behind. "Improvised weapon?"

"And who exactly am I looking to stab in my own house?" His hands moved quickly as he sliced an onion, the half-circles cut so thinly, you could see through them.

"I feel like I've brought you to the brink of wanting to stab me a time or two." I tried to make light of the situation, though my chest constricted. I wasn't here to joke around or pretend. I was here to see if I could even do this whole trust thing with him. I needed to see if he even deserved it.

"You're not wrong," he said, dropping the last of the onions

230

into the pan. "However, I spent a lot of money on this knife, and I wouldn't risk dulling it just because it was convenient. I would just steal whatever weapon you had on you instead."

"Poetic." I crossed my arms, lingering by the round dining table a few feet away from the kitchen area.

He wiped the knife off gently before resting it on the cutting board, picking up the roasting pan and shoving it in the oven behind him. "Is there a specific reason you wanted to stop by?"

Here we go.

"Well, um, I wanted to..." I couldn't believe I was struggling so hard to say such simple words. "Talk. About what happened. Yesterday."

The muscles in his neck constricted, his throat quivering. "Oh, okay."

My stomach churned. "Unless you don't want to?"

"No, no! I do, I promise!" He braced his hands on the counter. "I'm just surprised you came by so soon."

I chuckled. "I know, I just...knew it was the right thing to do. But if you're too busy cooking..."

He wiped his hands on a towel before tossing it back on the counter and removing his stained apron from his waist. "The meat needs to roast for a bit in the oven anyways."

He crossed the room, meeting me in the open dining area before pulling a chair out, gesturing for me to take a seat. I swallowed down sarcastic words at the gentlemanly gesture and sat. He took the seat next to me, angling so we faced each other, our knees barely grazing. A shock rippled up my spine at the contact, reminding me of what had happened yesterday.

"What would you like to talk about?" His brows curved inward.

"Well, first, I wanted to say thank you." A blush crept up my clavicle. Great. "I didn't realize how much...anger I had built up until you let me kind of take it out on you."

He leaned back in his chair, rubbing his hand across his jaw, lips pressed together tightly as if trying to conceal a laugh. "Well, you had taken it out on me emotionally over the past few weeks, I figured physically couldn't hurt me that much more."

My chin fell to my chest, a groan escaping my lips. "Oh, Goddess, Nolan..."

"Hey, I'm kidding," His hand gripped my knee, shaking it slightly, his touch burning through my dark pants. "I'm sorry, I can tell you're trying to be serious. I shouldn't be making light of the situation."

"No, it's not that, I'm just so sorry for the way I've been treating you." Shame washed over me, flushing heat from my cheeks to my toes. "You didn't deserve any of that. I was just so bitter and angry and hurt by the High Faction, and you inadvertently represented that to me. I didn't want to accept that you deserved this posting. Which you do. You were obviously meant to be an Alpha, and you've taken the whole situation you've found yourself in quite well. Not many people would have been able to handle our crazy and lasted."

His teasing grin faded, relaxing into a genuine smile. "Thank you. That...that means a lot more than I expected it to."

I let out a breath. Part one of the conversation was done. Now, the hard part. "About the, um, kiss."

"Kasha, you don't..." he leaned forward, his hands hovering just above mine, as if he wanted to grab them, but he pulled away at the last moment.

"No, I really have to explain," My heart pounded in my ears, my palms sweating. This was the moment. My mind was screaming at me to run, to forget this dumb idea, but I pushed through; I listened to the whisper instead. "What I'm about to tell you is a big secret of mine. A terrible, shameful secret, and a part of me still can't believe I am about to tell you."

He sat up straight in his chair. "What is it?"

"Seriously, Nolan, I'm about to trust you," I said, my tone lowering, my fingers curling around my knees. "Please don't make me regret it."

"Never," he said, his eyes staring into mine with sincerity.

"I told you before that something happened about a year ago, a few months before my...hospitalization." He nodded intently, gesturing for me to continue. "Well, that was the last time I went to a Full Moon Camp."

"I had guessed that."

"What you don't know is...that was also the last time I had been able to shift to any part of my wolf form."

He blinked rapidly a few times. "What?"

"Something about that night forced my wolf to retreat inside, and I haven't been able to feel it since." My skin crawled like it was trying to shrink around my bones and muscles, suffocating me. But I persevered through it. "I haven't even been able to shift my eyes to their golden form."

Understanding began to sweep across his face. "So yesterday..."

"That was the first time my wolf had appeared to me in a year." Now that the truth was spilling out of me, it was like a tidal wave that I couldn't control. "It had just been so long since I had even slightly shifted, and everything was overwhelming me. The freedom, the wildness, the adrenaline. I needed to get it out

233

somehow. So, I did something I'd been doubting for so long: I listened to my instinct, I let it tell me the first thing I needed to do."

He bit his lower lip. "And that was to kiss me?"

I couldn't look at him anymore, my eyes misting over. I stared down at my lap, nodding gently.

I didn't have a reason or an explanation. I still had no idea why, in my first moment of freedom, all I had wanted was to know what his lips felt like. None of it made sense to me, and I wondered if it ever would.

"Are you alright?" he asked.

My hands twisted in my lap, my gaze lingering there. I didn't know how to answer.

"Kasha," his voice was tender, so soft and alluring. "Please look at me."

I didn't know what compelled me, although it wasn't him giving me a command. His voice just called to me, drawing me to look at him. It felt like safety whispering against my skin, beckoning me to come toward it. So, I listened, and I looked up into those beautiful forest-green eyes that were so full of concern and admiration. My heart skipped a beat before slowing to a normal pace.

"Are you alright?" he whispered again.

"I'm trying to be, you have no idea how hard I've been trying to get my wolf to come out this past..." My words were rushed, just as they felt stumbling through my mind.

"No, Kas, that's not what I mean." He shook his head, leaning forward. I caught a whiff of cinnamon as his hair fell gently into his eyes. "You just had some form of transformation for the first time in a year. How are you feeling after that?"

His clarification shocked me; even Liv and Eden hadn't asked me that.

"I—I don't know, to be honest." He reached out again, this time not hesitating as he laid his hands over mine. I don't know what came over me, but I flipped mine around, weaving them with his. Another wave of calm rushed through me, his touch bringing me strength to continue. "It enthralled me and gave me hope. It made me feel like myself again, alive. But it was over so quickly, a part of me is even wondering if I just dreamed it up."

"You didn't." He shook his head, his hands squeezing mine. "I saw them. Your eyes glowed, bright and beautiful and perfect."

"It was probably just a fluke." A tear finally slipped from my eye, my own words slicing through me like my Amalgam Blade pierced my chest. "It's been a year and that's all I've been able to accomplish. Maybe it's just time I start accepting that my wolf has abandoned me."

"You're looking at this all wrong," he said. "You shouldn't be thinking this is all that happened, you should be celebrating that it did happen."

I sniffed. "What do you mean?"

He brushed a piece of hair behind my ear. Apparently, me kissing him had dropped a bit of a physical barrier for us. I was surprised it didn't scare me, having a man touch me again, but it didn't—not with Nolan.

"Your wolf eyes came back to you. Maybe just for a moment, but they did." His own eyes lit up, the green illuminating in the light. "That means that your wolf is still inside of you, it's still a part of you. It may not be completely ready to come out yet, but it's trying, just like you are. It's giving you a sign, letting you know that you aren't alone."

235

"Yes, I suppose that's true."

"I don't know what happened to you a year ago," My stomach lurched, a part of me wanting to look away, but his gaze held mine steady. "But whatever it was, you're still healing from it. Maybe that's what your wolf is doing, too? Healing from what happened. And when it's ready, when it's healed, it will come back to you."

My breath hitched at his words, the truth in them bringing me a sense of clarity that I had been missing for so long.

"You are strong, Kasha, you are a survivor—that I can tell." Awe lit up Nolan's features. "You are a fighter and a leader and I am honored that you are my Beta."

His words took my breath away. I had been so worried that he would judge me, I had never realized that he was the only person who didn't know me before. He only knew this Kasha, this moment, and yet he still saw me as strong—and I had been so cruel to him for weeks. I didn't know if there was anything I could do to make amends for my treatment, but I was going to try my hardest to find a way.

"Thank you," I whispered, biting my lip. "I don't deserve your kindness after everything."

"You do. After what I witnessed with the High Faction, you deserve so much more than just my kindness, but it's all I can offer right now."

"Thank you all the same," I said. "I wish there was something I could do to prove just how thankful I am that you made me feel safe trusting you right now."

"Just don't hate me for what I'm about to do."

He leaned forward, my breath catching, wondering if he was going to kiss me again, contemplating if I would let him or not. But instead, he wrapped his arms around me, pulling me to the

236

edge of my seat. His legs sat on either side of mine, my cheek pressed lightly into his chest, one of his hands gently stroking my hair. He smelled of warmth and comfort and bright summer days. He was safety, a place I hadn't found myself in for a long time.

"Thank you," he whispered against the top of my head.

"For what?" I mumbled into his shirt.

"For giving me your trust, or at least a part of it." He rubbed his cheek gently against my hair. "I promise to cherish it."

I choked back a sob. I had no idea what was happening in this moment; all I knew was that something was shifting between us, and only time would tell what direction we were now heading in.

Chapter Twenty-Nine

Somehow, it was easier to breathe walking around the Compound the next morning.

My bag was still slung over my shoulder when I walked from the tiny kitchen to my office, a steaming cup of coffee clutched in my hand. Yet, as I was about to turn inside, I hesitated, my ears perking up at the oddest noise coming from down the hall. It was almost like...a snore? I walked toward it, the slight wheezing growing louder as I approached the slightly-ajar conference room. I pushed it open, peeking in, and tried not to laugh at the sight I caught.

Nolan. Lying across the conference table, one arm slung off the side and his mouth slightly opened, sleeping as if in his own bed.

I could just shut the door and let him sleep; it was obvious by the case file lying on his chest that he'd been working all night. However, that would've been just too easy. So instead, I walked forward, staring down at his peaceful face for one more moment before giving a swift kick to one of the table legs, the whole thing moving half an inch at the impact.

He jolted upright as if being attacked, eyes darting around the room before settling on me, wide and frantic. "What's going on?"

"You know, even I've never found myself so tired that this table looked comfortable, and I work late nights and don't live here anymore." I dropped my bag in one of the chairs. "What are you doing? Your cozy bed is only steps away from here."

He sat all the way up with a groan, bending his knees and wiping his hands up and down his face a few times. "I didn't even realize I fell asleep. With the High Faction's visit, I got behind on reviewing the autopsy report from Elliot's most recent victim."

"Looks like you could use some coffee." I smirked at him over the rim of my mug before taking a long, drawn-out sip.

"Rude." He grumbled, a glint of amusement in his eyes. He shoved off the table, walking down the hall toward the kitchen. I didn't follow, as there was no need when you could talk telepathically. *"I don't like that I fell behind."*

"He's a serial killer who's been on the loose for ten years," I said to him, shuffling coming from the kitchen. *"You have to give yourself a break. Overworking yourself is not going to make catching him any easier."*

"When did you become so concerned for my health?"

"When I stopped resenting you." I laughed, trying my best not to think about the kiss we'd shared only a few days ago. *"I didn't lie last night, you deserve to be the Alpha, even if I do want the post someday. The only way we can continue earning each other's respect is by being open to it and working together."*

239

"Aw, you really do have a heart." He walked back through the door, a full cup of coffee in hand, the scent of sweet cream wafting from it.

"Behind the guarded, sarcastic exterior, yes I do." I rolled my eyes. "Did you even remember what the report said?" My eyes trailed him as he walked around the conference table to stand in front of investigation board.

"The last thing I remember was reading over the toxicology portion." He picked up a piece of paper from the floor before perching on the edge of the table. "But no surprise the only thing found in her system was wolfsbane absorbed through skin contact."

I walked around to sit next to him, the overwhelming investigation board staring back at me. "There is one thing I noticed with the past two victims, about the wolfsbane."

"What's that?" Nolan asked, still staring at the board and taking a sip, fingers mindlessly playing with the chain of his necklace. My heart shook, remembering what hung at the end and all it represented for him. We needed to catch this man, now more than ever.

I shook my head, refocusing on my theories. "This isn't the first time I've dealt with people using it to stop our tracking, but it is never as potent on the bodies as it is with Elliot's victims."

"How so?"

"In the past, it's uncomfortable to be near, sure, but it doesn't burn my nostrils to the point where it's overwhelming. The amount he uses is more than just a quick wipe down. I wondered if maybe he bathes the bodies in distilled wolfsbane after death."

"Huh." Nolan leaned back. "It's excessive, but it would be on profile for a man like him. Every piece of this is a game he's determined to win no matter what. If bathing the bodies gives him extra security that we can't find him, allowing the game to continue, I wouldn't be surprised if that was the case."

"That does lead me to ask how he gets his hands on so much of it." I took a step forward, my eyes scanning over one of the maps. "Distilled wolfsbane can hold its potency for over a year if properly brewed, but it would probably lose efficacy with each person he dipped in it."

"Xoblar and other Factions have theorized that he must brew it himself with the amount he uses, so as to not leave any witnesses or gain attention for how much he needs." Nolan pointed to the list of theories ever growing on the board, walking over to stand next to me. "It kind of makes sense with the gaps he takes in between location shifts. He would need time to set up any type of field or greenhouse and grow his crops before they were ready to distill. Although it still seems like a large venture to take on."

"He's a narcissistic sociopath. His concern isn't time, it's perfection," I pointed out. "Which leads me to question two things. One: if he's brewing it, what if he's also selling it?"

"Interesting." Nolan rubbed his chin with his free hand. "He does stay in areas for long periods of time, he would need some way to make money."

"My thoughts exactly," I said. "He probably has another job too, but this would most likely help supplement the high cost of actually having to make the liquid, especially if he needs enough to bathe his victims."

"What was the second question?"

"What if these aren't all of his victims?" I looked up at him, my chest tightening.

241

"These are all known cases where his markings are present. He's too much of a narcissist not to include it in one of his kills."

"True, but like we've been saying this whole time, this is a game to him, something to win." I turned toward Nolan, his brows furrowed as he looks down at me. "What do you do before you enter a game? You practice. What if there are other similar victims out there, while he was attempting to figure out his perfect method of killing? He wouldn't have marked them and risked staining his perfect record now."

"And maybe it's in one of those cases where we find a clue that can finally move this case forward." Nolan clapped his hands together, his body almost buzzing as a smile spread across his lips. "This could actually be a lead."

I tipped my mug to him, giving him a wink, my stomach flipping at the gesture. "You're welcome."

"Ollie was right, you are a master at case puzzling." He began to move around the room, pulling files and papers from different boxes. "We need to send messages out to all of the Factions and have them do a case review. Any cases from between eleven and fifteen years ago need to be reviewed for certain aspects pertaining to Elliot."

"The Isle of Kazola is about to despise us," I laughed, writing down a few notes that sprang into my mind.

I tried to focus on the work that needed to be done and the rushing high that came with a break in a case. I wasn't thinking about how easy it was to work with Nolan now that I'd decided to trust him, how effortless it felt brainstorming with each other about a case that had racked us for weeks. Thinking about that brought a different kind of pressure to my chest, and I didn't particularly need that distraction.

Nolan pointed his stilo at me. "Let's split the country into fours. Each Keturi member and their seconds can oversee contacting a handful of Factions and then going through their files when they arrive by Falcon Mail. That way, hopefully, we can go through the files quicker."

"Perfect." I spread my attention down the hall to hear if Emric or Beckett had arrived yet. "Emric's in his office and Beckett should be here soon. We can get them in on this right away."

My skin buzzed, my fingers flying to write down the list of steps I'd have to take for the rest of the day. A surge of energy raced through me, my mind and body almost feeling like one again. Not quite, but it was a step in the right direction, giving me hope that my wolfish flare the other day wasn't as much of a fluke as I originally thought. Maybe, just maybe, I was starting to take the right steps forward.

Maybe solving this case would help get me there.

"We should also follow up on the idea that he's selling drugs on the side," Nolan said without looking up from the table, breaking into my excited thoughts. "Although how we'll ever find someone to help us with those details, I'll never know."

"Oh, Goddess above." My stilo hesitated over my notebook, and I looked up to the ceiling as I chuckled.

"What?"

"I know someone who can help." The laughter bubbled up from my chest. "But you're not going to like them."

"My favorite words," he challenged. "Can't wait."

I rolled my eyes once again, hoping he didn't regret those words when I introduced him to one of the banes of my existence: Mylo, head of the Bralechi family, notoriously known as Seathra's

243

biggest drug trafficking pack.

***

The whole day was spent contacting every Faction in Kazola, telling them the parameters we needed them to look for when researching potential early cases involving Elliot. We were able to narrow it down to a five-year timeframe, meaning we would hopefully have some potential reports in our offices by the next day.

The next few days were going to be important as we gained new information about Elliot and his demented, twisted ways. Hope bloomed in my chest—maybe we would be the ones to take this sick man down.

I couldn't get too far ahead of myself, so I focused on the task ahead for that night; forcing Mylo into a little meeting, hopefully ending with some answers. But first, I had to talk to someone about this new idea of mine.

I knocked on the office door, grumbling from the other side telling me to come in.

"Hey." I walked a few paces in, Eden and Greyson looking up at me, eyes glazed over from a full day of work. "How are you two progressing?"

"As well as I suppose we can." Greyson shrugged his broad shoulders. "Still waiting to hear back from our territories."

"Good work, though." I smiled tensely. "Gray, can I have a minute with Eden?"

"Uh-oh, I'm in trouble," Eden teased, dropping her stilo on her desk and leaning back in her velvet cushioned chair.

"Nothing like that." I shook my head. "Just need to talk."

"Alright," Greyson said, standing up and walking toward the door. "Just come get me when you're done, Edie."

The door clicked behind him.

"What's going on? Are you alright?" Eden asked, gesturing for me to sit.

"I'm fine, I promise, I just needed to update you on something." I sat down, my hands twisting together in my lap. "I have to go and visit Mylo tonight."

Her face darkened. "What? Why?"

"A lead for the Elliot case." I leaned forward to rest my arms on the edge of her desk. "You know I wouldn't be going there if it wasn't important."

"I know, I know." She shook her head, letting out a deep breath. "If you're asking me to go with you..."

"You know I would never ask that of you."

Her shoulders loosened. "Good, thank you."

"But I shouldn't go alone. So, I'm taking Nolan with me."

Her eyebrows shot up, eyes wide. "Oh, really now?"

I tried not to laugh. Of course, that was what she was focusing on. "Stop it. He was the smart choice. Mylo doesn't know who he is yet, and this is a prime opportunity to use that against him and his crew to get the answers we need."

"Keep telling yourself that, Kas." She gave me a knowing smirk.

I swallowed a lump in my throat, trying not to think about the knot of nerves tightening in my stomach. This was oddly a big step forward for the two of us. Not only were we working together on Compound, but I had invited him to follow a lead and be my partner for the day.

And every moment of it felt extremely...natural.

I shook it off, focusing on Eden. "Either way, he's going to meet Mylo tonight. And I didn't want you blindsided if he brought it up at some point tomorrow."

"Thank you." She looked down at her lap. "Just...don't tell Nolan about...my past with that family. I know I have to tell him, and I will soon, I just want to be the one to tell him. In my own words, no one else's."

"I promise." I nodded. "And I'll try my best to keep Mylo under control so he doesn't give anything away."

Eden scoffed, rolling her bright green eyes. "Good luck with that."

"Are we okay?" I asked, leaning forward to grasp her hand.

She squeezed it back. "Of course. Just keep me updated on how it goes and let me know if he steps out of line."

"I will," I chuckled, patting her hand one last time before standing and heading for the door.

The moment I stepped out of Eden's office, Nolan was walking down the hall. "You ready?" he asked, a gentle smile on his lips.

I took a deep breath, matching his smile with sincerity. "Let's go."

Chapter Thirty

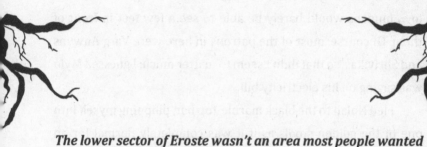

The lower sector of Eroste wasn't an area most people wanted the Onyx Guard to be. Although it looked well put together with its white brick buildings and bright shop windows, everyone knew the truth about what happened in the alleyways or in back rooms; drug trade, sex trade, any kind of deplorable trade you could think of, all hidden behind opulence.

Nolan followed me silently, not speaking once as I led him through the area on our lectracycles. Finally, I pulled up in front of a black-painted brick building standing out like a beacon in the bright streets. It was the place everyone avoided unless they were invited or desperate or both.

The *Black Howl Tavern*.

This was going to be a fun evening and, even though he had no idea what we were walking into, there was a gleam of anticipation in Nolan's eyes as we locked our bikes up. He could tell something entertaining was about to happen, and he seemed just as excited as I was.

"Ready?" I asked, straightening the leather breastplate of my full Onyx Guard armor.

"I suppose," he laughed, following me over the threshold.

The inside was as dark as the outside, decorated in a pitch-black-and-gold color palette. The black marble floor was swirled with bits of gilding, matching the painted metal tables and chairs. Chandeliers hung from the ceiling, the electric light dimmed so low, humans would barely be able to see a few feet in front of them. Of course, most of the patrons in here were Varg Anwyns and Shrivikas, so that didn't seem to matter much; I guessed Mylo was saving on his electricity bill.

I led Nolan to the black marble-top bar, plopping myself into one of the golden stools as if it was completely normal for an Onyx Guard to be a patron of this deplorable place. My eyes scanned the room, recognizing a few people I had either arrested, saved from overdose, or both. My heart lurched a bit at that; Kazola had a free detox program for anyone who wanted to get clean off of wolfsbane or blackthorn. I always tried my best to get people into the local program, but it seemed a few had found themselves sucked back in.

Others I recognized as some of Mylo's pack, their movements subtle but predatory, striding around the room like guards of the kingdom—Mylo's kingdom. It would only be a matter of time before one or two of them made their way to whatever back room Mylo hid himself in. Lucky for me and my heightened abilities, it would be easy to track their movements to him if I concentrated hard enough.

"Two pints of ale, please," I ordered for Nolan and me, my stomach clenching at even the idea of having alcohol in front of me—but it would look odd if I sat here without anything. So I kept my face neutral as the bartender begrudgingly slid two crystal pint glasses in front of us, giving nothing more than a grunt before disappearing down the bar to serve another patron.

"So, now that we're here, are you going to explain how being in this depressing place is going to help?" Nolan asked, his gaze lingering around the room, tracking people's movements.

"How much research did you do about Seathra's crimes before you came here?" I asked.

His glance slid to me before returning to the front of the room. *"A little."*

"Hear anything about a family known as the Bralechi?"

"Oh, yeah, I remember reading about them. They're a Varg family that runs drug trade, right?"

"That, and a few new ventures over the past few years." My lips tightened, my fingers tapping against the cold pint glass I hadn't taken a sip from. *"Their reach goes past Seathra when it comes to where they peddle their drugs, but they started in this territory and continue to run the operation from here."*

"If it wasn't my job to hunt these people down, I'd be impressed." Nolan took another silent sip. *"Why are we here?"*

"If anyone has come in and disrupted trade on the streets, the Bralechis will know about it." I scanned the room. "What do you think of the bar?"

His eyebrows rose. "Seems a bit solemn based on where it's located in town. You'd think there'd be music or something to help the crowd."

"Yeah, you'd think." I turned back toward the bar, making sure the bartender was still intently watching us. "Of course, Mylo has always enjoyed his atmosphere quiet."

The air in the room shifted from wearily uncomfortable to viciously tense. Conversations halted, people went from stealing subtle glances to outright staring at me. My skin prickled at all of the attention I wished I didn't have to put on myself...but it was a necessary evil if I wanted to smoke out Mylo.

"Oh, is that the owner of this establishment?" Nolan asked, playing along well. "Would love to meet him someday and give him a little constructive criticism about how he chooses to run a tavern."

"Maybe he'll be kind enough to show himself," I said loud enough for plenty of people to hear. "I'm sure he'd love to see me again."

"Oh? He knows you well, Kasha?" Nolan smirked at me. Damn, he was good at this.

"We've crossed paths once or twice." My fingers clenched around my mug. I knew the final step to get him to run, but it felt like a betrayal. "Of course, Eden knows him better than I do."

Gasps rang through the room before two men abruptly stood and walked to the back, disappearing behind a curtain. I counted out thirty seconds before swiveling in my seat and hopping off.

"Let's go," I said, dropping a few coins on the counter and walking out the door.

Out front, I focused for a moment, listening through the walls, picking up muffled voices. I couldn't make out the conversation, but I recognized one of them as Mylo. He sounded aggravated and annoyed. Perfect.

"Stay here," I whispered to Nolan. "I'm going to circle around to the other side of the alley and block his escape."

"Got it." He nodded, positioning himself at the entrance.

I took off quickly around the building, leaping over a low wall and turning a corner to the back entrance to the tavern. I propped myself against the wall opposite, my nose crinkling at the overwhelming stench of rotting food and sewage. Only a few minutes passed before the door burst open.

"Hello, Mylo," I smiled sweetly, although his unamused scowl made it clear he knew it was all fake.

"What would you like, Kasha?" He stalked forward a few steps, arms crossed tightly against his broad chest.

I tried not to be rattled by the beachy blond hair, bright, bottle-green eyes, and the dark olive skin tone I'd come to know well in another person. I shook it off, noticing the differences instead. The sharp, squared jaw and wide build; the jagged scar that ran along his forehead to his left eye. The menacing expression lingering on his features.

"I had a few questions for you." I took a step forward. "About some wolfsbane."

Without warning, yet no surprise, he took off down the alley, jumping over the wall with ease even though his black trousers and shiny, polished shoes looked difficult to maneuver in. I sighed loudly and took off after him, barely even breaking a sweat before I caught up. He skidded to a stop when he noticed Nolan blocking his way, turning around as if to dash back the way he'd come.

"No, no, no." I blocked Mylo's path. "I think you'll stay right here."

His eyes flashed golden, his teeth sharpening. "You have no reason to hold me."

"That's not true, I just can't tie you to any of those reasons." I leaned against the wall, the moist brick slick against my

251

shoulder bracer.

"Then what do you want?" He widened his stance, arms crossed again. Mylo always tried to act tough around me, but we had crossed paths too many times for me to find him intimidating.

"I didn't come here to try and arrest you," I finally admitted. "We're looking for answers from the streets, and in the past I've found you are a wealthy source of information on that subject."

He smirked. "I suppose I am. I'm glad you're finally recognizing me for my talents."

Nolan snorted. *"Seriously, who is this guy?"*

"A complicated pain in my side," I said, because it was the only way to explain Mylo.

"What happened to those annoying twins that usually follow you around?" Mylo stuck his thumb over his shoulder, nodding to Nolan.

"Lucas and Taylor were busy." I laughed at Mylo's disdain for them. "Besides, I assumed you would want to welcome the new Onyx Guard Alpha of Seathra."

"Ah, I see." Mylo turned to Nolan, only inches apart as they sized each other up. "Well, then, welcome to my city."

"Your city?" Nolan snorted. "Yeah, keep telling yourself that."

"As I've mentioned to your Beta here many times," Mylo flourished his palms, "my hands are very clean of the deplorable things she tries to pin on me. I am nothing more than a restaurateur, dealing with the day-to-day pleasures of running a little tavern."

"And it will be my pleasure to prove what a lie every word you just spoke is." Nolan leaned himself against the grimy wall of the alley, his posture relaxing. "However, that will have to happen another day. More important things have come to light."

"What can I help my local Faction with?" Mylo took a step forward, turning so he could look at both of us. "I am your humble servant."

"Alright, Mylo." My insides ground at his cockiness. I wished he wasn't the one I had to talk to, but he was the best person to tell us what was really changing on the streets. It was one of those moments where a necessary evil would help save the country from an even bigger threat. "Have you or your crew heard anything about a new wolfsbane distributor taking over the streets?"

Mylo stiffened, his eyes flashing panic for a moment before returning to their cool mask. "Why would you ask about that?"

"Confidential," Nolan said. "Now just answer the question."

"Of course, I wouldn't know as I personally don't deal with any of that deplorable substance." He placed his hand over his heart, as if swearing an oath.

"Yeah, yeah." I waved off his lie. "Get to the point."

"Based on what I've heard from some people, there has been a new player on the streets...though no one knows who it is." His fingers twitched at his side, his foot tapping a random pattern against the damp ground. "But that's not even the worst part. Not only are people losing customers, but those customers have also seemed to disappear from the area altogether."

"What?" Nolan straightened, his hands balling into fists. "Have any of them shown up dead?"

"Not to my knowledge. First, they stop going to their normal dealer, but are obviously still strung. Then their presence lingers before they just vanish." Mylo fidgeted a bit, my eyes narrowing at the show of unease.

"What else?"

He sighed. "A few of my people have disappeared. Three as of right now. I'm trying to keep a tighter surveillance, but there is only so much I can do."

The timelines were lining up that Elliot was not only killing, but using wolfsbane distribution as a way to make some extra money—maybe even lure some of his victims. This helped; it meant we had another lead to pursue, another chance to find a weakness in Elliot's perfect killing spree and exploit it.

"Thanks for the information," I pushed off the wall, walking to the entryway of the alley. "Looking forward to arresting you one day soon."

"Kasha," Mylo called out, Nolan and I turning around to look back at him. "I need you to give a message to Eden."

My eyes narrowed as I took a step toward him, his shoulders slumped. "This better be important. If not, I'll be giving you a few choice words before refusing to pass it along."

"It *is* important." Mylo let out a deep breath, rubbing his hand across his forehead, fingers pulling a few pieces of well-manicured hair from its styling cream. "Those people who have gone missing over the past few weeks? One of them is Lila."

My heart bottomed out, my throat closing in on itself. I rushed forward, slamming Mylo into the wall, his head hitting it with a loud thump. He didn't fight me, his body just sagging in my hold as if he was resigned to whatever attack I wanted to inflict.

"Didn't think to lead with that little fact?" I yelled. "Goddess, Mylo, how long has it been?"

He hesitated for a moment. "Three weeks."

"*What?*" I screeched.

Nolan took a step forward. "Who's Lila?"

254

"A long story." I looked over at him, his face pinched in confusion. I was sure this whole situation was utterly impossible to follow along, but it wasn't my place to tell him the whole story without Eden here. He would find out soon—just with his Gamma present as well. "But what matters is she's important to Eden. You should have reported her missing the moment you realized it."

"You know I couldn't do that," Mylo whispered. I could see the guilt and worry swirling in his eyes, his face paling. "I've had my people searching for weeks, but nothing has come up. I'm worried. She's disappeared at times on a bender, but she's never been gone for this long."

"You are damned lucky she's important to one of my best friends," I said through clenched teeth. "I'll make some calls, see if anyone has a report of her being checked into a detox center. But you and I both know that's a long shot."

"I know." Mylo's head hung low.

"And I'll tell Eden." I got closer to him, our noses grazing. "But this news shouldn't be coming from me."

"And you know she won't see me even if I say it's an emergency." Regret filled his eyes. "Just, please, tell her."

"Fine, but I'm not doing this for you." I gave him one last shove into the wall before walking down the alley, Nolan close behind as we disappeared into the streets.

Chapter Thirty-One

"We should go back to the Compound so I can talk to Eden." I didn't know how I was going to explain everything to her.

I'd assumed Nolan would learn that Eden has some connection to Mylo—which was why I'd let her know before I left—but I wasn't expecting the admissions he gave. I didn't know how she would react, and the unknown made my heart beat a little too fast.

"She's not there," Nolan said, already straddling his cycle. "The Rystin Faction agreed to start looking for potential files for us if we agreed to go and pick them up. Eden and Greyson left soon after we did. They won't be back until morning."

I huffed, throwing my head back. "Wonderful."

"Look," he leaned forward, his arms braced on the handlebars of his cycle, "I don't know exactly what I witnessed back there, but it's obviously important."

"This isn't something I can explain without Eden." I threw

my leg over my own cycle, but we kept them off.

"I'm not asking you to." He shook his head, his dark hair falling into his eyes. "All I was going to say is, it's obviously important, but there is nothing you can do at this exact moment. It doesn't sound like the type of conversation that should be done over a Comms Unit."

"Absolutely not." My imagination tried to get the best of me, thinking about how Eden would react to the news. No, in person was much better.

"Then the best thing you can do is try and get some rest and take time to think about how you're going to explain this to her in the morning." He punched me in the arm playfully. "You'll survive, hopefully."

I snorted a laugh. "With any luck, between now and then I don't overthink too much."

Like that would even be possible. *Overthinking* could be my middle name.

"I'm going to head back to the Compound and write out some of the new details and next steps," Nolan said, flicking his lectracycle on. "Although, if you prefer, I can wait until tomorrow so we can work on it together."

I looked up at him, my heart skipping a beat. He looked ahead, his words casual; yet I couldn't help but wonder if his cheeks had been that red the entire time.

"Well, I'm actually off tomorrow. Besides stopping by to talk to Eden in the morning, I have plans most of the day." I had counseling midmorning before I planned to go to Nana Aggie's. It was her birthday, and Ollie and I had promised to have lunch with her and spend the afternoon helping around the house.

"Oh, well," he rocked back and forth on his seat, "I guess I'll work on it tonight then."

"Unless you want to come back to my house with me?" The words slipped out before I even realized what I was offering: to bring Nolan into my sanctuary. To a place only those closest to me had been able to visit.

Why was I doing this?

He perked up in his seat, a smile spreading across his rosy lips. "That would be great. That way we're on the same page when you're off tomorrow."

Bile rose in my throat; it was too late now to take it back. Nolan was coming to my house.

Nolan, the man I'd hated only weeks ago and randomly kissed, was coming to my house.

"Great," I managed to get past my lips, hoping desperately that it didn't come out as strained as I heard it. "Follow me, then."

As we sped away from the *Black Howl*, I was convinced this idea was going to kill me.

***

My throat dried, my fingers tingling as I guided him through the streets. I kept telling myself we were just going to my house because it was convenient, and we needed to work. I kept saying it was the logical thing to do, and it was. Why go all the way out to the Compound when there was a perfectly good place to talk about next steps right down the street?

Yet, no matter how many times I repeated that to myself, a little voice in the back of my mind was telling me to stop this, to not let him in. He could learn too much about me and exploit that; he could betray me. If he saw too much truth about me, would he run?

Was I even ready to know the answer?

I ignored the voice, just as I'd been doing ever since it had led me down the path of almost-destruction. That voice wasn't the voice of reason and happiness, it was the voice of darkness, determined to swallow me whole. I wouldn't let it take me. Not again.

Once we arrived and parked our bikes, we gave a quick hello to Lea, Nolan asking her how she felt after the hostage situation. She waved us off, her smile perky and happy as if nothing was bothering her. And she said as much, rambling on about how she felt perfectly normal and my worry was unnecessary.

I had been keeping a closer eye on her for the past week, my gut telling me that this was only the beginning. What Lea went through wasn't simple, no matter how much she tried to convince herself it was. With the wary glance Nolan gave me when Lea's back was turned, it seemed he was thinking the exact same thing.

After a few more minutes of small talk, I led Nolan upstairs to my bedroom. I told myself the logical truth: we couldn't talk about case stuff in front of Lea, we had to keep it private. And the only private place was my bedroom. Nolan wouldn't do anything, not with Lea in the house.

Hopefully.

No. I shook that thought away. *Practice trust.* I'd told Nolan I would practice trusting him, and that was what I would do.

I walked into my room as if it was completely normal that he was following, milling about to light my fireplace and a few oil lamps to help illuminate the space as much as possible. When I finally finished, I turned around to see Nolan looking over the dozens of books on my shelf.

"Do you like to read?" I asked awkwardly, not exactly sure how else to talk to him at that very moment.

"Yeah, some." His fingers skimmed over the titles. "I recognize a few books here, but not all of them."

"Probably because some of them are imports from other continents." I rummaged through my desk, looking for a notebook and stilo for us to use.

"You're kidding!" His eyes went wide as he bent forward to get a closer look. "How did you get these?"

"I like to visit rare bookshops." I shrugged. "They have some good titles. Some are amusing."

"How so?"

"Plenty of other continents have rumors of Shrivs and Vargs, although in their stories they call us by different names." I smirked, turning toward him. "You wouldn't believe some of the insane things people make up about us."

His eyebrow perked. "Examples?"

"Well, in some, Vargs can only turn during the full moon, as if having this form is a curse or something," I laughed, although my stomach squeezed at the mention of my wolf form that still evaded me. I shook my head, putting that thought away. "And Shrivs are apparently allergic to the sun to the point where they burst into flames if they walk into direct sunlight."

"I'm sorry...what?" Nolan flipped through one of the books, his expression puzzled. I couldn't help but laugh a little. "How does that even make sense?"

"Not sure." I shrugged. "Although it gives me a better understanding why outside of Kazola people are terrified of our kind. In their books, we're depicted as monsters who want nothing more than to kill and eat humans. Doesn't matter that we're people too, we're dangerous in these stories."

"Like how humans saw us in the Ancient times." Nolan set

the book he was looking through back on the shelf.

"Exactly." I nodded, sitting on my bed, gesturing to the desk chair across from me for him to sit on. "It makes me wonder if the rumors were started by Kazolanians from the Ancient days who escaped the Isle and spread vicious rumors with their ignorance."

"It's possible." He settled into the seat, leaning back to look at me. "Alright, so, what are the new investigation tracks we discovered today?"

I perked up, my mind ready to go back to work and move away from all this personal talk, even if my body was at ease. We effortlessly found ourselves back in work discussions, debating over the exact details we needed to look for in past cases, how we could use these to our advantage, and the best way to divide the work to help research go quicker. Somehow, an hour passed us by, pages of my notebook filled with our ideas, which Nolan planned to update the rest of the Hierarchy on tomorrow at a morning meeting he would call.

I wrote down the last few to do list items, scribbling into the notebook. When I looked back up, I caught Nolan studying the artwork framed on my wall.

"My grandmother made that for me," I said, not sure why I was explaining it. It must be because of how quizzically he stared at it.

"It's like your tattoo on your left shoulder." He pointed to it, his fingertip grazing the swirl of the word. "The word 'moonlight' surrounded by poppy flowers. The styles are different, but the concept is the same."

"That piece of artwork was the inspiration, but Lucas is the one who created my tattoo." My shoulder tingled.

"Lucas is a tattoo artist?" Nolan turned to me.

261

"He was certified right before joining the guard with Taylor," I explained. "He doesn't take commissions anymore, but he does keep his skills up by tattooing the Faction."

"Huh, I'll have to remember that." He scratched his chin. "May I ask what this means?"

My lip trembled a bit, wondering if I was ready to tell this. I reasoned with myself that it was far from a secret—most of the Hierarchy was aware of its meaning. "It's for my mother. She used to call me Moonlight growing up, and poppy flowers were her favorite. We would give them to her for any occasion we could think of."

"Oh, that's beautiful. I remember Ollie telling me about your mother...she didn't deserve to be taken from you that way."

"Thank you." A tear stung the corner of my eye. "It's still odd to think that you knew Ollie so soon after it happened."

Her death had been a traumatic experience for all of us, but that was the risk for those in the Guard. We garnered enemies, and sometimes those enemies took revenge. And on that night so many years ago, one of her past enemies had taken the final revenge, stealing her from us forever.

Ollie had been sixteen when Mama passed, and like Caleb and I, had joined the Guard once he turned eighteen. A big portion of his grieving had happened when he was training. Sometimes, on special occasions like Mama's birthday or the anniversary of her death, he would come home to be with Father and me. But grief was never a consistent thing; sometimes it could hit you for no reason at all. Ollie never talked about how he handled it when he was away, but he had mentioned that his friend Carragan was a good person to talk to. I had always been thankful for that.

"He's my friend, and he needed support. I did what anyone

else would do," Nolan said, as if it was completely normal. But it wasn't. He didn't have to be there for Ollie. He didn't have to be here for me now, yet here he was.

This man was still the goofy yet confident Alpha I'd met on his first day, but he was so much more than that. My heart shuddered at the thought—one I needed to keep at bay. I enjoyed working with him, this whole day of collaboration proved that, but these stirrings inside me, these attractions I couldn't seem to control, they had to stop. I couldn't want this; I wasn't ready.

"You know, this isn't how I pictured your room would be." Nolan walked the small space, glancing over my piano and the stack of sheet music all the way over to my crammed bookshelves.

My mouth hung open. "You pictured my room?"

"Oh, um...no, not exactly..." He blinked as rapidly as he spoke. "I meant this wasn't what I was expecting when I came here. I thought it would be more...minimalist."

I gave a small laugh. "I get that, you've only really seen me in a professional environment and I can be very...rigid when I'm determined."

"I remember this book." Nolan said, changing the subject as he pulled the oldest book from my shelf, the spine well-worn, the pages tainted yellow from age and wear. "My fathers used to read it to me when I was growing up."

"My mom used to read it to me as well," I leaned back against my headboard, ignoring the voice trying to tell me I was getting too comfortable with Nolan being in my space. "I love the story about Lunestia and Firenielle."

The brown leatherbound book had been passed down in my family for years, full of the stories from Ancient times, from the

263

creation of Kazola to the day the first High Faction was created. The stories were our history; they told the truth of who we were to our core and how our peace came to be. It was the reason for the Onyx Guard, it was our ultimate drive.

Tsio a Chisain. Protect the Peace.

As a child, growing up with two Onyx Guard parents, I knew what my destiny was. These stories had filled me with joy and excitement as I counted down time until the day I could protect the way my family did. I wanted to be a part of that legacy for as long as I could remember.

This was who I was meant to be.

Nolan sat back down in the chair, his legs sprawled out in front of him as he leaned back. He flipped through the pages for a few seconds before smiling. *"The truth of Kazola comes down to one word: love."*

"What are you doing?" I sat up a little, my cheeks numbing.

"I'm reading you a bedtime story," he said, a wicked grin on his face, eyes brightening with that forest-green sunlight that made my heart leap.

"Um... why?" I threw my legs back down on the ground, attempting to stand, but he placed a gentle hand on my shoulder, keeping me seated.

"Looks like you could use something to relax you," he said. "Maybe this will help."

"I'm fine...re—really. You don't need to..."

"I know I don't need to. I want to." His brow crinkled. "Is it really so hard to believe that people want to help you, Kasha? Is it so wrong of us?"

A part of me wanted to scream at him, to tell him it was none of his business. He didn't have a right to question what I wanted, to act as though he could help the mess of emotions and thoughts that I battled every day of my life. But I didn't say those things, because in truth, he wasn't questioning what I wanted; he questioned why I resisted help, why I was convinced I had to do everything myself.

It all came from everything that had happened this past year. Yet, my heart and mind were starting to crack against the hardened walls I had erected around them for protection. They didn't want to be smothered under the weight anymore, they wanted to feel again. They wanted to be free.

I couldn't go back to being the person I once was, but maybe, just maybe, I could teach this new self how to move forward, how to let others in. Maybe not completely, but in small ways to start.

So, I chose to take a step I had been refusing for so long. It would be harder when it came to work or my health, but this was a first step. This one, I could take.

I leaned back, curling up against my pillows, lying on my side so I could face Nolan and watch him.

"Wonderful." He leaned back in the chair, reopening the book. "*The truth of Kazola comes down to one word: love. When Firenielle, the God of Blood & Truth, met his one true love, Lunestia, the Goddess of Moon & Hunt. Their bond was destined from the beginning of time, and when it finally came to pass, they chose to celebrate by creating life...*"

I couldn't remember at what part of the story it happened, but I drifted off into sleep, visions of Lunestia watching over me as I ran freely in my wolf form comforting me throughout the whole night.

Chapter Thirty-Two

As promised, Nolan was right beside me the next day, walking toward the front door of Eden and Greyson's house.

"Are you sure it's okay that I come?" Nolan whispered, leaning down a bit closer, my spine tingling at his nearness.

"You witnessed things last night." I turned my neck to look up at him. "I knew bringing you there risked you finding out a few things, but I wasn't expecting everything Mylo said. If she really doesn't want you to know the truth, she'll kick you out."

"Fair enough." He shrugged one shoulder.

With one final deep breath and a prayer to the Goddess, I rapped my knuckles a few times against the door. Footsteps approached, my heartbeat kicking up its pace with each one that drew closer. The door finally opened, revealing Greyson standing on the other side, a frown pulling at his lips, obsidian hair sticking up at odd angles and dark circles rimming his dark brown eyes.

"Good morning!" I said a little too cheerily, my voice pitched higher than normal.

Greyson narrowed his eyes at me. "What's wrong?"

"Nothing," I sighed, trying to let out a bit of the tension crawling up my shoulders. "Is Eden here? We need to talk to her."

"She's not in the best mood, but sure." Greyson opened the door wider, welcoming us in. "I warn you though, she doesn't like either of you particularly right now."

"She's mad about traveling all night?" Nolan asked as we walked down the hall toward the kitchen.

"I think she's more upset about having to read cold case files all day. She's just a bit more vocal about it because we're both running on little sleep."

"Wonderful," I thought, letting only Nolan hear it. He glanced over his shoulder, giving me a sympathetic smile before we crossed the threshold into their kitchen, multiple boxes already littering the dining table, stacks of papers and folders spread out across the surface. Eden sat at the table, her legs curled up so her arms rested on her knees, a cup of coffee clutched in one hand and an open case file in the other.

"I hate you both," she grumbled without looking at us, her red hair piled on top of her head in an unkempt bun and her over-sized, sleeveless, sage-green shirt wrinkled and looking like she stole it from Greyson's closet. Knowing her, she probably had after running out of clean clothes.

"Hello to you, too." I took the seat across from her, my palms sweaty. Nolan sat next to me. "I'm sorry you didn't get much sleep last night."

"You should be apologizing to Greyson." She stuck her thumb over her shoulder toward Greyson, who was leaning against the wall behind her, rummaging through a box. "He's the

267

poor soul who gets to work with me all day."

I let out a halfhearted chuckle. "This isn't actually what we came to talk to you about."

"What's wrong?" Eden tossed the case file on the table, dropping her feet to the ground and leaning forward. "You look paler than normal and your heartbeat is erratic. Did something happen?"

"I don't know how to start."

"What is going *on*?"

"Remember how I warned you yesterday I had to stop by the *Black Howl* on a possible lead?" I began.

"Yeah," Eden scoffed, leaning back in her chair, arms crossed. "Although you didn't specify exactly why you needed to visit that Goddess-awful place."

"We had questions about wolfsbane distribution, but that's not the important part..."

Eden jumped out of her chair, the whole thing falling over as she began to pace in front of us. "Let me guess, he was an arrogant little criminal who acted all higher than—"

"Eden." I leaned forward, grasping her hand to pull her attention back to me. "He told me Lila's been missing for three weeks."

Her steps froze, eyes widening. "What?"

"I'm so sorry." I tugged her forward, Greyson picking the chair up and gently helping her sit back down before settling into the seat next to her.

Her jaw trembled as I went into all the details I knew, even though I didn't have much. She was trying to hold strong, but her eyes glassed over, tears threatening to spill. My heart broke with each word I spoke, my fingers trembling in my lap.

"Oh, my Goddess." Eden dropped her head into her hands, silence filling the room as the three of us let her process this overwhelming information. Finally, she looked up. "I need to start reaching out to centers..."

"Taylor and Lucas are already on it." I'd asked them to begin the research before I headed over here. "Catch up with them for updates."

She nodded, her eyes not focusing anywhere specific. "Good, that's good. Did Mylo mention if he reached out to any of his contacts in other territories? Maybe she went there trying to find new people to scam into giving her more wolfsbane? She always had a way with charming people..."

"Eden." I shook her hand across the table, snapping her out of her rambling thoughts. "We'll find her."

"I'll even tell Mylo your idea." Greyson wrapped his arm casually around her shoulders. "That way you don't have to talk to him if you don't want to."

She looked at Greyson, smiling. "I think that would be best. I don't want to see him."

"Alright, then." I nodded. "See? You won't be alone in this."

"Thank the Goddess for that." After a few moments, her shoulders stiffened, her eyes looking up at Nolan, who had been silently observing this whole time. "How much do you know?"

"About your connection to these people? Basically nothing." Nolan shook his head. "Kasha refused to say anything without your permission."

She laughed, a little smile peeking out. "Thanks, Kas."

I gave her a smile back. "You always know your secrets are safe with me."

"I do."

"You don't have to tell me anything," Nolan assured her, hesitating for a moment before he reached out to pat her shoulder. "Your past is your own, it doesn't affect the way I respect you in the present."

"No, you deserve to hear this." Eden wiped her hands down her face before looking back to him. "It's something you should have known a while ago, I was just scared to tell you."

"Alright," Nolan said calmly, bracing his arms on the table. "I'm listening."

"My name now is Eden Remalle, but I was born Eden Bralechi. Mylo and Lila are my older siblings."

Nolan nodded solemnly, his eyes soft. "No wonder I thought he looked a little familiar."

"Our parents were arrested when I was ten, caught in a huge drug bust that the Guard had been working on for months," she continued. "It was a big deal back then, but my Uncle Clay was the head of the family at the time, so the guard wasn't able to completely take down the whole operation.

"But the Guard knew they couldn't give custody of the three of us back to the family, so a pair of retired guards took us in instead." She leaned back in her chair, rubbing her hand across her face, redness pooling in her cheeks. "Mylo was seventeen at the time and Lila was fourteen. They both had already learned so much from our family and their corrupt ways that when they turned eighteen, they both went back. Mylo eventually took over the family when Uncle Clay retired."

"But you didn't follow them," Nolan said—not as a question, because he already knew the answer.

"I couldn't." She shook her head. "Ellie and Kayla basically raised me, and they used to tell me stories about being in the

Onyx Guard. The way they helped people. It would excite my soul in a way my family's 'business' never had. I finally started to realize what was right and what was wrong, and I couldn't follow my siblings back.

"So, I took my foster parents' name and joined the Guard. I hoped I could make up a little for the decades of crimes that my family has committed." She shrugged, her eyes lowering to the table. "I know it sounds lame, but it's the truth."

"From what I've been told and what I've witnessed over the past few weeks, you absolutely have done that," Nolan encouraged, my cheeks warming at the kindness in his words.

"How can you even say that after meeting my brother? After learning about my family's past and my connection to them?" She shook her head in disbelief. "How can you even trust me now?"

"You aren't your family, Eden." Nolan smiled at her. "If I've learned anything over the past few weeks of working with you, it's your passion for being a part of the Guard and keeping this country safe. I promise, I will never doubt your allegiance."

"Really?"

"Yes." He stood, walking around the table to pull Eden from her chair and wrap her in a hug. "I trust you. And on top of that, I couldn't have asked for a better Gamma. I'd been telling myself for weeks I was the luckiest guy for getting you and Greyson as my seconds."

"Thank you." She sniffed, pulling away from him, wiping a stray tear from her eye. "I'm sorry I acted so horribly when you first arrived."

"Eh, you were wary of me," Nolan laughed, his shoulders relaxing. "Just another sign you're good at your job."

"Speaking of our job, we need to get back to searching these

271

files." Greyson cleared his throat, his posture rigid in his seat. "The sooner we do, the sooner we can focus on Lila."

"Yes, we do." Nolan tugged his seat from around the table so it sat next to Eden's. He began pulling stacks closer to himself and rifling through papers, Eden's eyes widening as she watched him.

"I have to go." I stood up, my eyes stinging. "I have counseling, but call me on my Comms if you need anything. And I promise to help search for Lila with you."

"Thanks, Kas." Eden wrapped me in a hug, her face buried in my neck for a brief second. "You are the greatest friend a girl could ask for."

"Back at you." I kissed her temple lightly before she pulled away.

I turned to leave, casting one last glance over my shoulder—watching her walk back to her seat between Greyson and Nolan, the three of them passing around files and bickering like three partners that had worked together for years.

Chapter Thirty-Three

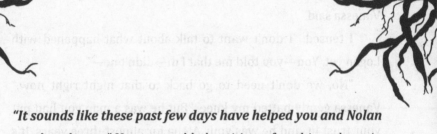

"It sounds like these past few days have helped you and Nolan get along better." Vanessa nodded, writing a few things down in her journal. I had told her about everything that had happened over the past week, from the High Faction's surprise visit, to my wolf eyes reappearing briefly, and Nolan and I kissing—ultimately leading to a few days of very successful investigation.

"They have." I stared mindlessly at the floor. At least she hadn't said I told you so about letting go of my anger. Even though she had told me it would help, I still couldn't shift, which meant anger wasn't the only emotion I was struggling to accept.

"What do you think helped break a bit of that barrier?" Vanessa asked, pulling me out of my thoughts.

"Besides the fact that I made out with him?"

She chuckled. "Yes, besides that."

My fingers traced my lips as I thought back over the past week. "Learning more about him helped, I suppose...knowing the real reason why he wanted to be transferred here."

"Was that the only thing keeping you from trusting him?"

"I had plenty of reasons not to trust him right away." I looked up at Vanessa. "I'm not saying all of them were logical, but he was a new person who came to take over, something we hadn't seen in a long time. Made me wary that he was a High Faction plant of some kind. He was taking the job that I was originally slated to inherit..."

"And the fact that your last Alpha betrayed your trust," Vanessa said.

I tensed. "I don't want to talk about what happened with Logan yet. You—you told me that I di—didn't ne—"

"No, we don't need to go back to that night right now." Vanessa gently patted my knee. "But he was a man you had put your trust in, and he was your Alpha for almost three years. It's okay to admit that trusting another Alpha felt not only impossible, but morally wrong."

My stomach rolled at the words, my vision blurring. There was merit to the idea—I had admitted it to myself a few times— but never had I said those words out loud. It all just seemed so much more complicated in my mind, like a tangled web of truths and lies.

I looked back on my time with Logan, wondering when it all went wrong. I was an investigator; I should have recognized the signs sooner so I could protect myself, but I had let my trust in him keep me blind to who he really was.

He hid in plain sight from a lot of people.

"It wasn't just my trust he broke." My shoulders shook. "He betrayed everyone that night. The Faction, our friends, Caleb..."

"He made a choice that caused a lot of pain," Vanessa said.

"You were the one the stone struck, but everyone else felt a ripple from the impact."

"Not Caleb." The words came out strained, high-pitched and struggling on soundless tears turned to sobs.

Vanessa pulled her chair forward. "Caleb made a choice to ignore the truth."

He was choosing to ignore a lot of things about Logan, and every day that went by, I felt more and more betrayed.

"*Take care of my sister,*" I whispered into my hand, the sobs still racking my body.

"What?" Vanessa squeezed my shoulder.

"That's what Caleb said to Logan when we celebrated our promotions." I moved my hand away so she could hear my words loud and clear. "*Take care of my sister.*"

"He broke that promise," Vanessa said. "He took advantage of the trust you built in him and he broke the promise he made to your brother."

"I know." I sniffed, wiping away the stream of tears. "I've always known that. What crushes me is that Caleb doesn't think he broke that promise."

"We can't control what other people think, even if their thoughts are misguided or clouded. This past year has forced you to lose people you once trusted. That type of trauma can force us to reevaluate the way we see people, especially when we first meet them. It's alright to be cautious when new faces enter your life."

"Then why does everyone joke about needing to be more trusting?" I looked up toward the ceiling, hoping it would help dry some of the tears. "People say it, not just to me, but to anyone who doesn't 'let loose'. It's like it's a flaw to be wary of people when they enter your life."

"It's not." Vanessa shook her head. "Just because most people find that kind of caution funny, doesn't mean it isn't valid. You have plenty of reasons to not trust people when you meet them. You not only work in a job that constantly asks you to question everything and see the worst kind of people in our country, but you personally experienced trauma and betrayal of trust in a compressed period of time. Your mind needed to do something to protect both itself and your heart from further pain, and the way to do that was to put up barriers, to allow your trust to be earned, not gifted easily. And that's okay, Kasha, it is okay to set that boundary for yourself."

I sniffed. "It is?"

"Those who care about you, those who are really worth your trust, will stop at nothing to earn it." She smiled at me.

The words washed over me, the truth of them settling on my heart and mind, validating something deep in my soul.

I was allowed to set boundaries. I was allowed to tell people that they needed to keep a distance as we got to know each other. Sure, I could go about doing it in a better way, cut the sarcasm and maybe be a bit more honest about my need for that boundary, but it didn't make the validity of my need any less real.

It was alright that I hadn't trusted Nolan right away—that wasn't wrong. It was wrong of me to be mean to him, to push him away, to treat him like the enemy. I at least felt a little settled that I had apologized for that this week; it made accepting all of this even easier, being able to see the errors of my actions but also noticing the efficacy of my needs. It was alright that I needed time. It was alright, and I could accept it.

I accepted this new part of me, and let the stress of my denial free.

"It looks like you just let go of something else," Vanessa whispered, holding up a small mirror she pulled from her pocket. I took it, my hands shaking, but what I saw was crystal clear: for the first time in a year, I saw myself with bright gold eyes.

For the first time in a year, I was reminded how beautiful I was.

Chapter Thirty-Four

My mind and body were equally exhausted after my counseling session.

Vanessa was kind enough to find an empty room by her office for me to lie down in, allowing me a two-hour nap before I had to leave. She even woke me up just in time to hop on my lectracycle and start my drive over to Nana Aggie's. My mind was still foggy, my muscles overexerted like I had just worked out all morning—without actually doing anything. I had to push through it, though; today I was celebrating my grandmother's birthday, and I wasn't going to let my mood ruin her day.

As usual, I caught up with Ollie on the road, the two of us racing toward Nana's place. I was too exhausted to jest and bait him into a race. I just wanted to enjoy the whipping of the wind against my cheeks and the pumping exhilaration of the speed we rode at. He didn't question my quiet, closed-off thoughts with odd looks, just followed along as we broke through the town lines and wound our way down the streets. We pulled up in front of Nana's house, parking our cycles in the drive, and my stomach dropped at an odd sight.

A third lectracycle was already there.

"What the...?" Ollie trailed off as we both stared at the extra cycle. Our gazes caught for a moment, and I assumed he was thinking the same thing as me: only those in the Guard were given cycles, which meant another Ibridowyn was here. And since Aggie lived in my territory, I would've known if someone was here to talk to her officially. Leaving only one other person who might come visit.

Without a word to each other, we rushed to the door, heading straight to the dining room. I shouldn't have been as shocked as my frozen muscles reacted; I'd known the moment I pulled into the drive. Yet my heart raced, my body numbing from my toes to my ears at the sight of Caleb sitting at the table with Nana, the two of them sipping cups of tea clutched in their hands.

They both looked up at us, Nana's eyes widening. "Oh, Goddess, did I lose track of time? I wasn't expecting you two so soon."

"It's fine, Nana." My words came out shaky, but that was the best I could do in the moment. I was just happy I was able to get anything out at all.

"What are you doing here?" Ollie sneered, taking a step forward, partially blocking me from Caleb as if he needed to protect me. And honestly, maybe a small part of me needed to be, my legs shaking at the sight of my brother sitting in front of me for the first time in months.

"I'm visiting our grandmother on her birthday." He stood slowly from his chair, his schooled features giving nothing about

279

his thoughts away. Part of me wanted to reach out and knock on his mind, try and get an understanding of what was swirling within him, but even if I tried, he would keep me locked out.

Lunestia was testing me today—throwing my problems in front of me, baiting me to come to terms with the wicked mess that still hid in my soul. Even though I was starting to accept it piece by piece, this was completely different. I wasn't ready to face Caleb, to tell him how his utter betrayal had broken me and I was still trying to bring the pieces back together. I wasn't ready for him to see me like that—not again.

"Kas shouldn't be that surprised, she's the one who reminded me." Caleb pointed to me, Ollie turning around with a questioning glance.

Those words certainly snapped me out of my silence. "I reminded you to send a gift, not come for a surprise visit."

"How was I to know the two of you would be here?" Caleb stood up straighter, crossing his arms. "It's not like you expressly told me to stay away."

"I live the closest to Nana, Cal, what did you expect?" I countered. "You've made excuses every year as to why you can't be here for her birthday, why in the Goddess would I assume this year would be any different?"

"Maybe this is the Goddess telling us it's time for a talk." Nana stepped forward, putting herself between Caleb and us. "As the family we all are."

Caleb shot us a smug smile. "I am more than willing to put the past in the past."

"Of course you are," Ollie grumbled, his head shaking.

"That's not what I meant, Caleb." Nana's voice was calm, but fury built in her eyes. "You need to listen to your sister, you need to hear her story."

"I don't need to hear the story, Nana, I know what happened." Caleb shook his head. "I read the case file, I saw the evidence, and I stand by my decision."

"What does that even mean?" I yelled, the little control I had over myself snapping just a bit.

"You're an investigator, Kasha." He looked me up and down, lips frowning. "You should know that only compelling evidence would have swayed the High Faction to make their decision."

I scoffed. "And an influential uncle like Cole to cover up for his disgusting nephew."

"That's speculation, and you know it!" Caleb shot back. I had to suppress a growl at the typical weak response to that defense.

"Then give me something that isn't speculation." I took a step forward, building up all the progress I had made over the past few weeks, pulling at my instincts to finally push Caleb to explain why he had chosen against me. What had swayed him? There must have been something besides blind faith in Logan.

Or, at least, the last shred of hope I had for my brother depended on that theory. And Goddess above, did I need it to be true.

He crossed his arms, staring down at me with those judgmental silver eyes. "Such as?"

"What made you choose him?" I kept my shoulders pulled back, not cowering away from the question I had been too scared to ask in the past. "How did he get you to believe him?"

"Classified evidence."

"It was my case!" I argued. "I had access to all evidence, so what Goddess-blessed evidence was so compelling that you chose *him*?"

Like the rest of us in the Guard, Caleb was well-trained at lying and diversion. But I knew his tells, I knew them as well as my own, having observed them throughout the years. So, when he didn't answer, and his fingers twitched subtly next to his thigh, I finally pulled one truth out of him.

He was hiding something.

"I had access to all of the evidence, didn't I, Caleb?"

"Of course," he struggled to get through his lips.

"You're lying." I took a step back, a weight bearing down on my chest. "You're lying to me."

He had never lied to me.

"No, I'm not." He shook his head, but his fingers twitched again.

"Are you kidding me, you bastard?" Ollie shot over to him, his words helping to keep my spine straight, even though my insides were starting to crumble again. "Why are you doing this?"

"You wouldn't understand," he mumbled. "I did what was best for our family, that's all I could do."

Something cracked within me at that. Maybe the part of me that had held a shred of hope that he would see the light, that he would believe me. I had been denying it for so long, letting it hide behind the hurt and anger I had suppressed. But after my talk with Vanessa today, it couldn't hide anymore. I missed Caleb, I wanted him back in my life, but not like this—where I had to pretend that he didn't betray me or treat me like a liar.

Caleb was my brother, my blood, but he wasn't worth my soul.

"Caleb, please..." Nana's shaking words crushed my heart even more. She had been putting on a strong face for me these past few months. I should have known she missed Caleb almost as much as I did; Father was an only child, we were her three grandchildren. A tear slid down Nana's face. "This isn't what your mother would have wanted for the three of you."

"No, Nana, you're right, it isn't." Ollie took a step forward, his posture rigid. "But I also know with my whole heart that Mother would be disgusted by the way Caleb has acted."

"Take that back," Caleb snarled, closing the gap between them, their chests only an inch apart. Nana backed away, thank the Goddess; an electric pulse of rage swirled in the air around them, edging on dangerous territory.

"Make me," Ollie challenged. "She wouldn't even recognize you anymore, protector of nothing."

That was all it took for Caleb to lash out, his fist arcing toward Ollie, eyes glowing gold as he connected with Ollie's cheek. Ollie didn't even flinch before sending his own punch back, the crack of Caleb's nose echoing in the small space, blood gushing from the wound.

This was wrong. This needed to stop—but I was frozen, unable to control my own movements, forced to watch as my brothers fought on opposite sides of a terrible family war. A war I had created.

Ollie growled as he sidestepped Caleb's right hook. He ducked down, his claws extended as he swiped at Caleb's ribs; his right ribs to be exact, shallow clawmarks now scraped across them. Caleb's shirt tore open, revealing the now-damaged, script tattoo written across his torso.

Born by Blood. Bound by Loyalty.

Our tattoo, our promise to each other almost ten years ago. My arm burned at the sight of his mutilated inking, as if it had somehow affected my own.

"Did you forget that promise? The one you believed in so deeply, you branded it on your own skin?" Ollie snarled, his chest heaving as he continued to throw punches. "Did you forget what that word *loyalty* means?"

Caleb said nothing, face set in determination. I crumbled inside as I watched them continue to throw and dodge each other's strikes, my mind begging them to stop but my lips unable to say the words out loud.

"Oh, Goddess, save them, please save them," Nana sobbed from the corner.

Her words echoed in my mind, her glistening tears ripping into me, snapping me to attention. This wasn't right. No matter how angry and hurt we all were, this wasn't the time or place to hash it out. I needed to stop this—if not for my brothers, then for Nana.

"Enough!" I shouted, throwing myself between them, Ollie barging into my back, but my strong stance kept me upright. Caleb's arm was already cocked back ready to throw another blow, but he hesitated at the sight of me. "Go ahead Caleb, hit me. It couldn't possibly hurt any worse than what you've already done."

His fist shook, eyes still vividly golden as he stared down at me, every muscle tense and ready to fight. I stood my ground, even though my insides begged to cower away from him. I didn't want to fight Caleb...not now, at least.

Finally, his eyes flickered back to their cool silver, his arm falling to his side before he took a few steps away. I let out a deep breath, Ollie's heat bleeding into my back as his hands came to rest on my shoulders.

"Are you alright?" He whispered just to me.

"No," was all I could say back before turning my attention to the one who mattered.

"Oh, thank you, Kas," Nana stepped forward, her fingers clutched against her sternum, chest heaving.

"Sit, Nana." Ollie put his arm around her, guiding her back to her seat, pushing her cup closer in silent suggestion to drink. She took it, taking a few shaking sips. Ollie kneeled in front of her. "I'm so sorry, that got out of hand. That wasn't fair to you."

"Yes, I'm so sorry." Caleb walked the table, grabbing a cloth napkin and pressing it against his bleeding nose. Ollie didn't even look in his direction.

Nana cupped Ollie's cheek. "These wounds should be punishment enough. You two hotheads have more of your father in your blood than you like to believe some days."

My nerves were fried, my mind spinning and dark. Color was draining from all around me, the bright space graying in the haze of emotions I was trying to get under control. I couldn't stay here, not after all of this. I wanted to be here for Nana, but I couldn't, not today—it was too tainted now. The least I could do was give something to her; even if it wasn't the three of us, she deserved to be with at least one grandchild on her birthday.

"Visit with Caleb." Ollie's eyes widened at my words. "He deserves time with you, too, but that doesn't mean I have to stay. I'm sorry, I just can't do this right now."

"Moonlight..." Nana reached out to me, but her hand shook for a moment before falling back to her side. She stared at me, into what I could only assume were exhausted, resigned eyes. She gave me a nod before turning back to the table.

"Goodbye, Caleb," I managed to get out before I turned on my heels, desperate to escape the smothering space.

"Kasha…" His voice drifted to me, stopping me in my tracks.

I looked over my shoulder, glaring at the man I no longer recognized. "You want to do what's right for the family? Then go back to Crelanti and continue to be Father's perfect little soldier boy. That's all you're good for anymore."

A bit of hope flared in my chest as I watched his shoulders slump in defeat before I turned back to head outside.

"Wait up." Ollie leaned down to give Nana a kiss on the cheek before coming up next to me, slinging his arm around my shoulder, guiding me back out the door.

Chapter Thirty-Five

Ollie wasn't ready to go back to his Compound, not after everything. I wasn't sure if it was for his own needs or if he was concerned for mine, but I was happy to have him around.

Once we got back, part of me wanted to work, lose myself in the research I knew the rest of the team was doing. Ollie convinced me otherwise, reminding me that I would be of no help in my current state and that I should focus on getting my own needs in order before attending to others.

For once, I listened to him.

We spent the rest of the afternoon in the training building, sparring hand-to-hand and practicing our aim with various weapons in the shooting areas. The focus and repetition of everything helped to calm something in me, to at least bring a sense of relief deep within my chest. After we had successfully run our bodies to their physical limits and cleaned up, a few of the Hierarchy invited us to join them at the *Blood Moon*;

apparently all of them needed a break as well.

Most of me hadn't wanted to be there, surrounded by the rowdy crowd with the pulsing music played by a vivacious band. But I could tell Ollie wanted to go out, his extroverted nature begging to be around people to distract him; and I could have said no, retired to my house while he went out with some of my team. They had known him for a while, it wouldn't have been odd. But I didn't want to be away from him, not after the day we had together.

So, I found myself seated in the corner of the tavern, nestled between Taylor and Ollie in a round corner booth, Lucas, Greyson, and Eden on the other side of the half-circle. All of them were on at least their third drink while I was enjoying my cool glass of sparkling water with lime, trying my best to ignore the buzzing in my fingertips at being around so much alcohol. As long as I didn't consume it, I'd be fine. Safe.

My past does not define me. I am stronger than my past.

I shook off the edge, remembering that going out tonight was supposed to help me relax, not make the anxious ticks and nerves worse. I leaned forward, wrapping my hand around my glass, allowing the ice-cold surface to snap me back to reality.

"So, you still hate me?" I threw a crumbled-up napkin at a frowning Eden, her bottle-green eyes detached and glazed over. After what I told her this morning, I worried how she faired the rest of the day. At least I was a bit comforted knowing she'd had Greyson and Nolan with her, even if it was sifting through reports.

Her eyes slowly found their way to me, clearing up as a weak smile tipped her lips. "A little, but I'll get back at you eventually."

"I'm sure you will." I laughed, taking a sip of my water.

"Let me guess, the Elliot case keeping you busy?" Ollie asked, all of us mumbling an affirmative. "I've heard stories from my Hierarchy. Some of them were in Vapalles when Elliot struck. A part of me feels lucky I never had that responsibility on my shoulders."

"You have no idea how lucky you are." I poked him in the stomach, a laugh escaping him. "The more you learn about him, the more drive there is to remove him from the streets, but he's like a ghost...impossible to catch. Every lead we think we get, barely pans out. Forces you to get creative with the way you investigate."

"Leading members of the team to curse our Keturi's names with the number of cold cases they've forced us to sift through." Eden stuck her tongue out at me.

"Ah, I see." Ollie said, bringing his glass to his lips to hide a smile.

"And with everything else we have to keep in order," Greyson knocked his head lightly against the wall behind him, "I'm surprised none of us have tried to kill one another."

We all laughed, cracking the weariness and exhaustion in our voices. It wasn't just me who needed a night away from Compound, away from the stress and triggers of what we worked on constantly.

"Surely the Deltas can handle most of the cases while you all focus on Elliot?" Ollie asked, taking another sip of his ale.

"Most of them do," I informed him. "Although my boys over here are technically still working on this hostage case we handled a week ago."

"Ah, heard about that." Ollie nodded. "A few strung Shrivs attacked a tavern?"

289

"Yeah that's it. Seems like an open and shut case except for..."

"We're still trying to figure out those blasted words," Taylor mumbled into his glass, before downing the rest of his whiskey.

Lucas leaned back, his fingers tapping against his own glass. "We're convinced they mean something, but until we can find someone to translate them, all signs point to their acts being nothing more than a drugged bender gone wrong."

My fingers drew circles along the rim of my glass. "Did you ask Emric if he knew anyone?"

Taylor nodded. "Waiting to hear back still from a few linguists at some of the other universities."

"What do you need translated?" Ollie asked.

"*Chu Fui na Déithe*," Lucas sighed. "We assume it's Ancient Kazalonian."

"It is," Ollie said. "Means, 'For the Blood of the Gods.'"

All of us froze, staring at him with wide eyes.

"How do you know that?" I demanded.

He shrugged, his expression puzzled, shoulder still slumped against the chair nonchalantly. "We had a robbery and murder case about two years back at a jewelry store. The robber had written it across the walls in the owner's blood. Took us a while to get it translated, too, it's not known by many."

"But it's still found its way into two cases in two different territories?" My mind stuck to that question. It couldn't be a coincidence.

"I suppose..." He trailed off, eyebrows crinkling as he stared at me.

"Kas..." Eden leaned forward. "What are you thinking?"

"Shh." I held up my hand, cutting everyone off so I could

think; then I closed my eyes, trying my best to picture the details of the Elliot case board.

For months, I had been telling myself that I needed to listen to my instincts more and stop second guessing; so that was what I did, I focused in on the path he had taken over the years, his movements between the territories and where his hits had been.

Elliot was tracked in Vapalles seven years ago, killing thirteen people over an eight-month period before disappearing for a year.

This robbery had happened two years ago.

"Have you had any other cases besides the robbery that had those words in it?" I asked Ollie.

"Uh...I don't think so, not based on any of the research I did during the investigation."

"That's it." My eyes shot open, my heart pounding.

It was all too coincidental; it was all too perfectly timed. Nothing was ever this easy. Which could only mean...

"Move." I pushed Ollie's shoulder, trying to get him out of the booth so I could escape.

"Ow!" he chided, even though my little push barely hurt him.

"Move! I need to call someone!"

"Alright, alright. Calm down." He shook his head, standing up and clearing the path for me to dart out of the booth and through the crowd.

I rushed out the door without another word, my mind racing. I had to let Nolan know my theory, let him know that we might just be one step closer to figuring out Elliot's identity.

The outside was still rowdy with people, crossing by in drunken hazes from one tavern to the next, laughing boisterously. I needed somewhere quiet, so I rounded a corner, cutting down an alley off to the left of the tavern, the noise dissipating slightly. I struggled to get my Comms out of my pocket, fingers shaking as I typed in Nolan's name. I was so wrapped up in the building pressure of excitement in my chest, I was barely paying attention to what was around me.

Just as I was about to hit the call button, something slammed into my side, throwing me stumbling back into the wall, the unit falling from my hands.

"What the—" A blow cut off the words, the punch aimed right at my nose, the quick impact whipping my head backward, cracking it against the stone wall behind me.

I struggled to get my bearings, blood trickling down my face as I scrabbled for my Amalgam Blade and triggered the release on the silver dagger. Even if this was a Shrivika, I could do some serious damage.

The figure in front of me was hooded, the dark navy cloak covering most of their face, their snarling lips the only thing visible. Even though I couldn't see them, I could guess they were a female, based on their height being and their slight, curvy build under the thick cloak. I took a deep whiff, wanting to commit this idiot's scent to memory just in case. But, no matter how many deep pulls of air I took, all I got was the dank and dirty alley, nothing of the person standing in front of me.

That couldn't be right. I couldn't catch their scent.

I shook my head, trying to clear my bleary vision from the two blows this woman somehow got on me. I stumbled forward, feeling separated from my upper half.

Damnit, she must have given me a concussion. I slashed with my blade, trying my best to connect it with any part of my attacker, but my movements were sluggish, my arms slow as if

292

the air around me had been thickened with honey.

"Help!" I screamed to everyone in the tavern. *"Attack!"*

"Kas?" Lucas's voice filled my mind, but I didn't have time to respond; the hooded figure was too quick. I just had to hope they would find me.

My attacker could tell she had the advantage, her triumphant snarl cutting through the fog that still tainted my vision and mind. I kept trying to block her precise strikes, willing every bit of my training to my aid until the group got here. I just need to delay—

I screamed into the darkness before I even realized where a sudden burst of pain radiated from, my eyes flicking down just in time to watch the woman pull her dagger from my side, above my hipbone.

"Help." I whispered again to all of them, my hand pressed against the gushing wound, blood already soaking half of my tunic.

"Where are you?" I heard Ollie first.

"Alley," was all I could get out as I staggered clear of another swipe. *"Attack. Backup."*

"Hold on."

I gave all of my attention back to the attacker in front of me; she thought she had the best of me, but she didn't know me.

As she tensed to strike, a cackle escaping her smirking lips, I lunged forward with the last of my strength, my blade slamming into her shoulder.

She shrieked into the night sky, stumbling backward. The two of us stared at each other, nothing but our heavy breathing filling the air between us. Neither of us moved for a second, until the pounding of my friends' footsteps round the corner.

293

My attacker straightened at the noise, giving me one last snarl before running in the opposite direction, jumping over the low wall and disappearing from sight.

I finally allowed myself to collapse just as the group reached me. "Go..." I coughed on my own words. "After..."

Lucas and Taylor didn't say anything as they dashed down the alley, jumping the wall with ease, disappearing from sight.

"We have to get you back to Compound. To Beckett." Eden moved my hands from my side, pressing hers into the wound. Ollie and Greyson crouched on either side of her.

"No, I need to see Nolan..." I coughed a few more times, blood bubbling from between my lips. The wound was deeper than I'd thought. "Theory..."

"Kas, you have a hole in your side!" Ollie grasped my face between his hands, forcing me to look at him, his face blurry in my impaired vision.

"I'll be...fine." They knew that too. Only a blow with the Ogdala Blade could kill me. This wound, although painful and burning along half my body, would be gone soon enough.

"Nolan is back at the Compound with Beckett," Greyson said. "Talk to them together if you want, but either way, we have to get you back."

"Drink first." Eden pulled out her blade, slicing a shallow cut just above her wrist. "It's the only thing that will stabilize her enough. Ollie, go find a carriage, she won't be able to ride a cycle safely. Grey, clear the area in front of the tavern and make sure there's space. After that, connect with Taylor and Lucas and tell them to return to Compound once they're done with their hunt."

Both men nodded, rushing off.

"You're so bossy," I laughed weakly, numbness spreading
294

through my fingers and up my arm.

"Don't act surprised, now do as you're told." Without another word, she shoved her wrist into my mouth, forcing me to drink until I could once again feel my whole body.

Chapter Thirty-Six

"Kasha, will you just stay still?" Beckett growled, pushing me back into the infirmary bed.

Of course, that didn't stop me from shooting myself back upright, trying to swing my legs onto the ground. "I told you, I'm fine!"

"You have a gaping hole in your side." He pushed on the wound to keep the bleeding contained.

I inhaled sharply. "It'll heal."

"I need to disinfect it, there's dirt and God-knows-what-else from that alley." He shook his head slightly to get a piece of wayward white-blond hair out of his face. "Then you need to drink more blood to help slow the bleeding and close it a bit before I can stitch it up to help it heal faster."

"Beckett, that's not important right now!" I tried to wiggle free of his determined grip. "I need to go to the investigation board and look into my theory. I swear, I have a breakthrough."

"And you will still have the breakthrough in an hour." He loomed over me, his dark eyes forcing me to still. "Even if this wound can't kill you, it can still get an infection. If it gets an infection, then it won't stop bleeding, or heal up, and then you'll be forced to stay in this bed even longer, which means you won't be allowed to prove your theory outside of this Compound. So, either hurt yourself more because you have no patience, or sit still!"

His firm voice chilled me to the bone. I flopped my head against the pillow with a grunt of surrender.

"Wow, you *can* listen." He sat in his chair next to me, pushing the blood-soaked fabric of my shirt up to just below my breasts. He pulled on a pair of gloves, then picked up a vile of clear liquid and a handful of clean linen. "You know the drill, stay as still as possible while I clean."

"Yes, sir," I grumbled, crossing my arms behind my head to keep them out of the way.

The first burning sizzle of pain engulfed my stomach as he poured some of the disinfectant onto it, my blood bubbling for a moment before calming down, bits of dirt and gravel floating to the surface. Beckett took his time, gently pulling the rocks out with tweezers, wiping away the clouded blood and repeating the process.

Minutes passed, my mind focused on keeping every inch of my body still, although it didn't stop a few grunts of pain from escaping my lips or my legs from squirming. Eventually, rushing, heavy footsteps echoed from the floor below us, signaling that someone else had entered the building. I let out a sigh; in a few moments, there would be two more people here to try and coddle me.

"Three, two, one..." I mumbled just as the doors to the triage room burst open.

"Ollie called and said you'd been stabbed!" Nolan rushed in, eyes wild, flashing gold.

"I'm fine!" I propped myself up on my elbow, staring at Emric and Nolan standing at the foot of my bed. "It's not as bad as it looks, I barely feel it."

"You have a hole in your side!" Emric pointed to where Beckett's hands wiped away the last of the dirty blood.

My shoulders sagged. "I'm really sick of everyone pointing out the obvious."

"What happened?" Nolan's hands curled around the metal footboard, turning his knuckles white. "Who did this to you?"

"That's not important right now," I said. "I need..."

"She was attacked in the alley behind the *Blood Moon*." Beckett didn't even look up as he threw a few soiled cloths into a bin by my bedside. "Perfect timing, Emric, she needs fresh blood."

"Here, Kasha." Emric walked right over to me, rolling up the sleeve of his purple button-up, baring his wrist to me.

I knocked it away. "I don't want blood right now! I need to tell you about my new theory—"

"Drink, Kasha." Beckett shoved Emric's wrist back in my face, my body tingling at the smell of it. It was a natural reaction after injury, and it was only exacerbated by the sweet, rich scent of my Consort's blood right under my nose, the thump of his pulse echoing in my ears.

My fingers curled into the bedsheets. "Nolan, please, I think this is a lead for Elliot. We need to contact the other Factions again—"

"You need to heal yourself first," Nolan interrupted, his

jaw tense.

I gaped at him. "But this is time-sensitive—"

"Not as sensitive as your health." Nolan walked around the bed to stand next to Emric. "I refuse to listen to this theory until Beckett says it's okay. So, either drink and move the process along, or keep yelling at us, but we won't listen."

"*Fine*." These three could probably kill me quicker than the wound, if I could die that way. I stared at Emric's wrist. "I...um...need you to..." I struggled to say the words, and all three of them stiffened.

I needed him to cut himself, because without access to my wolf, I couldn't transform my teeth sharp enough to break the barrier between his sweet blood and my lips. Emric's eyes softened before he brought his wrist to his lips, biting down quickly and returning the wrist to me, a trickle of blood sliding down his skin.

My instincts took over, and I clamped my lips around the wound, sucking the warm, luscious blood from Emric's veins. There was nothing as delectable as fresh blood, still warm against my tastebuds. Unlike the bagged blood we stored for regular nourishment, this tasted divine, making it easy to get lost in the pleasure that came with feeding. My mind spun, craving more and more of the delicacy, my hands grasping onto Emric's arm to tug it as close to me as possible. I relished the rush of power surging in my veins, bringing back strength to my tired muscles, sharpening my mind. Colors seemed brighter. Scents seemed stronger, the aroma of cinnamon drawing me in.

I looked up, finding the evergreen eyes I searched for. My heart thumped, body flooding with heat as we stared at each other. He'd no doubt seen someone do this before—in fact, he'd probably fed from someone plenty of times—but something about the way he watched me, as if engrossed by some performance I was putting on just for him, sent a jolt through my spine.

I didn't know why it kept happening. When my impulses took over, my mind went to him, and I couldn't seem to stop myself.

"That's enough," Beckett said, snapping me away from the tug Nolan had on me and solidifying me back into reality.

I pulled away from Emric's wrist, my chest rising and falling heavily. "Thank you."

"You're welcome." Emric gave me a quick wink, wrapping a cloth around his wrist to stanch the bleeding, the wound already starting to close.

"Here." Nolan grabbed a few pillows from the neighboring bed and helped me prop them behind me, allowing me to sit up in a more comfortable position while keeping the wound available for Beckett to stitch up. After I was situated, Nolan sat on the edge of the bed by my feet while Beckett worked and Emric remained standing. "Alright, what is it?"

Finally. My mind sharpened, the details I had lined up only an hour ago rushing back to the forefront of my mind. "I think the hostage situation we had a few weeks ago is connected to Elliot."

"What?" All three of them said together, their wide-eye stares directed at me.

I explained everything Ollie had told me at the *Blood Moon*. The words tumbled out, and for all I knew, in the haze of blood loss, they made no sense. Beckett continued to stitch me up, but his hardened expression told me he was listening to every word; Emric paced next to me, and Nolan was as still as a statue.

"It can't be a coincidence," I finished my longwinded explanation, my mind and chest feeling lighter now that I'd finally been able to speak it out loud.

"So you think Elliot isn't working alone?" Nolan leaned forward.

"No, I think he has a Clan, and they all work together somehow," I said. "Think about it, it adds up a few things: how there's no definitive victim profile, how he can move an intricate operation from Territory to Territory so seamlessly. He's not working alone, we just always thought he was because of the brandings."

Beckett leaned back in his chair, pulling off his gloves, observing the thin stitching now running an inch up my side from my hipbone. "He must feed off of the homicidal tendencies of others, bringing them together and teaching them how to kill or attack without detection."

"Exactly!" I threw my arms up. "We need to contact the other Factions again, see if they have the same pattern."

"This could be so much bigger than we even realized." Nolan rocked back and forth, his eyes glowing amber.

"This is only just beginning, it seems," Beckett whispered, before the four of us dove right into devising a plan.

***

We only worked on the plan for an hour before Beckett pushed the other two out of the infirmary, insisting I needed to rest. He kept me overnight, staying with me and observing me as the wound healed itself at an accelerated rate.

By midmorning the next day. he was able to remove the stitches, but still insisted I stay in bed until it was nothing more than a scar, wanting to be safe in case any internal damage was still healing. I was in and out of sleep for most of the day, letting my mind wander with potential ideas on what I could do with the investigation when I was able to leave this bed. I could check missing person files, trying to find potential Clan members, maybe set up a canvassing search around the territory for any kind of wolfsbane farm that might have popped up, or I could—

My thoughts were cut off by the loud buzzing of Beckett's Comms, sitting on his desk. Beckett sat forward, answering it immediately. "Yes?"

"Sorry to interrupt, *Ar Dtus*, but my name is Major Crillian of the Dornwich outpost." The voice drifted to my bed. "We've found another body."

Chapter Thirty-Seven

It took ten minutes of arguing that I was healed enough to travel to the crime scene, the rest of the Keturi unsure it was the best idea. Finally, we agreed to a compromise that I wouldn't drive—which was how I found myself on the back of Nolan's lectracycle, air whipping around us as we sped through the streets.

My blood pumped loudly in my ears, my mind going through all the possible horrors we might be about to walk into. They hadn't given us many details about the victim, just that it was a male Varg, and they had found Elliot's crest. Something felt off to me, and though it could have been exhaustion from everything that happened since yesterday, my mind still spinning over the whole ordeal…that wasn't it. Something in my soul was unsettled, nagging at me and grating on my nerves. It felt like a warning, the alarms in my mind telling me to turn back, to not continue forward.

I pushed through the doubt and tightened my grip around Nolan's torso, his abs flexing under my touch. He reached down with one hand, gently squeezing mine. Seemed I wasn't the only one worried; my heart settled a bit knowing I wasn't alone.

We rounded the corner into the outskirts of Dornwich, tall brick warehouses taking up the space. Officers and soldiers milled in and out, not many civilians in sight. We parked near the military wagons and walked straight for the group.

Major Crillian grabbed our attention right away, his cheeks flushed and eyes filled with haunted fear. What were we about to walk into?

"I don't know how to explain it, so I think it best just to show you," he said solemnly after introduction, leading us to a side entrance and through a storage area of crates and boxes stacked on top of each other. The faint scent of herbs penetrated through the cargo; we were in some kind of mass market apothecary, most likely for some of the more popular tinctures that local shops preferred to outsource in larger batches based on high demand.

We made our way to the back of the room where the victim had been found, all of us stopping instantly in our tracks, taking in the scene.

This was unlike any of the other victims we had seen. This man was mostly naked, in nothing more than an undergarment concealing his intimate areas. His sun-kissed skin was drenched in sweat and blood, most of his body covered in deep gashes and brutal bitemarks. Unlike past victims, where the bites were clean and precises, these looked like the attacker had tried to rip his skin clean off his body, thrashed and jagged. In the center of his chest, an R had been carved, Elliot's crest branded right in the center of the letter's curve. The whole room reeked of wolfsbane, his body still slick with the milky liquid.

This wasn't calculated or specific, but erratic and brutal. Something about this man had set Elliot off, and we had to figure out what it was.

But it wasn't the intense mutilation of this poor man that made my heart pound and my stomach threaten to release its contents. It wasn't the burning pain of the wolfsbane still lingering in the air that spun my mind with lightheadedness. What made me stop in my tracks, bone-chilling fear burying itself deep within me, was the victim's completely unmarked face.

He was maybe in his mid-thirties, his well-defined, sharp jaw, and full lips contorted in a half scream, showing just how much pain Elliot had put him through. His dirty blond curls were matted to his forehead by sweat and blood. His amber eyes still shown with hints of gold; he had fought to the end.

And dear Goddess above, he looked like Logan.

I knew it wasn't him; I would never forget that man's face no matter how hard I tried. But with all of those similarities, every memory of him, good and bad, flashed before my mind, pulling at the deeply dangerous emotions I tried to keep settled.

I felt a few eyes lingering on me before Beckett and Emric took control of the scene, distracting the different officers and soldiers who were scattered around us. I didn't know what I was doing to make people look at me; everything felt so far away.

"Kasha?" Nolan whispered only to me, keeping everyone else out.

I couldn't respond, even within the privacy of my mind. It all seemed too much, too overwhelming, too many thoughts trying to take all at once. My fingers shook at my side, pressure building to an unbearable pain in my chest.

"I think I saw something over here." Nolan cocked his head to the side building. "Kas and I are going to check it out."

"Sounds good," Emric said, Beckett giving us a knowing nod before returning his attention back to the body.

Nolan put his arm around my shoulders, guiding me away from the group. We went around the building where a small opening of tables and chairs was set up haphazardly, obviously a place where workers ate their meals during shifts. Luckily, no one was out there.

My movements were barely under my control as Nolan brought me to one of the chairs, pushing gently on my shoulders so I'd sit. The cool metal seeped through the fabric of my pants, a bit of moisture from a past rainstorm staining the back, but I didn't care. It helped in a way, bringing the spinning fog back to reality a bit, my fingertips starting to tingle.

"What happened?" His voice was calm and low as he dropped onto one knee in front of me, our heads so close the tickling of his hair brushed lightly against my cheek.

I leaned forward, bracing my elbows onto my knees and dropping my face into my hands, fingertips rubbing circles against my throbbing temples.

"He—He—He..." Sobs started to rack through me, tears escaping from my eyes. I cursed under my breath, chiding myself for being so weak, so out of control of myself. This wasn't alright, not during an investigation, at a crime scene no less. What had I done to deserve this? "He...looks..." My breath hitched again, the squeezing in my chest tightening even more. "Lo—looked like...like Logan."

"Logan?" Nolan asked. I peeked through my fingers, the

confusion creased on his forehead. "Your old Alpha?"

All I could do was nod.

Nolan leaned back on his haunches, eyes focused on nothing in particular on the ground. I bit my lip as a range of emotions and thoughts rippled across his features. Finally, after a few moments of silence, he looked back to me. "You don't have to tell me anything, but...did he do something to you? Hurt you in some way? At the Full Moon Camp?"

I wasn't even surprised at this point. He was a sharp investigator, born to find any answer with the clues and hints fed to him over time. It was only a matter of time, even if he didn't know the specifics. My heart loosened a fraction, a shaky breath escaping my lips.

Slowly, I gave him one more nod.

"To the Goddess above, Kasha," he whispered. "No wonder you didn't want me here."

Somehow, I blubbered out a laugh, the most inappropriate thing, but it was all I could do. Nothing was right in my mind, nothing was making sense. I tried to focus on something, anything. Of course, I went right to the here and now, concentrating on what was in front of me, the concern bubbling to the surface.

"Di—did any-anyone notice?" My voice barely sounded like me, so weak and terrified. "Th-th-the other off-officers?"

"No," Nolan assured me. "I think Beckett and Emric did, but they must have seen the similarities too, because they looked just as shocked. The other officers just seemed to be waiting for us to say something. Once Beckett and Emric did, they didn't even pay attention to us."

I let out another deep, shaking breath. "Good."

"Let me take you home." His hand moved up and down my bicep with just enough pressure to help soothe my nerves a fraction. "You don't need this right now."

"We need to help."

"It's one crime scene, Beckett and Emric have it completely under control."

I shook my head, unable to say anything else.

"If you don't take time to let yourself unpack everything that's happened to you over the past two days, you won't be able to investigate this properly." He crouched down a bit, forcing our gazes to catch. "You have one of the sharpest minds on the team, we need you to be at your best. It's alright to admit you need to rest to be able to work efficiently. That isn't weakness, it's a natural need."

I let his words seep into my mind, rolling them through and agreeing with the logic. He knew I wouldn't go off of an emotional appeal, but a reasonable one; right now, I was far from my best. Rest—and something else I couldn't seem to name—was what I needed. Something to distract me.

I looked back up at him, blinking a few times before I stood up, every muscle in my body feeling unbearably heavy. "Alright, let's go."

He gave me a smile, but not his usual, wickedly-teasing grin. This soft, warm smile made my heart flip a few times as he took my hand and guided me back to the front of the warehouse, not even going to the crime scene but right to his cycle. We mounted it, and I internally prayed to Lunestia as we left this whole mess behind.

Chapter Thirty-Eight

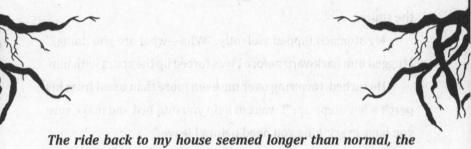

The ride back to my house seemed longer than normal, the speed and wind doing absolutely nothing to calm my nerves like they usually did. Instead of giving me a sense of freedom, a taste of what I used to have, the sensation just reminded me of what I'd lost. My mind kept spiraling with each mile we rode.

Nolan wound us through the empty roads and streets of Eroste, doing exactly as he'd said and taking me home. The weight of everything settled on my shoulders as Nolan parked in what was typically my spot, dismounting his bike with me.

"You don't have to come in." I said, my voice raspy and harsh from my panic attack.

"I know I don't have to." He shoved his keys into his pocket and walked straight to my front door without missing a step.

I sighed, following him and unlocking the door to push our way inside. The house was dark and quiet, and even before I found the note tacked to the banister, I knew Lea had gone out for the evening.

"Are you hungry?" Nolan leaned against the doorframe. "I could cook you something."

I shook my head, crumbling the note and shoving it into my pocket. "I'm too tired to eat. I think I just need to lay down and end this day as soon as possible."

His face softened. "Understandable. Let's go."

He grabbed my hand, tugging at me slightly as he headed up the stairs.

My stomach flipped violently. "Wha—what are you doing?" I tugged him backward before I was forced up the stairs with him.

He turned, towering over me even more than usual from his perch a few steps up. "I want to help you into bed and make sure you have everything you need before I leave."

"Nolan, this is very sweet of you..."

"I know," he teased, sending me one of those grins that once upon a time grated on my nerves.

Not anymore, apparently. I ignored that, looking up at him. "But I can handle myself. You don't need to burden yourself with my problems."

"You are never a burden, Kasha, not to those who care about you." His words swept over me, sending a shiver running up my spine. "And if I haven't made it abundantly clear by this point, I do care about you. I would never forgive myself if I left you here to fend for yourself, not after everything you were forced to go through. So, if you don't want to do this for yourself, then look at it as doing it for me. Alright?"

Usually, I would fight him off, tell him it was none of his business. I was strong and capable and could put myself to bed. Yet, a whisper in the back of my mind tried to break through the

310

stubborn fog, telling me it was alright to lean on someone else, to admit when I needed help.

I decided to listen to the voice, nodding silently. He winked before turning back toward the top of the stairs, leading me the rest of the way and pushing the door to my bedroom open as if it was the most casual thing in the world. But that wasn't what bothered me; what made my pulse speed up was how natural it was to have him here, in my space, standing beside me, giving me his strength in ways I seemed to need.

This whole forty-eight hours had been nothing short of a disaster for my emotions, stripped bare of their protections and put out for all the world to see. My body felt raw, sensitive to even the slightest breeze that rustled along my long-sleeved undershirt. I headed straight for the oil lamp on my bedside table, igniting it with my flint and adjusting the lighting to give the room a soft glow. I turned back to the fireplace, ready to light that as well, my typical routine feeling more burdensome than usual.

"Just relax, I'll get this lit." Nolan grabbed the flint from my hand, crouching down in front of the fireplace. I sighed, plopping down onto my bed, my numb fingers tugging at the bracers on my arms.

I tried to look back on the last two days' events, but even starting at the beginning felt like an impossible mountain to climb. Everything was spinning out of my control, and yet I didn't see any solution on how to rein it back in. I didn't want to be burdened any longer, I didn't want to linger on these terrible, dark thoughts; I wanted a taste of freedom from everything that clouded my mind. From the pain and heartache and mental torture I found myself in some days.

The last time I had felt good, not caring about the tangled

mess my life had become, was when Nolan had helped me with my pent-up anger. When we had sparred, and my eyes had flared back to life.

When we had kissed.

My heart fluttered at the idea, heat flaring in my cheeks at the memory of his luscious lips moving against mine. That moment had been chaotic and exhilarating in ways I never knew I needed. It had ignited something in me; I wanted him again and I was too tired to try and convince myself otherwise. I wanted Nolan; no matter how much I tried to deny it for weeks now, it wasn't going away.

The last time I had given into that lust had been more than I had ever imagined. What would happen if I gave into it again?

I watched him fumble with lighting the pyre, a laugh escaping my lips.

"Goddess, this is impossible," he grumbled.

"I can do it, you know."

"No, I've got it." Finally, after a few more failed attempts, a spark flew from the flint, landing on the stacked wood and igniting, the crackling and warmth slowly filling the room. He turned back to me, a smug smile settled on his lips. "Told you."

"Well, I'm failing, can you help me?" My voice was low and raspy as I held up my arm weakly to him.

He chuckled. "Sure." He sat beside me on the bed, gently cradling my arm in one hand while the other quickly removed my bracer. He worked silently, removing all my black armor, placing the pieces on the floor at the foot of my bed with gentle care. "Better?"

My heart pounded violently, daring me to make the move my mind was telling me to take.

Instead of answering him, I leaned forward, cupping his scratchy cheek in the palm of my hand. His body tensed under my touch as I stared into his intoxicating eyes, those forest-green irises igniting with a heat I remembered well.

My body ached to lean in, to feel that fire once again. I wanted it, I craved it in a way I never thought possible. I didn't want to think, I wanted to forget about everything terrible that had happened. I wanted just one moment of unbridled joy before I ended the day. Nolan could give me that; we could give it to each other.

That was all I could think about—forgetting it all—as I leaned toward him, pressing my lips against his.

I groaned the moment they touched, deepening the kiss instantly. The heat, the desire flared to life in my core, flowing through me and snaking up every inch of my body, leaning me closer to him. My thoughts dulled, my mind only focused on one thing: tasting more, touching more, getting lost in Nolan. A low buzz hummed in my chest, that all-too-familiar stir jolting at me, igniting every little movement of our lips against each other. It was perfect, it was everything I had wanted. It was doing exactly what I needed; I was forgetting, getting lost in the pleasure.

Yet, after only a few seconds, he stiffened against me.

"Kas..." he mumbled, his hands flying to my shoulders, gently pushing at me. "Kas, stop."

My body froze, my lips stilling against his. "Wh—what?"

"This isn't right." He leaned away, an unreadable mix of emotions crossing his handsome face. "You've been through so much..."

"Yes, and this is making me feel better." I leaned forward. "Please, Nolan, help me feel better."

I stared at him, pleading silently. It had all felt perfect, right, and beautiful, and he was pulling away. I needed him, I wanted him—did he not want me?

He closed his eyes, letting out a deep groan, shaking his head slowly, my throat closing at the simple movement. He stood, taking a few paces away and leaning against my desk.

"I can't." He looked down at me, his body still tense and rigid. "Not like this."

Icy chills swept through me, the sting of his rejection piercing through the last shred of hope that I had given myself. Why did I think he would ever desire the broken, weakened mess that I was?

Fine, if he didn't want me, then I didn't need him—no matter how much my body still ached for his touch to return. I curled my arms around my torso, staring at him, waiting for him to run away. But he didn't move, he just looked at me from his perch on my desk.

I didn't like it, my skin crawling with each moment he stayed in the room.

"Why aren't you leaving, then?" I growled, shooting him a withering stare that, in the past, had made others run away in fear. But not Nolan; he stood his ground, his fingers digging into the sides of my desk.

"Because I want to be here." He refused to break eye contact no matter how much it made my skin crawl. "I won't abandon you."

"Your actions just now told a different story." My insides squeezed at the immaturity in my words. I was better than this, but I didn't make a move to retract my ignorance, my mind too exhausted to care.

"Just because I won't take advantage of you, doesn't mean I'm not here for you." He crossed his arms. "I know you didn't always like me, but give me some credit."

My throat closed, guilt twisting at my insides. I had lashed out like a petulant child when he had done nothing but be kind to me, reverting back to my embarrassing habits from when he first arrived. He wanted to do right and treat me with respect. Somehow, I was surprised. His pulling away wasn't a slight, it wasn't a denial; it was protection, it was kindness. Why was I expecting something different?

Maybe because my last Alpha wouldn't have been so considerate of my needs.

That thought slammed into me, stealing my breath and last shred of sanity. I stared down at my feet, rocking myself back and forth. Months of not seeing him, and yet his poisoned actions still ruined me. His choices forced themselves on me, reshaping how I viewed everything, even people he had never crossed paths with.

"I—I don't..." I stammered, my throat tight and scratchy.

"Kasha, just lie down." Nolan's hand was heavy on my shoulder, pressing lightly, guiding me to lie down on the bed before he lifted my legs so I was curled up on my side.

"I ne—need to explain." I didn't know if I could fall asleep without explaining, even if my words were barely coherent. I didn't want him to think less of me.

"You need to rest." He sat down on the side of the bed, pulling the covers over my shaking body. The warmth enveloped me like a cocoon, settling my pulse slightly. He tilted his head, hands moving slowly up my arm and toward my hair, his fingers gently brushing the strands in a smooth rhythm. "Just sleep. I'm not going anywhere. We can talk tomorrow."

There was sincerity in his voice, a promise laced through the words he would not break. I let myself sink lower into the soft mattress, pulling the blankets tighter around me. He continued to stroke a reassuring pattern up and down my hair, his fingers lightly scratching at my scalp in the most unexpectedly soothing way. I didn't know what it was, the crackling fire, the overwhelming exhaustion, or the calm flow of his fingers, but before I even realized it, sleep took me into its clutches.

Chapter Thirty-Nine

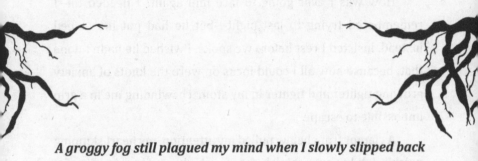

A groggy fog still plagued my mind when I slowly slipped back into consciousness, a groan escaping my lips as I rolled over to welcome the next day.

My mind and body were out of sync, my movements lethargic and slower than normal. I kicked the covers off, pulling at the sweaty black under-armor that I hadn't taken off. My mind tried to push through the fog, attempting to remember everything that happened.

Counseling. Caleb's unexpected arrival. Being stabbed by a mystery assailant. The crime scene.

Dear Goddess above, a week's worth of stress rolled into one terribly short time period.

Then the final moments of the day came rushing back to me, my body shooting upward at the memory that made my cheeks redden with shame. "Oh Goddess," I groaned, dropping my face into my hands. What was I thinking?

I had thrown myself at Nolan, when all he was trying to do was help me. I had tried to use him to numb my pain, not even caring what he wanted in that moment. How could I even cross that line? It had happened once before, but this was different. I knew what I was doing last night, and still I'd made the choice. I had risked my reputation in the Guard and my newly developed friendship with Nolan...not to mention my pride.

How was I ever going to face him again? I needed to—I remembered trying to last night—but he had put me to bed instead, insisted I rest before we spoke. I wished he hadn't done that, because now all I could focus on were the knots of anxiety growing tighter and tighter in my stomach, winding me in a grip impossible to escape.

A clamor from below pulled my attention, my heart skipping quickly. I didn't even think before I rushed out of bed, heading for the staircase.

I padded downstairs, my bare feet slapping against the smooth wood of each step, mouthwatering at the scent of fried eggs and bacon before I even made it to the lower floor. Was Lea still here? She was usually at her forge by this time. I headed for the back of our house toward the kitchen, the crackling of fat sizzling in a hot pan beckoning me forward.

But as I rounded the corner, a new scent that caught my attention, the cinnamon-citrus aroma intoxicating in a completely different way.

"Morning," Nolan said, his typical grin welcoming me into the sunbathed kitchen. He stood behind the counter where I usually found Lea. His hands moved expertly, one with a spatula flipping a few pieces of bacon out of a cast-iron pan, another lightly seasoning a heaping stack of scrambled eggs.

318

He acted as though it was completely normal for him to be here when it was anything but.

"What...did you come back?"

"No, I never left." He turned his back for a moment, grabbing something off the back counter before facing me with a steaming mug in his hand. "I crashed on the couch after you fell asleep. Gave Lea a scare when she came home, but I made it up to her by feeding her breakfast before work this morning."

"Wh—why?" My pulse picked up speed, my weight easing back and forth on each foot.

"Well, seemed like the right thing to do since I scared her witless at two in the morning."

I shook my head. "No. Why did you stay?"

"I told you last night, I'm not abandoning you." He pushed the mug toward me, the nutty roast of the coffee wafting into my nose. "Come and sit. I already ate, but I wanted to make sure you ate, too. After yesterday, you need it."

My cheeks heated at his nonchalant nature. He was one of the most infuriatingly kind people I had ever met. I had embarrassed myself utterly with him yesterday, I had desperately thrown myself at him, yet here he was, refusing to let that affect the way he treated me.

Why couldn't he just give me a taste of my own medicine? Goddess knew I deserved it after all this time.

"Will you just stop being stubborn and sit down?" he laughed, shaking his head as he dropped a plate of food next to the coffee. "Or are you going to let all my hard work go to waste?"

His light laughter helped to loosen some of the tension in my muscles, my shoulders relaxing. Finally getting control over my feet again, I slid into the high stool perched in front of the counter, the food and coffee tempting my growling stomach. I took a few hesitant bites, the eggs perfectly seasoned and the bacon crispy. My stomach gurgled again, begging for more; I picked at the plate, staring down at it. "I'm sure you have some questions about yesterday. About why the victim...affected me that way."

He stared at me from over the counter, his bright forest eyes softening. "Kas, you don't have to tell me anything."

"How can you even say that now?" My stomach churned as I took another bite. "After everything you witnessed yesterday?"

"Your past is your story to tell." He wiped his hands on a cloth before tossing it on the counter. "I would never force you to tell me anything until you're ready."

"That seems unfair. You told me about Cleo when I asked."

"That's different." He stole a piece of bacon off my plate and ripped a bite off. "I knew going into that bet there was a high probability you would ask me about my connection to Elliot. I was ready for it, expected it, and I still made the choice to take the risk. I've had time to mourn Cleo, to accept and recover from my trauma. All of that coping makes it easier to tell the story. If you're not ready, then I understand."

His words hit me with a force unlike any other. This man, who I had shown so much anger and resentment toward, continued to surprise me daily.

"Why are you so kind to me?" I just didn't understand. I didn't deserve it.

"Because I like you," he said without hesitation, his bright gaze steady, holding mine. "I see you in a way I don't think many people, including yourself, do. Strong, capable, utterly intoxicating, fascinating. You have a mind unlike any other, and a drive that could change the world if you wanted to. How could I

320

not want to be around that? How could I not be drawn to that?"

His words left me speechless. Darkened whispers once again tried to tell me they were all lies, pretty words meant to deceive; yet, for the first time in a while, those terrible thoughts were the quite ones. A stronger, more loving voice told me to listen, to look. Everything about him in front of me, his posture, his eye contact, the passion behind each word spoken, told only the truth.

He meant every single thing he had just said about me.

"Doesn't mean I deserve it," I mumbled, unable to control the waver in my voice.

"You do." He leaned his elbows on the counter, sliding one arm over to cover my hand with his. "I don't know everything, but I have witnessed enough over these past few weeks to get an understanding of why you acted the way you did at first. Plus, I knew you were passed over for promotion—I was given warning about that. I sort of expected you to be...less than thrilled when I came into it."

"And yet you still came?"

He smirked, a wicked glint in his eye. "I knew my charm would eventually win you over."

I scoffed. "Still as confident as ever."

"As if you'd want me to change." He winked.

Heat spread into my cheeks again, flushing down my chest. "No, I suppose not."

"Anyway," he walked around the counter, dropping into the chair next to me, angling himself so we faced each other. "I don't need answers until you're ready, but trust me when I say I see you. I see all of you. I see the reason for being weary of trusting outsiders, of not wanting to risk yourself after everything you seem to have been through. You have an army of people who

321

would lay down their lives for you, literally. You don't need me, I get that. I know your trust isn't easily earned...I get that too. But just know, I hope to one day be considered part of those trusted people. I hope one day I can earn that privilege."

I stared at him, my mouth slightly gaping as I took in all of the beautiful, honest words he had just spoken to me.

He was right, in a way. The rest of my Faction, my friends who had been nothing but a protective support through everything I had gone through, would never waver from me. I trusted them, but I had gained that trust before my life came tumbling down.

Nolan was the first person in the past year that I'd attempted to form a bond with, something that had seemed pointless at the beginning. In a way, it made his presence different than the others. He hadn't known me before, he hadn't known the woman who walked around the Compound with nothing but surety in her heart and unwavering confidence in her veins. He only knew this broken, tattered version where I barely felt like a complete person some days. Yet, he still saw these unimaginable traits in me and spoke of me with nothing short of awe in his voice.

He saw all of me, the weak and the strong, and still he wanted to learn more.

He wanted me to trust him. Not only that, he had put in effort to help bring me to a place where I could. It set a fire inside of me, my mind spinning as I came to terms with what I had been denying for too long. Vanessa's words from the other day rang in my head: *"Those who care about you, those who are really worth your trust, will stop at nothing to earn it."*

If I believed in the power of clairvoyance, I would be utterly convinced that Vanessa had that ability. Somehow, she had known exactly what I needed even before I did.

Nolan cared about me. He was determined to prove that to me every day, with his words and actions. He had listened to me, he had pushed me to places others feared would break me, he gave me excuses when I needed them, a shoulder to lean on when support felt impossible, and he never seemed to ask for anything in return. He was a confident man who liked to tease and play games. Yet, with all of that, he held so much kindness and selflessness within him. I was unsure what it was about him that made me feel so out of control and yet completely safe at the same time. I may have been resistant at first, but slowly we had found ourselves in this place.

Which meant he was worth giving my trust to.

The thought was an unprecedented one for me, but my heart and soul settled, the guilty tension easing the moment I accepted it. He did deserve it, he had earned it, and I would cherish it for the gift it was.

My gut was telling me this was the right thing to do. Trusting my instincts, I pushed forward.

"I want to tell you." I looked up, my words full of determination, my heart still beating steady at the declaration.

"Are you sure?" He asked, his voice soft and soothing, beckoning me with its comfort.

I nodded, taking one final breath before I began. "It all started about a year ago, on the night of a full moon..."

Chapter Forty

My pace slowed, my soft silver fur rustling in the wind as I finally came to a stop after my race with Logan. It was an odd tradition we had started when I became his Beta, one we always did. I leaned back on my hind legs, my neck craning to look up at the full moon, basking under the protection of its glow.

"You are such a cheat," Logan teased me before he rounded the corner, coming into my view, his silver-and-brown fur windswept.

"You're just bitter I won again." I knocked my muzzle against his neck, pushing him slightly.

His laughter filled my mind. "You tripped me!"

"You got in the way!" I laughed back, rushing to tackle him; but he evaded, sidestepping to the left. "Let's get back to camp, I could use another ale."

He nodded, and I trotted behind the giant oak where I had stashed my clothing before transforming. I shifted, feeling the pull and twist of my limbs melding into their second form, just as true as the first, just as much a part of who I was deep to my core. My fur shrank toward me before smoothing out to reveal my creamy, pale skin, my spine straightening until I was standing upright, the only sign that I had just been a wolf the thin layer of sweat from my run and the tingling that came with my glowing yellow irises.

I rolled my shoulders a few times, adjusting before picking my undergarments up, pulling them on to cover the most intimate parts of myself.

Behind me, leaves crinkled. I jerked around to find Logan rounding the tree, eyes glimmering roguishly in the moonlight, his half-smirk plastered on his lips.

"What do you think you're doing?" I punched him in the shoulder, rolling my eyes. "I'm still getting dressed, you degenerate."

He always liked to laugh when I got heated, especially during the full moons; this was just him playing a trick on me, trying to get a rise so I would tackle or mock-fight with him.

But he didn't move, he just stared at me, his form hulking over mine as he took a few steps forward. The skin on the back of my neck prickled as I looked down. "Did you misplace your clothes or something?"

I had seen him naked before—it was a hazard when you were born a Varg Anwyn—but this was different. He didn't seem in any rush to put his clothes on, let alone feel any shame to be standing there. My stomach churned, the smell of...arousal mixing with the complex scents of the forest. I dared not to look further down, I didn't want to confirm what I already knew.

I took a few steps back, but he matched them with longer strides, his body pushing mine against the tree, my exposed back scratching against the rough wood as he pressed us together.

"Where you going, Kas?" he whispered against my cheek.

"Back to the camp?" I didn't know why I asked it like a question or why I just stood there, the heat of his body pressed against mine, and...other parts of him. "Can you get off me, please?"

"You're so beautiful, Kasha."

"Logan, please, just stop." I wiggled around a bit, trying to get my arms in between us, but it was no use.

"Why?" His lips brushed against me, his left hand skimming up my body, disgust running along with each graze of him. I was in shock, in utter disbelief—that was the only way I could comprehend my stillness, my utter lack of action. Why wasn't I moving?

"I don't want this." I shook my head, hoping he would see how badly I just wanted him to step away, to feel the cool air between us so I could finally breathe again.

"That can't be true," he chuckled. "You flirt with me all the time."

"No." I shook my head more vigorously, my voice weak, heart pounding in my ears. I had no idea what he was talking about. Yes, I teased him and messed around with him, but it was never anything sexual or romantic. It was the same way I treated the other members of the Hierarchy. It was how I treated Ollie and Caleb. What could I have done recently to make him think that this was alright?

My skin was crawling, my insides twisted. Nothing about this was alright.

Finally, something snapped me back to attention and I pushed against him, my pinned arms working against his strength to free me. And I almost did.

His hand took hold of my throat and forced me back against the tree, pinning me there. His grip flexed, my airways constricting a bit. "Shh, don't talk or make a noise. To anybody."

It was a command from my Alpha. I wouldn't be able to fight it; no matter how hard my mind wanted it, my wolf would obey. I was officially cut off from everyone, out loud or mentally, my communication gone. The words and screams that I was desperate to release sat in my mind, but only silence surrounded me in my isolation.

It was just me and Logan.

"It's going to be alright, don't worry," he whispered against the base of my throat, his lips burning against my flushed skin.

I knew what was about to happen, and I prayed to Lunestia that I was wrong. But I knew it was a pointless prayer, I knew it...

I wanted to scream into the darkened sky the moment his teeth sank into my skin where my throat met my shoulder, but his Alpha command kept it buried deep in my chest, silent tears running down my face. He didn't draw blood or try and drink from me—no, this was different. This was a Mark, this was a branding. It was what Vargs did with their sexual partners, just before they gave into lust: they bit them where all eyes could see that this one was taken.

It was a primal drive buried into the animalistic parts of us. It's what we did.

He was marking me, trying to claim me as his own. Maybe not forever, but for tonight, this bite mark meant I belonged to him and him alone.

No, this couldn't happen. Not to me, not like this. I wouldn't let it. Even with his claiming me, I did not accept it; I would never accept it.

I did the only thing I knew to: I fought.

I clawed at him, my nails growing into their sharp form, my teeth elongating as I thrashed, trying to bite or kick my way out of his pinning assault. He struggled to keep me in place, releasing his teeth from my tender flesh but keeping his hand firmly grasped around my throat, the pressure tightening as he tried to control me. Tried to use me.

To take me.

"You're so vicious," he growled in my ear, my blood still dripping from his smirking lips. He sounded amused, almost approving of my fight. "Now, stay still."

No...no, no, no, no.... another Alpha command.

I couldn't do anything, I was at his mercy.

I felt my golden eyes flicker away as I retreated within, letting the darkness of what was happening take me.

***

The words left my lips, that part of my story finally out in the open between us. So many emotions tried to assault my body, my stomach threatening to release my breakfast, my mind trying to convince me this was a mistake as seconds of silence continued to pass by. Nolan stared at me, his face twisting in an unreadable way, full of emotions that could either be supportive or disgusted; my nervous mind couldn't read them in the moment.

"I will kill him." Nolan's voice was low and menacing, eyes flashing from bright green to glowing gold. "He doesn't deserve to breathe after what he's done to you."

"You aren't the only one to say that to me," I mumbled, remembering what had happened when I was finally able to escape him, even though it had been too late...

***

328

Just make it back to the townhouses. That's all you need to do, make it back.

I kept repeating that, telling myself that I would be alright if I made it there; it helped me put one step in front of the other. Dirt was sweat-smeared across my face, twigs and underbrush knotted in my long, hip-length hair that he had pulled free sometime during...it.

Bile rose on my throat, my mind unable to say the word. The act. The shame.

The world was a haze around me, the moonlight still beaming down across me. Usually, I would feel strong under it, I would feel like myself, but not now. All I wanted to do was hide from it, I didn't deserve Lunestia's protection, I didn't deserve her love.

I just needed to get inside.

The row of Hierarchy townhomes came into view, a whimper escaping me at the sight. But I didn't go to mine, I went to the only other one where I would feel safe. What if Logan went to mine? What if he tried to find me again?

Salty wetness seeped through the crack in my lips. When had I started to cry?

I couldn't seem to focus. All I could do was pray that Beckett and Liv's door was open.

Thank the Goddess it was.

I rushed inside, not even capable of turning a light on. I hurried to the corner of their common area, a little nook between the wall and the couch the perfect place to huddle as I waited for them to come home.

Or to hide from Logan.

I settled in, pulling my legs to my chest, rocking myself back and forth and I waited.

And I kept waiting...

I didn't know how long passed, hours, minutes, days, until I heard the click of the front door. My body tensed; I should be able to smell who was about to cross the threshold or hear the voices drifting behind the door, but I couldn't. Everything was dulled and gray and lifeless.

"Kasha?" A voice cracked through as the door closed. My heart skipped a beat: it was Beckett.

"Kas?" Liv's lighthearted voice broke through as well. "Where are you?"

I could call out, answer even within our minds, but I didn't. My voice was gone, along with so many other things.

"Kas!" Beckett was the first to find me, I looked up to see him staring down at me, his footsteps bringing him too close.

I cowered as near to the wall as I could, and he hesitated in front of me.

"God, Kasha!" Liv gasped, her hands flying to her mouth. I hadn't seen what I looked like, but I could only imagine with the things caked all over me. "What happened?"

I began rocking again, huddling my head between my knees, my whimpers growing in strength, tightening my chest.

"I can smell Logan on her," Beckett mumbled, and I covered the fresh bite mark bleeding from my neck.

"Futeacha," Liv cursed. "I'm going to rip his throat out with my teeth."

"Stop." Beckett took another step closer before crouching down. "Kas, can you look at me? You don't need to talk, just look at me."

His voice washed over me, the deep, slow words sending calming energy brushing against me. I had come here because

330

Beckett was a physician. He could help me. He could protect me.

My dirt-crusted fingers shook as I finally peeked up. He was almost eye level with me, but still a comfortable distance away.

"Did Logan do this to you?" he whispered. "Just nod yes or no."

The tears free-fell as I slowly moved my head up and down.

His head fell to his chest, eyes closing as he shook it a few times before looking back up to me. "Can I take a look at you? That's why you came here, right? So I could patch you up?"

He was right; he knew me so well. But new voices were starting to whisper in the back of my mind; dark, inky voices telling me Beckett could hurt me too, that trust wasn't worth anything.

I tried my best to ignore them. I tried to fight them, so I nodded yes again.

He reached his hand out to me, and I took it.

"Liv, grab my bag," he whispered, pulling me to my feet. "And make sure there is a sexual assault kit in there."

***

Nolan swiped his fingers through his hair, mussing up his bedhead even more. He let out a deep, ominous breath. "I want to say I'm happy someone took care of you, but that just seems so weak and wrong."

I played with the remnants of my breakfast, tapping a half piece of bacon against my plate. "I understand the sentiment, and I was lucky that even after that, I felt safe to go to Beckett. He made sure to check on me as I healed and helped me figure out my next steps with everything."

"What do you mean?" Nolan's brows crinkled.

"He convinced me to report it, to fight." I swallowed a lump in my throat, bile rising behind it. "But it was a pointless one..."

***

"What do you mean the case has been dismissed?" Beckett growled—he literally growled—at my father, who stood in front of us in Beckett's office.

"Did I stutter, Ar Dtus?" Father glared at him. *"Kasha's accusations against Logan have been dismissed, and he will be reinstated to his post effective tomorrow."*

No, no no no no…

Was this really happening?

"This is disgraceful!" Beckett slammed his fist against his desk. *"The High Faction is supposed to protect its own. We gave you everything necessary to win that trial. Evidence, witnesses, and you're telling me that wasn't enough?"*

"I'm telling you what Cole, our Varg Tribune, has said." Father's face was as hard as stone, not giving away anything. He had always been difficult to read, even to me, but this was different. This wasn't professionalism.

This was hatred. This was disgust. This was disappointment.

And I could feel it directed not at the situation, but at me.

"Futeacha," Beckett swore under his breath, although there was no hiding it.

"Prepare for his return, and make sure he receives a warm welcome." Father straightened the jacket that he never took off. *"He is not to be treated as anything less than the Alpha he is."*

With that, he walked out of the room. I had no idea why I followed.

"Father!" I yelled, chasing after him. *"Father, please! Just look at me!"*

"I can't." He stopped, but didn't turn, his voice rumbling from deep in his chest. *"Not after the disgrace you put our family through."*

"I had to," I whispered, tears once again threatening to escape. I had cried so much over the past three months, ever since that night. I was surprised I still had more to shed.

"No, you didn't," was all he said before he pushed through the door and out of the building.

Somehow, I ended up back in Beckett's office.

"We'll fight back, Kasha, we won't let him win." Beckett leaned me against the edge of his desk.

"No, we won't." Cole was Logan's uncle and the head of the Varg Anwyn branch of the High Faction. I should have known this would happen, but I had been ignorant. I had believed all the pretty lies I had been fed for years—that the High Faction protected. That they believed in justice.

"Kas..."

"No, Beckett, I'm too tired to fight." I shook my head. "I just want to be done with it all."

"If that's what you want." His tone was suspicious, but I couldn't find it in me to care.

I could never seem to find the strength in me to care about most things nowadays.

"Do you have the training files?" I asked, changing the subject. "I need to review the assignments before I pass them on to the recruits."

His face crinkled, his white-blond bangs falling gently into his eyes. "I left them in my office at the infirmary. I'll go grab them for you."

"Thanks." I watched him walk out the door.

The truth was, I didn't care about the files, but I had seen him working on them in the infirmary and I needed him to leave his office. I needed to be alone so I could walk around his desk and take *my lockpicks out, prying open the bottom drawer.*

I reached in, wrapping my hand around the sheathed dagger within. The Ogdala Blade. The one weapon that could hurt me, that could inflict a mortal wound that actually stuck.

I stared at it for a moment before shoving it in my boot and walking out the door.

***

"No wonder you and your father were so distant when he was here a few weeks ago." Nolan's eyes flashed gold once again. "No one should treat their kin like that. He should have supported you."

"Yeah." The word felt completely useless. I wasn't ready to face that skeleton in my closet yet, especially since there was more to the story.

His jaw flexed, hand shaking in a fist on top of the counter. "Why did you take the Blade?"

He was asking, but he was already aware of the physical reason why I took it; so I explained in a different way. "Because I was tired of trying to fight." I rubbed my face, scratching at my knotted hair. "Every day felt consumed with the desperate need to survive, and I just wanted a moment of peace."

His face softened, hands flexing on the countertop. It was clear he wanted to reach out to me, to comfort me with his touch, but didn't know how to react. So I showed him it was welcomed and reached out to him myself, wrapping my fingers with his on top of the counter. His shoulders loosened a bit at the contact, his grip squeezing mine, the subtle movement releasing a bit of the pressure on my chest.

"You asked me once why the secrets of the Faction seem to revolve around me." It was time to give him the whole story, my soul settled knowing the rest of the team would be alright with me saying these truths. "It's because you were right, and it all started because of what happened later that night..."

***

The knife shook in my hand, my body full of nothingness. I couldn't go on, I couldn't face tomorrow. This was the only way.

I had lost everything.

My dignity. My comfort. My strength.

My wolf.

News would soon spread through the Faction, everyone learning about why Logan was suspended. What he did to me. How he got away with it. How I was just a shamed, weak little Brido that didn't deserve the title of Beta.

I just wanted peace. Maybe in Lunestia's arms, forever in the glow of her moonlight, I could find it.

A whisper in the back of my mind was trying to build to a scream, to warn me that Lunestia wouldn't approve of this. She wouldn't want me to give up. She would want me to fight. She would give me the strength to fight.

But I was just so tired.

I put the dagger to my neck, to the place where Logan had held me down and marked me against my will. I lined the shining, sharp edge to my pulse.

And I pulled, ripping it in two.

I didn't know what I was expecting. Pain. Agony. Regret. But none of that came as I settled down on my bed, letting the minutes pass me by.

I felt my heartbeat slow. I felt the warmth of my blood pooling around me and sticking to every inch of me. I wasn't cold. I wasn't warm. I was peaceful as darkness slipped across my vision...

"KASHA!" a voice boomed, trying to pull me back from that darkness.

No, I wouldn't let it.

"What did you do?" I felt pressure against me, but I still couldn't see anything, darkness was still master of my sight. "Kasha, what did you do?"

"I knew something was off. I knew it..." The voice was trying to do something, he must be, because it was tethering me to this place, keeping me here longer, my slipping soul hesitating between this world and the next.

Rustling came, then a sharp intake of breath before I felt something drip onto me.

Onto my lips.

It was blood.

"No..." I croaked, not realizing my voice still worked. I clamped my lips down, rolling my head back and forth to avoid the sweet scent that was dripping across my face.

"Yes, drink, Kas, it's the only way for me to fix the wound." It must be Beckett saying these things. It was the only thing that made even a little sense in the overwhelming peace of darkness.

But I still refused to open my mouth, even for him. If I let him drip blood into my mouth, if I drank, I would heal. I would survive.

I didn't want that.

"Don't let him win, Kas," Beckett whispered in my ear. "He tried to take so much from you, don't give him this, too."

The words somehow made it through the haze of blood loss, through the darkness, silencing the voices that had been encouraging me to do this for so long.

If I did this, Logan would win. He would have taken it all from me. I would be giving up.

336

And I didn't give up.

I fought.

What was happening? I couldn't seem to figure out how I got here, how I had fallen so far. So much of the past three months had been nothing but a thick gray fog that I was lost in. I couldn't find my way out; I had succumbed to it.

But I didn't give up. So why was I giving up now?

I wouldn't let him win, I couldn't. Not if I wanted to go to the Afterlife, to Lunestia, with my whole soul intact. Parts of it were still in this world and I needed to find them. And the only way to do that was to survive.

And to fight.

So, I did the only thing that I could. I clamped my lips around Beckett's soft wrist, and I drank.

And I drank. And I drank. And I drank...

Chapter Forty-One

"So that's why you were in the hospital," Nolan whispered, not as a question but as a fact he already knew.

"The first two weeks were for my body to recover." I scratched my arm. "The other two and a half months I was in the psych ward, mandated by the High Faction. They said if I refused treatment, then there was no way I would be allowed back in the Guard."

"*Futeacha*," Nolan swore, gripping my hand tighter.

"It was the right thing to do," I whispered—and it was the truth. Those months had been torturous, being locked up, but they did help. They gave me a safe space to start my recovery, to at least begin facing what my future would hold.

"Doesn't mean that blackmailing you into it was the right thing to do," he said.

"I suppose." I shook my head. "After my life attempt, and coming back from basically the brink of death, all of the Hierarchy found out what really happened to me."

"Let me guess—they reacted the same way I did."

"Some did. I wasn't there to witness most of it, I was brought right to the hospital after Beckett stabilized me, but they've told me the stories. Beckett threatened Logan and almost slit his throat with the Ogdala Blade the next day...apparently my blood was still on it."

"Good for him," Nolan mumbled, my chest squeezing at his words.

"Liv was the one to pull him off of Logan." I wished I had been there to see that whole moment. "I guess Logan made some kind of crude joke about Liv being the only sane one, so she punched him and kneed him in the groin. Told him the only reason she was saving his life was to save her husband's. If he wouldn't be punished for slitting his throat, Liv would've had no problem watching Logan's blood spill. Or so she says."

"Wow." Nolan's face dropped in awe. "Liv doesn't strike me as the bloodthirsty type."

"She's not."

"So, how did life continue on after that?"

"Logan tried to act like it was completely normal that I was gone after that night," I said, my chest burning with the fury I felt every time I thought about it. "But the rest of the Hierarchy wasn't having it. Taylor and Lucas went on leave, refusing to come back until I was reinstated and Logan was gone. Beckett and Emric left Logan out of as many cases and responsibilities as they could, effectively cutting him off from his title. Eden and Greyson tried their best to refuse as many of his orders as possible, and sometimes he forced them to with an Alpha command. Eden was much more vocal about it, but Greyson searched Logan's office for any shred of evidence that would prove my claims. His own quiet way of being rebellious."

"Goddess, I love those two." Nolan shook his head with a smile.

"They all wanted to fight for me while I was gone, but the problem was, the High Faction stood their ground on Logan's side," I sighed. "They started writing up the Faction, labeling us defiant and belligerent. They threatened to force everyone through the removal, but the Hierarchy wasn't scared to push back. They threatened to spread the truth about everything, how the High Faction didn't even protect one of their own, that they let a rapist go free. The High Faction acted like it didn't bother them, but in the end, no one was fired."

"So, how did the post become available?" Nolan asked.

"Honestly, none of us know whose decision it was in the end, Logan's or the High Faction's." I rubbed my forehead with my free hand. "Two weeks before I was set to be released from the hospital, Logan visited me and told me he was taking an Alpha post in Dalchus."

"He had the nerve to come close to you again?" Nolan growled, his eyes flashing once again.

I nodded. "Acting like it was completely normal that he was coming to say goodbye. He tried to explain his reasons for leaving, but honestly, I don't remember, the whole visit is just a haze by that point."

"What a soulless bastard," Nolan mumbled, and my heart warmed at his words.

"After he left, my father came." Tears pricked my eyes, the memory still fresh as if it only happened yesterday. "He was so cold, just like he had been ever since I brought the investigation

340

to them."

"I'm so sorry, Kasha," he whispered, his hand squeezing mine once again.

"He gave me a choice: either leave the Guard and tell my story, or accept my posting back and sign a non-discloser agreement." Shame washed over me, remembering the day I had made what felt like an impossible decision. It was one of the hardest choices of my life, deciding between owning what had happened to me or going back to the job that had been my dream and purpose for my whole life. "Obviously, you know what I ended up choosing."

I had been so lost when I made that decision, broken and splintered in a way that had felt impossible to come back from. I needed safety and normalcy, and the Guard was always that for me. I needed to go back to a place where I felt strong, and if I had given that up, I would have lost myself completely—most likely attempting suicide again.

Although I cursed the names of those who silenced me, I did not regret the choice I'd made. I had done good in the Guard, and it was my purpose to continue forward. If I left, who would fight for any others the High Faction wished to silence? Who would use their power to fight for change? I couldn't leave that behind.

So, I'd stayed silent in one way, but continue to fight in others; even when I felt broken, I fought for those who might come next.

Nolan wiped his hand over his face, our other hands still link together. "I expected it to be bad, but this...this is deplorable."

"I know."

"Please tell me you don't believe the lies they tried to feed you?" Concern filled his eyes.

"I'm starting not to," I said, and for the first time, I actually believed the words. "I'm trying, at least. Surprisingly, my sessions with Vanessa have been helping. Fighting for others helps. The strength of my friends helps. That includes you now."

His cheeks pinked, his lips twisting up into a warm, handsome smile. "I'm glad I could help."

"I'm still fighting for myself, and most days still feel bad compared to the good." I stared out the window for a moment, a bird perched on the windowsill outside the kitchen. "But at least the good days are coming back. At least I'm starting to accept this new me, no matter how different she is from who I was before. I know she's here to stay, and it's time I welcome her, not force her away."

The words seemed foreign on my tongue—something I had feared I would never be able to admit again. But it felt right. I had grown, even though through the journey it didn't feel like it. I still had miles to go, but it was a start, and that was what mattered most.

"I wish I had something more to say." Nolan rubbed his chin, his foot tapping against the floor. "Anything to show you that I'm fighting for you, too."

"You don't have to say anything." I stood. "Just...thank you."

His brow crinkled as he looked up at me. "For what?"

"For listening." I laid my other hand on his shoulder. "For accepting me for this broken person I've become."

"You aren't broken, Kas," he rose as well, our chests grazing. "And I will spend the rest of my time here helping you remember that."

My heart leapt at his words, my throat tightening. I'd thought Lunestia had abandoned me after that night, but maybe, just maybe, she hadn't. Instead of giving me a direct answer, she had given me exactly what I needed to grow into who I was meant to be—and he was standing right in front of me.

Chapter Forty-Two

"Do you have a moment?"

I looked up from my desk to find Nolan peering around my door. My heart flipped at the sight, still unable to control itself ever since yesterday.

It was a moment that had broken everything between us, removing the last bit of tension that had settled since his arrival. Now, in its place, my heart didn't know how to react whenever he was around me; yet I felt comforted by his presence at the same time. It was a swirl of unknown brewing in my chest, forcing me to try and decipher yet again what my soul was trying to tell me.

It was annoying and thrilling all at once. But mostly annoying.

"Sure." I dropped my stilo, gesturing for him to sit in the chair across from me. He didn't hesitate, closing the door behind him and crossing my office in three quick strides to drop into the chair. "Is something wrong?"

"No, nothing like that." He waved his hand quickly before dropping it back in his lap. "I've just been thinking since yesterday, going over everything, and it helped me come to a decision."

I swallowed a giant lump in my throat, the words almost impossible to get out. "And that is?"

"I want you to know, once the Elliot case is either solved or moved to another Faction, I'll be transferring away from Seathra." His eyes didn't reflect a wicked glint or his lips their usual smirk. He just stared at me in resignation.

He was telling the truth. He was leaving.

My heart dropped, my fingers going numb. My mind lost all ability to create cohesive thoughts, just reciting one sentence: *he's leaving you.*

Not that he was leaving the Faction. Not that he was going away. No, what I couldn't stop thinking was, *he's leaving* you.

After all the barriers we somehow found a way to break through, he was leaving.

"O-okay." I looked down at my lap; I couldn't look at him if I wanted to actually speak. "I...I understand. We haven't made it easy for you, me especially. I'd hoped that the work we've done together over the past few weeks would help show you I'm trying to be better, because you really do deserve this post...that wasn't a lie, and I just want you to realize you didn't deserve..."

I couldn't seem to stop rambling until the warmth of his hand gripped mine on top of the desk. I froze at the touch.

"Kasha." His voice was soft and calm, urging me to look back up at him. "I'm leaving so the post will open and I can recommend you for the job."

My eyes widened, my mouth falling open but unable to take

345

in a breath as I processed exactly what he was saying.

He was leaving, not because he wanted to get away—but so he could give me the Faction back.

Why didn't I feel elated? Why wasn't I jumping out of my seat to thank him, even hugging him? Why was this pressure settling in my chest and throat making me feel like I would cry?

The answer was obvious, yet a part of me tried desperately to ignore it. I didn't want to believe it, but there was no denying the truth: I didn't want him to go.

He stared at me, his gorgeous green eyes searching for something, for any reaction to the kindest, most selfless words a man had ever spoken to me. I wanted to give it to him, but I couldn't seem to muster up even fake enthusiasm. Because that meant I would be celebrating his departure, and the weight of that truth was crushing my heart and soul in a way I never thought I would feel again.

This wasn't just attraction. It wasn't just physical, I couldn't deny it any longer. My heart was called to him in a way I had dreamed about as a child and in recent months believed I would never experience for myself. He was an odd culmination of traits—one moment a confident, teasing trickster and the next selfless, helping me any way he could. He could rip my throat out if wanted to, but instead he comforted me with a gentle touch that set my body aflame.

He was a dichotomy even my investigative mind still couldn't figure out, and I was drawn to it, desperate to be around him and learn more. To feel his strength and kindness and to talk to him for hours about complex topics or benign ideas. He was everything I had ever wanted and didn't realize I needed all in one.

346

I didn't deserve him.

So I knew what I had to do to show him how much I cared about him, how much my heart called out to him, even if I didn't deserve to be with him.

I perked myself up slightly, turning my hand over to wrap our fingers together. "I'm sorry, I think I'm in shock," I shook my head, dragging up my lips. "I didn't expect this to happen. Ever."

A sweet, lopsided smile grew on his face. "Looks like I accomplished my goal, then."

My brows furrowed. "Excuse me?"

"I made you smile." He winked, a sliver of laughter escaping him at his own stupid joke.

I flopped back in my chair, biting my lip to conceal a laugh. "You're so weird."

"We both deserve this job, Kas." His voice lowered back to its serious, honest tone. "It's not fair you were passed over for the actions of others. If anything, it should have shown the High Faction that you deserve the posting. No one has fought harder for it than you, no one has proven their strength more than you have. I need to stay to put Elliot behind bars if we can—I wouldn't feel settled if I didn't. But after that, I want to step aside, let you take the place you've earned."

No words could describe the swirl that brewed in my chest, how much gratitude I had for this man—so I did something else instead. I walked around the desk, my feet heavy as I approached him. I didn't think, pulling him to his feet and wrapping my arms around his torso. His arms didn't hesitate to embrace me back, the light pressure of his cheek resting on my forehead comforting me even more.

"Thank you," I mumbled into his shirt, the smooth cotton

347

brushing against me.

"You're welcome," he whispered into my hair, stroking the back of my head.

I didn't know how long we stayed like that, how long we embraced and relished in each other's warmth. It was a moment I wished I could freeze in time, a place I could always go back to once he was gone. It was a memory, along with many others, I would cherish forever.

"I should let you get back to work." He pulled away, hands warm on my shoulders as he looked down at me. "The sooner we solve this case, the sooner you get your job back."

I let out a stream of forced laughter, trying to make it sound as light as possible. "Seriously, Nolan, thank you. Not just for this, but for everything."

"For you? Of course." He gave me one more wink before walking away and closing the door. My body fell against my desk, perching on the side as I stared blankly at the wall.

So much had happened to me over the past year, and I was finally starting to understand the emotions and the repression all of it had caused, and face who I was forced to adapt into. But somehow, in that moment, in Nolan's selfless act, he showed me that it wasn't each individual emotion I was repressing that made me struggle the most, but a truth that encompassed all of them together.

I just wanted to feel whole again, that was what I had been unable to decipher for so long. It was an impossible reality to face. Yet, this entire time, I couldn't seem to accept that just because I had changed, that didn't mean I was less of a person or less than whole, even if it didn't feel that way all the time.

And there it was, the final tangled piece I hadn't been able to figure out.

I stared at the door for Goddess-knew how long. A deep, rumbling pressure tore at my insides, desperate to escape, to be set free for the first time in over a year. A renewed strength coursed through my veins and muscles, a light buzzing tingling across my arms and torso, snaking upward to ignite my cheeks and brighten my eyes into their sharpened, golden hue.

This was it; it was the moment to finally try and transform, to let my wolf run free once more. I had accepted the truth about myself and set it free. I had removed the chains from that part of myself, and it was ready to express its gratitude.

And I was ready—I was itching to let it free. I could run to the woods right now and feel my limbs crack into place, the tufts of my fur growing across my body, the crunching of freshly fallen leaves under my paws as I dashed through the forest, the entire space surrounding me in a cocoon of comfort and peace.

It all sounded perfect.

But I hesitated; there was an even better time to let it out. A better moment to reclaim who I was. I just couldn't face it alone.

I picked up my Comms from the side of my desk, dialing a familiar name.

"Hey, little shadow, to what do I owe the pleasure of your call?" Ollie teased, his typical goofy grin plastered on his lips through the screen.

I let out a shaky breath, tapping a finger against the side of my unit. "I need a favor."

Chapter Forty-Three

The moonlight welcomed me as I trudged through the woods the next night, my heart beating erratically with every step closer to my destination: The Full Moon Camp.

For the first time in over a year, I returned. Not only would I be reclaiming my wolf form, but I would be reclaiming an event that I used to love every month. I'd no longer let Logan's choices ruin mine. This was a place I used to let go and relish in my freedom, and tonight I would face my fear and take back what was stolen.

I stopped short of the clearing, my breath hitching at the sight of it all. The burning embers of the small fire pits, the clinking of bottles as people passed around ales and different drinks to imbibe in, and the whistling of the wind crinkling in the leaves and branches above us overwhelmed my heightened senses.

Everything about it was familiar, riddled with years of

wonderful memories. But that didn't seem to matter as the dark part of my mind reminded me what had happened last time.

"It's going to be alright," Ollie's low, soothing voice whispered in my ear. His hand rested on my lower back, rubbing a gentle circle, releasing some of the tension. Thank the Goddess he was able to come with me, to lend me some of his strength. I was going to need it, especially if the night didn't go as planned. "You have as much right to be here as everyone else."

I let his words repeat in my mind. I deserved to be here; nothing about my past made me any less worthy.

My past does not define me. I am stronger than my past.

With a few more breaths to calm my shaking fingers and nerves, I broke through the trees and into the clearing, taking a few tentative steps into the gathering. Ollie stayed by my side while I looked around, catching a few glances from some of the younger Faction members.

"Kasha!" Eden was the first to spot me, running over and throwing her arms around my neck, crushing me close to her. "I am so happy you're here!"

"Thank you." Her warm, enthusiastic welcome did just a little bit more to help calm some of the fears I had been harboring for too long. She pulled away, a wide smile on her heart-shaped face, eyes stuck in their golden hue most likely for the whole evening.

"Welcome back, Kas," Greyson said from behind Eden, his own golden eyes partially flecked with silver. "It hasn't been the same without you."

"Come on, let's get a drink." Eden linked our arms together, dragging me farther into the throng of people, Ollie and Greyson following behind us.

My stomach clenched. "You know I don't drink."

"I know, that's why I had the youngsters make sure to pack a few bottles of that sparkling lime water you love so much." She leaned down into the barrels packed full of ice and glass bottles, an array of imported ales and other meads chilling and waiting for the Faction to consume.

"How did you know I was coming tonight?"

She shrugged, popping the cap off the clear bottle, bubbles crawling up the side of the glass. "I didn't. We've had them pack it ever since you returned to active duty, just in case you showed up."

"Oh, my Goddess," I shook my head, taking the offered drink from her hand before she popped the caps off a few ales for the rest of them. This little group of people were more of a blessing in my life than they even realized. I never would have found myself back here without them.

Ollie threw his arm over my shoulder, pulling me close to his side and holding his bottle up in between the four of us. "To Kasha's triumphant return!"

"Hear, hear!" Eden yelled before we all clinked out bottles together. The rest chugged back a few swigs while I took a refreshing sip of my own beverage.

The four of us fell into a comfortable conversation, others coming and going over the next hour to welcome me back. Taylor and Lucas made a quick appearance, Taylor picking me up and twirling me around until I laughed and Lucas squeezing me so hard, I almost choked on my own breath. Beckett and Liv eventually joined us, Liv's face flushed and Beckett's hair a haphazard mess with a few leaves stuck in the back, letting us know exactly what they had been doing. We all laughed, Beckett's cheeks turning a bright crimson as if this was the first time we caught them, even though it was a typical occurrence at these things. After a while, my entire body was buzzing, my fingers twitching at my side.

It was time, I knew it.

I looked around, searching for the one person I needed to take this final step.

Finally, I spotted him: Nolan, standing with a handful of Omegas and Fledglings. My heart skipped a beat at the sight, for nothing more than he was close by once again.

I walked up to him, my hand gently brushing against his elbow to get his attention. He turned away from the group, a bright smile on his lips, his golden eyes beautifully contrasted against his bronzed skin glowing in the bright moonlight.

"Welcome back," he whispered, his body lingering near mine.

"Thanks," I smiled back up at him, my stomach doing a few flips. This was the right decision to make. "Can you walk with me for a minute?"

My heart stuttered waiting for his reply.

"Of course." He chugged back the final sips of his ale before throwing it in one of the bins we collected the empty bottles in. He gestured for me to lead the way, my fingers twisting in front of me as I walked to the edge of the camp and ducked into the thicket of trees. He followed silently, not even questioning where I was leading him. I needed to be alone, to make sure it was just the two of us for a while.

I'd realized that to make this work, to make this memory the best it possibly could be, I needed it to be with someone who wasn't there the last time. I did not blame my friends for what happened to me; I never had. But they were inadvertently tangled into the mess of tainted memories. I wanted to create this one in a way that no reminder of the past could ruin it. I needed someone to lean on, to have their strength with me if necessary. There was only one person I knew could be there for me, and that was Nolan.

I stopped about a mile away from the group, their voices and laughter finally dissipating. I couldn't sense anyone else near us, letting me know we were finally alone.

I turned back to him, heat flooding my core at the sight of him basking in the moonlight. Like most of the wolves, he wore minimal clothing, just in case of an overexcited transformation that would lead them to being ripped off. His arms were completely exposed, the tight black tank top conforming to his well-defined torso. A twisted runic-patterned tattoo decorated his left bicep, swirling inward to frame a single word: *Cleo*. It rested right below the Onyx Guard crest tattooed proudly on his shoulder. His loose linen black pants hung low on his hips, a strip of tanned skin peeking out from under his shirt. That was all he wore, his feet bare, eyes glowing a deep shade of gold, his typical wicked grin gracing his lips as he stared at me, his posture relaxed and waiting.

"What?" My eyes darted around, my skin prickling at his intense gaze.

"Nothing," he shrugged taking a few tentative steps forward, "just looking at you."

My cheeks flared with heat. "Stop it."

"Nah, I'm good." He offered his hand to me. I didn't hesitate, reminding myself to follow my desires and drives as I laced my fingers with his, allowing him to tug me forward so we stood only inches apart. "Did you need me for something?"

"Yes," I whispered, tingling with every slight breeze that grazed across my skin. I didn't know why I was suddenly feeling shy, but I averted my gaze to the forest floor. "I...I didn't want to be alone when I tried to transform for the first time."

His body stiffened. "And you chose me to be here?"

I nodded, brewing the courage to look up at him, his eyes searching my face. "I did."

"I'm honored."

"I mean, I want to do it privately, behind a tree...like I normally would..." My words stumbled over themselves, my whole body flashing with heat at the idea of being naked in front of Nolan. "I just...I don't want..."

"Kas, I get it." His thumb rubbed a small circle on the back of my hand. "I'm gonna go over here," he gestured to a large oak behind him, "just take your time. Listen to yourself and for Lunestia's calling. We're in no rush tonight, but I'm here. Alright?"

"Alright." I sighed, letting the cool air tamper down the fever growing inside me. He gave my hand one final squeeze before pulling away and disappearing from sight.

I walked around behind one of the other trees, my fingers shaking as I unlaced the front ties of my midnight-blue shirt. I couldn't bring myself to dress down tonight—that would have been too far for my comfort. Once the laces up top were loosened enough, I pulled the half-sleeved shirt over my head, the cool air sending ripples of gooseflesh crawling up my chest and stomach. I bent down, making quick work of my boots and kicking them off, shoving my socks inside them. My fingers shook when I reached for the laces of my pants, but I found the strength to shed them from my body. With one final uneven breath, I removed my undergarments, my entire self now exposed to the night breeze and the calming glow of the moon above.

It was natural, thank the Goddess. It was right and normal; like this was exactly where I needed to be in that very moment. I eased my body back against the tree, looking up into the moon above; my eyes instantly glowed at the sight, the whispers of Lunestia calling me forward.

The first trigger came naturally. All I needed to do was take the final step.

I evened my breathing out, my bare back resting against the scratchy bark, toes digging into the soft dirt below. I breathed and I breathed and I breathed...but I didn't feel anything. No stirring, no transformation. Nothing.

Rustling came from behind me, the light tapping of paws against the underbrush inching closer. Nolan must have finished transforming already; my heart pressed against my chest tightly, my murky thoughts trying to convince me this was a failure. I dug my fingers into the tree, looking up at the moon, to Lunestia, for any guidance.

"Just breathe, Kasha," Nolan's voice drifted into my thoughts. *"Don't overthink it, just feel it."*

I closed my eyes, taking his words as the guidance I had been praying for. I let myself feel it all—the sensory assault of the forest around me and the swirling of emotions deep inside. I didn't repress them, I accepted them, just as I had been doing for the past few weeks. I let myself know this is who I was now. This is who I had become and that was okay.

Maybe, just maybe, this was exactly who I was meant to be.

A burst of energy exploded in my core seconds before my arms and legs cracked into new places. I howled, the noise

356

ripping through the open air as my limbs morphed downward, my body falling forward onto hands and knees. My back arched, skin on fire, but in the best way possible. My fingers shrank down toward my palms, tufts of silvery gray fur growing quickly from the creamy flesh until it had completely taken over. Moments passed, my body snapping and popping, and before I knew it, calm washed over me.

I panted, my tongue hanging out of my muzzle as I stared at the ground, at my front paws shaking, but still holding me up.

I did it. I transformed.

My wolf was back.

I let out another howl, a bright burst of triumph singing through the air for everyone to hear. Echoes of other howls joined me, celebrating with me, welcoming me back.

"Congratulations," Nolan said, his voice laced with awe and pride even within our minds.

After a few more moments alone, I emerged, my paws padding against the earth, an extra bounce in my step. My gaze came up, stopping short as I fell back on my haunches to look at Nolan.

This was the first time I was seeing him in his full wolf form, and it absolutely took my breath away. Just like in our human form, he towered over me, a vision of dark black fur with speckles of white peppered throughout. His muscles flexed, ready to blow off steam as his front paws clawed at the soft earth below. His eyes grazed over me, taking in every inch of my wolf.

We sat there for a few moments, not talking or playing or moving, just staring. I didn't know what he was thinking as he took in this other side of me, but I didn't care; I relished finally being able to show him all of me.

My body buzzed, the current running along my skin and pulsing in a way I hadn't felt in a long time. I needed to move, wanted desperately to feel the rush of strength and power that I had missed; I craved it. I lifted off my haunches, taking a few trots forward until my nose gently touched Nolan's, his eyes widening.

"I'll race you." I nudged him with my muzzle before taking off into the trees.

"You little tease," he laughed, not missing a stride as he rushed after me, his long gait catching up to me quickly. I pushed harder, the muscles in my rear legs screaming at the power and aching for more as I picked up speed, determined to win.

A part of me feared that this would trigger something, since I used to race with Logan; but in that moment, I chose to let my happy, free thoughts take control. I chose to let myself feel and enjoy. I was taking power back from the man who tried to steal it from me a year ago. It wasn't his to own, it was mine, and I would enjoy every moment of this night despite his efforts to ruin me.

He hadn't ruined me, and he never would.

"First back to the starting point wins," I baited Nolan, circling around toward our final destination.

"You're on," he chuckled, never losing stride as we set our sights on the course ahead, our feet pounding the earth, echoing around us.

My chest tightened with each labored breath. I didn't let it slow me down, pushing myself further and further, bringing myself to the brink of my strength, feeling that power course through my muscles. We were neck and neck, each of us determined to get there first. Laughter bubbled in my chest, the freeing tingle speckled all along my long body.

The area was only about fifty yards away when something

slammed into my side—Nolan's broad shoulder banging into me. I stumbled only for a moment before I righted myself and pushed back on the course.

"Cheater!" I squealed, but it was too late; he had the edge, pulling himself forward to clear the finish line first.

Oh, if he thought he could get away with that, he was sorely mistaken.

I didn't even hesitate as I came to the clearing he'd stopped in, leaping through the air and landing on top of him, the two of us tumbling across the forest floor, our laughter filling our minds. We finally stopped, my back against the warm earth, my four legs bent toward my chest as I stared up at him; Nolan stood over me, staring at me with a fire in his gaze, his chest heaving, mouth slightly open.

My legs were shaky and muscles on fire from most likely pushing too hard in the race. I could have convinced myself that's why I didn't move, but it would have been a lie. I let myself stay there, basking in the moment we had found ourselves in, a desire pooling within me, burning and begging to be released.

Goddess, I didn't want him to leave.

Maybe...maybe he didn't have to...

I barely had time to process that shocking thought before howls filled the air, drifting to us. Taylor and Lucas's were instantly recognizable, their concerned warbles shattering the moment. They were calling everyone back, the deep low resonance of their outcry letting us know something was wrong.

My gaze caught Nolan's for a moment before we rushed back to where we'd ditched our clothes, transforming back into our human forms and dressing privately before returning to the camp together.

Pandemonium had erupted, people putting out the fires while others collect the food and drinks, shoving them haphazardly into packs and boxes.

"What's going on?" I asked as we approached the cluster of Hierarchy members off to the side, Ollie among them.

Beckett turned to us, his face grim. "Another body has been found."

Chapter Forty-Four

We kept the group as small as possible, only the Keturi members quickly changing into our full Guard uniforms before racing on our lectracycles to the crime scene. The rest of the team stayed behind; Ollie even offered to help with clean up before heading back to his own Faction for the night. All our Gammas and Treasus began preparing for another body to be brought to compound along with any preliminary setup for the additional case.

The tension was palpable between all of us as we whizzed through the streets, our bikes picking up speed. Something was off tonight...maybe it was the full moon or my instincts and body still abuzz from my first shift in a year, but I couldn't help but feel uncomfortable at the tiny pinpricks crawling along every inch of my body.

Part of it was certainly how quickly Elliot was killing, which just seemed off with his patterns. Everything about his time here in Seathra was slowly slipping from his normal, and for someone who thrived on details, it made my insides crawl. He was making moves quickly and erratically, yet with plenty of expertise to not give anything away before he wanted to. He was in control of this whole situation, and if we didn't hurry, he would win.

I would not let him win. I would bring him down if it was the last thing I did.

We rounded through the empty streets and crossed the threshold into the town of Trudid. Our bikes were most likely waking up plenty of people so late at night, but there was no way around it. We were needed, we had a case, and nothing would keep us away.

We made it to the residence where the body was found, the typical local guard and spectators milling in and out of the front door. The lieutenant in charge brought us through, giving us all the details: twenty-something Varg Anwyn female, found by her human husband after he had reported her missing three days ago. She had been completely drained of blood and drenched in wolfsbane before being brought back to her house and laid out on her bed, Elliot's crest found branded on her neck. It all sounded fairly straightforward—as straightforward as one of these mind-bending cases could be.

But when we got to the body, it was clear this was nothing like before.

This young lady had been handled with extreme care. Her body was peacefully resting on the bed, hands gently folded on her sternum, neck propped lovingly with a pillow, wearing a new lace-and-silk black nightgown. Her curly red hair was brushed and gently laid out around her like a halo. It was once again a perfect crime scene, the wolfsbane burning my nostrils and making me want to gag, but I was able to tamper down the urge.

"What is he doing?" Emric mumbled as he took another step into the room, rounding the bed so we could all get a good look.

"No idea." Beckett shook his head, a fang biting gently at his lower lip. I took in my fill, scanning the body for something, anything we could use.

That's when I finally saw what was setting this victim above the rest.

She had a fresh laceration, the only wound besides the bite marks on her wrists. Typically, it wouldn't bother me, but today it did—because the thin mark was just above her right shoulder, running about four inches long, a perfect slash to the carotid artery.

It looked eerily similar to my scar. Not just similar...almost identical.

Panic clawed at my throat, but I held onto the strength my shift had given me only hours before; although my anxieties were valid, they did not control me. Beckett, as always, moved to the body first, examining it with his physician eyes; I took the opportunity to tug on Nolan's arm, gesturing for us to talk out of earshot. He shot me a confused look, eyebrows scrunching, before shrugging and following me to the adjoining room.

"What's wrong?" His deep voice was filled with concern, probably still partially on alert since my reaction at the last crime scene.

"You'll tell me if I'm crazy, right?" I held his gaze to show him just how serious my question was.

He narrowed his eyes. "Of course."

"Then, please, tell me I'm crazy when I say that the marking on the body looks like my scar." I pulled down the collar of my

363

undershirt, exposing as much of the long, pale, thin line as possible before it disappeared under my chest plate. I had been so relieved when I had put the uniform on for the first time after the attempt, seeing that the combination of the underclothes and armor kept the entire mark covered. At least when I was out on professional matters, people didn't have the opportunity to balk or question or give me wayward glances over my own weaknesses.

But at that moment, I couldn't be afraid to show it. My mind was spinning, going to the worst possible idea: that somehow, Elliot was trying to connect me to these victims.

I hadn't noticed it at first, but after the brutal murder of the Logan lookalike, and now this, I couldn't let the thought slip away. But Nolan would tell me right to my face that I was being too self-absorbed or paranoid; he would tell me the truth, put this stupid idea to rest, and then we could go off and do our jobs properly.

Yet, the silence continued to stretch between us as he stared at my scar, his eyes flicking between it and the room holding the body. His face paled, his lips pressing into a thin line.

My stomach dropped out. "Nolan? Tell me I'm crazy."

"I can't." He reached out to push my collar back in place, hiding my scar. "You're right, they look identical."

"Oh, Goddess." I covered my mouth, muffling my labored breathes. Why was this happening? Why me, of all people?

"It'll be alright," he soothed, his warm hand resting heavy on my shoulder. "It will all be alright, you know we'll never let anything happen to you."

I nodded, looking down at the ground as I got my breathing under control.

"Do you think all of them are connected to you?" His voice

stayed calm in that serene way I remembered him talking to Lea. The warmth and caring laced within it helped my nerves just enough to focus on the question and contemplate an answer.

"I'd have to go over them again," I said, trying to think about the first two victims, but my mind was too murky to remember any details that stood out. "But the last one, yes. He looked like Logan."

Nolan's posture stiffened. "Right." His jaw tensed, eyes closing for a moment before opening back up to look down at me. "By the way I came to learn about it, I would have to guess that was very...privileged information about your past."

"Yes." My voice shook over the word. "But I did file reports, so those closer to the High Faction could have found out. Or from a rumor I was unaware of."

"Alright." He nodded, his face twisting in thought. "Still, I know it's hard to hear, but he's trying to get your attention."

"Now we need to figure out what kind of attention he wants."

"Kas, I'll understand if you need to take a step back from this." He looked me straight in the eye, holding my gaze so I could see how sincere he was. If this was too much, I could back down, act more as a witness than an investigator. A small, nagging voice told me to let the others handle it so I didn't risk hurting myself even more.

But I couldn't listen to it. I was the Beta of this Faction. Elliot was terrorizing not only me, but my territory, and I would not back down.

Chapter Forty-Five

Somehow, I made it through the rest of our time at the crime scene.

Nolan had tried to convince me to search in other areas of the house or head back to the Compound while they finished up, but I couldn't bring myself to leave. I wasn't sure if Elliot had chosen this woman to kill purely to get my attention, or if the attention-grabbing was just an addition to his disgusting plans; but somehow, I was involved, and I would not let him get away with it. I would not let him get the best of me and watch me cower from his breed of evil. I would face it head on.

By the time we made it back to the Compound, the full moon was setting, the sun attempting to break through the horizon, bursting with deep lavender and orange skies. We were all exhausted, barely able to keep our eyes open, but we didn't have time to sleep. We needed to work, to solve.

The entire Hierarchy sat around the conference table,

myself at the head while their bleary, exhausted faces looked up at me, listening to my theory. Even with Nolan telling me at the crime scene that he thought the idea had merit, I still hoped someone would tell me I was crazy, that there was no way this was possible.

But they just stared at me, wide-eyed, mouths gaping. Beckett and Emric confirmed my suspicions, backing Nolan up; they saw the same perfect resemblance that we did, bringing this whole mind-bending idea to truth: somehow, Elliot was trying to connect me to these cases.

"Alright, let's break this down." Nolan sat to my right, his chair a little closer than the rest, but I didn't mind. I liked the proximity, it helped keep my mind rooted in the now; and his questions were keeping me sane. "First victim wasn't on your radar yet when he killed her, so how do you think the second victim was linked to you?"

My eyes drifted over to the case board, reminding myself about the first victim I had laid eyes on, her past, and the crime scene. What about it could have been linked to me?

"The hair." I squinted at the question on the board, asking why Elliot had modified her that way. "Her hair was cut and dyed to look like mine."

"By the Goddess, how did we not notice that before?" Liv seethed, her fist pounding gently against the table.

"Why would we? It's not like my hair is uncommon or odd, plenty of people have hair like mine."

Liv mumbled under her breath, the scowl on her face making my stomach do flips.

"Alright, alright." Beckett slung his arm behind Liv's chair, rubbing gentle circles along her back. "Third victim?"

I stared at the board, shaking my head. "I don't know. I was so busy making sure Lea was alright, I didn't pick up anything too odd about it."

I turned back to my Faction, all of them looking as stumped as me—except one, who couldn't seem to make eye contact.

"Eden?" I glared at her, her hands twisting together on top of the table. "What are you hiding?"

"Nothing." She shook her head.

"Eden," I snarled. We didn't have time for her silence—we didn't have time for games.

She sighed, shaking her head. "It really could be a coincidence..."

"Tell us anyway."

"The third victim," she couldn't seem to look up, "the one you weren't able to join us for, at the crime scene. I did the background check on him. He was the oldest of three, with a younger brother and a younger sister."

And there it was—the link to me.

"Fourth was the Logan victim." A shiver ran up my spine at the casual mention of his name, forcing myself to swallow down the bile crawling up my throat.

"Now we know what the R must have stood for," Nolan mumbled. I squinted at him for a moment, his gaze catching mine as if to tell me the answer was obvious.

Then it hit me: *Rapist.*

"In the name of the Goddess, how did he know?" My body ached, my mind spinning. All of this was just too unbelievable. "Why me? Most of the details are common knowledge, like my scar and hair. But everything with Logan and Caleb? I keep that a secret. How could he have known?"

My chest was beginning to hollow, the darkness creeping into my mind telling me this was hopeless, to give up. I tried to ignore the notion, to fight it.

"Think, Kas," Nolan urged, leaning forward. "You're a puzzle master. Think about who could know these details. Who had the opportunity to learn them either from you, from others, or from overhearing it somewhere? Think about the past few months. Who could have heard?"

I let his words run through me, using them as a weapon against the sinister thoughts. I rubbed my temples with my fingers, staring down at the dark wooden table in front of me.

I just had to *think*.

I thought about everyone who I'd told all of these details to, but unfortunately, most sat in this room. Ollie, Lea and Nana were the only others who knew about me hating my natural hair color; Caleb and Father couldn't have been bothered by that, and we never had a decent enough conversation for something so trivial to come up. Possibly, someone could have overheard some things in public, like the hair or my problems with Caleb, but no one would have known anything about Logan's attack.

Who was it? Who else had I been talking to?

Talking to...

Icy chills ran through my veins as something clicked, something that made me want to throw up and pass out all at once. There was only one person who I had been talking in detail with, who knew my innermost thoughts and had helped me open myself up. One person who just always seemed perfect...too perfect.

"Vanessa," I whispered, my fingers shaking as I rubbed them across my face. Everyone froze at the one name, the one suspect that I was bringing forward.

"Your psycho-physician?" Lucas asked, leaning forward on my left side.

I nodded, looking up at the dazed faces surrounding me. "It's the only explanation."

"Haven't you been going to her for a while?" Nolan asked, his brow creased. "It wouldn't match up with Elliot's timeline."

"No, Vanessa and I only started talking about a month ago now...it matches perfectly." I shook my head. "Plus, she was here in Seathra for a good two months before she started taking patients. It would give her enough time to get that first kill in before I saw her."

"But she was assigned by the High Faction, I thought," Beckett said carefully. "It might not be her."

"Maybe she's a part of his Clan," I pointed out. "There's no one else who would have had access to these details, told or untold."

"Untold?" Eden questioned.

"We haven't gotten too into Logan and who he was," I said, my fingers tapping against the table. "But I had with my last psycho-physician, and like an idiot, I signed a release form allowing Vanessa to take a look at my last physician's notes and treatment plans."

I dropped my head forward, banging my forehead lightly on the table. How could I have been so stupid—trusting a complete stranger with all of those detailed, intimate parts of my life they hadn't earned? My chest was burning, tearing at me from the inside, a growl rising in my throat, but I forced it down. I was happy my wolf was back, but this was not the time to let her free.

"You're not an idiot," Emric said. "You trusted the

recommendation of the High Faction and your last psycho-physician, anyone would have done the same."

"All of these ideas are circumstantial, Kas," Beckett said warily. "Without something to bring us doubt, we can't search her office, arrest her, even set up some kind of sting without more solid evidence to imply motive or opportunity."

My shoulders perked up. "What if a patient stumbled across something suspicious? Would that witness be enough?"

"No." Taylor was the first to speak, his blue eyes flashing with worry. "You aren't going back there."

"I am," I said, leaning back in my chair, spine straightening. "First off, if I'm right, it will look suspicious if I stop going to my High-Faction-mandated counseling. We can't risk that. Second, Vanessa willingly invites me into her space. I can figure out a way to get her to leave the office for a while so I can search it."

"What makes you think she keeps anything in there?" Taylor asked. "Why not at home?"

"The area she works in has a lot of security," I said. "If she was trying to hide something, it would be safest there."

"Anything you find in there without a warrant would be evidence most likely dismissed in court," Greyson pointed out. "You would compromise it by searching without a warrant."

"But if I find something and give a witness statement, it should give us enough tangible doubt to get permission for a sting operation," I urged, filling my words with equal amounts logic and passion to drive the point home. They needed to listen; they needed to see this was the only way. "If we can do that, I can go into a session bugged and get her to admit to something that gives us cause to arrest her."

Silence fell again, a mixture of tense emotions filling the

space between us all. This was the right move, the only move at this point. We had gotten nowhere, but Elliot had finally shown his weakness—and it was me. We couldn't let this opportunity get away from us, it was our only lead and we needed to see it through. This was the perfect way to do that.

By the wandering gazes, I knew I wasn't the only one to think so, even if others weren't ready to say it out loud.

"I say we vote." I looked around the room. "Keturi vote first. Beckett?"

He looked at me from across the table, his onyx eyes swirling with pain. "I'm sorry, Kas, I can't send you into a risky situation without more tangible evidence. I vote no."

My heart fell, my jaw tensing.

Beckett's concern came from a place of love, and in some ways even trauma. He had been the one to find my almost-lifeless body bleeding to death, he had been the one to feed me and stabilize me so I could survive. He had every right to want to keep me as safe as possible, to keep me away from the person who was apparently calling me out.

Still, it stung. But I didn't have time to think about it.

"Emric?" I turned to him, praying to Lunestia he was on my side.

His face was stern, lips in a thin line. "I'm sorry, no."

Damnit, Emric. I wanted to question him, but I didn't think my quivering heart could take it.

One last chance. All of my hopes rested on the man who I thought I despised, yet came to adore and admire. Would he try to keep me safe, or would he trust in my strength? Only one way to find out.

"Nolan?"

Nolan looked at me, his gaze hot. "Are you sure about this?"

"Yes." My voice didn't waver, my breathing even. I held his gaze, showing him just how much I believed in this, how deeply I knew this was the right move.

He sat silently for a few more seconds before turning back to the group. "I vote yes."

I sighed in relief. "You all know my vote, so someone grab the cards."

When the Keturi was at a standstill with a vote, a random name was chosen from the seconds and their vote was the deciding one. I knew some of them agreed with me, but even so, they might side with their Keturi member out of obligation or dedication. I just had to have hope that my gut was telling me the right thing—that this was the right move and we would make it happen.

Eden grabbed the stack from one of the cabinets in the room, the black cards plain on one side and each second's name scrawled on the other. She shuffled it a few times before placing it face down in the center of the table and fanning the cards out.

Since I was the one who called the vote, I was the one to pull the card. I took a deep breath, standing up to lean forward and pick one a few spots from the left. I flipped it over, revealing who would break the tie.

Alivia.

My heart sank. Liv might be my best friend, but she was Beckett's wife. She trusted him in everything, and she knew the pain he went through when he saved me.

It was over.

Her gaze shifted between Beckett and me before she sat up straight, looking into the group. "I vote yes."

373

I almost fell out of my chair.

I had won. I would be going back to Vanessa to search her office, to find proof she had betrayed me. I had trusted my instincts, and Lunestia had blessed me for it.

"Livie," Beckett breathed, his brown eyes full of the sting of betrayal. "Why?"

"I trust you, Beck, and I know you're just trying to protect her." She looked over to me. "But she made logical points, and we need to believe in her strength. We keep telling her she still has it, and we need to show her that we have faith in our own words."

Beckett looked away, his expression pensive as he fell slack into his chair, shoulders drawing in. I would talk to him later, I would help him to see that this was the right decision, making sure he was at least partially comfortable with me going in there.

"Your plan will go forward," Nolan said, turning to me. "But just because you'll be going in there, doesn't mean you're going in without backup."

"What do you mean?" My muscles tightened.

"I'm going with you."

Chapter Forty-Six

It took most of my strength to keep my fingers from shaking as I walked through the long halls of the clinic to Vanessa's office.

No matter how many times I went over my theory in my head, trying to come up with any other suspect to take her place, I came up empty. All I could do was hope and pray that I wouldn't find anything today.

"It's going to be alright," Nolan whispered, keeping pace with me as we wound through the halls. He reached over, grabbing my hand and giving it a tight squeeze, the pressure helping to slow my racing heart.

"I know." But still, my mind wouldn't stop. It retraced every moment with Vanessa, looking for any shred of doubt that my theory was wrong.

"Just stick to our plan," Nolan leaned in as we walked up the final set of stairs, stopping just outside the waiting room door, "and it will all work out the way it's supposed to."

I gave his hand a squeeze back, nodding before I pulled away and pushed the door open, finding the waiting room empty as usual. We both sat, letting the silence fall between us as I counted down the seconds until my appointment would begin.

A little too soon, Vanessa came out, the picture of perfection as always. Her hair was secured in a twisted ponytail at the base of her neck, layered in soft curls today. Her tan slacks were tailored to sit right above her hips before flowing down to her ankles, a pair of matching beige heels complimented by a silk button-up sky-blue-and-pastel-pink striped blouse.

It took every bit of my strength to keep my shoulders from tensing, to restrain myself from yelling at the mere sight of the prospective betrayer.

I reined it in and swallowed it down. I was a soldier, a fighter, and I would not let my emotions get the best of me.

"Oh," Vanessa stopped in her tracks, her eyes wide as she stared at Nolan. "I see you brought a friend today."

"Vanessa, this is Nolan." I gestured to him, a sly smile spreading on Vanessa's lips. "He's just going to wait out here for me, if he's allowed."

"Oh, of course." She looked between us. "Is everything alright?"

"Absolutely." Nolan nodded, giving her one of his irritatingly charming smiles, eyes glistening in the harsh overhead light. "Somehow, I convinced Kasha to go out to lunch with me. I wasn't going to give her an opportunity to take it back." He winked, prompting me to roll my eyes.

Vanessa just laughed, smoothing her blouse. "Well, then, the sooner we start the session, the sooner you two can enjoy your day." She opened the door wide, welcoming me back.

I turned my back to her, looking to Nolan. "I'll be quick," I said, only the two of us knowing the underlying meaning of the promise.

"Take all the time you need," he said, leaning forward and placing a kiss on my cheek, my body flooding with heat at the gesture.

We had not discussed *that*.

I stared at him wide-eyed, a smirk spreading on his lips at what I could only assume was a hilariously shocked expression on my face. Even in the middle of a mission, he found a reason to flirt.

Arrogant man.

I shook my head a few times, clearing it before turning and walking into the lion's den that was Vanessa's office.

She laughed, clicking the door shut behind us. "Seems a lot has happened in the past week."

"You could say that," I mumbled dropping into my normal seat.

"So, we established a while ago that things have been evolving between you and Nolan." She took her seat, grabbing her journal and stilo from the table next to her, gently placing them in her lap. "But it seems you have become more intimate since then."

My cheeks burned. "Yes."

"What helped with such a change?"

I took a deep breath. Here we go. "Well, it all started at the last full moon." I looked her straight in the eye. "I was able to transform."

Her face brightened, eyes shining full of happiness. "Oh, Kasha, that is wonderful news. Such incredible progress...which is a testament to your strength and determination."

"Thank you," I mumbled. "But when I decided to, I asked Nolan to come along..."

Bile crawled in my throat as I started telling her about that night, a feeling of betrayal rising in my stomach at the idea of talking to a suspected traitor about such an important moment in my life. But I couldn't do anything that might raise suspicion to her. If I suddenly closed myself off, unwilling to talk about things, she would question it. So, instead, I used my triumph as an excuse to prattle on, standing from my chair and beginning to move around the room.

I continued detailing the events, pacing between our two chairs, keeping my posture rigid. This wasn't unusual for me, the desperate need to move as I talked about my emotions. But today was different; today, I was doing it on purpose. As I took my next turn, I mis-stepped, my thigh banging into the small table next to Vanessa, effectively spilling the glass of water right into her lap.

Perfect.

"Oh, Goddess!" I slapped my hands to my mouth as I stopped in my tracks, staring down at her. "I am so sorry!"

She just laughed, standing up as a pool of water dripped from her pants onto the floor. "It's no bother, mistakes happen. I keep a set of clothes, just give me a moment to go to the changing room."

"Do you have any towels I can use to clean this up?" I lifted a book from the table, as if trying to save it.

"Not in here." She shook her head, pulling her soaked blouse away from her, the bright, shining fabric sticking to every curve of her body. "I'll bring some back, though. I'll just be five minutes."

She gave me a gentle smile, reassuring me that my mistake

was forgiven, before opening the door to her office. Silence fell in the space as she clicked the door closed.

I didn't waste a moment, rushing right to her desk to begin my search.

"Five minutes," I said to Nolan. *"Keep a lookout and warn me as she gets closer."*

"Got it."

A sense of protection engulfed me, and I used it to focus on the task. I rummaged through all the drawers, finding nothing but office supplies and other journals, each marked with a patient's name, just like mine. I searched for anything—a false bottom, a hidden safe. I even crawled under the desk, feeling across the floor for any kind of misplaced floorboard that could be hiding something, but I came up empty.

I couldn't keep wasting time on the desk; it was too obvious anyway. I crawled out from underneath it, my foot catching on her chair. I stumbled backward, my shoulder slamming into the wall behind me.

"Futeacha," I cursed, terrified that the pieces of art would come crashing down and I'd have a lot of explaining to do. My heart steadied as I noticed none of the paintings moved from my clumsy impact, their frames secured by strong bolts in the wall.

All except one.

I stared at the painting that hung behind her desk: the bright blue and white sky melded perfectly into the dark waves of the Vapalles coastline. Memories flooded through me, from family vacations to the beach growing up to late night bonfires with Ollie and Caleb when we went to celebrate Ollie's promotional transfer to the Faction there. It was a popular design to say the least, one that wasn't necessarily misplaced in an office.

379

Yet, an office was a special place, and the artwork one chose to hang within that space said a lot about them. When first learning about Vanessa, I had been told she had transferred from Ochrat. So why did she proudly display a picture of Vapalles?

Even more important, the other paintings were bolted to the wall. So why had this one moved?

I pushed the frame, the whole painting giving way slightly.

My heart sped up, and I pushed the painting just a bit farther to reveal a weakened stone in the wall. This was it, it had to be. My fingers tingled; using one arm to keep the painting propped up, I tried to pry the stone free from its holding.

"Two minutes," Nolan warned, the urgency apparent even within our minds.

"I think I found something,"

"Well, hurry, I can smell her scent starting to drift down the hall again."

My pulse sped up as I stopped trying to be delicate, using all of my strength to rip the stone out, bits of dust escaping and falling against the wall in white and grey plumes. I stuck my hand inside, pushing it farther and farther back into the hole, feeling around for anything that wasn't the cold, musty rock that should be there. I let out a gasp when my fingers brushed against something smoothly textured, with a familiar, dry crinkle. Parchment paper?

I gripped it, just in time to hear the clicking of heels entering the waiting room. My time was up.

"Stop her!" I yelled into Nolan's mind without a second thought.

I sucked in a breath, my hand still half in the hole when the doorknob rattled.

380

"Oh, Vanessa wait!" Nolan's voice came from behind the door. "You have…"

"Keep distracting her," I whispered to him, pulling whatever I had grasped in my hand out of the small space.

The stack of papers were covered in crushed stone dust from their hiding space, my fingers sifting through them, my soul stirring with each one I read.

They were fake ID papers and birth certificates. Each one within the same birth year but different names, all of them around the same age I would guess Vanessa was. There were at least a dozen. There could be plenty of reasons why she had all of these papers, few of them good, but it didn't necessarily lead me to believe that she could be connected to Elliot.

That was, until I got to the last sheet of paper, by far the oldest in the stack judging by its crinkled yellow edges. My throat closed as I read the name scrawled across the top.

Haelyn Vanessa Wells.

Chapter Forty-Seven

Our hallway of offices was in a frenzy by the time Nolan and I returned from my counseling session.

The whole team had been notified before we even got back to Compound, Nolan finding privacy while I finished my session out. I had been trained for years to go undercover; this wasn't my first time having to fake it through time with a suspect, pretending that everything was perfectly fine. However, this had certainly been the hardest.

A part of me had still hoped that I was wrong, that Vanessa wasn't hiding anything. In the short time we had been meeting, somehow, she had helped me better understand the toxic decisions I had been making. She had helped me unpack my emotions, showed me how to advocate for myself in a way. From the beginning, it had always seemed like she was genuinely trying to put me and my healing first.

I felt like a fool for believing that my luck had just been that good, to find a psycho-physician that I had clicked with so quickly, especially after never fully trusting my last one. I had thought it a blessing from Lunestia, a sign that my healing journey was ready to move forward; and even though it had, it was still too good to be true.

Vanessa was hiding something.

Nolan hadn't left my side since I walked out of her office, even making sure I had a few bites of food at the *Blood Moon* before we returned to the Compound. I had tried to convince him that I could handle coming back, but he wasn't buying it. In his exact words, "We can't trap her for another week, so you might as well enjoy a decent meal after such a terrible session."

The food had tasted bland, but at least my head wasn't as foggy with a hearty meal in my stomach.

We walked down the hall, Taylor and Eden the first to greet us, both of them pulling me into a hug.

"Are you alright?" Taylor whispered in my ear.

"As alright as I can be, I suppose," I sighed into his chest, Eden rubbing circles along my back. "At the very least, I can find some gratification in knowing we've gotten closer to taking Elliot down."

They both pulled away, Eden saying, "Beck and Emric are waiting for the two of you in the conference room. They thought it would be best to keep this conversation between the four of you. Hopefully make it quicker, so we have plenty of time to plan."

"Let's go, then," Nolan said, his hand on the small of my back guiding me to the end of the hall. We went right in, finding Beckett and Emric sitting at one end of the table, their eyes immediately finding ours.

"Enough doubt for you now?" My words emerged a bit

383

harsher than they should've been. Though they had just been trying to protect me when they'd voted against this operation, a little flame inside of me burned with satisfaction that I had proven them wrong: I didn't need to be coddled, I was strong enough for this job.

"I still hate the idea of you trying to trap her," Beckett admitted, his arms crossed tightly against his broad chest as Nolan and I sat across from them. "But you were right, it was the best decision. Which is why we need to start preparing for the sting."

"Should I try and make an earlier appointment?" My fingers twitched on top of the table.

"No." Emric shook his head, pushing his glasses up the bridge of his nose. "We can't risk any suspicious behavior on your part. Unless you think she would take you scheduling a last-minute appointment as normal."

I scoffed. "Probably not."

"Then we keep your regular appointment for the week," Beckett said, jotting down notes in a journal in front of him. "Honestly, we probably need the time to make sure we have everything perfect. This is a big moment for our Faction."

He was right. After the past few months, after all of the threats and labels, we could demonstrate that we weren't the misfit insubordinates the High Faction was trying to make us out to be. We were on the side of truth, and we would never back down from doing the right thing. Bringing in someone close to Elliot, this was something no other Faction had accomplished. If we could do this, we could prove ourselves again as strong, well-managed soldiers. No one, not even the High Faction, could doubt us again.

***

My fingers shook as I checked my Comms unit for the fifth time.

The week had passed by too fast, to a point where I was convinced we had missed something in developing the operation. The plan was simple enough: I would go in with my Comms unit connected to Beckett's, which was set to record the entire conversation with Vanessa. Everyone would be stationed within a two-mile radius of the clinic, our telepathic link keeping them informed on when it was time to close in, just in case of an emergency. Once she incriminated herself, we would move in, arrest her, and figure out her connection to Elliot—if she wasn't Elliot herself.

I could do this. And once I did, the High Faction could no longer deny my strength. They could no longer tell me I was too weak to be an Alpha, not when I had such a big hand in taking down a criminal no other Faction was able to capture.

The silence was deafening in the conference room after our final briefing, some people already heading out to their posts around the city while others closed up a few things in the office before taking their spots. I fiddled with the wire inside my shirt in their absence, giving my hands something to do.

"Need help?"

I whipped around to find Nolan leaning in the doorway, arms crossed as he stared at me.

"Is my wire puckering in my shirt?" I looked down at my loose-fitting plum blouse where the wire was secured, muting any noise from Beckett and his surroundings without muting myself to him. "I don't want it to look obvious."

"It's not while you're standing." He walked toward me, his forehead wrinkling as he stared at the front of my shirt. "But you'll be sitting for a good portion of the session. Let's see if that changes anything."

"Good point." I pulled out a chair and turned it toward him before sitting down, trying to relax into it like I would in the session. "How about now?"

"Hm." His fingers tapped against his lips, his gaze fixed on me. "Looks fine from here, but..." He trailed off as he grabbed a second chair, moving it to sit across from me, our knees knocking together. "Fine like this, too."

"You thought of everything," I chuckled nervously, surprised I hadn't thought of those details myself.

"When your safety is involved, I'm not going to take any chances." He leaned forward, elbows braced on his knees. "Are you ready?"

I mimicked his posture, leaning on my own knees so our faces were only inches apart, his minty breath wafting over my face. "Yes, I am."

The room melted away, allowing me to relish in another moment of just the two of us, our strengths and weaknesses blending together inexplicably. With Nolan, I had support when I needed it but encouragement to stand on my own. I had a person who had only known me at my self-proclaimed weakest time, yet still saw something genuinely strong about me. It was exactly what I needed to snap me out of my fog, to help me find that extra push to fight the darkness that still brewed within me.

I might have been the one to help myself, but having him by my side was exactly what I needed to feel safe enough to explore that terrible place within me. I would always be grateful for this man. Maybe one day, I would even find the strength to tell him exactly what his presence these past few weeks had meant to me.

But this was not that moment; this was a silence to get lost in.

He reached out to me, hesitating for a moment before cupping my face, his thumb stroking my cheek. The warmth seeped into me, and I nuzzled into his palm.

"Do you believe in me?" I whispered, my insides quivering as I waited for his answer.

"Always."

I didn't know who moved first or what drew us, but within the serene silence we were pulled closer, inch by inch, our breaths mingling until there was nothing between us, our lips pressed together in a sensual, intoxicating dance.

This was different from our other desperately-heated kisses. Although it didn't lack passion, it was softer, more alluring, his lips slowly exploring every inch of mine. Heat stirred low in my belly, churning and spinning, allowing me to relish every moment. Each small move of his lips and flick of his tongue against mine jolted me into a frenzy, pulling me in, reminding me of how far I had fallen for him with each day that passed.

After Goddess-knew-how-long, we drew apart, the room blurring back into existence, the weight of my responsibilities once again settling on my shoulders.

He pressed his forehead against mine. "Take her down."

"Trust me," I whispered, squeezing his knee, "I plan to."

Chapter Forty-Eight

I barely remembered the journey to the clinic or even through the hallways and into Vanessa's office. But the moment I stepped across the threshold, my senses sharpened, my instincts driving to high gear as I prepared for whatever battle I would need to fight within these walls.

"You seem stressed today, Kasha." Vanessa looked me up and down, tilting her head. "Anything on your mind?"

Plenty, but that wasn't the point.

"Work is just stressing me out." I leaned back in my chair, my neck resting on the cushioned back.

"Moreso than normal?"

I nodded. "I can't talk about the details, but it's this case."

"Oh?"

"Everything is just evolving so quickly." I lifted my head up slightly, catching a peek at her crossing her legs back and forth as if she couldn't get comfortable. I sat up again, hunching my shoulders. "I've never struggled this much before. I feel like I can't keep up no matter how hard I try. Every move I make seems just too slow."

"Sometimes we feel that way, when in reality, we are moving at the exact pace we're meant to."

"I've never had to work on such a high priority case before." I shook my head, taking in a deep breath and letting out a loud sigh. "I just don't know how to handle all the pressure. I feel like I have to keep it all inside, since I can't talk about it to anyone outside of the Faction."

"Careful, Kas." Beckett's voice drifted to me, warning me not to take this too far, but it was too late now. She needed a nudge to show a weakness in her secrets.

"Well, why not them?" Vanessa tapped her foot against the floor.

"I know it probably sounds petty, but a part of me believes they don't trust my judgement anymore." I had warned my team beforehand about the tactics I was going to use; I hoped none of them were taking this lie personally. "I've stopped giving them my theories, because I just don't see the point when they won't listen. But they're just eating me up inside. I can barely sleep some nights, and I feel sick to my stomach."

She stared at me pensively; I stayed hunched over, attempting to seem burdened by the whole ordeal. I had set the trap, I just had to see if she took the bait.

"You know," she leaned forward, looking me up and down slowly, "anything you say in here is completely confidential. If you want to talk about specifics, I won't tell anyone."

I got her.

My chest tightened, pushing down the glee that rose up in

389

me, keeping my features as tense as possible and trying to show that I was struggling with the idea of opening up about this. I twisted my fingers in my lap, staring down at them, shifting in my seat. Finally, I whispered, "You promise?"

"Of course, Kasha." She smiled. "You can trust me."

My blood boiled, but I smiled anyway, pretending that I actually believed her—as if she could take advantage of this completely fabricated weak moment. "I have a theory that whoever this killer is, they aren't working alone." I gripped my knees, looking up at Vanessa. "I think they have a Clan helping them."

"What brought you to this theory?"

"It just seemed like so much for one person to handle. With that and the lack of consistency in the kills and victims, it makes sense that it's multiple people working together under the guise of one person doing it alone."

"I see." She nodded, looking down to write something.

"I want to arrest one of them so I can track down the leader. I have a plan to hunt them down."

Her forearm tensed, the tip of her stilo cracking off.

"Oh, God above," she mumbled, throwing the broken stilo onto the table. "Keep going, I'm listening."

My eyes trailed her as she moved across the room, opening the top left drawer of her desk and rummaging through it for what I could only assume was a new stilo. Was that the drawer she had stored them in?

"I wanted to prove to the High Faction that we're doing everything we can," I said, my pulse pounding in my ears. "I just know that once we discover who some of these accomplices are, we'll be able to take them all down. I just need my Faction to listen."

"I see," she mumbled, returning toward her seat, arms behind her back.

I needed to push her. I could lure her in, I just needed to be a bit weaker.

That was the only reason I turned my back to her, rubbing my forehead like I couldn't bear the stress anymore. "I just can't wait to arrest these terrible people."

Silence fell at my words, the tension pressing into me, attempting to drown us, time falling still as I waited.

And waited...

My skin prickled, alerting me to danger right before I caught sight of Vanessa's clamped hand fly right for my throat.

I grasped her wrist just in time, the shining tip of a needle protruding from the side of her fist. A full vial connected to the end, a swirling, milky-white liquid inside that could only be one thing: wolfsbane.

She had tried to drug me.

Well, I wasn't expecting that, but attacking an Onyx Guard was certainly cause for arrest.

Vanessa didn't even hesitate, taking advantage of her towering form over my sitting one, ripping her wrist from my hold. Taking a few steps backward and raising her arm again, she swiped the needle in an arc toward me, a growl escaping her lips, eyes shifting to the deep burgundy red of a Shrivika.

I jumped to my feet just in time to miss the dripping tip of the needle and slammed my fist into her open solar plexus, her body doubling over as she coughed for air. It gave me an opening to slam my elbow into her wrist, the needle flying from her hand. I rushed forward, intending to take her down, but she recovered quickly. Her lips curled upward in a snarl as she rushed me, fists bared and ready to fight.

"Close in!" I screamed.

The entire team confirmed all at once how long it would take for them to get there, a few of them promising to be there within a minute.

I just needed to hold her off that long.

My feet moved quickly, arms raised to protect my body as she kept throwing punches. I let her take the offensive stance, not wanting to risk her safety when she came at me.

I didn't want to hurt her. Partially because I didn't want to wait to interrogate her and the other, quieter part that was still telling me to keep her safe. Could I have pulled my weapon and easily overpowered her? Yes. Could I have thrown a few well aimed punches and knocked her out? Also, yes. But that wasn't the point of this mission. The point was to get answers, and hurting her would just delay that. I couldn't risk it.

So, I kept the defensive lie up, letting her think that she was winning the fight, when in reality, she had already lost.

It would be a lot easier to overpower her when the rest of the team arrived, but the least I could do was set us up for success. I kept dodging, moving with each throw she took, inching us around until her back was to the door. She didn't even notice the trap I'd set, too preoccupied with trying to take me down.

"Stop fighting, Vanessa." Her name tasted like acid on my tongue; I pushed away the thought that it most likely wasn't her true identity.

"Never." she growled. "I can never stop."

She threw another flurry of jabs, one of them connecting

with my side.

I growled; this was not how I'd expected things to go.

"Anytime now, team," I yelled.

The door slammed open after far too many moments, my Faction pouring into the room. Beckett and Millie were the first to get to Vanessa, taking both of her arms and ripping her away from me. She flailed as she tried to break Beckett's hold, but his grip was relentless, holding her wrists behind her back and pushing her over so her torso and head rested on top of her desk. She snarled at him, legs kicking, body writhing against the surface.

The violence escaping her perfect facade stunned me; I couldn't turn away from the whole ordeal unfolding in front of me, dizziness overtaking me from the adrenaline coursing through my veins and overwhelming my whole system.

My theory had been true, or at least a part of it must be if Vanessa had felt so threatened that she needed to risk drugging me. She was hiding something, and she was fighting with everything she had to protect that secret.

I would make sure it wasn't hidden for much longer.

Liv and Nolan rushed toward me, their voices drifting around me asking if I was alright, but all I cared about was bringing this part of the mission to a close.

"No," I growled, pushing Liv and Nolan out of the way. "Let me."

I took over Beckett's hold on her, wrapping her wrists in a tight grip so she couldn't escape. She struggled, still kicking the wooden sides of the desk, her hair coming loose of the tight bun on top of her head.

"You don't understand," she hissed, her voice muffled

against the desk.

"Vanessa Relantis," I kept her face down on the surface, my chest heaving as I grabbed the pair of metal cuffs from Lucas's outstretched hands and secured her wrists behind her back, "you are under arrest for accessory to murder and treason against Kazola."

Chapter Forty-Nine

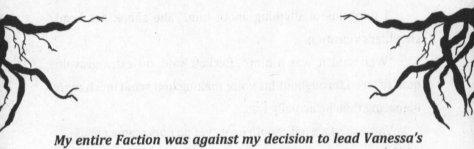

My entire Faction was against my decision to lead Vanessa's interrogation.

They said I shouldn't come in, tried to convince me that others would be better fit for this, but I couldn't let that happen. This might be our battle to fight, but our enemy had made it personal, and I wouldn't stop until I put this whole ordeal to rest.

Vanessa sat across from me in the plain, dark interrogation room, mostly empty except for the long wooden table and three chairs that took up the claustrophobic space. Beckett sat beside me, his posture rigid, eyes trained on the tousled woman in front of us. I had never seen her so disheveled; her typical perfectionist air quickly shattered the moment she showed her true colors.

"What do you want from me?" Vanessa broke the silence first. Excellent, she was nervous, eyes darting between the two of us, attempting to hide her shaking fingers beneath her long-sleeved shirt.

"You attacked an Onyx Guard member," I said blandly, keeping a chill to my words. "We have every right to hold you here."

"Fine, but I don't know anything."

"Well, that can't be true." I leaned forward, forearms braced on the table, breaching her personal space by a few more inches. "According to our investigation, you seem to be connected to someone we've been hunting for a while now."

"I don't know anything about him." She shook her head, shoulders vibrating.

"Who said it was a him?" Beckett said, an extra gravelly quality laced throughout his voice making him seem much more menacing than he actually was.

Vanessa's face fell, mouth open, yet no noise came out as she realized the first mistake she'd made.

"Are you Elliot Wells?" I asked, the one question we were all on the edge of our seats to know the answer to.

No surprise, Vanessa kept her mouth clamped shut, cuffed and chained hands curling into fists on the table, her eyes shifting to bright Shrivika red. She was struggling, but she was determined to keep her mouth shut.

"Do you know who Elliot Wells is?"

No words escaped her lips, but she pulled them even thinner, almost disappearing between the sharp confines of her fangs.

"Is he threatening you?"

Her cheek twitched, showing the distress my question caused her, but still no words.

I could read her body language all day long, but we didn't have time for that. I didn't have the patience. I needed answers—

we all did.

So, it was time to stop playing nice.

"You're a Shrivika, Vanessa," I leaned forward, dropping my voice a few threatening octaves. "You know we have a way to pull the truth from you. So, you can either answer our questions, or Beckett here will make sure you give us what we want against your will. What's your choice?"

Fear rippled across her features, that perfect façade breaking just a little bit more as she sat up straighter. "You have no idea what you are doing." Her eyes clouded with a darkness only found in those who hid secrets for far too long. "Don't do this, and we'll all be safe."

"We don't have time to waste on pointless interrogations and warnings, so we're getting right to the point." I nodded to Beckett, who dragged his chair around the table to sit right beside Vanessa; her eyes widened, knowing exactly the tactic we were about to use.

The *Firinne na Fola*—The Blood Truth.

Shrivikas were extremely heightened beings with a taste for blood unlike any other. Not only did they need blood to survive, they could also taste every little detail and flavor in one's blood. They could taste your fear, your hormones, and even diseases that spread throughout your body. This incredible ability came in handy when we wanted to interrogate people; just a small taste, and Beckett would be able to know if Vanessa was lying, measuring spikes of hormones coursing through her blood with each answer she gave.

She struggled in the cuffs, desperate to get her arm as far away from Beckett as possible, but it was no use. She was at his mercy as he unhooked the one closest to him, holding it in a

397

secure grip. He flipped her hand palm-up before lowering his lips, his fangs piercing the fleshy part just below her thumb, a line of blood beginning to trickle down her wrist. He nodded to me, eyes steady.

We were ready to begin discovering the truth.

"Are you Elliot Wells?" I asked again.

Vanessa screeched, flailing in her seat like a wild animal trying to escape its cage. She kicked and bucked, one hand still chained to the table so she couldn't escape, but she did whatever she could to keep herself away from her blood being taken. Beckett struggled to keep his grip on her arm, let alone getting his teeth close enough to taste the truth. She let out a howling screech as she kicked, the thump of her feet thrashed under the table before she connected with my shins, a sharp pain radiating up my leg. I banged my fist on the tabletop, grunting.

I had no more patience left for her.

"Liv," I called out through my teeth.

Aliva's tall, menacing form emerged right away on the threshold. She glided across the room to stand behind Vanessa. Without warning, she grabbed Vanessa, wrapping her long arms around her torso and shoving her back into her chair, one hand flexing around Vanessa's throat. Vanessa struggled against her, but no longer with as much vigor now that Liv has her in a sensitive position.

"Relax," Liv barked, her muscles flexing under her armor, sweat slowly beading along her dark forehead. "Either sit still and behave, or we tie you to the chair. Your choice."

Those words seemed to get through to Vanessa, her body going limp within Liv's grasp, although she kept a hold on her just in case. Vanessa gazed up at her, nothing but desperation now in her eyes. "Please."

There was no point to the single pathetic word. She would get no sympathy from any of us, no matter how hard she tried.

"One more time." I clenched my fists on top on the table, staring down my prey. "Are you Elliot Wells?"

"No!" she said, shrill and shaking.

I looked to Beckett, his lips already covered in a few drops of her blood. "Truth."

Damnit, if only it could be that easy. But it didn't matter; she was connected to him somehow.

"Is Vanessa your real name?"

Her jaw quivered. "Yes."

"Lie," Beckett said, his grip on her wrist and Liv's on her throat tightening as she once again tried to yank away.

Vanessa's fear pushed a dose of fire through me. "Are you a part of Elliot Wells's Clan?"

"No." She shook her head.

Beckett's brows creased. "Truth."

That wasn't possible. "Are you somehow connected to Elliot Wells?"

"No!" she screamed, her next jerking movement pulling a few more pieces of hair from their containment.

"Lie." Beckett's lip quirked, attempting to hide a smile just as I was.

Now we were getting somewhere.

"*Were* you a part of his Clan?" I balled my fists on the table, my heart thumping loudly as I waited for the answer, hoping my newest theory was correct.

"No."

"Lie." Beckett growled, no longer able to hide the smug

399

smirk.

"How long were you in his Clan?" I asked, trying my best to keep my voice steady.

A few wayward tears slowly began to spread down her cheeks, her gaze lowering to her lap. "Please..." she begged, shaking her head.

"You could make this so much easier on yourself, Vanessa." Beckett leaned in closer, drops of her blood still on his lips—a reminder that her lies couldn't be hidden from us. "Tell us what we need to know. Cooperate, and maybe we can help you."

She scoffed, her bright eyes dulling with hopelessness. "No one can help me. None of you can understand what you are attempting to discover."

My cheek twitched, red-hot fury simmering just below the surface, but I reined it in. We didn't have time for loss of control. "Well, what we have discovered is far from appealing." I looked her up and down, unable to stop my heart from twitching at the obvious fear now spreading across her features. Whatever Elliot had done to her, it wasn't good. Just as Logan had left his mark on me, Elliot had left a mark on Vanessa.

"You can't stop us," Beckett added. "So, you might as well talk."

"I can't." Her voice was courser through the tears that blotched her face.

"I still believe you want to help people." I softened my posture and voice, lowering both to a soothing level. We'd successfully scared her and caught her in enough lies; she knew she wasn't going to be able to escape this anymore. Now was the time to show sympathy, that we were not an enemy unless she made us one. "So, please explain to me how you are connected to this man. You could save so many people. You could help."

Betrayal still coursed through me, a pain I struggled to accept pulling at me over everything Vanessa had done. Yet, she had truly seemed genuine from the beginning; she had helped me break through so many walls around myself. She obviously enjoyed helping others, or she wouldn't be a psycho-physician.

But maybe it wasn't as pure as I once thought. Maybe it wasn't a calling, but penance for something she had done.

And I knew deep in my soul that that something was connected to Elliot Wells.

"Why did you try and drug me?" I asked the selfish question I desperately wanted an answer to.

"To escape."

Liv's hold on her loosened as she straightened up, placing her hands on Vanessa's shoulders in warning.

"From him kidnapping you? Killing you?" I guessed.

"There is so much more to him than any of you even realize." Her gaze went vacant, her face slack. "I've seen things I can never unsee. I've done things I can never take back."

"Then let us help you," I pleaded.

"No one can help me." She shook her head, looking right into my eyes, her void gaze chilling me to my bones. "I'm already damned. If I can't run, then I'm as good as dead once I'm no longer of use to him."

"What does that mean?"

"Protect yourself, Kasha," she warned. "That's all I can say."

"You need to give me more." I leaned across the table. "Tell us how he's threatening you or what he's done. We can protect you, we can take him down if you just help us."

We stared at each other, and for one brief second, I hoped

401

that she could see I was determined to protect her from this man who obviously brought her nothing but fear.

"Even in your deceit, you helped me, Vanessa," I said. "Please, I want to return the favor. Just let me help you."

"I can't." She shook her head, her fingers starting to bleed around the nailbeds as she picked at them. "I just can't."

Her stubborn, heartbreaking words pierced through something in me, opening my eyes to the whole situation. We had discovered a lot in the short time we'd talked, but it was nothing of substance. Still, she was obviously convinced she was in danger, even with the protection of the Onyx Guard and the Compound surrounding her. I could see the struggle just below the surface: she wanted to help, but she had to decide between her own safety and the safety of others.

She was choosing her own safety. For now.

"Should we keep going?" I looked to Beckett and Liv.

Beckett stared at her for a moment, licking the last few drops of blood from his lips before turning back to me. "She's terrified, and convinced that nothing we say will calm it. Right now, we've pushed her as far as she can handle today."

"Damnit."

"We still got plenty to hold her," Liv said, pulling a cloth from her pocket and handing it to Beckett, who wiped at the cut on Vanessa's hand, the shaking of her fingers slowing as she realized we were coming to an end. "She's connected to Elliot somehow. It will just take us a bit more time to discover what exactly it is. Once she realizes she has no other options, I'd bet money she'll start opening up more."

I nodded, letting the truth of their words wash over me before I turned my attention back to her. "Maybe a few days in the cells will change your mind."

"Kasha..." She tried to reach for me, but I yanked my arms away, abruptly standing to put distance between us.

"Don't," I snarled. "Unless you're ready to tell me the whole truth about your connection to Elliot, then we have nothing else to talk about. Consider this my resignation from your services."

And without another look at the woman who'd betrayed me, I walked out of the room, slamming the door behind me.

Chapter Fifty

The Blood Moon was full of life as we took over the entire space for the evening.

Elliot might not be caught yet, but we had taken far greater steps than any Faction before us. We had found one of his cohorts, we had them in custody, and now we would be able to track this man down and put this whole case to rest. It was cause for celebration—our team had earned it. The drinks flowed freely, laughter and high spirits filling the room with the most infectious energy, everyone couldn't help but smile at each person they talked and laughed with. Music thumped around me as I pushed my way through the crowd, the bar within my sights.

"Can I get more water, Benji?" I slid my empty glass across to him.

He gave me his typical, flirtatious smile. "Of course, lovely." He filled up the glass, even adding in a slice of lime like I enjoyed, mixing it all together.

I gripped the cold glass, stirring the drink before taking a few refreshing sips and turning back to the room. I took a moment to decompress from all the conversations I'd had since I arrived, trying my best to enjoy the moment even though my mind tried to wander to harder topics.

I fought to ignore thoughts of Vanessa, to not give her betrayal the power of my emotions. It was a night to celebrate, to spend time with my friends and their loved ones, not to think about what she had done.

Tomorrow, we would do the final questioning and get the truth. I just had to make it through until then.

Someone nudged into my shoulder, pulling my attention to Beckett standing to my left. "How you doing?"

"The best I can," I answered honestly. He knew when I was lying, so it was never worth the effort. "This is helping distract me a bit."

"Your pensive look before says otherwise," he teased.

I rolled my eyes. "Can't help that I'm a workaholic."

"We'll get him, Kas." Beckett slung his arm over my shoulders pulling me into a warm side-hug, loosening the tightness in my chest.

"I know. We'll crack her tomorrow. I know we will."

He gave me a classic Beckett smile, full of hope and love and encouragement. "Well, looks like someone is ready to whisk you away."

"What?"

He gestured with his free hand to Nolan heading our way, his eyes trained on his intended destination: me.

My heart flipped at the sight, pumping faster with each step he took. By the time he was in front of me, I was surprised it hadn't burst from my chest. With Beckett's hand on my shoulder, he could certainly hear the pick-up of my racing pulse.

"Hey, there," Nolan said, his green eyes glimmering in the dimmed lighting around us, a teasing smile on his lips. "Would you honor me with a dance?" He gestured to the dance floor, the music slowing to a gentle song.

Beckett burst into laughter, his hand flying to cover his mouth.

"Shut it," I mumbled.

"What's so funny?" Nolan looked between us.

"I'm sorry," Beckett wheezed. "You've just asked the one musician who somehow has no rhythm to dance with you."

My shoulders hunched, my fingers tightening around my glass. "I'm not that bad."

"As someone who has danced with you, I can honestly say, yes, you are that bad."

"I just can't time myself well, that's all." But Beckett was right; the last time we'd danced, I was surprised I didn't break any of his toes with how many times I stepped on them.

"Maybe you just haven't found the right partner to teach you." Nolan swayed from side to side, his body perfectly timed to the music. "I've taught even the most helpless of dancers, so you couldn't ask for a better partner."

I cocked my head, suppressing a laugh. "Do you ever make attempts at humility?"

"Seems like a waste of time when you're this perfect." He winked, my stomach twisting at the sight. Why in the Goddess was that attractive? "So? Dance with me?"

His hand was outstretched, begging me to accept. I tried to act like it was a difficult choice, but my quivering legs made it clear it was the only place I wanted to be in that moment—as close to him as possible for the last few weeks we probably had together. Another fact I'd tried not to think about all night.

I dropped my half-empty glass on the bar top before taking his hand, his grip strong leading me to the dance floor.

He twirled me around, my feet stumbling over themselves before he pulled me back toward him, one arm snaking around my hips, the other still gripped tightly in mine. I hesitated for a moment before sliding my free hand up to his shoulder, our chests touching as he swayed us to the beat of the music.

"Wow, you, uh, really are a little clumsy on the dance floor." He laughed, the sound low and rough, his forehead barely brushing my own.

Heat washed over my cheeks. "I prefer fighting over dancing."

He pulled me close against him, his grip tightening on my hip. "Stay close. I'll keep you safe in this dangerous place."

"Such an arrogant man." I shook my head, finally relaxing a bit.

"You wouldn't want it any other way." His hand squeezed mine.

Silence fell between us as we just moved with the music, other couples dancing and swaying around us to the slow, heart-pounding tempo that engulfed us. His arms were warm, safe. They were a place I'd never expected to find myself, yet I relished every moment I got to spend in them. I was...comfortable. Content. My mind wasn't moving a mile a minute or expecting something terrible to happen, needing to be constantly on guard.

At that moment, with him so close, I found myself lost within my own happiness, a place I hadn't been in a long time.

Those intoxicating forest-green eyes stared down at me, barely blinking. They were so easy to get lost in, to find myself pulled to discover everything that lay behind them. Yet, my heart lurched at the sight of something buried deep within his gaze, something I could tell he was trying desperately to hide in such a perfect moment.

"What is it?" My throat dried at the conflict raging across his handsome face.

"I just..." He shook his head, staring up at the ceiling before looking back at me. "I don't know where to start."

"Try the beginning," I teased, but my voice was strained, my mind getting a bit dizzy.

"I never expected to find us here." He chuckled, smirking at me. "You, willingly dancing with me, seeming to enjoy yourself."

I bit my bottom lip. "I *am* enjoying myself."

"You've captured me since the day I met you, Kasha." His words were so pure, full of absolute honesty. They set my whole body alight, heat swarming me, making me desperate for more. "You fascinate me, you push me to my limits and show me I'm strong enough to bear the pressure. You challenge me in a way I crave, but then you make me laugh and feel at ease at almost every turn. When you asked me to be with you the other day during your transformation...you have no idea what that meant to me. To know that you trusted me with that, it was a gift I've cherished every moment since."

My heart raced, palms sweating. What was he trying to say? Was it what I'd been thinking myself, too scared to say out loud?

"I know I made you a promise to leave when Elliot is caught." He took a deep breath, closing his eyes. "And I will keep that promise. But..."

"But?" I prompted, my eyes refusing to leave his, everything around me blurring.

"But if I'm being honest, I don't want to go." He rested his forehead against mine. "I'm not ready to leave you."

We kept swaying to the music, somehow my legs finding the strength to keep me upright after his confession.

"If you want me to go, I will." He kept me close, lowering his lips so they brush against my ear. "But if you would let me stay, then I want you to know my intentions."

I sucked in a shaky breath. "Which are?"

"I want to pursue you romantically." His breath tickled my neck. "I want us to discover exactly what's growing between us."

"Nolan, I—"

I had more to say, more to admit; but words eluded me, my mind hazing over sharply. I shook my head a few times, trying to clear it, but that only made it worse, my stomach churning at the quick movement.

Nolan stopped us. "Kas?"

I leaned my hand against his shoulder, trying to get myself together. "Sorry."

His words were beautiful, but something was pulling my attention—this overwhelming spinning of the room, my vision struggling to stay focused. Everything was off, events flowing around me, my body struggling to keep up. If I didn't know any better, I would've guessed I was close to blackout-drunk, but all I'd had was water.

What in the Goddess was happening to me?

Nolan gripped me tighter, helping to keep me upright. "Are you alright? Did I say too much?"

"N-no, it's no—" I gagged, my stomach churning, my cheeks

tingling, "y-you. I ju—" I coughed, my lungs struggling to draw in air. "I need the washroom."

I bolted away before he could say anything, stumbling and crashing as I headed to the back of the bar. Voices swirled around me, muffled, asking if I was alright, but I couldn't even find the strength to answer. I finally stumbled into the back hall, the door at the end of the short span seeming miles away. I rested my hands against the wall, trying to use it as a guide to my destination. All I needed to do was get to the washroom and purge whatever I'd consumed to make me like this. Just make it to the washroom and everything would be alright.

I collapsed about ten paces from the door, my hands scratching at the wall, head resting against it to try and find my balance, but it seemed almost impossible. Dread overcame me. I desperately tried to figure out what was happening, but it was no use. Whatever had taken over my system was spreading rapidly, to the point where thinking felt like the most strenuous activity that existed. My muscles shook as I fell to my knees, sobs escaping my lips, trying to find any shred of strength to call out to my friends.

But it was no use. Something had taken control of me, pulling me into its clutches, and I had no idea what it was.

"Hello, lovely," a voice whispered in my ear before darkness engulfed the world.

Chapter Fifty-One

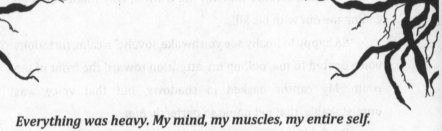

Everything was heavy. My mind, my muscles, my entire self.

My head rolled side to side, and I coughed as dust erupted around me in a cloud. Where was I?

I blinked to clear my vision, forcing myself to pull in my surroundings so I could assess the situation I had found myself it.

Crates were stacked around me, the stale scent of musky fabric and rotting wood filling my dulled senses. I tried to sit up, but every micromovement took all my effort, a groan dragging involuntarily from my lips. Somehow, I was able to prop myself against the wall behind me, my head rolling against the dirty surface as I looked around.

I was in a warehouse of some kind. If I didn't know any better, I would think it had been abandoned for a while, with its broken ceiling beams, busted light bulbs still in the fixtures above, and plenty of mismatched graffiti littered along the walls. Yet, the crates looked new, the wood freshly-polished and no dirt littering their surfaces.

I tried to find any clue as to where I was; my breath escaped in a rush as my eyes focused on the scrawled writing across the wall in front of me.

Chu Fui na Déithe. For the Blood of the Gods.

I was in a den of vipers, in the darkened lair of the man I'd been hunting. For some unknown reason, I had been drugged and dragged to this place, and I would not waste it. With the Goddess as my witness, I would find out the truth of why Elliot has been calling me out with his kills.

"So happy to finally see you awake, lovely," a calm, flirtatious voice drifted to me, pulling my attention toward the front of the room. My captor basked in shadows, but that voice was unmistakable, that pet name so perfectly *him*.

"Benji." My voice was hoarse, my throat raw.

He came into the light, his steps slow, making his way over to me and crouching with his fingers laced together as he looked me up and down. "How do you feel?"

"Like I was just drugged and kidnapped," I growled. "Oh, wait, I was!"

"Necessary evil, darling." He shrugged, his cool features giving away nothing. "We won't be here long, I promise."

"My Faction will find me," I threatened, clawing at the floor below me.

"Oh, I know. I was planning on that."

I balked at his confidence. "What?"

"Trust me, if I wanted us to disappear without a trace, it would have been simple." He took in his fill of my weakened state. "This was merely an intimate moment for us to officially meet."

My blood boiled at his nonchalant demeanor about

kidnapping me. I wished I could lunge forward and scratch his eyes out, but whatever he'd drugged me with still had me within its hold, my body weakened, impossible to hold itself up without the wall behind and the floor below. "Do you work for Elliot?" I demanded. "Who is he?"

He smirked, a treacherous laugh escaping his lips. The evil sound danced across my skin, realization snaking through my slow, clouded thoughts.

He wasn't working for Elliot.

He *was* Elliot.

"What in the name of the Goddess did you give me?" I snarled, my frozen muscles sinking lower as if I was melting into the concrete floor below.

"Sedative-soaked lime." His smile was the most disgusting combination of pride and cruelty, my stomach lurching at the sight. "One of my simpler ideas, but effective at getting the job done."

"Why?"

"I kept trying to send you messages," he tsked, a fresh wave of nausea rolling through me at his apathetic reference to the murders. "But I suppose my methods were just a bit too subtle for you to draw a quick conclusion. So, I figured it was easier to finally show you exactly who I am."

My insides quivered. "So, you were calling me out?"

"I suppose that's one way of putting it." He shrugged. "I considered it more of an invitation."

"I thought you were smarter than this," I spat. "Was I truly such a weakness for you that you had to reveal your identity to a guard?"

"You have no idea how special you are." He dropped onto his

413

knees, leaning forward. "You and I...we are destined."

I wanted to vomit at his words, my skin crawling. "You are delusional."

He laughed again, eyes dancing with unbridled passion. "I know it seems that way now, without the proper knowledge of what you were born to do. But don't worry, when the time is right, I will teach you everything. About your strength, your calling from Lunestia, and how we are the chosen children of the Gods."

My head spun from the combination of the sedative and his trickster words that didn't make sense. "Why now? After hiding for so many years, why reveal who you are?"

"Because you are ready, along with the rest of Kazola." He leaned forward, hands skinning across my cheek, my body recoiling from the touch. "To learn the truth."

"About who you are?"

"And what we are meant to do for Kazola." He smiled. "And we can't do that if you have no idea who I am."

"But you're letting me go?"

"You must stay out in the world to truly understand. You need to experience firsthand the beginning of my plans to get a full idea of why you're needed to save this country."

"You're a lunatic!"

"You may think that now," he tilted his head, "but you won't forever. As you watch the truth unfold in the streets, as you see Kazola's secrets come out of the shadows the High Faction is desperate to keep them in, then you will be ready to take your place next to me."

"And what place is that?"

"As the savior you are meant to be."

414

My sluggish mind couldn't keep up with his delusional ramblings. I couldn't make any sense of them, no matter how hard I tried. The first time I had seen Benji—no, Elliot—was in the bar. I tried my best to focus on the past year and a half he was here, to think of anything I could have done to garner this kind of taunting, fanatical attention. My head pounded, my chest heaving, breath becoming increasingly difficult to pull in. "Nothing you're saying makes any sense."

He just shrugged. "For now."

Luckily, we were interrupted by a man emerging from the same direction Elliot had come, his hulking figure dwarfing both of us. The hood of a dark cloak covered his face, but that was all it hid of his monstrous, boulder-like build.

"Sir?" The ogrish man cleared his throat.

"What?" Elliot barked, darkness twisting his features.

"Guards have been spotted about a mile away." The man's voice tensed, like a soldier reporting to their commander. "They will be upon us in a matter of minutes."

Elliot sighed, turning back to me. "It looks like our time is up."

I growled, trying to lunge forward and punch him; but it was all in vain, my body crumbling like a flailing fish. "You will not get away with this."

"There is nothing to get away with. My plan has already been signaled to begin, and nothing can stop the true heart of Kazola from taking back what is rightfully ours." His corrupted smile shook me to my core. "Just as the Gods blessed it to be, centuries ago."

I snarled, swiping my clawless hand at him, but he just leaned back, dodging it effortlessly. The man beside us

415

stiffened—not at my weak attack, but something else.

A noise gained on us, closing in around whatever disgusting place they had taken me. My skin prickled as I used all my strength to focus on what I thought I was hearing.

Finally, I confirmed exactly what it was: footsteps.

"Sir," the brute growled. "We have to go."

"Oh, very well," Elliot sighed, as if his impending capture was nothing more than a fly on his shoulder. He leaned forward, pulling in a deep, bone-chilling breath, capturing my chin between his fingers. "Until next time my lovely *Rogthna*."

His suave voice froze every inch of my body, I could barely register that he had called me a name I didn't understand.

Rogthna. What did that mean to him?

He leaned forward, placing a delicate kiss against my cheek before releasing me and rising. He gave me one final look before walking away, two goons by his side as they disappeared together into the shadows.

I wanted to run after him, to tackle him to the ground and arrest him, but my body just wasn't strong enough—too weak to fight, too drugged to even stand. I tried to focus on what direction they were going, tracking their scent...but just like the mystery person in the alley, they didn't have one. They disappeared like shadows chased away by the light, making me wonder if they were ever here at all, or if my hazed mind had caused me to hallucinate the whole encounter.

I fell back against the wall; voices drifted to me, but the sedative still had a hold over my senses, the words so muffled that I couldn't make them out. Finally, after several seconds, the words became clearer, booming toward me from what I had to guess was the floor below.

"Come out, Wells, you coward!"

My heart lurched at the anger laced in every word. He was here.

Nolan had found me.

"Nolan, calm down, she's here! We can smell her." Greyson. I tried to figure out how many were running, but I lost count after five.

A small smile pulled at my lips; they were all here for me. My friends. My family.

Footsteps pounded closer and closer, a whimper of relief escaping my lips at the sound. I used every bit of strength I had, bracing my hands and legs to drag myself from behind the stacked crates, my eyes set on the center of the room in hopes they would see me the moment they came inside.

"I'll kill him!" Nolan's words matched the frantic beating of feet on stairs coming from my left. "Do you hear that, Elliot? If you've harmed one hair on her head, I will rip your throat out!"

"Keep it together!" Liv said; then a smack echoed from not too far away, the distinct sound of flesh against flesh. Had she slapped him?

He snarled, "Get out of my way."

Finally, they turned the corner, all of them rushing into the wide-open space. They were all here to save me, but my eyes went to the wild one in the center: Nolan.

He was a frenzy of energy, eyes wild, hair disheveled and windblown, a sheen of sweat covering his skin like they'd all run here. His Amalgam Blade was clutched in his white-knuckled fist, the wood blade protruding from one side. His eyes darted around the room, low snarls escaping his lips with every breath. He was so lost in his own mind, his desperate attempt to get to me, that

417

he couldn't even see that I was right in front of him.

"Nolan," I whispered.

He whipped around to face me, eyes going wide, his blade clattering the ground the moment he caught sight of me. He stared at me for a moment, blinking a few times as if he was trying to decide if I was real or not.

"Thank the Goddess." He bolted across the room, sliding on his knees to close the last few feet between us before pulling me into his arms.

Without hesitation, he crashed his lips to mine, fingers reaching up to tangle in my dirty hair, pulling me closer. I melted into his embrace, not caring that all of our friends were watching us from across the room; I ignored them, letting them melt away as I took in all Nolan was pouring out to me. We didn't hold back, our tongues and teeth licking and nipping, consuming each other in a burst of need to remind ourselves that we hadn't lost each other. I clawed at his shoulders, fingers bunching in the soft cotton as I pulled him as close to me as possible.

I needed to feel every inch of him pressed against me, his warmth seeping into me, letting me know that I was no longer alone.

Finally, we pulled apart, his strong arms gathering me into his lap, pulling me close and cradling me protectively. I let the tension in my tingling muscles loose, my heavy body aching as the effects of the sedative finally started to wear off.

"I've got you. I've got you," he chanted as he rocked me back and forth; my pulse beat a bit, knowing his words weren't only for my comfort but his as well.

"It's okay," I whispered, trailing small kisses along his jaw and throat. "It's going to be alright. I'm safe now. You've got me."

I cupped his face in my hand, my thumb drawing small circles along his cheek, his muscles loosening a bit.

We were safe for now. But I couldn't ignore the chilled, foreboding sense that even though Elliot had showed me who he really was, this hunt was far from over.

Epilogue

My vision tunneled as I stormed through the Compound, my clothes still covered in dirt and grime from the warehouse, my face smeared with sweat and dust. I should go and clean up before I did this, but I didn't care. I needed answers, and I would not back down this time.

I went straight for our office building, but instead of heading up, I headed down, to the below level: the prisoners' cells.

The Delta guards on duty jumped to attention at my arrival, their uniforms rumpled, eyes wild when they saluted me. They weren't expecting me, but neither was she.

"Keys," I barked. The guards scurried, one of them yanking the ring of heavy iron keys from the wall and handing them quickly over to me. I grabbed them without hesitation and descended into the row of cells.

The entire space was eerily quiet as I walked to the end, the thumping of my boots echoing off the walls. But I wasn't alone in this dank, miserable place. One more person was here, residing behind the bars—her new home.

Vanessa sat on her cot, knees pulled up to her chest. She no longer looked like the perfectly-quaffed physician, but a prisoner. Her hair was a tangled, mottled mess, her eyes dry but cheeks still stained from what I could only assume was hours' worth of tears. Her white silk shirt was smeared with sweat and dirt, the pocket of her pants ripped. She was a mess, but she was here. She knew the truth, she knew *something*, and I wasn't playing games any longer.

"You knew," I growled, my fingers curling around the bars, my eyes glowing brightly, my wolf no longer scared of this new person I was becoming. It was here for me, just in time to face the storm that loomed ahead, the battle waiting on the horizon. "You knew who Elliot was this whole time."

"Yes," she whispered, her lips pressed against her knee; but I still heard the admission of guilt. "But it's not like you think. None of this is what you think."

I shoved the key into the door, ripping it open and storing in. It was completely idiotic to be here alone, but the rest of my Faction wasn't far behind. And I couldn't wait. I needed answers.

"Did you know he was after me?" I kicked her bed, attempting to get her to focus on me, but still she just stared at the floor. "That he was obsessed with me?"

Her chin lifted from its perch. "What are you talking about?"

I narrowed my gaze, evaluating her tone. She really didn't know the answer to that particular question.

No matter, there were still plenty I could ask.

"Tell me everything," I demanded. "Everything you know about him and what he's planning to do to Kazola. No more lies, no more secrets. The truth, Vanessa."

We stared at each other for a few fleeting moments, a battle of wills clashing in the air between us. Conflict flashed across her face, twisting her features as she decided what was the best choice for her own safety. I let out a low growl, a warning that the only way forward for her was with the truth.

"Elliot isn't who you think he is," she finally said. "He is a mastermind, a leader. He is much more dangerous than the petty murderer you all believe him to be."

"And why is that?"

"Because he is leading a revolution." Her frown deepened, her eyes igniting as she stared straight into mine. "And if you don't hurry, he'll end us all."

End of Book One

The Story Continues...

Kasha, Nolan, and the whole Faction will
return in book two of the Kazola Chronicles

Marked by Truth

Coming Fall 2023

Acknowledgements

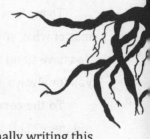

I am always in awe when I get to the point of finally writing this special section of the book! And in honesty, this has been over ten years in the making, when I first came up with the idea at the age of 21. So, this one is a bit extra special to me, as I never believed that this story would one day be published.

First, I want to thank my amazing family. My loving husband Nathaniel, my incredible sister, Liz, and my supportive parents, Mark and Ellen. For always believing in me, celebrating every step along the way, and encouraging me to follow a dream that I used to believe was impossible. You have always driven me to be my best and to follow the path that would make me the happiest. I wouldn't be here without you.

To my incredible editors, Cassidy and Renee. Kasha's story and the journey she takes wouldn't be the same without you two. Not only am I lucky enough to have such incredibly talented writers assisting me with this book, but I am forever grateful to call you both friends.

To my fabulous CP, Brianne. For being there to talk when I second guess myself, being Kasha and Nolan's biggest cheerleader and listening to me endlessly bounce ideas off of you. When I doubt, when I struggle with imposter syndrome, I know you are always in my corner to help lift me when I'm down. Thank you for always being you. This book would not exist without your constant support.

To my best friends Alyson, Chelsea and Meaghan. I know, no matter what, you are by my side, even if you live so very far away. You have stood by me through the best and worst of times. Thank you for always giving me a reason to celebrate.

To the cover artist who has perfectly captured (see what I did there? Lol) this story and gave it a beautiful book cover to go with it. Jupiter, you saved me during a particularly stressful moment and blew me away with your talent and collaborative work ethic. I cannot wait to work with you again soon and see all the other beautiful covers you will create throughout the years!

Special shoutout to my proofreader Roxana, my map designer, Vanessa, and my Beta Reader team. You all made sure that this book had those perfect finishing touches.

And finally, as always, to you beautiful readers, who took the time to pick up this book. This dream of mine would not be possible without you. Thank you for reading a book that holds a special place in my heart. I hope Kasha's journey gave you an escape you needed, filled your heart in a way only a book can, or just gave you a few hours of entertainment. Her journey is still going, and I cannot wait for you to read what comes next.

Until then, happy reading!

About the Author

Kathryn Marie is the indie author of the fantasy series, the Kazola Chronicles and the Midnight Duology. She began writing at the young age of thirteen, when she was stuck in bed recovering from spinal surgery. Ever since then, she's loved creating stories and characters for others to enjoy. When she is not at work or busy writing in her home office, Kathryn can be found spending time with her wonderful husband or friends, experimenting with new makeup techniques, or watching reruns of her many beloved TV shows.

Follow Kathryn on social media for updates!

__Website Newsletter:__ www.authorkathrynmarie.com
__Instagram:__ @author_kathrynmarie
__TikTok:__ @author_kathrynmarie
__Facebook:__ @authorkathrynmarie

CPSIA information can be obtained
at www.ICGtesting.com
Printed in the USA
BVHW030246260423
663086BV00017BA/91